"A great read; you can really picture the characters and their surroundings. I'm looking forward to the movie."

Toni Courtier
Marketing Director, Crawfordville, Florida

"*The Potter's Wife* draws you into the story and fills your senses. Reading this book becomes addictive—you won't want to put it down until the very end, and then it leaves you wanting more. Nobody gets to the heart of human emotion, frailty, and courage like Cindy Neel."

Rue Luttrell
PR Director, Tallahassee, FL.

"It was very easy to identify with Cindy's characters, she made them come alive; and the setting evoked memories of many sea-side vacations. Hope she will write a sequel—I didn't want it to end."

Ruth Pokorski,
Loan Processor, Ochlocknee Bay, Florida

"Cindy Neel has created a wonderful, romantic tale of life, loss, love, and redemption set on the beautiful coast. She is an exceptional storyteller, and the reading was a true pleasure."

Jan W. Gorman,
Gallery Owner, Apalachicola Florida

the
potter's
wife

Published by Tate Publishing & Enterprises, LLC
127 E. Trade Center Terrace | Mustang, Oklahoma 73064 USA
1.888.361.9473 | www.tatepublishing.com

Tate Publishing is committed to excellence in the publishing industry. The company reflects the philosophy established by the founders, based on Psalm 68:11,
"The Lord gave the word and great was the company of those who published it."

Book design copyright © 2008 by Tate Publishing, LLC. All rights reserved.
Cover design by Lance Waldrop
Interior design by Tyler Evans

Published in the United States of America
ISBN: 978-1-60799-000-0
1. Fiction : Romance : Contemporary
2. Fiction : Religious
08.12.22

Acknowledgment

The journey that took me down the road of *The Potter's Wife* was a journey that would forever change my life. Though my childhood was littered with abuse, pain, and family secrets, fifteen years before his death my father gave his life to the Lord. He changed as the darkness changes to light. He was a wonderful soul, and God allowed deep healing to take place in my heart where he was concerned. I came to know this son of a sharecropper to be a wonderful, loving, caring person.

When we found out that my father had terminal cancer and there was no curative treatment for him, I knew that my life would forever be changed. The grief I felt for the loss I was about to incur was overwhelming for me. He had become my encourager, my critic, and my friend. He was about to leave me forever, and I could not bear the thought of not having him around to give those hugs of approval and encouragement.

As the days passed and the grief grew more intent, God put *The Potter's Wife* in my heart, and I began to write about life after grief. Little did I know at the time it would be the tool God would use to heal the brokenness I felt and replace it with joy knowing I would have accomplished that one thing God had placed me here on this earth to do—tell stories, stories that would touch the hearts of others as He has touched mine.

I dedicate this book to the loving memory of a man who gave his life making me who I am today, my father, Paul A. Trull.

Chapter 1

The morning sun was bright; the cool brisk breeze sent a chill down Mandy's spine as she surveyed the dusty potter's shop. It was silent except for the sound of the birds singing outside. A beautiful melody began to unfold as she sat by the potter's wheel. She tried to picture Clay sitting in this very spot, feeling the warmth of the sun on his face as he created beautiful pots and vases. She could almost feel his presence in the room with her.

The tears began to fill her eyes. *Why did I come in here?* she thought. The wound was still too fresh. Her brokenness took over again, and she began to sob uncontrollably. "Why did you leave me, Clay? We had such plans, you and I. We were supposed to be together forever." She could hear herself talking out loud as if he were sitting there, as though he would answer her. No answer came. He was gone, forever.

She felt the warmth of the sun on her face. Her mood was broken when a tiny bird flew in and perched on the ledge of the open window. She peered at the bird. What did he want? It was as if he had perched there just to comfort her. She smiled, and the bird flew away.

She surveyed the room. Beautiful pottery lined shelves covered in red dust. This was his life—how Clay had loved it in this room. This is where he spent most of his time caressing the clay in his hands, sweat rolling down his face, singing with the birds.

She took a dusty rag from the pottery wheel and started to dust the shelves. She cleaned for what seemed like hours when she heard a faint voice coming from inside the house. She put the rag down to go see who it was when a petite lady stuck her head in the door.

"I'm sorry to just barge in…but the front door was opened, I knocked—"

"That's okay."

"I saw the sign down by the road, 'The Potter's Shop,' and I just had to come see. I love pottery," the petite lady rattled on. "Please forgive my manners. My name is Grace, Grace Howard. We just moved in down the road. I was taking my morning walk when I saw the sign. Hard at work are we?"

"Well, no—yes, I mean—I'm not the potter, if that's what you are asking. My husband was—"

"That's perfectly all right, young lady. Do you mind if I look around?" She began to move around the shop. "Such beautiful pieces they are."

"They're not for sale," Mandy broke in. "The shop is closed."

"Well, why on earth would you close the shop when you have all of this beautiful pottery to sell?"

"Well, as I said, my husband was the potter, and he's not here anymore. So I've closed the shop. May I show you out?"

"Left you, did he? Don't know what to think about men these days. Here one minute, gone the next."

"No, it's not like that," Mandy stammered. "He died a year ago. Today is the first day I've been in here. I just was trying to straighten up when you came in."

"Sorry to hear that, little lady. What did you say your name was?"

"I didn't, please forgive me. My name is Mandy Bowls."

"Name fits."

"I beg your pardon."

"Bowls," she said, as she picked up a bowl from the shelf.

Mandy began to laugh. This little old woman had made her laugh for the first time in a year. "Please come into the kitchen, and I'll fix us something to drink."

"Kind of cool outside, got some coffee?"

"Coffee it is."

They both headed for the kitchen. "Where did you say you moved into?" Mandy fixed the coffee.

"The ole Boyd place. Mr. Boyd died about ten months ago, and the kids didn't want the ole place, so I bought it. We've been restoring it for a couple of months; moved in last week. I love it here by the Gulf. I've always wanted to live here, just never could afford a place."

"Mr. Boyd died? I didn't know," Mandy replied in bewilderment. How could her neighbor have died and she didn't even know?

"Yes, it's a beautiful place now." Grace broke Mandy's thoughts.

"Yes, I always liked the Boyd place. You have a beautiful view of the lighthouse, don't you?"

"Yes, we do. I love spending my evenings sitting on the back porch watching that ole lighthouse guiding the way for the boats that didn't make it ashore before dark."

"Welcome to the Cove. I think you'll love it here. Clay and I have lived here for ten years or so. We've always loved it here, even in hurricane season. The rock levee keeps out most of the floodwater. I don't think you'll have a problem either."

"Wouldn't matter to me much; I love the place. Got to take the bad with the good. Life don't pick and choose, you know."

"No, I don't know what you're talking about."

"Well, it rains on the just and the unjust. Thanks for the coffee. Better be going now. I've taken up enough of your time. I'll be seeing you around. You ought to reopen that Potter's Shop." With that, she was gone.

· · · · ·

Walking down the road to her house, Grace knew she had her work cut out for her. She couldn't let Mandy close that shop. She knew it would be just the tool she and the Good Lord needed to bring Mandy out of this depression she was in; to be able to move on and stop living in the past. "Yes, Lord, these young people think their lives are over when tragedy comes along. They don't know that it's a growing experience for them. Help me, Lord, to do what you would have me do to help this little lady." Grace smiled; she knew that everything would be all right.

· · · · ·

What a strange morning, Mandy thought, learning her neighbor had died, the house had been sold and remodeled. Where had she been? She had gone into town to buy groceries, pick up supplies. How could she not know what was going on around her? Were people that stand-offish to her? Had she become a hermit, locking herself into a world that no longer existed?

The phone ringing shook her out of her thoughts.

"Thought maybe you'd like to come over for lunch," the voice on the other end of the phone said. It was Grace.

"Well, I'm really not hungry, but—"

"No buts. Come on over. I have a nice salad, and we can eat out on the porch. Come on over now, no excuses. I won't take no, you hear?"

Who was this old woman, and why did she have to invade Mandy's solitude? "I'll be over in a minute," Mandy replied.

Walking down the path to the road Mandy could see the old sign hanging on one hinge. "The Potter's Shop." *I need to take that down,* she thought.

The sun was up high now, and the warmth it gave soothed her soul as she walked down the dirt and shell road to the Boyd place. It was a wonderful old place, she thought as she walked up the front porch to the door. *The beautiful trees; the green grass; those lovely flowerbeds and the old cypress house with a wrap-around porch...*

Mandy and Clay used to come over and have tea in the evenings with old Mr. Boyd, a very pleasant man who lived a simple life. His children would come in the summer to spend a week or two. Other than that, he lived alone. He would tell them about the lighthouse and the times it saved wayward fishermen from crashing into the rock levee, guiding them safely to port. Mandy realized she was smiling again. She reached up and knocked on the door. She could hear Grace inside humming an old hymn. She couldn't recall the words, but it was sweet to hear.

"Come on in, make yourself at home," Grace said, opening the new screen door.

"The place looks beautiful," Mandy said as she looked around at the renovations. New floors; and the old torn wallpaper had been replaced with new paint. The whole house looked different, yet somehow it still had the same homey feel. *Peaceful,* she thought, *just as it was when Mr. Boyd lived here.*

"I guess this is the Howard place now." Mandy laughed.

"Well it's my little piece of heaven here on earth. I still can't believe I live here. Still got a lot to do, but it's coming."

The two of them sat on the back porch talking about the lighthouse and the scenic view, enjoying the fresh, cool salad Grace had prepared.

Spring was in the air. The cold of winter had finally passed. The breeze warmed her inside; she knew she had found a new friend. Mandy welcomed the thought for the first time since Clay had died.

On her way home, instead of going into the house and shutting herself up, Mandy took a stroll on the beach. The seagulls were squawking, and the sandpipers were hunting for lunch in the sand as the waves washed away at the shoreline. The tide was starting to change; the wind had picked up. It had a chill in it even with the sun bearing down. She shuddered and started up the hill to her house.

What an interesting day, she thought. It had started out like every other day for the past year. But it had changed; Grace had changed it.

Mandy went back into the pottery shop; she had accomplished a lot this morning in her cleaning. Things looked better already. She continued on her quest, cleaning, moving, and reorganizing. Perhaps that was what she needed, being in the place Clay loved the most. She had locked the door the day he died and had not been inside it since.

She noticed the sun going down on the horizon. She was tired but pleased. In a spirit of peace, she smiled as she surveyed the room. Everything was in its place and was organized. It was a good day, a productive day.

She would go into town tomorrow and pick up supplies. She needed to; she needed to reenter life again. She didn't know how, but she needed to.

• • • • •

The morning sun broke through the thin curtains hanging over the window in her bedroom. It was bright; *bright*, that was a new thought for her. Things had been so dark for so long. Today she was going to start over. Grace had given her a sense of life. She was still alive, though life hadn't run through her body in so long, just the pain. *Pain*—she didn't want the pain anymore. She poured a cup of coffee and walked into the pottery shop. *Yes, this is more like it. I must fix that old sign too,* she thought. Clay deserved better than what she had done, shutting herself away from the world. There was a world out there still going on, even though she thought it had left her behind.

She hurriedly dressed and headed for town in Clay's truck. It felt nice to get out of the house and wander around town. People smiled as they passed, bidding her good morning. *Life. This is life without Clay,* she thought.

"I can do this." She knew these people; they knew her. Sure, she had been antisocial this past year; she had even been short with some of them. But surely they understood and would except her.

"Good morning, Mandy," a voice invaded her thoughts. She turned to see Mrs. Morrison from the County Store standing next to her.

"Good morning." Mandy smiled.

"Spring is coming early this year, don't you think?"

"Yes, and I welcome it. The winter didn't seem it would ever let up."

"It's good to see you out. We've all missed you and Clay so much … oh, I'm sorry."

"It's okay. I know you hardly ever saw one of us without the other. It's okay. Nice to see you, Mrs. Morrison." Mandy turned to walk away.

But was it okay? Would everyone respond to her the same way? Was she no one without Clay? The familiar tears began to stream down her face as she hurried away.

Back at home, she let her emotions go. Her sobs were broken by the sound of Grace's voice calling from the front porch. "Mandy? Mandy, is that you in there making all that fuss?"

She didn't want to see Grace today. She tried to quiet herself. Perhaps Grace would go away. No such luck; she came through the door and made her way into the bedroom where Mandy was lying across the bed.

"Now, now, what is all of this about?" Grace comforted her as she tried to raise herself from the bed.

"I thought you were past all of this. What's got you all in a tizzy?"

"I went into town. I needed some things. Life is just not the same. Why didn't I die that day too?"

"What in the world are you talking about, little lady?"

"Clay. It was my fault, you know."

"You're not making any sense. Slow down and tell me what you're talking about."

"That day on the rock levee, I went up there to think. Clay and I had had an argument. The water was rough that day. I knew better than to go up there, but that's where I went…when Clay and I argued. I was coming down when a big wave swept me off into the water and started beating me up against the rocks. Clay saw me from the pottery shop window and ran down to help me. He jumped in and pushed me onto the rocks. I climbed up the levee, and when I turned to help him, he was gone. I was going to jump back into the water to find him, but there was a riptide, so I stayed on the levee. I didn't know there was an undertow. I thought he was playing with me, you know, getting me back for being so angry with him. But then I realized that it was no joke. I screamed and screamed for someone to help me, but the people who came to help weren't able to find him. They found him three days later in the Gulf. That was the day my life ended too." Mandy sobbed.

"Your life hasn't ended, dear. You're still here. The Creator has a reason for you being here."

"The Creator. You mean God. Where was God that day on the levee? Where is God every night when I lie down in my sorrows?"

"Well, he's right there with you, darlin.'"

"Please, I don't need this today."

"This is exactly what you need today. You've been grieving over this long enough. It wasn't your fault—it just happened. Life is like that, you know? We can't explain everything. There's not always a reason for why things happen. They just do."

"Clay was a much better person than I am. Why didn't God take me and leave him?"

"Because, God's not through with you yet. Come on now, let's get some tea, that'll make you feel better."

"Nothing is going to make me feel better—"

"You felt that way yesterday too, but I saw lots of smilin' and even heard a laugh."

"That was yesterday. This is today."

"Well then, we got to make it a new day."

Mandy knew it was hopeless trying to convince this old woman. She dragged herself up and made her way to the kitchen. "I don't have any tea. I went to town today, but I didn't get anything I needed. Could I get a rain check?"

"No clouds in the sky today. Let's go get you some tea," Grace replied, getting up from her chair and heading for the door.

"I can't go back into town now," Mandy whined behind Grace.

"No better time than the present. When you fall off a horse, the best thing to do is get up and get right back on that critter, or you'll never ride again. Yes, now is the best time. Come on now, before the stores close. I won't have any fussin,' come on," Grace insisted.

Mandy and Grace climbed in Clay's old truck and headed to the County Store.

· · · · ·

"Good afternoon, Mandy, I'm so glad you came back. I felt so bad about this morning. I wanted to apologize, how could I be so—"

"It's really fine," Mandy interrupted.

"No, it wasn't." Grace walked into the store. "I came in and found her just a bawlin.' Lying about the way we feel isn't good, little lady. If you can't be honest with yourself, how can you be honest with others?" Tears filled Mrs. Morrison's eyes; she felt terrible about the slip of her tongue earlier.

"Mrs. Morrison, I know you didn't mean any harm to me. I know you meant well," Mandy defended herself.

"If this nice lady here wants to apologize, let her. It'll make her feel better and you too." Grace put her hand on Mandy's shoulder.

"Thank you for your kindness, your words of wisdom," Mrs. Morrison said as she busied herself. "What was it you needed, Mandy?"

"I need a lot of things. Let me shop and I'll be right back."

"That's the spirit, honey." Grace winked at Mrs. Morrison.

Mandy hurried off to gather the things she came for. Shopping was not on her mind, but God was. Grace had defended God to her earlier. What did Grace know about her relationship with God? She and Clay had attended church regularly. They both were very active in the church. Where were those people when she had needed help? Sure, some of them came by, all of them came to Clay's funeral, but she couldn't recall them reaching out to her in her time of need. Or had they, and she had rejected them the way she had rejected everyone since Clay's death?

She had rejected God too. She hadn't been back to church nor had she tried to keep in touch with the other members or the pastor. Pastor Johnny had been a good friend to her and Clay. He and his wife had dined at their house many times. Clay had made all of the flowerpots and garden décor for the church. He loved God so; he would sit at night and read her the Bible. He could make the stories sound so real, as if you were right there. She finished her shopping and loaded the groceries into the truck.

On the way home Mandy felt release. She was unsure of what had just happened, but she knew that it was a good step in the right direction.

The sun was beginning to hide behind the trees now, its rays sparkling off the still water in the bay. She watched the seagulls diving for their last meal of the day, singing to each other as they caught their prey. *The sights, the sounds, that's why we moved here*, Mandy thought as she drank in the beauty of the evening. The day was going to sleep and the night awakening. Two different worlds that coexisted together but never touched.

"Where're you at, little lady?" Grace broke into her thoughts.

"Oh, just enjoying the beauty of the evening falling," Mandy directed her attention back to the road.

"Did you say 'enjoying'? A far cry from where I found you this afternoon."

"Thank you, Grace. I'm so glad you came into my life. I've only known you for a couple of days, yet I feel we have been friends forever," Mandy said as she dropped Grace off at her driveway. She really did like the ole woman; she just seemed to invade her life at the most inopportune times.

"I feel the same, little lady." With that Grace was on her way to her little piece of heaven. She was glad she had been able to get through to Mandy. *That little lady has a lot to offer. The world will be a better place with her in it*, she thought. She knew the grief Mandy was going through. When her own husband died she had shut herself away for years. It was only by the good graces of God an old woman came into her life to show her the way back into life. She would return the favor by helping Mandy. Though, she knew Mandy was a much better person than she had been at the time. With the help of the Good Lord she knew all would be well.

She pulled weeds from her flowerbeds, making preparations for spring. *It wouldn't be long now*, she thought. Spring was in the air already, and she was glad.

Chapter 2

As the days passed Grace and Mandy became closer, spending their afternoons together, working to complete the renovations on Grace's house. Long walks on the beach and laughter were a regular part of Mandy's days now. Grace insisted that laughter was healing, and Mandy was beginning to believe her.

Standing in the pottery shop drinking coffee had become a morning ritual for Mandy. She felt close to Clay, but the pain was not there. It was replaced with the fond memories the two of them shared together. She even found herself chuckling as she remembered the blunders Clay made with some of his creations. He used to tell her he meant it to turn out like that. "See the artistry in this piece," he once said as he showed her a warped bowl with a long crack in the side. "This is pond pottery, see, it looks good. You can even make a water fountain with it. See, water will pour out the side." Both of them had roared with laughter. Laughter was a big part of those memories, lots of it.

After her first cup of coffee Mandy decided a morning walk on the beach would be a good way to start her day. She ran in to put on her shorts and shirt, and down to the beach she went. The tide was low and you could see the fiddler crabs scurrying back to their holes for safety. The sandpipers ran back and forth with the waves, ever so careful not to get wet as they plucked the sand fleas out of the sand for breakfast. The sun was already hot, even though it was early.

In the distance she saw a man sitting on the beach staring out at the water. He looked so sad, as if he were not here at all, but somewhere far away. He didn't even notice as Mandy got closer.

"A beautiful morning, isn't it?" Mandy asked as she waked up to him.

The man didn't reply; he just kept staring out at the water. Watching the waves roll onto the shore. Blank, as if he were imprisoned. The beauty of the morning was far from him. *Where is he staring? What is he looking at?* Mandy looked in the direction he was looking to find nothing. Just open water, or perhaps he was watching the lighthouse. No one was on the rock levee so he couldn't be looking at tourists.

"You're new around here, aren't you?" Mandy again tried to strike up a conversation.

"Yes, I'm new around here," the man uttered.

"Just visiting or do you live around here?"

"Are you writing a book?" the man snapped.

"No, no I'm not. I was just trying to be neighborly, that's all."

"Good, you've been neighborly. Now you can go on your merry way," the man replied, not even looking up at her.

She continued on her morning walk, a little taken aback by the strange encounter. *What did I do wrong?* she thought. *Perhaps I shouldn't have interrupted him.*

She looked down the beach to find Grace sitting on her back porch. She scurried up the sand dunes to where Grace was sitting. "Top of the morning to you, old woman."

"Top of the morning to you, little lady," Grace replied with a wave. "I just had the strangest encounter on the beach," Mandy started as she and Grace walked inside the house.

"Oh, what happened?"

"Well, I was taking a walk down the beach this morning…"

The strange man on the beach walked in the door right past where Grace and Mandy were pouring a cup of coffee. Silence fell over the room. The man walked up the stairs and was gone.

"You were saying," Grace said, breaking the silence.

"Who is that?" Mandy was surprised to see the stranger in Grace's house.

"Oh, that's my son, Ben. Came down for a visit. He works in the city, you know. He's the one who helped me restore this ole place. Hard worker he is. He needed a break, so he decided to come down and see me. Not much company, though. Never says too much, just drowns himself in sorrow. Pretty much like you when I first met you. You were telling me about your strange encounter this morning."

"Well yes, I was, but it was really nothing," Mandy replied, her face blushing ever so slightly.

"Go ahead, don't mind Ben," Grace insisted. "I've spent three years minding Ben. He's no better off today than he was three years ago. I just can't seem to reach him."

"What in the world happened to him?"

"Wife died of cancer three years ago. He's never gotten over it," Grace answered. "Are you going to tell me about this strange encounter or are you going to make me wonder all day?"

"The strange encounter was with your son," Mandy quietly answered.

"Oh, I see. No matter, what's up for today?" Grace left it at that and busied herself cleaning up the last of the breakfast dishes.

"I was thinking about learning the trade of pottery. I went out on the Internet last night, and with what I learned working with Clay, I think I can do it. I have to do something. The insurance money is about gone, and I thought it would be good to learn the pottery business. I mean, I do have all of the equipment."

Grace noted the pride in Mandy's voice as she spoke. "Little lady, I couldn't think of a better trade for ya. Going to start today?"

"Yes, I thought I'd repair my sign, then get started."

"I'll send Ben over to help you with the sign."

"No," Mandy replied quickly. "That won't be necessary. I think I can do it."

"It's no trouble. He needs to do something besides mope around here."

Mandy hesitated. "I guess that would be all right then, if you're sure he won't mind."

"He won't mind a bit."

Mandy excused herself and set out up the hill to her house. She went into Clay's tool shed and found the tools she needed to fix the sign and headed down the driveway. She saw Ben sitting beside the sign when she reached the end of the drive.

"Good morning, again," she said as she got closer.

"Morning. Sorry about earlier. It's just not a good time for me. I didn't know you were the little lady my mom always talks about. You've been a great comfort for her," Ben answered.

"She's the one that's a great comfort to me."

"I know what you've been through; Mom told me. Doesn't change things, though. What is it you need me to help you with?"

"I was just going to fix this old sign. It needs it, don't you think?" Mandy tried to lighten the mood. "I really could do it by myself though."

"Fine," Ben said as he got up and started down the road.

Mandy watched him as he made his way down the road. She pulled the sign up and started to hammer the hinge back into place. She suddenly hit her finger with the hammer. Letting out a loud wail, she put her injured finger in her mouth.

Ben came running back up the road to see what had happened. "I told you I'd help," he said as her reached out to take her injured hand.

"I didn't want to be a bother," Mandy replied with tears in her eyes. "Look, I can see this is more than you can handle. So why don't you just run home to your mommy?"

"There is no need for all of that. I wanted to help."

"Then why didn't you just help instead of acting like this is such an inconvenience for you?"

"You acted like you didn't need any help, so I left."

"Just go." Her tone grew harsh.

Ben gently took the hammer from her and fixed the broken hinge. Handing the hammer back to her, he asked, "Can I assist with that hurt finger?"

"No, just go away."

"I'm sorry, okay?" Ben screamed.

"Don't scream at me …"

"I don't mean to, you're just … you're just. …" He stomped off.

Mandy gathered her tools and headed for the house. *What nerve,* she thought. *How could he be so cruel, so hateful?*

She went into the house and placed the tools on the kitchen table.

She found a Band-Aid, washed her hand, and placed the Band-Aid on her finger. She walked into the pottery shop and started to check the clay. Hard as a rock, she rolled the barrel outside and added water to it, covered the barrel, and walked inside. She sat at the table and cried for what seemed like hours when she heard someone at the door. She dried her eyes and surveyed her face in the mirror. It was obvious she had been crying. Her face was red and her eyes were swollen. *All I need now is company,* she thought as she made her way to the door.

It was Ben. She straightened herself up and opened the door. "Can I help you?"

"I felt so bad about the way I acted this morning. I wanted to apologize for my rude behavior," Ben said with his head hanging down. "Here, these are for you," he said, handing her the flowers he had hidden behind his back. "It's not much. I picked them on the side of the road. Well, here, I hope you will forgive me."

She felt her face get hot—not from anger, but she felt herself blushing. That was two times in one day this man had made her blush. She hadn't blushed since Clay. "It's okay, I know you're grieving. Thanks," she said, taking the flowers from him. "Please come in while I put these in some water."

"I need to get back to Mom's. Thanks anyway." With that he was gone.

She didn't know what to think about this strange man. She turned and went into the house. She put the beautiful buttercups in water and set them on the kitchen table. She went back into the pottery shop and started arranging the pottery into displays.

She opened up the outside door and placed an "Open" sign on the outside wall so any would-be customers could come in. She swept the walkway and pulled the weeds out from the flowers that were struggling to grow along the walkway. She was pleased with the work she had done. Everything looked so much better. When it was time to close the shop she would run into town and get new flowers to plant in the beds lining the walkway to the road.

Much to her surprise she had fifteen customers that day and made $960 off the pottery she sold. *Clay was so gifted,* she thought. Would she ever be able to recreate the beautiful pottery he had made? She shuffled around on his desk and found patterns for the mass-produced items. She felt much better; she checked the clay in the barrel and saw it was beginning to soften up. She took several large balls of clay from the barrel and placed them on the long worktable. She kneaded the clay as you would knead bread dough, working the moisture back into the clay. She took the rolls of freshly kneaded clay and placed them in another barrel, covering the barrel with a wet rag to keep the clay soft.

The sun was beginning to hide itself behind the trees. She was tired, her back ached, and her hands were sore. She stared out the large picture window in the pottery shop. *How beautiful the view is from in here*, she thought. It was enough to get your creative juices flowing. The lighthouse, the rock levee, the sun, and the birds—all of it was the foundation. No wonder Clay spent long hours in the shop. *The flowers,* she thought, as she looked at the clock on the wall. She still had just enough time to make it to the store before it closed. She hurried out to the truck and headed into town.

The County Store was the nearest thing to an old country store that you could come to. They stocked almost everything you needed. It was located on the outskirts of town and was run by Mr. and Mrs. Morrison. They had lived in the Cove all of their lives. Mr. Morrison's family as far as a few generations back had also run the County Store.

Mandy loved the little County Store. She loved the Morrison family too.

The County Store was just about to close when she pulled up. "Can I get some flowers before you close?" Mandy yelled to the back of the store where Mrs. Morrison was checking the day's tally.

"Help yourself, Mandy. I'll be done here in a minute."

"Thanks."

Mandy sorted through the flowers, picking out lots of bright colors for the walkway. She had never been much on plants, but they were pretty and that was all she cared about. She picked up some ground cover and mulching wood chips. Mrs. Morrison tallied up the gardening items, and Mandy loaded them into the truck.

As she was placing a last bag of mulch in the truck she turned and ran into Ben. "Oh, excuse me. I should look where I'm walking."

"That's fine," he said, chuckling at her.

"What's so funny?"

"I didn't know if you needed this or not," he replied, pulling a big piece of moist clay from her hair.

Once again she felt her face get hot, and she knew she was blushing. "Hazards of the trade," she said and got into the truck.

"Are you going to plant all these flowers by yourself?" He looked through the flats of flowers.

"Sure am, first thing in the morning."

"Do you need any help unloading the truck?"

"Nope, sure don't. Thanks anyway." She started the truck and backed out.

"Could I get a ride?" Ben yelled from behind. "I walked into town, and it's getting dark. I thought maybe since you were going my way ... "

"Hop in."

Ben got in the passenger side and looked ahead. "I know we kind of got off on the wrong foot. I'm really sorry about that."

"No need to be sorry, some people are just mean spirited."

"I'm not mean spirited," he snapped back.

She could feel his closeness beside her in the truck. She felt her heart begin to beat fast. What was it about this strange man that touched her so? She checked herself in the rearview mirror and realized she had clay smeared all over her face. Trying not to attract his attention to her, she smiled, knowing this was possibly the worst she had ever looked.

It was silent the rest of the way home. She dropped Ben off at the end of his driveway and hurried to the house.

Ben felt a strange sensation as he turned to see the truck speeding off. *This lady is special*, he thought as he walked slowly up the path to his mom's house.

Mandy unloaded the truck and went inside to take a long hot bath. As she soaked in the hot water, she reflected on Ben. How handsome he was, his dirty blonde hair, his ocean-blue eyes, the tiny cleft in his chin. She recalled the way it felt to sit next to him in the truck. She had not had feelings like this since Clay. She shuddered when she thought of it. A cold chill ran up her spine. She dressed for bed.

The next morning she arose early, excited about planting her new flowers. She went into the kitchen to get the coffee started when she heard a knock at the door. *Who is that this early? It must be Grace*, she thought. She went to the door and opened it to find Ben standing there.

"I thought you could use some help this morning," he said, smiling down at her.

She realized she still had her nightclothes on. "Thank you for the kind gesture, but as you can see, I'm not up for company yet," she said as she pulled the door closed ever so slightly so that just her head was showing.

"I understand."

Mandy closed the door and leaned against it. *What in the world is he doing here? Where is Grace? I could handle Grace this early in the morning. Not Ben.*

She hurried into the bedroom to change when she heard a dragging sound. "What in the world?" She looked out the window to find Ben dragging crates of flowers over to the sidewalk flowerbed.

He carefully surveyed the area and started placing flowers around inside the beds. The morning sun was hot; Mandy watched as he took off his shirt. Her heart pounded as she surveyed the rippled stomach and the huge muscles that surrounded his arms. She watched as he dug each hole and carefully replaced the soil around each delicate flower. She felt as if she couldn't breathe; stepping away from the window, she leaned up against the wall to catch her breath.

She made lemonade for the both of them. "Well, I guess you're going to help anyway." She laughed as she walked out the door.

"I just felt so bad about the way I treated you. I'm not mean spirited. I'm not a mean person. I just didn't want the invasion of my space. Mom told me you were not like that, that you had just began the healing process yourself. She told me about Clay. I'm sorry for your loss. I was so involved in my own grief that I couldn't see yours." Although he sounded sincere, he wouldn't look her in the eyes.

After trying to catch his eyes, Mandy looked away; the lump in her throat was so big she couldn't speak. She handed him the lemonade and sat back on the sidewalk, surveying his face.

"I'm sorry for your loss too. You must have really loved your wife. Your mom told me it's been three years," she heard herself say.

"Yes, yes I did. I still do. She was my soul mate, if you believe in that kind of thing. I could never love another. I will always love her. She told me before she died that she wanted me to move on with my life. Find someone else to share it with. I can't. I see her everywhere. I hear her voice. At first I thought I was going crazy. My friends did too.

I mean, I had these dreams. They seemed so real. Then I would wake up and realize it was only a dream."

She could feel his pain; her heart went out to him. She too had known those feelings. But Grace had been a godsend to her—helping her to move on, helping her to feel alive again. Making her realize that's what Clay would have wanted. *Why could Grace not help Ben? He is her son; he needs to hear Grace say all the things she had said to me,* she thought.

"We have to move on with life. God left us here for a reason." Did she hear herself right? Had she just mentioned God? Yes she had, and she knew as she spoke the words—Grace was right.

"I've heard all of that from Mom. The reason I didn't move here with her is because I couldn't stand the lectures anymore."

"They aren't lectures. They're truths. Your mom helped me to see that. I don't know what I would have done without her. She has been the greatest friend. I'm thankful to her. Well, if you're going to do this, I'm going to open the shop. I did real good yesterday."

"You go right ahead. I'll finish up here."

"Thanks. Are you going to send me a bill?"

"Not if you won't send me a bill for the counseling session."

They both laughed. It was nice to hear him laugh. His face radiated with joy; having someone to talk to was probably the best medicine for Ben.

She hurried inside to straighten up and get the shop ready for customers. Taking balls of clay from the barrel, she sat at the worktable and started to form the clay into bowls, setting each one on the shelf to dry for the second stage of processing. Before she knew it the shop was full of tourists asking questions about this piece or that one. She realized that she knew more about pottery than she thought. She had listened to Clay explain each stage to her. What she once thought were boring details she now realized were valuable facts; Clay had taught her the trade.

By lunchtime Ben was through with the flowerbeds. He called her to come outside to see the finished product. "It's beautiful, where did you learn to do this?"

"I have a landscaping business in the city. We do large corporate buildings, inside and out. We do all of the design and upkeep—my trade, where yours is pottery."

"My trade is not pottery. Actually I was an aspiring artist when I met Clay. I quit art when we married. We moved here, and I started being his flunky. Clay was the potter, not me." She laughed.

"You'd never know it. Look at the design of these pots you just made. They're very unique. Use your artistic skills to paint them. I think you're going to do just fine," he said, surveying the pots.

"Let's have lunch. I can see anyone coming up the walk through the window."

"Lunch sounds great."

Mandy prepared tuna sandwiches and salad for lunch. They sat and ate in silence.

When lunch was over, Ben got up and helped Mandy do the dishes. "Thanks for all of your help, Ben. You really did a wonderful job."

"You're welcome, anytime. I'm the one who should be thanking you. I need to go check on Mom. I enjoyed the company. I feel better. I needed this morning." With that he was gone.

As soon as the last customer was gone, Mandy closed up and headed for Grace's house. Mandy couldn't wait to see Grace and tell her about the strange yet wonderful morning.

She didn't even knock on the door; she just hurried into the kitchen where Grace was humming that old gospel hymn again. She still couldn't remember the name of it.

"Hello, stranger," Grace greeted Mandy as she walked into the kitchen.

"Stranger?"

"Well, haven't seen much of you the last two days. My son hasn't been bothering you, has he? Haven't seen much of him lately either."

"Where is Ben? Is he down at the beach?"

"No, he went back to the city early this afternoon. Busy season for him, you know."

"Oh."

"Just came for the weekend, he does that sometimes." Grace was staring at the shocked look on Mandy's face. "He'll be back when the notion strikes him."

Mandy could feel her heart drop to her feet. The excitement she felt drained from her innermost being. *What is this all about?* Mandy thought. *He's nothing to me.* Clay was everything to her, even now.

"Stay for dinner—keep an old woman company? Got a good one. You look tired. Sit down and let me fix you a plate."

She was hungry; the tuna sandwich and salad were gone. But the food seemed to get bigger as she chewed. She couldn't eat. A lump formed in her throat. She made passive conversation with Grace. After dinner Grace wanted to go out on the back porch to drink a cup of coffee and watch the lighthouse.

Mandy could hear Grace talking, but she had not heard a word Grace said. It was if she were not here at all but away in the city. Wondering what Ben was doing.

"You okay, little lady?" Grace finally asked.

"Yes, just a little tired. I think I'll go home and turn in. See you tomorrow," she said, getting up from the rocking chair.

"If it be the Good Lord's will."

"Pardon me?"

"You'll see me tomorrow, if it be the Good Lord's will," Grace replied.

"Yes ... yes."

Mandy walked slowly up the road to her house. The buttercups swaying in the breeze reminded her of the peace offering Ben had brought her. She felt sadness consume her. Why was she feeling like this? She felt like a schoolgirl who had lost her best friend. She soaked in a hot bath, trying to wash away the feeling of loss once more. This time it wasn't Clay she was thinking of ... it was Ben.

Chapter 3

The days flowed into each other. Time seemed to stand still. Mandy was getting good at the pottery business. She realized her art came in handy. The beautiful scenes she painted on her pieces were unique, just as Ben had told her they would be. Her customers really seemed to like them. Most of her pieces were seascapes; she loved the bay, and her work reflected it.

Spring turned into summer; the days were long and hot. Mandy spent long hours in the pottery shop, mixing the clay, learning the wheel, and painting. How she loved to paint. She had forgotten how fulfilling it was. She took long walks on the beach, gathering new ideas for her creations.

Grace was away in the city visiting Ben. Mandy missed their evening chats, the companionship, and the laughter. She longed for Grace's return, but she longed for word of Ben more.

Mandy slid down into a hot bathtub of water, her long curly brown hair tied up. Her skin had gotten dark from the summer sun. She noticed she had lost weight; she could see her bones. She had to start eating better, she thought. Most days, she would be consumed with her work and would forget to eat altogether. Grace had been the one who made sure she received a good meal every day. "Hurry home, Grace," she said out loud. "Hurry home."

She crawled under the cool sheets and tucked her head in the pillow. It was only about eight o'clock in the evening, but every bone in her body ached. The phone rang. *Who could that be?* she thought.

It was Grace. "I'm home, want to come over for some coffee?"

"Sure" she heard herself say.

She hurried up and changed clothes, making her way down the road to Grace's house in record time. She could hear Grace inside humming that old hymn.

"Good to see you, little lady," Grace said as Mandy came through the door. "Been a long trip for this old woman. Come on, let's sit on the porch and have some coffee."

Mandy complied with her request. She wanted to ask about Ben, but she didn't want to seem anxious. She let Grace go on about the airport and the new safety measures taken because of the terrorist attacks the year before. About the noise in the city, she went on and on.

"How was Ben?" Mandy blurted out.

"Well now, isn't that a coincidence? Ben asked me the same thing about you when I got there." Grace smiled. "He's doing much better thanks to you."

"Thanks to me? What do you mean, thanks to me?" Mandy asked in anticipation.

"Seems like you had an effect on my boy. He even smiles when he hears your name. Isn't that something, haven't seen the child smile for the better part of three years. Now he smiles all the time.

"I went down to that big fancy office of his and his employees said the trip he took down here was real good for him. Seems he's been in a good mood ever since."

"I'm glad I was able to help."

Life was changing for Mandy. She didn't know what the future would hold, but she knew life was different. Once she had thought she would never get over the hurt and guilt after Clay's death. But now she could smile and even laugh. Guilt seemed a thing of the past.

"God, bless Ben. Help him to feel your presence in his life as you have caused me to feel it. Thank you, God, for sending Grace to me. Thank you for the healing taking place in my heart, in my life." With that she was asleep. That night, sleep was peaceful.

Grace called early the next morning to let Mandy know Ben would be arriving that afternoon for a visit. She was hoping Mandy would be able to eat supper with them. "Supper would be nice. Want to come over and have a cup of coffee?"

"I can't right now, but I have a favor to ask of you. Could you pick Ben up at the airport in Spring Hill? I need to finish dinner and—"

"That would be fine. What time is he coming in?"

"About four-thirty this afternoon. Delta flight 2621."

"I'll pick him up."

Spring Hill, the closest city to the Cove, was about forty miles away. It would be nice to go into the city. Perhaps she would close the shop today and make a day of it. She could use some new clothes. The weight she had lost made her clothes hang loose on her. It was time, time to make the next move.

Mandy got dressed and headed for Spring Hill in her old truck. She wished she had a nicer car to pick up Ben, but the old truck was all she had. They had never needed anything but the truck for hauling supplies. It would have to do.

She treated herself to a morning at the spa; she got the works. She felt much better when she came out. She felt new and refreshed. She headed for the mall to buy new clothes. Styles had changed since she had been shopping. In the Cove pretty fancy clothes were not needed. She realized she and Clay had led a very sheltered life for the past ten years. Things were so different. She shopped around not knowing what to buy. She was thirty-two and all of the clothes seemed to be for much younger clientele.

A store clerk saw her dilemma and came over to assist. She showed Mandy all of the latest styles. Mandy was tall and trim; the new clothes made her look younger and much more sophisticated. She purchased new shorts, a bathing suit, and summer dresses. The dresses were so different from the frocks that she had been used to wearing.

She dressed in one of her new dresses and headed for the airport. She was a little early, so she shopped around the airport. She heard Ben's flight being announced over the loudspeaker and headed for his terminal. When she saw him, she waved. He walked right past her. *He didn't recognize me*, she thought.

"Ben!" she yelled.

Ben turned to see who was calling him. "Mandy, I was looking for Mom. Didn't recognize you."

"Your mom stayed home to make you dinner. So you're stuck with me."

He didn't respond; they walked in silence to the baggage center then to the truck.

Ben started to laugh, much to Mandy's surprise. "What are you laughing about?"

"Your new look doesn't go with this old truck."

She felt her face get hot. This time it was from anger. "Are you insulting me?"

"Well, you look so different in makeup, your hair all dolled-up. You look like a city girl. Not like the down-to-earth woman I met several months ago."

"You forgot the dress. Don't you want to insult my dress too?" Mandy fumed.

"The dress is nice. It's you, but all the rest—"

She stomped over to the driver's side, got into the truck, and started the engine. "Are you coming?"

Ben loaded up his luggage and barely got into the truck when Mandy took off.

They rode in silence; the entire forty miles the air was thick in the truck. Mandy was so angry she couldn't talk. All that money and time, she thought she was doing a good thing. She dropped Ben off at the end of Grace's driveway, luggage and all, and took off up the road.

Grace came running out when she saw Ben. "Where's Mandy?"

"At home, I guess," Ben said, giving his mother a big hug. "Good to see you, Mom."

They walked into the house together arm in arm. "She was supposed to have dinner with us. What did you say to her?" Grace inquired.

"She went out and had a lady's day in town I guess. She looked so different. I didn't mean to upset her. But I like the old Mandy better."

"You insulted her looks?" Grace questioned Ben as she put the final touches on the table.

"I just said her new look didn't go with that old truck, a fish out of water of sorts."

"Ben, how could you? That's probably the first time she's been to the city since Clay died," Grace scolded. "I'd better call her."

"You go call Mandy, and I'll put my things away."

Grace dialed Mandy's number; the phone rang and rang, and there was no answer. "I'm going up to see if she's okay."

Grace headed to Mandy's house when she saw her coming down the road. Her hair was tossed and she had washed the makeup off. She had on the same new dress. Her eyes were red from crying. "I'm glad you came down, Grace. I don't think I'm going to make dinner tonight. I'm really tired, and I have a lot of work to do tomorrow to catch up from today."

"Little lady, don't you let that son of mine ruin our evening," Grace insisted. "Now you come on, I've made a good dinner, and if I have to kick that son of mine out for us to eat it, we're going to eat it."

Mandy sighed and walked with Grace to her house. She tried to dry her eyes. She didn't want Ben to think she had shed one tear over him.

Dinner was quiet. There was quaint conversation between Grace and Ben, but Mandy didn't utter a word. When dinner was over she helped Grace clean up then excused herself.

How stupid she felt. How could she have been such a fool? *I just met Ben; what did I expect? Ben is nothing to me*, she thought as she readied herself for bed.

She couldn't sleep. She fired her pottery in the kiln at night. Sometimes, like this night, it made the house unbearably hot. She got up and decided to go for a walk on the beach. The sea breeze would feel nice, she thought.

The moon was high in the sky, its silhouette sparkling on the still water. There wasn't much of a breeze. The only sound was the slight lap of the waves on the shoreline. The sand was cool to her bare feet. She spun her hair around her finger and tied it in a knot to get it off her shoulders and neck. The sweat began to run down her chest. She could hear her heart beating in the stillness of the night.

This is so peaceful, I can almost feel God, she thought as she sat on the cool sand. "Lord, I'm sorry for the way I've acted this past year. Clay was the strong one, not me. I don't know what to do. I've made a com-

lady excused herself as Mandy sat stunned at Ben once more eavesdropping on her.

"I hope you're not going to make a habit of this!" she yelled over the roar of the waves.

Ben walked closer and sat beside her. "No, I'm not. I was coming out to talk to you when that lady walked up. I didn't want to interrupt you, so I waited."

"So you weren't spying on me again?"

"I wasn't spying on you the other night. I was going to apologize for my rude behavior."

"You're rude and selfish and anything else I can think of," she smirked, getting to her feet.

"Where are you going?"

"Away from you."

He grabbed her leg and pulled her to the ground, beside him.

She fell to the ground, sand covering her face.

Ben began to laugh at the sight of her. "Could you just hold on one minute?"

"You're the meanest person I know or have ever met. What's wrong with you? You could have broken my leg," she screamed.

"Calm down."

"Calm down? You just snatch me to the ground like that, look at me."

"I am looking at you." He roared with laughter.

Mandy began to laugh. "I must look a mess."

"You do," he said as he reached out to brush the sand from her face.

She drew back as he touched her.

"I don't bite. I was just getting the sand off your face."

"I'm sorry. I really need to go and clean up," she said, getting up. "Please don't pull me down again. People are watching."

He looked around to see a group of people gathering to see what was going on. "We're just playing," he yelled.

When he turned back she was walking down the beach to her house. He started to follow her, but he heard Grace calling from the porch for him. He watched her disappear behind the dunes before he heeded his mother's call.

"I thought maybe you could invite Mandy for supper," she said as he came onto the porch.

"She's already gone home."

"I'll call her and you set the table."

The phone was ringing when Mandy came into the house. She answered it. "Thought maybe you'd like to have supper with us this evening."

"I have to take a bath first, Grace."

"You take your bath and hurry on down, we'll wait."

Mandy took her bath and put on one of her new dresses she had bought in Spring Hill. The blue flowers accented her eyes; it flowed over her curves and hung to her knees. It was cool, and she felt like a woman in it. A woman. She had not felt like a woman for a long time. She looked in the mirror and surveyed her face; her long hair was tussled and hanging in her face. She pushed her hair back and was looking for what Ben was talking about. She shrugged, brushed her hair, and hurried to Grace's.

The table was beautiful, wine glasses, candles, dim lights—what was this? The view from the dining room was breathtaking. You could see the bay through the double glass doors facing the porch. The sun gleamed across the water as it set on the horizon, casting a bright orange silhouette in the sky.

"Grace," Mandy called.

Ben came down the stairs to see the same romantic surrounding she had seen when she walked in.

"Where's Grace?" Mandy asked.

"I don't know. She was here a few minutes ago."

There was a note stuck to the refrigerator. "Gone to Pastor Johnny's house. I forgot I had a meeting with him tonight. Supper's ready, enjoy."

Ben and Mandy looked at each other and laughed. "This looks like a set-up." Mandy laughed.

"Yes it does," Ben replied. "Let's see what we have here."

Mandy and Ben put the baked chicken, broccoli, salad, and rolls on the table. They both ate in silence. When dinner was over they both cleared the table and cleaned the kitchen. It was so strange being here with Ben alone like this. She didn't know what to say. She felt like a shy schoolgirl on her first date.

"Would you like a cup of coffee on the porch? The sun has already set, but the view is beautiful," Ben asked, breaking the silence.

"Sure why not?"

Ben made the coffee while Mandy enjoyed the beauty of the evening. It was peaceful here, tourists walking up and down the beach, birds flitting around before nighttime rest, the sound of the waves pushing against the shore. She leaned against the porch post; the warm breeze against her skin felt so good.

"Coffee, ma'am," he joked, handing her a cup of coffee.

"Thanks. It's a lovely night, don't you think?" she replied nervously. She could hear her voice shake as she tried to speak. All of this was new to her; she didn't know what she was supposed to do. She took her coffee and walked down to the beach, and Ben followed. She kicked her shoes off, set her cup of coffee down, and headed for the water. She ran out into the water and started to swim, turning to look at Ben. "Come on in, the water feels great."

He took off his shoes and followed her. "It's like a hot tub."

"It feels wonderful," she laughed, swirling in the warm water. The tide was going out; she sat down on the bottom. The water was up to her waist. "Come on, have some fun. Loosen up."

With that he came over and gently kissed her. She slapped him on the cheek.

"What was that for?" he demanded.

"I didn't say to kiss me—"

"I wanted to. I've waited months for that kiss."

"Don't do it again," she cried, getting up out of the water and heading to shore.

Mandy picked up her shoes and started running for her house. Ben ran behind and caught her. "What's wrong?" he asked, bewildered, turning her around.

"I don't know what you had in mind, the dinner, this … this—"

"I didn't have anything in mind. I care for you. I thought you cared for me. Your prayer, I heard you. You told God you cared for me. You looked so beautiful sitting across the table and standing here in the moonlight. Playing in the water, I couldn't resist."

"You need to control yourself—"

He grabbed her and kissed her again, this time she let him. "Now you can go home, goodnight." He turned and walked home.

She was stunned. She had asked him not to kiss her, but he had, and she wanted him to do it again. She slowly walked home. She could feel his warmth, his arms around her. She had never felt like this before. She had betrayed Clay. How could she fall for another? She couldn't—she was still Clay's. But Ben was the one on her mind.

She dried herself off and sat on the rock pathway to the beach. What was she supposed to do? She was confused, and yet she longed for Ben to come to her. She cried as she tried to sort through her feelings. "Oh God, I have made such a mess of things. Please help me to do the right thing. Help me to know your will. Help me to understand. Help me to let go of the past so that I can live today." She got up and started to go inside, when she heard Ben calling her name.

"Mandy...Mandy..." He stopped when he saw her standing at the top of rock pathway. "Mandy, I'm sorry if I hurt you. I didn't mean to be so forward..."

She walked down the pathway to him. "You didn't hurt me. I don't know what to do. I have never had any other man, just Clay. We were together since we were children. That's just the way it was for us..."

"You don't have to say anything else, I understand. I understand for the first time." He held her in his arms, and they cried together at the end of the pathway, both letting go of the past. They were exploring a journey together. Neither of them knew where it would take them.

Tourists walking by looked at them; soon they both started to laugh. They sat on the sand and talked for hours. Gone was the barrier that had separated them both from the rest of the world.

Chapter 4

The morning was beautiful as Grace fussed around in her garden humming that old hymn. Ben had just gotten up and walked out on the porch to watch his mother. "Where were you last night?"

"I forgot I had a meeting with the pastor. How was dinner last night?"

"Dinner was wonderful."

"How did things go?"

"What things, Mom? You mean the candlelight or maybe the wine or the delicious dinner? Which one of those things were you talking about?"

"You know what I mean, son—"

"No, Mom, I don't. Dinner was lovely, Mandy was beautiful, and I made a complete fool of myself."

"Now, how in the world did you do that?" Grace came closer to where Ben was standing.

"Well, you can't set up something that perfect and not expect something to happen."

"You didn't do anything stupid, did you? You know she's fragile right now"

Grace's eyebrow raised in suspicion. Ben chuckled as he waved away her thoughts. "No, I respect her too much to do that, but I did kiss her."

"And?"

"She slapped me."

"She did, did she?" Grace laughed to herself. "Full of fire that one is."

"She sure is, and she's the most beautiful woman I have ever laid my eyes on. My heart hurts when I get around her. She's so innocent, so real, so—"

"So perfect for you."

"I wouldn't go that far. Our lives are so different. She lives in a beach house and I live in a high-rise condo. She loves it on the bay. I love the city. I don't see how it could work between us. We are worlds apart." Ben walked back inside and sat at the table.

Grace came in with a basket of fresh vegetables. "Look at these tomatoes. Aren't they beautiful? I think this is the best crop I've had in a long time."

"Mom, I don't want to talk about tomatoes. I have to leave today, and I don't know how to tell Mandy. I can't live here in this place, all the sand and salt air, the endless flow of tourists. I can't ask her to leave this place either. She loves it here just like you do. What is it with you two women?" Ben replied, disgusted at the predicament he had gotten himself into. "I wish I had never met her."

"Ben, don't say that. I've seen you laugh and smile and enjoy yourself with this 'strange woman' as you call her. She has more caring in her big toe than most people have in their whole body." Grace sounded like a mother dog barking in protection of a pup.

"I just can't do this. Do you understand? I have to go pack. It'll be awhile before I come back."

"Are you going to tell Mandy you're leaving?" Grace asked.

"I don't know. I don't know what I'm going to do." Ben went upstairs. *Oh mercy me*, Grace thought. "What now, Lord?"

·   ·   ·   ·   ·

Mandy sprung out of bed and hurried to the bathroom to bathe. Today was her day off, and she was going to enjoy it. *Perhaps a picnic lunch with Ben would be good*, she thought.

"But first I've got do something to this house before I do anything. It needs a good cleaning." She hurried around and cleaned the house, throwing some clothes in the washing machine; the clay from the shop turned everything red.

She dressed in her bathing suit with shorts and a shirt over it. She hummed as she prepared the basket for a picnic lunch. She would surprise Ben with this peace offering, she laughed to herself.

Placing the basket in the back of the truck, she thought about taking Ben to the island for the day. It was only about twenty miles away, and it was so beautiful this time of the year. She knew places to go that the tourists didn't know about. *He will love it,* she thought as she backed down the drive.

She passed a taxi as she drove down the road to Grace's house. *Tourist*, she thought, *probably got lost*. Getting out of the truck, she saw Grace standing in the yard looking down the road.

"You saw that taxi too. Kind of unusual to see a taxi way out here," Mandy said as she approached Grace.

"Yes, I saw the taxi."

"Where's Ben? I thought we'd go for a picnic on the island today. It's such a beautiful day, don't you think?" Mandy rattled on.

"Ben's not here, Mandy. That was him in the taxi." Grace dropped her head and headed for the house.

"Where's he going? I could have driven him if he needed a ride … Grace?"

"He's gone home, honey. Had a big deal to close in the morning. He said he had to get back."

"Without saying goodbye? Why?" Mandy could feel her voice shaking.

"Men. Don't you know, little lady? Men."

"No, Grace. I don't know, tell me what happened?"

"Like I said—"

"I know what you said, but you're not telling me everything." Tears began to stream down her face. She couldn't control them. She felt her legs get weak, and she felt sick to her stomach.

"Please, honey, come inside. It's too hot out here."

Mandy dragged herself inside the house behind Grace; her head was spinning. She tried to recall last night and how wonderful things were. She tried to think if she could have said or done something to upset him. He seemed fine; her heart screamed in her.

"Coffee—"

"No, I don't want any coffee. I want to know what happened."

"I told you he had a big deal—"

"I don't want to hear about big deals, I want to hear about Ben. Please, Grace, tell me, please." Grace reached over and took Mandy's face in her hands. "He's confused, little lady. He's scared, and he thinks that you both live in two different worlds. He feels to lead you on wouldn't be fair. He's confused."

"Confused…he couldn't tell me that? He's just got to run off?" Mandy screamed. "Why, he's the one who—"

"I know, he told me—"

"He told you?"

"Yes he did. We've always been close, and we've always talked about everything together. He's not thinking straight if you ask me. But, little lady, you got under his skin…"

"I've got to go. I can't stay here. I'm sorry, Grace, I love you, and I hope you'll excuse me. I want to be alone."

"I understand."

Mandy ran out of the house to the truck. She couldn't think. She felt dizzy. She stopped in the middle of the road and cried. A car came up behind her and started blowing the horn at her.

"Hey, lady, this is a public road, move on," the driver hollered out the window.

Mandy got out of the truck and stormed toward the car. "This is *not* a public road. It's private. If you have a problem with that, turn your car around and go the other way. I'll move when I'm ready."

The man saw she was crying. "Is there anything I can do to help?"

"No, just go the other way or go around," she cried.

"Are you hurt, do you need a doctor? I'm a doctor, and I can help if you need help."

"I don't need help, please just go around." Mandy couldn't stop screaming, and soon her words were made up of incomprehensible syllables and shrieks.

"I'll wait while you take your bath and we can go together, doctors' orders. You shouldn't be left alone right now."

Mandy slid into a hot bathtub, reflecting on the day, what she could remember of it. *I should have known not to get attached. I don't know why I did.* She thought Ben was so kind and gentle. He had seemed to really care about her. Perhaps she had totally misread his actions. She reflected on the night before when he held her close. He had even kissed her. How could she misread that? She was old-fashioned and took it that he really cared for her. Or maybe he thought she was easy. Either way she felt used.

The restaurant was a tropical paradise. Large banana trees and all types of tropical plants made up the décor. They decided to take a seat on the deck. Caribbean music was playing. People were dancing and laughing. They seemed to not have a care in the world. She, on the other hand, was troubled. She wanted to put the whole thing out of her mind. This was ladies' night.

"Glass of wine?" Grace asked.

"Yes, a glass of red wine would be great."

"Wait, you took that medicine today. I don't know if you should drink anything or not."

"I'll have a small glass of red wine. We don't have to drink the whole bottle." Though she wanted to. She looked around and saw a familiar face coming over to their table.

"Why, ladies, what a surprise to see you here." Dr. Young smiled as he got closer to their table. "How are you feeling, Mandy?"

"Much better, thank you. I'm sorry about my road rage episode today. After all of that you helped me. I really appreciate it."

"Come sit with us, Doctor," Grace invited.

"Oh no, I couldn't intrude."

"Please intrude, we owe you so much," Grace insisted. "Anyway, I was wondering if Mandy should have a drink of wine after she took that medicine today."

"Perhaps she should wait on the wine. I wouldn't advise it. Perhaps some nonalcoholic champagne?" Dr. Young suggested, waving at the waiter. "A bottle of your best nonalcoholic champagne with three glasses, thank you."

"Yes, Dr. Young," the waiter replied.

"You're known here?" Grace asked.

"Yes, my wife and I have been coming here for years. After she died, I come here to celebrate for the both of us."

"Your wife is dead?" Mandy asked.

"Yes, six years ago yesterday."

"I'm so sorry."

"Thanks, but she's still in my heart so—"

"I think I'll have the lobster, what about you, Mandy?" Grace interrupted.

"Sounds good to me," she replied, still staring at Dr. Young. "You look so familiar to me. Do you work at Spring Hill Memorial?"

"Why yes, I do."

"Do I look familiar to you?"

"Not that I recall, but then I see so many people."

"You were the doctor that pronounced my husband dead a year ago. Remember, he drowned? They didn't find his body for three days. You were down at the marina when they brought his body in."

"Yes, I do remember. I remember you too. You blamed yourself for his accident. I gave you a sedative and they took you to the hospital in an ambulance," Dr. Young recalled. "It's nice to see you're doing better, though this morning you were a little upset, wouldn't you say?"

"Let's order now—" Grace interrupted.

"You look good. I hope all is going well with you. Losing someone that close is so devastating. When my wife died, I was a total wreck. My life had been dedicated to saving people, and the one person that I needed to save I couldn't. I thought about becoming a drunk. But I figured that wouldn't help either … so I decided that I would do everything I could to save the people I could and pray for the rest. We can't take responsibility for what God has planned. We just have to accept it. That's hard, I know, but it's the truth. Destroying my life wouldn't have brought Kay back. But I could use my grief to help others. Just as you have done, Mandy, your artwork is beautiful. Every time you sell a piece you bring joy to that person. You are a gifted woman. It's going to be great being your neighbor."

"My neighbor?" Mandy was confused.

"Oh, I forgot to tell you, Dr. Young is buying the house on the hill just up from you. He's going in with Dr. Hagen until he retires," Grace said, wondering if she was in this conversation at all.

"That's wonderful. We can use a little young blood around the Cove. Get it? Young blood?" Mandy joked. When everyone else merely grinned or nodded, she cleared her throat. "I noticed you mentioned God."

"Yes. Well, who else is in control? I don't know of anyone … do you, Grace?"

"I can't think of anyone." Grace felt grateful they had finally included her in their conversation. She was beginning to feel like a third wheel.

Dinner finally came, and they ate chatting about this and that. You could hear the thunder in the distance. The lightning created a light show in the sky. The deck was covered, but it looked like they were in for a summer storm.

"We really need to be going, Grace. It looks like the bottom is going to fall out and that old truck, well there's a lot to be said about that old truck in the rain. It was nice meeting you again, Dr. Young—"

"It's Westbrook … please, call me Wes."

"Wes it is. We really need to be going," Mandy said, getting up from the table.

"Dinner is on me, ladies."

"No, we owe you so much now—"

"I insist." Wes took the bill from Mandy's hand and held it to his chest. "It has been my pleasure to have had the company of two such lovely ladies."

"We're grateful," Mandy replied. "But it's not necessary."

"My pleasure. If you'll wait until I take care of this, I'll follow you ladies home to make sure you get there all right."

"Again we are indebted to you," Grace responded.

On the way home you could see that the storm was moving fast. The roads to the island were narrow and held a lot of water. Mandy knew she needed to get to the mainland before it hit.

"What a pleasant evening. Wes is a kind soul, don't you think?" Mandy said, trying to take her mind off the upcoming storm.

"Yes, he is a fine fella indeed. To buy our dinner, I think he likes you."

"Grace, if you don't stop your matchmaking, I'm going to have to put you out right here."

"With that storm coming?"

"You'd better lay off," Mandy laughed.

Grace was pleased to hear her laugh. After the day they'd had, she was thankful to have her here at all. She was so disappointed in her son. She thought she had raised him better than that. *It is that city life*, Grace thought as she watched the storm getting closer.

"Are you going to be okay by yourself at your house, Grace? You can always stay with me tonight," Mandy asked.

"This old woman has been through a lot of storms. I'll be fine. What about you?"

"I've lived by myself for a year, storms or not. I'll be fine. Let me get you closer to your house so that you won't get wet."

Grace got out of the truck and ran to her porch. "See you, little lady."

"Bye, old woman."

When Mandy reached the end of Grace's driveway she saw Wes waiting for her. She rolled down her window to see what was the matter. "Are you okay?"

"Yes, I just wanted to make sure you both got home safely. I'll follow you to your drive, and then I'll head home."

"Thanks."

Mandy pulled into her drive; she heard Wes blow his horn as he passed. She hurried into the house. The storm was right on top of them now. The thunder was deafening; the lightning was striking everywhere. She turned on the TV to see if they had a special weather report, and they did...severe thunderstorm and the possibility of tornadoes till midnight. About that time the power went off.

"Great, where are the candles?" Mandy said to herself, feeling around in the dark. She found the candles and started looking for the lanterns. She tried to call Grace to see if she was okay; then she remembered what Grace had said—she had weathered the storm before. She settled back in her easy chair and listened to the sound of the rain on the tin roof. She loved the sound of the rain; she loved the majesty of the thunder and the power of the lightning.

She could feel the wind shaking the house. She got up and looked out the back window to see what the bay was doing. She wanted to make sure the water wasn't rising. If the water started to rise she would have to move her clay barrels. The old shed she kept them in was prone to flooding. Clay was the one who always moved those barrels; she didn't even know if she could move them. She wouldn't worry about that now; the tide was low and she didn't have to worry about the water coming up until much later in the night when the tide came back in. And by the looks of the storm, it was going to move out rather quickly.

She settled back into her chair when she heard a knock at the door. She opened it to find Wes drenched standing on the front porch.

"I'm sorry to bother you, but it seems I've locked myself out of the house," he explained.

"Are you an axe murderer?"

"I'm afraid not, but if you want one, we could look one up in the yellow pages." They both laughed.

"Please come in out of the weather. The power is off, but I have lanterns and candles. So we have light."

"Hum, the power isn't off anywhere else that I could see. Forget to pay your power bill?"

"No, I don't think so. Anyway, they wouldn't cut it off at ten on Sunday night, do you think?"

"Have you checked your breaker?"

"No, grab that lantern and let's look."

Mandy and Wes made their way back to the pottery shop; she opened the big door to the breaker box. "Look at this." She pushed the switch and the lights came back on. You could hear the TV blaring from the living room. She ran in and turned it down.

"I guess the lightning flipped the switch. I didn't even think to look at the breakers. I just thought everyone was going to be in the dark."

"Not tonight. I think the rain is letting up some. The thunder is getting farther away. I need to borrow your phone if you don't mind. Mr. Harris has a spare key somewhere, and I don't remember where he told me it was."

"Go right ahead," Mandy said, showing him where the phone was.

She walked back into the kitchen so Wes could have some privacy. She thought about Ben and how he didn't even tell her goodbye. Why didn't he feel the need to tell her that he wasn't going to be around? She could feel the sting of tears filling her eyes. She gently reached up and wiped them away.

"Now, now, no crying on a rainy night. There's enough water out there without you adding to the problem." Wes interrupted her thoughts.

She smiled. "Did you get in touch with Mr. Harris?"

"Yes, I did, fair lady, and I thank you for your assistance. Take two 'thank-you-Lords' and get a good night's sleep," he said, patting her shoulder. "No more tears. Whoever or whatever it is, it's not worth shedding another tear over."

She smiled again and thanked him for his kindness. When he was gone she walked out on the back porch. The air was so fresh after a summer rain. Everything smelled so clean. She wished the rain could have washed away her hurt. Perhaps it was God's way of telling her she was on the wrong track.

"Lord, I know you have everything worked out, but if you could let me in on it, I sure would appreciate it."

She decided to take a walk on the beach, maybe even make sure Grace was okay. The sand was wet and cool to her bare feet. She walked near the shore, the waves washing up on her feet and legs; the water was warm. The night was still, just the sound of the waves lapping against the shore. Lights of the houses up and down the shore were the only light the night offered. The moon was behind dark ugly clouds. That's the way she felt, dark and ugly.

She didn't want to dwell on Ben, but her mind kept going back to him. She tried to search her memory for details, anything to give her a reason for him leaving her. She had kept herself away from people for a year. When she decided to reenter life, it had been a disaster.

She looked up toward Grace's house and could see her busy in the kitchen. *Good, she's okay*, she thought as she continued on her walk. Tourists were beginning to come out of the motel down the way to walk on the beach. She thought about just going home, saying two "thank-you-Lords," and going to bed. She turned around and started walking toward the house when she heard Grace calling her name.

She walked toward where Grace was standing on the back porch. She really didn't want to talk to anyone now, but she didn't want to be rude either. "I see you weathered the storm okay."

"Sure did. It was a bad one wasn't it?"

"Yes, it was. We really needed the rain, though."

"Yes, my garden will be happy. Want to come in?"

"I was just going home and go to bed."

"Tired?"

"I think I'm just drained. It's been a long, eventful day. Thanks anyway. I'll see you in the morning."

"It's a date. I love you, little lady. God does too. You remember that now, you hear. Don't go home and cry yourself to sleep over that son of mine."

Mandy chuckled at Grace; she always had to have the last word. She waved and headed down the beach toward home. She didn't intend to cry herself to sleep over Ben. She realized for the first time in her life that relationships were complicated when you're dealing with other people's feelings. One never knows what's in the mind of another human being. She just assumed that Ben felt the same way she did. She never stopped to realize that perhaps he didn't. She would never take anything for granted again.

The morning sun shining through the curtains was a welcome sight. The seagulls were squawking; a gentle breeze was blowing. The sounds of the bay didn't reflect that a storm had ripped through the night before.

People were walking on the beach to the sound of children playing. What a wonderful sound. She had never had children. She had never even thought about it. Her heart dropped as she thought perhaps she would never know the joy of having children. She and Clay thought they had plenty of time. She had married when she was twenty-one. She felt she was too young to become a mother; now she was thirty-two. Time was ticking away, with no prospect of her ever being a mother. She didn't know why she was having these thoughts now when there was nothing she could do about it. She should have had them earlier and she wouldn't be alone now.

She thought maybe she would get a dog for a companion. Dogs made good companions; they didn't require you to know what they were thinking or where their heads were at—they just loved you. "That's what I'll do, I'll get a dog," she said as she climbed out of bed. "I'll look in today's paper for one."

She made the coffee and took the paper out on the back porch to look for a dog. Looking through the want ads she found lots of puppies. *Puppy, lots of care,* she thought. *Maybe I should get one from the animal shelter.* You could get a full-grown dog that way. "No, I think I want to be the one to form its personality. What kind though?" There were big dogs, little dogs, fuzzy dogs, slick dogs, registered dogs, and non-registered dogs. "I didn't know there would be such a big selection."

"Selection, what are you selecting?"

Mandy looked up to see Wes in his jogging clothes running up to her porch. "Good morning." She greeted Wes with a friendly smile. "I see you found a way into your house."

"Yoo-hoo, anyone home?" Grace called from the front of the house.

"We're around back, Grace, come on out. Would you like a cup of coffee, Wes?"

"No thanks. Never drink the stuff."

"Grace, grab yourself a cup of coffee on your way out," Mandy shouted.

"Will do."

"Yes, I did. How are you this beautiful morning? You look great." He meant it; she was a beautiful woman. He was glad they were going to be neighbors. Mandy had a way about her that made people like her; she was a pleasant person with lots of love to offer someone. *No wonder Clay loved her*, he thought.

"Well, looks like we're having a party this morning. What are you looking for in the paper, little lady?" Grace asked, pulling up a chair to sit in.

"A dog."

"A dog? What do you want a dog for?" Grace seemed confused by the prospect.

"You know, man's best friend all that stuff." Mandy laughed. "I get lonely, and I thought a dog would be a good companion. You can't trust men, no insult intended, Wes."

"None taken." Wes smiled at the two women bickering over a dog.

"But a dog is there through thick and thin, rich or poor or—"

"Wait a minute, are you going to marry the dog or what?" Grace laughed.

"Well, I just might, you never know. It's according to how we get along, if he's a good boy." They all roared with laughter.

"I have a friend that has some puppies right now, if you'd like we can go over and look at them. They aren't registered or anything. I think they're just mutts," Wes suggested as he sat on the steps.

"Now that sounds like a good idea. When do you want to go?" Mandy was excited at the thought.

"I can go change and pick you up in half an hour."

"That sounds great."

"Half hour it is." Wes jogged back up the beach to his house.

"Do you want to come with us, Grace?"

"No, I think I'll go get ready. You two have a good time."

"Okay, don't say I didn't ask." Mandy laughed.

Mandy and Grace said their goodbyes, and Mandy hurried to change before Wes arrived. She put on shorts, a shirt, and sandals, brushing her long hair and pulling it back into her makeshift hairdo she always wore. She was ready to find her new companion. She rushed around in excitement at the prospect of not being alone anymore. She would have someone to talk to and hold. She would be able to love again.

Wes blew his horn to let her know he was there. She ran out and climbed into his new Hummer. "This is awesome. I've never ridden in one of these before."

"I like it. It helps having something to drive on these sand and shell roads around here," Wes replied. He could feel his hands start to sweat on the wheel. Just sitting next to her made his heart beat faster. He was hoping she was not aware of the way he felt about her. He had only known her for a couple of days, but he already longed for her.

He had not thought much about women since his wife died. He had buried himself in his work. He had not dated or even gotten close to another woman. But now, this young woman was making him feel like a schoolboy, and she didn't even know she had that effect on people. She was so innocent, so pure. The kind of woman any man would be proud to have, and she was sitting right next to him. Her excitement was contagious.

"This is not the car you had last night." She interrupted his thoughts.

"No, no, you're right. I have a car for special occasions."

"Oh, last night was a special occasion?" She smiled. "We must have messed up your plans."

"No, you didn't. Sometimes I just like to get in my car, let the top down, and go."

"Dr. Young, what should be said about you?"

He laughed at her; she was full of joy today. He was glad to see she had her feeling for this other person under control. He wondered if it was a boyfriend that had upset her the day before and he was interfering. Right then he didn't care, the other person's loss was his gain, and he was not going to let anything get in the way of enjoying someone who was so precious.

"Where are we going?"

"Well, Todd lives about five miles up the bay in a little place called Spring Creek. It's a fishing—"

"I know where Spring Creek is. The fishermen there are having a hard time with the government right now. They want them to only fish in season and with special nets."

"That's right. Todd is having it rough right now, but he has been saving money all his life. He's able to take care of his family. They used to be rather wealthy, now they are thankful to survive."

"That is so sad. To think God has been replenishing the bay for thousands of years for men to fish for food and now they think it's the fishermen that are hurting the ecosystem when it's all of the land developers, not the fishermen." Mandy was loyal to the locals. She too was a local and she knew the local economy depended on the fishermen.

Wes was surprised to hear Mandy talk like that. She was well versed on local issues to have been shut up for a year. "You're sure up on the news."

"Of course. I've lived here for more than ten years or so. We're all in this together. If the fishermen leave it will hurt tourism, and that affects my business."

He was impressed. "You need to run for county commissioner or mayor or something. I'd vote for you."

Mandy laughed. "What a joker."

"No, I'm serious."

"I am too, you're a joker."

She smiled that enchanting smile at him, cocking her head slightly each time she smiled. He could feel his pulse rate increase. *Calm down*, he thought as they turned into Todd's driveway. Todd's children were playing with the puppies in the front yard while Todd and his wife sat on the porch watching them.

"Wes, how in the world are ya?" Todd said, walking out to the Hummer.

"Fine, my friend. I see those little ones playing with your puppies, fine children you have," Wes said, watching the children rolling in the grass with the puppies.

"Yeah, they love them puppies. I keep telling them we have to find homes for 'em, but you know how children are. No, you don't, you never had any." He laughed, patting Wes on the back.

"Actually that's why we're here. This is Mandy Bowls, my new neighbor. She's in the market for a puppy. I told her about yours, and she wanted to come look at them."

"Help yourself. The kids can tell you more about them than me. They're a mix, just mutts."

Mandy got out of the truck and walked over where the children were. "Hello, my name is Mandy, and I sure would like it if you'd let me see those pretty puppies you have there."

"My name is Mary Margaret, and this is my puppy, you can look at them over there. I think you'd like them better. This here one you wouldn't like, 'cause he only likes me."

"Oh, I see," Mandy said, kneeling down to talk to Mary Margaret. "Which one do you think I would like?"

"That one over there. He's the runt. That means he's the smallest one of the bunch. He's sweet, but he don't like me, so I don't like him, so you take him," Mary Margaret instructed.

"What kind is he?" Mandy asked, picking up the little golden puppy.

"He's a Labrador mix. My daddy calls him a mutt."

"Oh, he does. I think I like him. See, he likes me too. What's your puppy's name?"

"Boo."

"That's a fine name for a friend, isn't it?"

"How'd you know he was my friend?"

"He is, isn't he?"

"He sure is." Mary Margaret smiled; you could see she was missing her two front teeth.

"Mary Margaret says this is the puppy for me. How much are you asking for them?"

"We ain't askin' nothin' for 'em. You want him, he's yours." Todd laughed. He was happy to get rid of the puppy. "One less mouth to feed."

"I'll take good care of him, what do you feed them?"

"Ain't never had a dog before, have ya?"

"No, this is my first one."

"You that pottery guy's wife, ain't you? Your husband drowned a while back, didn't he?"

"Well, yes, I am. Clay. Clay was my husband's name."

"Yeah, that was a fine man he was. I used to trade him fish for some of that fancy pottery he made. Gave it to the missis. She sure loved that stuff."

"I like fish, and she likes pottery. If she'd like to come by the shop, I'll be glad to keep up the tradition," Mandy said, glad that she could return the favor for the puppy.

"She sure will be glad of that. See here this pond piece? Your husband said you laughed at him when he made it. But it's real pretty in the missis' pond."

It was the warped bowl with the long crack down the side she had encouraged him to throw away. He had made this lady proud to own it and he was right; it was a lovely piece in her pond. Todd's wife had a beautiful yard; it was full of blooming flowers, statues, and pottery. She was glad to know Clay had blessed so many people. She would have to carry on his legacy.

"It was nice to meet you, Todd. You tell the missis anytime she wants to come by, come on and we'll wheel and deal. Thanks for the puppy."

"I sure will, Ms. Bowls."

Wes said his goodbyes, hugged Todd's neck, and climbed into the Hummer.

"What a wonderful family, Wes. Thank you for bringing me over. I didn't know Clay blessed so many people. I remember the day we laughed over the piece in his pond. I tried to get Clay to throw it out, but he wouldn't hear of it. I know why now. I think I've been going at this all wrong. I think of the pottery shop as a business and Clay thought of it as a life. Wow."

"They are fine people, a little rough, but they are fine people. I got to know them when their oldest son died of AIDS a couple of years ago. He was a hemophiliac, contracted AIDS through a bad blood transfusion several years earlier. They were devastated. They didn't have health insurance, so I rendered my services free. I got the hospital to hold a fundraiser for the rest of his medical costs and funeral." Wes' voice broke.

"I'm sorry. There seems to be so much death and hurt in the world. I thought I was the only one who was suffering, but I can see it's everywhere. Thanks again for bringing me."

"What are you going to name that little one?" Wes asked.

"I don't know yet. He's pretty, isn't he?"

"I think he's a fine one." Mandy played with the puppy as Wes drove toward home. "Would you like some lunch? I know a nice little place on the riverfront. You can even carry your mutt in."

"That sounds nice, but I need to pick up some stuff for him. You know, dog things. You do know what dog things are, don't you?"

"No, what are dog things?" Wes laughed.

"I don't know. I was hoping you knew."

"Let's stop at the County Store. Ms. Morrison knows what dog stuff is."

"Thanks, Wes."

Ms. Morrison did know what a dog needed. Mandy bought shampoo, a collar, a leash, dog toys, puppy food, and a puppy bed.

"That'll get you started. As he grows you'll know what he needs. He'll let you know. Dogs have a way of doing that. I think he's a fine young pup. What are you going to call him?" Ms. Morrison asked.

"I don't know. I'll have to think about it. Thanks for all of your help. See you soon." Mandy took her puppy stuff and got in to the Hummer.

"Ready to go?"

"Ready."

The Riverside Café was a quaint little place right on the river that ran into the Gulf. It was open to the outdoors; you could sit, have your meal, and watch the boats going in and out. It had a tropical appeal. You could carry your pet in if you had it on a leash. Mandy put the collar and leash on the puppy; they went inside and found a table on the riverside. It was wonderful; a cool breeze blew in from the Gulf. The people were friendly, the waiter even brought out a bowl of water for the puppy to drink while they ate.

"This is a wonderful little place. How did you find it?" Mandy asked, untangling the puppy from her feet.

"Todd and his wife brought me here after their son died. I've been coming here ever since. I know the owner pretty well. We go out fishing together on his boat. They catch all of their own seafood here, so you know it's fresh."

"It's so peaceful, look at that yacht going there. Wouldn't you like to take a cruise on that?" Mandy said, admiring the huge luxury vessel. "Those people act like they don't have a care in the world. Just think, you could get on that boat and set off for destinations unknown."

"I want to show you something after lunch."

"What is it?" Mandy asked in anticipation.

"It's a surprise. So just cool your jets, wait and see." Wes smiled at her child-like excitement.

After lunch they climbed into the Hummer and headed for the marina at the cove. "Where are we going, Wes? Come on, let me in on the secret." Mandy held the sleeping puppy on her lap.

"We're almost there. You'll see. You may be disappointed, though. Here we are," Wes said, pulling up to the marina where yachts were docked. "Follow me please, Ms. Bowls."

Mandy climbed out carrying the puppy and followed Wes into the marina. He walked up to the service counter; the man at the counter said, "Good afternoon, Dr. Young, everything is ready."

"Thank you, Don." Wes slipped him a twenty, took Mandy's arm, and led her out to the dock.

She was amazed at the size of the boats; they were huge. You could live on them, they were so big. People were everywhere up and down the dock. Others were lounging on their yachts, entertaining. Wes led her up to a large beige yacht with a full crew.

"Welcome aboard, Dr. Young. Everything is ready, just as you asked."

"You had all of this planned? You rented a yacht and everything? How wonderful," Mandy shrieked with excitement.

"No, I didn't rent a yacht, this one is mine. I had it pulled out of dry storage to take her for a cruise. I hadn't even met you yet. Would you like to go along? We're only going for a dinner cruise. You game?"

"Sure, let's go, Captain." Mandy gathered up the puppy and followed Wes aboard the yacht.

The *Katie I* was a beautiful yacht. She had brass-lined rails, sunning decks, and large living quarters, complete with all of the luxuries of life. You could disappear in this yacht and never miss the comforts of home. The crew consisted of a captain, chef, and two deckhands. All ready to meet your every need.

"Wes, I don't mean to be nosy, but where did you get the money to buy such a yacht as this? Just what is it you do at Spring Hill Memorial?"

"I work with cancer patients and cancer research, of course. One of the leading specialists in the nation. The yacht was a gift from my father to Kay her real name was Katie we called her Kay. He gave it to her when she found out her cancer was terminal. We sailed the seven seas," Wes said, pretending to be a pirate. "That was her dream, to just sail away. My dad is a world-renowned plastic surgeon. Need I say more? When Kay died, I put the yacht in dry dock, and she's been there ever since. I thought it was time to pull her out and see if she is still seaworthy. The marina checked and tested everything, put her in the water, and here we are. You can put the puppy down now," Wes instructed as he took the puppy from Mandy's arms.

"What if he has an accident? You know puppies." Mandy struggled to take the puppy from Wes.

"If he has an accident, Bo will take care of it. Right, Bo."

"Yes sir, Dr. Young," Bo responded.

"Now, my dear, if you'll follow Judy, she'll take you to the guest quarters where you can change if you like. I think you'll find anything you might need. If you don't find what you need, ring the bell and Judy will get it for you. Thank you, Judy, for your assistance," Wes said, taking the puppy back from Mandy.

Mandy followed Judy through the beautiful entertaining room. There was large lounging couches and fine furniture throughout, soft music playing, hors d'oeuvres on the table, a bar, tinted glass so that you could still enjoy the beauty of the voyage while being inside. A long corridor opened to a stairwell that led to the sleeping quarters. Judy showed her into the guest quarters. A large suite with a king-size bed, walk-in closets. It had its own bathroom and dressing room. For a moment she thought she had taken her into the wrong suite.

She walked into the closet; it was filled with ladies' clothes. Dressers were located under the hang-up clothes section. She felt strange going through the clothes in the closet. She wondered whose they were. If they were Kay's, she would feel strange putting them on. She decided to just keep her clothes on. She closed the door and went back upstairs where Wes was playing with the puppy on the deck.

"You couldn't find anything?" Wes asked, looking disappointed in her.

"I have on shorts, that's good enough," Mandy replied.

"I was planning a nice dinner onboard and thought perhaps you would like to dress for the occasion."

"You didn't tell me that. I felt a little strange going through some-one else's clothes." Mandy peered over the edge of the boat; she didn't want to look at him.

"Judy, could you please take the puppy and find him something to eat? I'll assist Ms. Bowls. Thanks," Wes instructed, giving the puppy to Judy and taking Mandy's arm. "Come on now, let's see what we have for you." He led her back into the guest suite, opened the closet, and began pulling out gowns. "Here, this one is nice. It would look lovely on you." He handed her an emerald gown, low cut in the back with a rope coil that wrapped around the waist.

The dress was beautiful; it seemed to be her size. She was surprised at the clothes he pulled out for her. There were matching shoes and jewelry with the gown. "Will this do for dinner?" Wes asked, admiring his choice.

Mandy clutched the dress and accessories next to her. "Whose clothes are these? I feel funny about wearing someone else's clothes."

Wes laughed at her as he started to leave the room. He looked back to ask, "Will half an hour be enough time for you to dress, or should I ask the chef to wait an hour before serving dinner? We're having guests, and I want to show you off."

"Wait, what do you mean, show me off?" She threw the dress on the bed. "Please don't get the wrong idea. I just meant some of my family is meeting us, and I want them to know the people, *ladies* if you prefer, from the Cove are fine people. I have been trying to convince my father that moving to the Cove is a good thing for me. He doesn't agree, and I wanted to make a good impression," Wes explained.

"I don't know." She felt strange about the whole thing.

"Mandy, please, it would mean so much to me. You are a lovely lady, and I just … I just … I understand all of this is a surprise—"

"That's the understatement of the year. I'm a plain person, Wes. I'm not fancy. I've never worn a gown in my life. Whose clothes are these?"

"They're my clothes. See, they still have the tags on them. That dress has never been worn. I don't wear them, of course, but like today, my father's yacht is meeting us. He just called in, and, well, you are onboard, and we have to have dinner. Just think of it as an adventure. I know it's a strange spot to be put in, but if you could just help me out, I sure would appreciate it," Wes pleaded.

"Well, okay, you helped me so I guess the least I can do is return the favor. Do I need to do my hair and face and—"

"Do the Cinderella thing, not that you need a fairy godmother or anything. You're already beautiful. You know what to do, you're a woman."

"What makes you think I know what to do? The closest I have come to rich people is the tourists that come into my pottery shop, and now you."

"You'll do fine, Mandy. We'll do fine. Half an hour or an hour?"

"When will they be here?"

"They will be here any minute. You can do this," he said, kissing her on the forehead.

"Half an hour."

"Wonderful. Thanks, Mandy, I really appreciate it."

"I'll let you know when the evening is over." She bit her lip and turned to the clothes on the bed. She walked into the bathroom. There she found designer makeup for every shade of skin, hair products, different Chanel fragrances—everything she would need for the Cinderella transformation. She pulled her hair back and started on her face. She pulled half of her hair back, placing emerald hair décor stones in her hair; she let the rest hang down her back. She put the gown and accessories on. Standing looking in the mirror, she felt like Cinderella, and her Prince Charming was waiting for her. She laughed at the thought and started up the stairs.

She could hear strange voices as she reached the top of the stairs. It was Wes and another man arguing. As she topped the stairs the two men stopped arguing. They both stood stunned looking at her.

"Good evening," she said, making her way into the room.

"Father, this is my friend Mandy Bowls. Mandy, this is my father, Dr. Raymond Young, III."

"It's a pleasure to meet you, Dr. Young."

Dr. Young walked across the room as if he was sure of himself. He was a very distinguished looking man.

"The pleasure is all mine indeed, young lady. Why, Wes, you didn't tell me you had such a lovely young lady as a friend. Please come sit over here beside me and tell me all about yourself." Dr. Young ushered Mandy to the sofa.

"Now, now, Raymond, you let this young lady alone. Hello, I'm Wes' mother, Catherine," Catherine said, holding out her hand to Mandy. "Come now, my dear, let's let these old men talk while you and I get to know each other."

Mandy looked back at Wes as she followed Wes' mother to the bar.

Catherine was a beautiful woman. She was tall and thin with long dark curly hair, coal black eyes, and olive skin. She had a heavy foreign accent when she spoke.

"Would you care for a cocktail, my dear?" Catherine asked, fixing herself a drink.

"No thanks, I don't drink."

"Now tell me about yourself and how you met my son."

"I own the pottery shop at the Cove. I've lived there about ten years. My husband died about a year and a half ago. I just stayed in the Cove after his death. I reopened his pottery shop about six months ago. I wanted to sell some of my late husband's pottery. I'm working at learning the business. I must say it's been interesting. I met your son quite by accident. He helped me out on a medical issue a few days ago."

"Oh, you've only known Wes a few days? Well, he's a wonderful man. He takes after me, not his father. You'll come to appreciate that. Wes is a very kind person. He's the apple of my eye, you might say."

"Is he the only child you have?"

"No, no, my dear, I have three sons. Wes is just the one I hold in my heart. His brothers are spoiled rich kids like their father. Wes never was. He didn't even want this yacht. His father insisted that all the Young men show their wealth. Wes wasn't interested. He went out and made his own mark in the world. Cancer research, you know."

"Yes, I know."

"Wes' father didn't approve of Kay, Wes' wife, until she was dying. Then he gave the yacht to her. She always wanted to bask in the families' fortune. Wes didn't, so they argued a lot about wealth. Wes worked long hard hours to give her what she wanted, but she was never satisfied. She wanted to be the wife of Dr. Young IV. That's not Wes. He's a wonderful man. Oh, I think I've already said that." Catherine finished her drink. While pouring her next, she offered again to Mandy. Mandy politely shook her head.

"You don't have to sell Wes to me. I like him. He's seems to be a fine man. I can see you're proud of him. He's simple, or at least I thought so until today. He bought the house just up the hill from mine."

"All of this fame and fortune doesn't affect him. He wants to be ordinary. His father won't let him. Regardless of what you may think, Raymond is proud of Wes. He calls him a chip off the old block, if you know what I mean. Sure you won't have a drink?"

"No thanks. I think what Wes does is most commendable. Cancer research is very important."

"I know, but Wes wants to be a small-town doctor. His father won't hear of it."

"He could still be a doctor and do cancer research at the Cove, don't you think?" Mandy's head was spinning from the movement of the yacht. She sat on one of the bar stools at the bar. The dress fit her snugly, and it was difficult to sit properly.

"Here, let's sit over here where it is more comfortable." Catherine motioned to the lounge area with her glass.

Wes walked over and sat on the arm of the chair Mandy was sitting in. "What are you two ladies taking about?"

"My favorite subject—you, darling," Catherine answered. "I think I'll see if I can't get Raymond settled. He's a little high strung today."

"You look beautiful in that dress, Mandy. You did a wonderful job dressing so quickly." Wes patted her shoulder.

"Wes, I don't know about this. I mean this isn't exactly my style. I'm a blue jeans and shorts kind of woman. This dress is so. ... " She pulled at the gown.

"You could have fooled me, and you did fool my father. He thinks you are the most beautiful woman he has ever seen."

"And you?"

"I've felt that way since the first time I saw you at the marina that day when you were yelling at me. They'll have dinner and leave. Then we can head back into port. I really appreciate you doing this for me."

"I think you're going to owe me one after this." They both laughed.

At dinner conversation was light. Raymond kept staring at Mandy. She felt uncomfortable; she felt like he was looking right inside her and knew she was just a plain country girl.

After dinner the Youngs excused themselves and boarded their own yacht, it was moored close by. Wes gave the captain orders to head to port.

"Can I take this dress off now?" Mandy asked, pulling at it again.

"Sure, you know where everything is, if you need anything—"

"I know, ring for Judy."

The trip in was wonderful. The sky was full of stars, and the Milky Way seemed to cover the entire sky. Mandy felt better in her shorts holding her new puppy. Wes sat next to her. They didn't need words, the night said it all. This was the life, she thought. Out here on the bay, the moon, the stars, the smell of the salt air. It was as if the whole world had faded and they were here in their own world.

"I think Duke would be a good name." Wes broke the silence.

"Duke. Why Duke?"

"Because he looks like royalty, a royal name for royalty." They both laughed.

"Sounds good to me," she said, holding the puppy up to her face. "I hereby name you Duke of the pottery shop." She held Duke close to her; she could feel his tiny heart racing. "This has been a big day for you, huh?" she said to Duke.

"It sure has," Wes answered.

"I was talking to Duke." They both laughed again.

Wes reached over and squeezed Mandy's shoulder. "I know we haven't known each other very long, and perhaps I'm out of line. Do you think we could go on a date?"

"I thought we were on a date. I mean, after all, I've even met your parents." She laughed.

"I'm serious, Mandy."

"So am I. I want you to know that I'm guarding my emotions. I've been too gullible. I don't want to mislead you. I'm not interested in a relationship. They're too painful. But we can be friends and go out. Will that work for you?"

"I guess it'll have to, won't it? I'll take what I can get."

"I can't give any more than that right now. I hope you understand."

"I don't, but like I said, I'll take what I can get."

Chapter 5

The sound of the birds singing woke Mandy, the bright sun shining through her curtains, the sound of the waves washing against the shore. *Home, I love this place. There is no other place on earth I'd rather be than right here,* she thought. She heard Duke whining from his doggie box. "Time to let you out for your morning bathroom run."

She picked him up, put him on the leash, and headed for the beach. Ever since she had gotten Duke, they took morning runs together. She had not heard from Wes in several weeks since the cruise. He had returned to Spring Hill to settle his affairs. But she was satisfied with her new friend. Duke didn't require much—just love, attention, and lots of puppy food. She was amazed at how much he had grown in such a short time. She had taught him to sit and to stay. They were still getting to know each other. He seemed to love her, and she knew she loved him. He never asked questions nor did he ever judge her. He just loved her the way she was.

He followed her everywhere she went in the pottery shop. The customers loved him too. He would get into her clay and string it out if she didn't watch him. She and Grace would joke about him being the next potter in the Bowls' family.

After her run she got into a hot bath. It was still early and she had time before she opened the shop. Business was good, and she was getting the hang of the business now. It was second nature to her. She read all she could find and experimented a lot. She made blunders, but she never threw them out. She knew special people would want her special pieces.

She heard a knock at the front door. She thought perhaps it was Grace. She climbed out of the tub, put on her robe, and went to the door. It was Ben. She stood at the door. She didn't want to open it. He knocked again. She cracked the door.

"Can I help you?" she asked through the cracked door.

"I came to see you. It's been a long time—"

"I'm not ready. I'll be with you in a minute." She hurried in to put on shorts and a shirt. Ran a quick brush through her hair and went back to the door where Ben was waiting. She opened the door. "Good morning."

"Good morning. I got into Mom's last night, and thought I'd come over and visit."

"You did, did you? So, what do you want?"

"What do you mean, what do I want? I just came over to say hi."

"Hi. Now I've got to get the shop open."

Ben followed Mandy into the pottery shop. "Oh Mandy, you've really gotten the hang of this, haven't you? These pieces are wonderful."

"Well, I've had a lot of time to work on it."

"Look, I know you are probably mad at me because I didn't say goodbye when I left, but—"

"You didn't say anything. You led me on then you left. I'm not mad, just wiser."

"What is that supposed to mean?"

"You're the big-city man, you figure it out."

Another knock on the door interrupted their conversation. "Excuse me," Mandy said sarcastically, heading for the front door. "Wes, when did you get back? Come on in, we can have a cup of tea."

"I have so much to tell you, Mandy. Who is this?" Wes asked as he followed her in.

"Oh, this is Ben, Grace's son. He came by to say hi. Say hi, Ben. This is Dr. Wes Young, my new neighbor."

"Pleased to meet you, Ben. Just call me Wes," Wes said, shaking Ben's hand. "Anyway, Mandy, the cancer research center is going to move my lab here to the Cove. They say research here will be an addition to the existing research because there have been so much data about sea plants and cancer—"

"I hate to interrupt, but I guess I should go." Ben felt out of place.

"Please stay and have tea with us. Any son of Grace's is a friend of mine. Your mom is a wonderful lady. If I was a bit older I'd have to ask her out." Mandy and Wes laughed. Ben didn't.

"I don't want to intrude. I should have called first." Ben started toward the door.

"Yes, you should have called first."

"Nonsense, you come on in and have tea. Mandy, you be nice," Wes scolded.

"Both of you come in and have tea and I'll open the shop." Mandy went into the pottery shop.

Ben watched as Wes followed Mandy around the shop telling her his news. He could feel his face get hot every time Wes got close to Mandy.

She laughed at his excitement and patted him on the back. "Well done, Dr. Young. See, I told you that everything would work out for you. I told your mom that they would let you do your research right here."

Once the shop was open, both Wes and Mandy came in and sat at the table where Ben was sitting.

"So, what do you do, Ben?" Wes stirred his tea.

"I'm a landscaper. I have a business in Boston. We landscape professional buildings." Ben couldn't take his eyes off Mandy.

"Have I interrupted something?" Wes noticed the way Ben was staring at Mandy.

"No, you haven't. Ben just came over to say hi. He came to see his mom, not me." Mandy tried to be reasonable, but she could feel the anger rising within her.

"Well, I really must go anyway. I have a million things to do. The trucks will start arriving soon with my equipment." Wes bent over and kissed Mandy on the forehead. "I'll see you." He was out the door.

They sat in silence for minutes, staring at each other. "Is that—"

"No, we're just friends." Mandy got up from the table and put the cups in the sink. "I don't know what you expected you'd find here, Ben, but what you did really hurt me. I couldn't believe you could just walk away like that without a word. Did you expect I would run to you with open arms?"

"I thought we had something."

"I thought we had something too, and then you just left without saying anything. You said nothing, you just left!" she paced the floor. "You led me to believe you cared for me. You knew what I had been through—"

"Please let me explain—"

"There's nothing to explain. You let your feelings be known loud and clear. I may be a country girl from the sticks, but I'm not an idiot. Do you hear me?"

"Yes, Mandy, and so does everyone else."

"How dare you come into my home and expect me to be the good hostess. Yes, Mr. Ben, whatever you say, Mr. Ben." Tears began streaming down her face.

He grabbed her and kissed her. She pushed away and slapped him. "I want you to leave, now."

"I'm not going anywhere until you let me explain."

"I don't want to hear your explanation. Nothing could explain what you did. Do you understand?"

"I was scared—"

"I was scared too. I just opened up my little heart and let you in. Now you're locked out."

"Please, Mandy, I want a second chance."

"You have got to be kidding. If you'd come to me and said, 'Mandy, I need time,' I would have given it to you. But you didn't say anything. You just left. It's as bad as someone dying. You don't know what happened, they're just gone. I can't bear the thought of getting close to you and you leaving again."

"I won't ever leave you again. I know what I did was wrong, but I—"

"Please, Ben. For my sake, please leave. I can't talk about this anymore. I don't even want to think about it. It took me awhile to get over what you did. I don't want to relive it, okay?"

The bell in the pottery shop rang to let her know she had a customer. She turned and walked into the shop to find Wes' mother standing there.

"I thought I'd come and visit you. We came into port last night. Wes is busy, so I thought I'd bother you until he's done," Catherine said, looking at the pottery on the shelves. "This is divine work. Mandy. You're very gifted."

"Thank you, Catherine."

"Why dear, you've been crying. Are you all right, do I need to call Wes?"

"No, no, I'm fine. It's been a really crazy morning. I'm so glad you came by." Mandy heard the front door close. She knew Ben was gone. She was glad he had left. She would deal with Grace later.

"Now, I just have to have one of these." Catherine picked up one of her most prized pieces, a tall floor vase that had a picture of the entire cove painted on it. It had the lighthouse, the rock levee, and the dunes, and in the distance you could see the marina. It had taken Mandy a week to paint it. It stood at the counter with long cattails and pompous grass in it. She had decided to use some of her pieces for decoration in the shop to make it more appealing to her customers; also she demonstrated ways to use her pieces. She hadn't really wanted to sell that particular piece, but for Wes' mother she would have to let it go.

"Please, darling, how much do you want, five thousand? Ten?"

"No, it's not that expensive. I was asking a thousand for it though."

"Sold." Catherine reached into her purse for her wallet. "Wrap it up. I'm going to put it on the yacht. Every time I look at it, I'll think of my dear Wes. Thank you, Mandy, you've made my day."

"I'm glad I could be of service." Mandy wrapped the beautiful vase for Catherine.

She started to take it out for Catherine when she stopped her and said, "No, don't lift that heavy thing. I'll get Charles to get it. Charles," she shouted out the door. "I need you to come in and get this vase for me."

Charles came in to carry the heavy vase to the car. "Careful," Catherine instructed. "This is a priceless piece."

"Yes, ma'am." Charles carried the piece to the car.

"Here's a thousand dollars, plus a tip for your hard work. I think the piece is worth much more than a thousand." Catherine handed her twenty hundred-dollar bills.

"Really Catherine, it's not necessary for you to—"

the last of the boats coming into the harbor, that old lighthouse directing it's path away from the rock levee. The moon was high overhead; the sky was full of sparkling stars, a soft breeze blew, and the sound of the waves washed ashore. In the distance you could hear the sound of children laughing.

Mandy lay back and watched the sky. It was an awesome sight. The heavens were full of blinking lights; you could see the airplanes flying to destinations unknown. "Isn't this wonderful? Peaceful?" she whispered.

"Yes, it is. I can understand why you and Mom love it here so much. It's so peaceful, so quiet." Ben lay back on the sand with Mandy.

You could hear the sound of footsteps rapidly coming up the beach, the sound of panting. "Good evening, guys." Wes flopped down beside them.

"Shh," Mandy whispered. "Come on, lay down here, Wes, and look at this."

Wes lay down beside Mandy on the cool sand. "Wow, so that's where God lives."

"Shh," Mandy whispered again. "Just soak it in."

This is letting life just happen, she thought. Moments like this would've been missed if they didn't just let it happen. About that time Duke ran up and slung sand on all three of them. They sat up laughing.

"Duke," Mandy reprimanded. "How did you get out of the house?"

"How *did* he get out, Mandy?" Wes held his collar.

They all three looked at each other, got up, and started running to Mandy's house. The back door was wide open; she started inside, and Wes stopped her. "Let Ben and I go in first to see if anyone is inside." Ben and Wes went in and checked the whole house. Ben found a note on the table in the living room. "Look at this, Wes. I think it's for you."

Wes read the note. It was from Todd's wife. She had gone by his house and George told her he was here. There has been an accident; Todd was hurt and needed the doctor.

"Mandy, you can come in now. It's Todd. He's been hurt. I've got to go."

"What if we all go? Do you think we could be of some assistance?" Ben asked Wes.

"I'll go get the Hummer. Wait for me at the end of the road, and I'll pick you both up," Wes said, hurrying out the door.

Ben and Mandy waited with anticipation for Wes to arrive. They piled in the vehicle and headed to Spring Creek where Todd lived. There wasn't a word spoken during the entire trip. When they pulled up in the yard they could see a crowd of people gathered around. "I'm a doctor." Wes pushed through the crowd. Mandy and Ben followed.

Inside they saw Todd lying on the couch. Blood covered his leg. It was running down on the floor. "Step aside and let me see. Todd, what happened?"

"The boom on the shrimp troller broke and came crashing down on my leg. I think it's broke, Doc," Todd struggled to say. He was pale, and sweat was pouring down his face.

"It's more than broke. You've cut the main artery in your leg, and we've got to stop the bleeding, so you lay back and let us help you, my friend." Wes helped Todd lay back.

"Mandy, I'm going to put a pressure bandage on this. I need for you to hold it into place. The nearest hospital is eighty miles away. We don't have life-flight out here, so I need to get him to my office as soon as possible. I have everything there I need to stop the bleeding and set his leg."

Four men gently lifted Todd into the back of the Hummer. Mandy crawled in beside him, holding the bandage in place. Ben, Wes, and Margaret, Todd's wife, rode up front as they headed for Wes' office. The four men followed them in a truck. Todd groaned in pain every time they hit a bump. The roads were rough and narrow.

At the office they carried Todd inside. Wes set up a makeshift operating room. "Mandy, Ben, I'm going to need your help. In the cabinet you will find surgical scrub sponges. I need you to scrub from the elbows down with the scrubs. There's a sink right over there." Wes pointed to a stainless sink in the corner. "Margaret, you wait outside with these gentlemen until I call you."

"Okay, Doc Young." Margaret walked out with the men.

Wes scrubbed himself and started the tedious task of repairing the injured artery. Mandy kept the sweat wiped from his face while Ben handed Wes the instruments he asked for. Minutes turned into hours. Wes had given Todd a shot to make him sleep. They worked into the wee hours of the morning before Wes said, "Okay, that's it."

Wes had repaired the artery and set Todd's leg. "Now, someone want to call 911?" Wes smiled as he sat on the stool next to Todd. "We'll let him rest. You can go out and get Margaret now, Mandy. She can come in and sit with him."

Mandy went out into the waiting area and called Margaret. "Wes says you can go in and sit with Todd now."

The four men excused themselves and left. Margaret went into the room and sat beside the bed where Todd was lying.

Wes, Ben, and Mandy walked into the kitchen area. "Tea, anyone?" Wes asked.

Ben and Mandy answered at the same time, "Sure." They all laughed.

"That was incredible what you did in there tonight, Wes." Ben sat down with a cup of tea. "I've never seen anything like that before except on *Emergency* 911, you know, that show on TV."

"This is what I do, Ben, just like you make the world a beautiful place to live in. I couldn't do that. I'm all thumbs when it comes to gardening."

Mandy sat and listened to the two men share their experiences. They talked like they had known each other all their lives. It was amazing how the morning had started off in chaos and now here they were—the three of them all together. She smiled. Grace was right again.

"I need to fix Margaret a place to sleep here tonight. Mandy, could you help with the linens, and Ben, could you help me carry a bed into the room where Todd is?"

"Sure, where are the linens?" Mandy followed Wes.

Wes showed her the linen closet as he and Ben went down the hall to retrieve a bed. Wes checked on Todd. He hooked him up to monitors so that he could keep tabs on his vital signs until an ambulance could get there. When they had gotten Margaret settled in, the three of them walked out on the porch.

"It's late. Mandy, you take the Hummer and drop Ben off, and I'll have it picked up tomorrow. You're off tomorrow, aren't you?"

"Yes, two whole days." Mandy yawned.

"As soon as the ambulance gets here to pick up Todd, I'll be through for the night, and perhaps tomorrow we can all go for a cruise, if that's okay with you, Ben."

"That sounds nice. Not too early, though."

Mandy and Ben rode back to the Cove in silence; they were both exhausted. She knew something had happened tonight, something that would change the rest of their lives. She dropped Ben off and headed home.

She fell into the bed. Duke started to whine. "Oh, Duke, what do you want?" Then she realized he just wanted to be close to her, so she let him sleep on the bed with her.

Mandy awoke to Duke licking her in the face. She heard a knock at the front door. "Who could that be?" She dragged herself out of bed. The sun was up high; she looked at the clock on her way to the door. It was noon.

"Wake up, sleeping beauty." It was Wes all dressed for the cruise.

Mandy opened the door for him and headed for the bathroom to take a bath and change. "Make me some coffee. I'll be out in a minute."

"Sure thing, lady," he hollered from the kitchen.

"Could you let Duke out back in the fenced yard? He probably needs to go."

"I'll do it. Hurry up, Ben is waiting."

"What do you have up your sleeve today? Last time—"

"I know. I thought since you're off tomorrow we could spend the night on the yacht and come back Monday afternoon. Ben thought that was a good idea too."

"I'll bet he did," Mandy muttered to herself.

"What was that? I didn't hear you."

"Nothing. How is Todd this morning?"

"He's fine. No more bleeding. I called the hospital this morning, and he's in good condition, and they should let him go home later today."

"That's wonderful." Mandy walked out of the bathroom and ran right into Wes holding a cup of coffee. She had never noticed how handsome he was before. His dark wavy hair, coal-back eyes, olive skin; he had a small cleft in his chin and dimples in both of his cheeks when he smiled. He had the body of a runner.

She felt her heart race as they stood staring at each other. "You spilled your coffee." He handed her the cup.

"You're something else, you know that?" She smiled and gathered some things in a bag for the trip. "I don't know if I should stay on that yacht with you two guys."

"Judy will be there to protect your honor. We'll be gentlemen, honest." He smiled, picking up her bag. "Let's get Duke and we're ready."

Mandy locked the house and climbed into the Hummer where Ben was waiting. "Has Wes told you about his boat?"

"No, but I'm looking forward to seeing it. Is it a skiff, Wes?"

Mandy looked at Wes and laughed. "Yeah, it's a skiff."

At the marina the yacht was ready for them to board. Mandy and Wes boarded while Ben stood in amazement looking at the huge yacht.

Wes motioned to Ben. "Come aboard, mate."

Ben walked up the ramp to the yacht. He couldn't believe his eyes. "This is what we're going out on?"

"Yes, why? Is it too small? I mean, I know it's not the skiff you were expecting." Wes laughed. "If you'll give your things to Bo, he'll take them to your quarters."

Mandy was talking to Judy about her honor. The two ladies laughed as they watched the men. "It's you and me, girl," Mandy said to Judy, patting her on the back.

It was a beautiful day, not a cloud in the sky. The Gulf was calm; the water was so slick it almost looked like a piece of glass for as far as you could see. There was a gentle breeze blowing; the dolphins were swimming right along side the yacht, singing to each other and dancing in the water. They put on a show for them. The three of them watched in awe. Duke was running back and forth barking at them.

Lunch was served on the deck. Including Duke, he had his own bowl with his name on it. "Where did that bowl come from? It looks like the one I made for him."

"It is the one you made for him. I packed his things while you were dressing."

"Wes, you're too much, you think of everything."

"I'm a doctor, I have to."

Mandy sunned on the deck after lunch while the men fished. Ben caught a large grouper; Wes didn't catch anything but pinfish. Wes told Ben to give the grouper to the chef for dinner. You would have thought it was a trophy fish the way he handed it off to the chef. They decided to anchor at Bullocks Bluff, a small island off the coast. The palm trees waved in the wind, and the sand was crystal white, almost like sugar. They had decided to go ashore to have dinner on the island. The chef prepared a wonderful dinner and had it served on the beach. Music played; they were like children in their own world.

Ben kept watching Judy; her long blonde braids hung on her dark brown skin, and her emerald green eyes sparkled in the moonlight. She was tall and lean, her legs were muscular; she was beautiful.

Mandy almost felt a tinge of jealousy rise up in her, but instead she smiled at Ben. She knew from that very moment that she and Ben were not meant for each other. "Ben was meant to be with another, and so was I," Mandy caught herself saying out loud.

"What?" Ben asked.

"Nothing."

Wes came over to the fire where Mandy was sitting; he reached down and took her hand. "Let's go for a walk."

"That sounds good to me," she said, getting up.

"Looks like Ben has an eye for Judy."

"You think?"

"He's been watching her all day. Judy's like me. She wants her own life far from all the glitz and glamour of her family. She asked me about this job when she graduated Harvard three years ago. She loves it. Her family thinks she's traveling abroad. Instead she lives on the yacht and serves as my assistant. She puts on a show for my guests, you know, like calling me Dr. Young and stuff. When everyone is gone we laugh about it."

"Why haven't you and she ever—"

"Well, she's more like the sister I never had. I don't look at her as a woman but like a sister. Our families have always been close. We grew up together. I'm several years older than she is. It's just the way it is. She loved Kay. My family didn't like her. They thought she was a gold digger, after the family fortune. When she got sick they changed the way they treated her. It really upset me. Why couldn't they have loved her when she was alive? To hear my family now that she's dead, she was an angel. Crazy, isn't it?"

"Yes, I'd say so. Your mother told me some about her—Kay, that is—when we were on the yacht before."

"She did?"

"Yes, she told me pretty much what you just told me."

"Leave it up to dear ole Mother."

"She really loves you, you know."

"I know, she calls me the apple of her eye. Let's lie here and look at the stars."

"Sounds good to me."

They both took off their shoes and lay back on the cool sugar sand. The sound of the wind blowing through the chimes on the yacht was mesmerizing. As they listened to the soothing sound of the waves rolling on shore, Wes moved closer to Mandy. He reached out and took her hand. "This is perfect."

"Yes, it is." She responded by squeezing his hand.

"You know I love you, don't you?"

"Yes, I do."

"How do you know?"

"The way you look at me, the way you always want to be close to me. You know, little things. A girl can tell."

The sounds of night filled their ears. Mandy sighed in contentment. "I care for you too."

"I know."

"How do you know?"

"The way you let me look at you, the way you always allow me to be close to you. A guy knows, you know."

With that, they embraced each other, holding each other tight. "I don't know if I would fit into your family, Wes. They're a little too much for me."

"You don't have to worry about my family. I live my own life, in my own way. My family loves you, my father went on and on about you. My mother thinks you are the most gifted artist she has ever met. But most important, I love you."

"You're right. That is what's important." She kissed him on the forehead, on each cheek, then on the lips. "I never thought I would feel this way about anyone, ever again. I'm so glad God brought you into my life."

"So you think God did this?"

"I know he did."

"Me too." They fell asleep in each other's arms.

Duke awoke them the next morning by licking their faces. Once he was sure they were up, he ran around the little clearing, wagging his tail and barking. They laughed.

"He must be happy for us too." Mandy pushed Duke off them.

"He must." Wes laughed.

"I guess we should get back." Mandy got to her feet.

"Before we go, can I ask you a question?"

"Sure, anything."

"That day on the road, the day we met. Was it Ben that you were so upset over?"

"Yes, it was." She put her hand over his mouth before he spoke. "That was then, this is now."

He pulled her to him and kissed her. "Thank you for being honest."

"It's the only way I know to be."

"I know, that's one of the reasons I love you so much." He kissed her again, and they walked back to where they had left the others. There was no one in sight. The dingy was attached to the yacht. "I guess they left us," Wes said, scratching his head. "How are we going to get to the yacht?"

Bo was walking on deck with his morning coffee when he spotted Wes and Mandy waving at him from the beach. "Be right over to get you, Dr. Young."

On board again, Mandy was glowing. It didn't feel like her feet were touching the ground. *Could I be in love?* she thought. If she was, she wanted the world to know.

"Let's go down and shower before breakfast," Wes suggested, dusting the sand out of his hair.

"Sounds good to me," she said, grabbing his arm.

"Where are Ben and Judy, Bo?" Wes asked, looking around the deck.

"I think they're still asleep, Dr. Young."

Mandy and Wes crept down the stairs to the guest quarters. They opened the door to Ben's room. He was sound asleep, Judy by his side. They smiled at each other and closed the door.

"God works in mysterious ways. Looks like they enjoyed their evening" Mandy said. "At least now I know for sure he wasn't for me."

"What do you mean?"

"Just something a wise old woman once said to me."

"Let's shower, and I'll check on things on the deck when we're done."

"See you soon," she said, kissing him on the nose.

He smiled at her, and they went their separate ways.

At the breakfast table, Ben held a cold glass of juice to his head. Judy dragged in and grabbed a cup of coffee. Wes and Mandy watched them.

"We sure had one heck of a party last night. Where did you guys get off to?" Ben said, taking a drink of the orange juice.

"I think you both need something more than coffee and orange juice. I'll be right back." Wes went it to the kitchen and made a concoction for Ben and Judy. It looked like tomato juice.

"Drink this, it'll help."

"Thanks." Judy drank the concoction.

Ben looked at the glass Wes set in front of him. "What's this?"

"Don't ask questions, just drink it," Judy said, putting her glass down. "I'm sorry, Wes, I just love this man. He's so funny. You should have seen him last night. He was going to ride a dolphin. Have you ever heard of such?" Judy laughed as she reached over and patted Ben's head.

"Careful, love, that part of my anatomy is very painful this morning. What did you put in those drinks?"

"I'll never tell," she said, kissing the top of his head. "Is this where it hurts?"

They all laughed as Ben drank down the last bit of his hangover remedy.

"What's up for today? Anyone have any ideas?" Wes asked, rubbing Mandy's arm.

"Let's take a cruise. Wes, you're not officially open. Ben is visiting his mom. Judy, you live on the yacht. and I'm my own boss. What's stopping us?"

Everyone agreed it sounded like a good idea. They would cruise down to the Bahamas and spend the week, enjoying the last of the summer together. Mandy was excited about the trip; she had never been to the Bahamas. They would have to cruise around the tip end of Florida over to the Bahamas. The trip would take two days, if the weather was good. It was hurricane season, but so far the weather report was favorable for the trip.

As they cruised down the West side of the Florida peninsula, Mandy and Ben realized they needed clothes for the trip; neither one of them had been prepared for the extended trip.

They went into port at Tampa Bay. It was a beautiful old town that catered to the tourists. Sand and sun was its main attraction. Beautiful sugar sand beaches, crystal blue water. *It is almost as beautiful as the*

Cove, Mandy thought, weaving her way through the tourists to a main street where they could hail a taxi to the mall.

She and Ben went into town together; Wes and Judy stayed on the yacht.

"Well, well, what's up with you and our doctor friend?" Ben got into the backseat of the taxi.

"What's up with you and Ms. Judy?" Mandy climbed in next to him.

"She's beautiful, isn't she, Mandy? We like the same things, we both live away from our parents. We both like to party—boy, that woman can drink. She drank me right under the table. Things work out for the best, don't they? Who would have ever thought?"

"Not me, I'm just a dumb country girl who doesn't like to party, who doesn't drink."

"Now, now let's be friends."

"You jump from one thing to another. A few days ago, you'd thought I broke your heart. Today you're in heat with a deckhand. Who knows about you? I'm glad I found out now, before I entrusted myself to you."

"Mandy, you know I'd never hurt you."

She looked at him with angry eyes. "You mean, you wouldn't hurt me again?"

"Yes, that's what I meant. So, you got yourself a rich doctor."

"Please, Ben, let's try to be civil. Wes really likes you, and I'm trying to. So let's just leave it at that. Let's get our clothes and get back to the yacht."

"You're right. I'm sorry for picking at you, but I just wonder what did he get that I missed."

"You haven't missed anything. I'm not that way, if that's what you're implying. He's a better man than that. You're so superficial. This is a side of you I didn't know existed. I do now. I'm glad for you and Judy. Just leave Wes and I out of it," she snapped.

"Hey, hey, calm down. We're going to be on that yacht a long time together, let's have a truce." He defended himself, holding up his hands.

When they arrived at the mall they agreed to meet back out front in two hours. They parted and went their separate ways.

She went into several shops, picking up a piece here and there until she decided she had enough clothes for the boat trip. She would buy more clothes in the Bahamas if she needed them. She looked at her watch and noticed she had been in the mall almost two hours. She hurried to the front door where Ben was waiting for her.

"I've already gotten a taxi for us. Are you ready to go?"

"I think I have everything I need. Thanks for getting the taxi. About earlier, I'm really sorry," she apologized.

"That's perfectly okay. I thought maybe you might be a little jealous, but I found out you weren't. You really care for this guy, don't you?"

"Yes, I really do. I think if he were the poorest of men, I would love him."

"Love, that's a strong word."

"That's the way I feel, and Wes feels the same about me."

"I'm happy for you both, really I am. I know I was a little hard on you earlier, and I want to apologize."

"I accept your apology." She smiled and patted his hand.

Back at the yacht Judy and Wes anxiously awaited their return. When they saw the taxi drive up, they both let out a sigh of relief. They had been talking about the situation while Ben and Mandy were gone. Wes had told Judy about the night before on the beach. How he had declared his love to Mandy and she declared her love to him. Judy was happy for Wes.

"Ahoy, mates, we're back, clothes in hand," Ben yelled from the dock, holding up his bags. The people on the dock stared at him.

"That's my man," Judy proudly announced.

Mandy rolled her eyes at him. "Thank you, Lord, for showing me the truth before it was too late."

Back on board Ben asked, "Hey, Doc, could we stay here tonight so that Judy and I can paint the town?"

"Sure." Wes helped Mandy with her bags.

Ben and Judy hurried and dressed to go ashore. "Don't wait up for us," Ben yelled as they ran down the dock laughing.

Wes waved at them. "Have a good time."

"We will," Judy shouted back.

"I think I understand what you meant when you said God works in mysterious ways. I look at Ben and I just can't for the life of me picture you two together. You two are so different," Wes said, watching the two of them playing with each other as they got into the taxi.

"I was desperate." Mandy laughed. "There was never anything romantic between the two of us. It was a strong friendship. Both of us were still grieving over the loss of our spouses. When Ben left that day without even a goodbye, I knew I had confused what feelings I really had for him. Then God sent you into my life that very day, though I didn't know it then. I was too broken. I guess God needed to break me to make me, if that makes sense."

"It makes all the sense in the world. I'm glad we had our little road rage incident. I would have never met you if you hadn't just stopped in the middle of the road. It's strange how things work out, don't you think?"

"Yes, I do. What would you like to do this evening?" she said, resting in his arms, looking at the beautiful bay.

"I'd like for you to put on one of those lovely gowns, we can have a romantic dinner, dance, and—well, whatever."

"I'd like that. I think I'll pick out my own dress if you don't mind."

"I don't mind at all. You go get dressed, and I'll make the magic happen."

"You do that." She kissed him on the nose.

Mandy looked through the beautiful gowns that hung in the closet of her quarters. She found a red velvet one she really liked. She took off her clothes and draped the gown over her slim body. *This is the one,* she thought. She took the dress and gently laid it on the bed. She went into the bathroom and settled into the large garden tub for a good long soak. The hot water felt so good. She was tired from her day's shopping. The sound of a yacht's horn blowing brought her back to reality.

She dressed and combed her long brown hair; she adorned it using red stones that matched her dress. She took one last survey in the floor-length mirror before going upstairs. When she arrived she noticed the room was dimly lit with soft music. The chef had laid out a beautiful table of silver and fine crystal. She could see Wes standing on the deck in his tuxedo talking to someone off the yacht. She wandered outside to see who he was talking to. To her surprise it was his parents; he was explaining to them he had a romantic evening planned and asking if he could get a rain check on their visit.

Wes' mother took one look at Mandy and pulled her husband away. "We understand. We were just cruising the coastline after we saw you in the bay. Your father thought he saw you and decided to come over. We'll see you, son. Have a wonderful evening. I'm going to make your father take me out for dinner and dancing."

Wes turned and saw Mandy standing in the light of the sunset in her red gown. He was speechless.

"You clean up very well, Dr. Young. Mind if I spend this evening with you?" she slowly walked over to him.

"I wouldn't have it any other way," he said, pulling her close to him. He held her so close; she couldn't breathe. She could feel his heart beating next to hers. It was as if they were one entity standing there in the sunset. "This isn't a dream, is it, Mandy? I mean, you're real, right?"

"I'm real, this is real," she whispered. "Look at that beautiful sunset, Wes, it's almost like the movies."

They danced together on the deck. People passing stopped to watch them. The ladies reached out for their men. They laughed together as they watched couples holding hands as they passed.

"This is like Cinderella," Mandy whispered.

"And I'm your Prince Charming." Wes took Mandy's hand and led her into the dining area. The atmosphere was perfect. They were alone for the first time since Wes had told her he loved her. He led her to her chair—pulling it out for her and making the gesture for her to sit—then he seated himself next to her. He rang the bell and the chef delivered the first course of the meal. It was lobster bisque soup. The second course was a seafood salad that was superb; the main course was lobster and shrimp in a white sauce over pasta.

Dinner was wonderful. When they were finished the chef cleared the table and Wes dismissed him for the evening. Wes poured them both a glass of nonalcoholic champagne, and they sipped champagne and danced together to soft music. Mandy felt lightheaded, being so close to Wes like this. She held him closer. They waltzed to the music for hours. The moon was up; the light of it cast a glittering silhouette across the water. This was the most romantic evening she had ever had, dancing in the light of the moon. Everything was so perfect.

Loud hooting coming from the street broke the mood. It was Ben and Judy; they were drunk. They staggered up the boarding plank.

"Well, well, look here. Look at the way these two are dressed. May I have this dance?" Ben said, reaching for Mandy.

Wes grabbed his hand. "You're drunk, my friend. Let's get you two into bed." Wes looked back at Mandy as he led Ben to his quarters. "Mandy, would you mind helping me with Judy?"

"No, of course. Come on, Judy, let's go nighty night." Mandy helped Judy down the stairs to her sleeping quarters.

When they were both settled in, Mandy excused herself to her quarters. She was angry that their perfect evening had been spoiled. She got ready for bed and crawled into the satin sheets. She was just about asleep when she heard her door open. She sat up, startled.

"It's just me, Mandy," Wes whispered. "May I come in?"

"It's late, Wes, and I'm really tired. This evening was wonderful. Let's leave it that way." She lay back down, facing away from him.

"Can I just lie with you a little while?"

"I don't believe we should do this, Wes. Go back to your quarters," she insisted.

She felt him lay next to her. "I don't want sex. I just want to lie next to you," he whispered. "I don't want this evening to end."

"Well, Ben and Judy made sure of that."

"Is something bothering you?"

"No, I guess the clock just struck midnight, and things are back to the way they were."

"Things will never be the way they were, Mandy. Life has changed for both of us."

"I know," she said, tears streaming down her face. She was so afraid of allowing him to get close to her. Though things seemed so good right now, she was waiting for reality to hit. Here they were on this wonderful cruise, but when they returned home, things would be different. She was a common country girl. How could she compete in the world Wes lived in?

"I don't want the others getting the wrong idea. Could I just be alone right now?" she asked, pushing him away.

"I understand," he whispered.

She heard the door open and close. She cried herself to sleep.

Wes walked back to his quarters. He looked around the big luxurious suite; it felt so cold and lonely. Sitting on the side of the bed, he hung his head. "Lord, I don't know what just happened, but I know I love that woman. I have kept to myself since the day Kay died. I have longed for a mate, and now I've found her. Please help me to understand what she's going through. Help me be the gentleman she needs me to be. Don't let this be the end of us." He lay back on the bed and wept.

In the morning she sat on the side of the bed not wanting to face the others. Her eyes were swollen; it was obvious she had been crying. She got up and locked the door. Crawling back into bed she could hear Judy and Ben running down the hall through the quarter's section of the yacht. She held her breath as she heard footsteps stop at her door. She saw the door handle turn and then the footsteps went up the stairs.

"I can't do this!" she cried out. This was not her life; it couldn't be. The sound of footsteps came running down the stairs. A knock on the door let her know everyone had heard her.

"Mandy, are you okay?" Wes asked in desperation.

"I'm fine."

"Can I please come in and we can talk?"

Mandy walked over to the door and unlocked it. She walked back and sat on the bed. Wes opened the door; she noticed his eyes were swollen and red. He looked like he hadn't gotten much sleep either.

"Was that you?" He walked over and sat beside her.

"Yes."

"Are you okay? What's wrong?"

"I was letting out my frustrations. I thought this yacht would be soundproof."

"Why are you so angry? Have I done something to upset you? Has anyone done something to you? I don't understand. If you don't tell me what's wrong, I don't know how to fix it."

"That's just it, you can't fix it. It's fate."

"What do you mean, it's fate? What is fate?" Tears started streaming down his face. "Mandy, it has taken me six years to find you. I don't intend to lose you without a fight. If that means fighting you then I will. You've got to talk to me—"

"I'm not used to having anyone to talk to. Especially a man. I'm sorry. This is a very scary thing for me. We live in two different worlds. We are so different."

"No, we're not. I can't help that my father is wealthy. But I can help who I am. I'm not my father. I'm me, Mandy. You know, the guy you said you loved two nights ago. Has that changed?"

"No, that hasn't changed. I do love you. But I've learned I can't trust my emotions. They're all too new to me. While you went on with your life, I was a hermit for over a year. I didn't talk to people. I stayed at home alone, alone. That's what I'm used to."

"Is that the way you want to live the rest of your life, alone?"

"No, I don't want to live the rest of my life alone. But I don't want to be hurt anymore."

"That's not reality, Mandy. Pain is part of life. Pain is what lets us know we have happiness. Without pain, how would we know happiness?"

She couldn't answer his questions; she knew he was right.

"You want a guarantee, is that what you want? Because I can't give you a guarantee; neither can you. There are no guarantees in life. We just have to live each day as it comes." He reached down and rubbed Duke's head.

"We're on this cruise and everything is so wonderful, it's like a Cinderella fairytale. I'm scared that when we get home everything will change."

"What if it does? We're still going to love each other. Sure, things will come up, but we'll deal with them together. The cruise was your idea. I could be building my practice. But I love you, woman, and you wanted to go, so we're going. Are you saying you want to turn around and go home?"

"No, I want us to slow down and deal with reality. I'm a plain country girl, but you're a successful doctor."

"Is that all it is? Because you're an artist, and you create beautiful artistic pottery? You're a successful businesswoman. I'm starting over in my practice, that's scary to me, but it doesn't stop me for reaching for what I want."

"All of this, this is just so new to me. I'm not used to wealth. Servants people waiting on me. I cook my breakfast, make my bed, do my laundry, and I … Oh, let's go have breakfast. Duke is hungry," she said, patting Duke's head.

"Does that mean the conversation is over and we've solved what is bothering you?"

"Yes, I guess that's what it means." She reached out and took his hand. "Let me change and I'll be right up."

"I'm taking Duke with me. You'll have to come up now." They laughed. He reached over and kissed her on the forehead.

It was quiet at the breakfast table. Judy and Ben looked at each other as Wes entered the room. They knew something was wrong.

Mandy had not come out and Wes had hurried downstairs; now he had come back alone.

"Is everything all right, my friend?" Judy asked, taking Wes' hand.

"Yes, everything is fine. What's for breakfast this morning?" he asked, laying his napkin on his lap.

"Wes, I've known you all my life, and the only time I have ever seen you cry is when Kay was dying. I see that same look on your face now." Judy moved to the chair next to Wes. "Ben, would you mind excusing us for a minute?"

"Sure, I'll go check the weather. We should get to the Bahamas today," Ben said, getting up from the table.

"Wes, I'm sorry for the way I've acted on this trip, but we both know that I'm just hiding out here from my parents. You know I'm a wild and crazy girl. I know we interrupted your evening last night. It looked like one of those serious evenings too, but you've got to get a hold of yourself. Relax—don't take things so serious. She'll get over whatever it is that seems to be troubling her right now. Look, we'll be in the Bahamas today. She'll be fine, and so will you."

Wes looked up at Judy. "I know you mean well. You're so young. How does one explain real life to someone who lives in a fantasy world? You do, Judy, you think life is one big party. It's not. There are real things happening out there. There are real issues in life, you know? You may not know that now, but you'll learn. Ben is older than you. Right now he's having the time of his life with a wild and crazy girl—"

"Woman."

"Okay, woman, but the time will come when feelings are involved. When that happens, the wild and crazy party is over, it's reality."

About that time Mandy came into the room. "Good morning, everyone."

Wes and Judy looked up. Mandy looked stunning. She had makeup on, her hair was rolled into a bone braid, and she had on tropical attire. She walked over and kissed Wes on the forehead before she seated herself next to him. "Thank you, Wes, for bringing Duke up for his breakfast. You look well this morning, Judy, especially after the night you had. Where's Ben?"

"He's on the deck," Judy stammered. "Wow, you look great."

"Thanks. What's for breakfast? I'm starving." She placed her napkin on her lap.

Ben walked in; he took one look at Mandy and his mouth fell open. "The weather is going to be great, no small-craft warnings. Smooth sailing all the way into the Bahamas. The captain said we should be there by lunch." He hadn't taken his eyes off Mandy. She was beautiful; he wasn't laughing now. He realized what he had let slip through his fingers.

Judy reached up and pulled him beside her. "Hey, don't you know staring is rude?"

Mandy smiled at Wes. "I'm looking forward to getting there. I've never been anywhere for a vacation. This is exciting."

"We'll be there soon, my love. Your wish is my command." Wes squeezed her hand.

Chapter 6

The islands were beautiful; the marina where they docked was lined with large yachts. The captain had radioed ahead to reserve a spot for them. They were staying a week; that would give the crew time to restock the yacht with the supplies they needed.

Wes gave the crew their instructions for restocking the yacht. He told the captain to see if he could hire a new deckhand to replace Judy, as she would be a guest now and not part of the crew.

Wes and Mandy gathered up Duke and headed ashore. She was amazed at the array of tropical plants, large birds, and beautiful trees that were here. The Cove had the appearance of being tropical, but this was the real thing. There were so many people. The islands were so nice. The locals catered to the tourists. Everywhere you turned locals were assisting you with whatever you wanted; open markets on the street; restaurants that overlooked the beautiful clear blue water; the warm breeze—it was intoxicating.

"Oh, Wes, this is more than I ever dreamed of. I want to go into those markets over there. Look at the beautiful hand-carved statues.

Oh, look at that pottery shop. Can we go inside?" Mandy squealed with excitement.

"Yes, yes, we can do whatever you want to do," Wes said, trying to keep up with her. He didn't realize she actually had never been anywhere. He watched the wonder in her eyes as she sat down with the potter and showed him how she created her bowls. He showed her new techniques she could use to make abstract pieces. They worked together all day. By the time she was satisfied she had learned the new techniques, it was getting dark.

"How long was I in there?"

"About seven and a half hours."

"What? Oh, Wes, I'm sorry."

"That's okay. We have all the time you need. We'll go into the markets tomorrow. My butt is sore from sitting on that hard stool all day. Duke and I are hungry. Let's go to the yacht and eat something," Wes said, pulling Duke along behind him.

"Don't you want to eat on the island?"

"I have a surprise for you, if you can wait."

When they got near the yacht she could see bamboo oil lamps, funny lights strung around the exterior deck, a real Bahamian band playing music, and tables of the local food.

"I have something special for you in your quarters. We'll slip in the back. You go change and come back to me, okay?"

"Okay."

In her quarters she found beautiful Bahamian attire for her to wear. There was even a special collar made for Duke. She hurriedly dressed and made her way to the top deck. Ben stopped her in the living room area inside.

"You're sure enjoying all of the attention, aren't you?" he said eying her up and down.

"Excuse me, Wes is waiting for me. I would imagine Judy is waiting for you too." She pushed past him.

Judy stood in the doorway watching the two of them. When Mandy had left the room, she walked over to Ben. "What's up with you? Why are you giving her such a hard time? Is there a past I need to know about here?" She was frustrated.

"There's nothing you need to know about. Want a drink?"

"No, I think I've had too much to drink on this trip," she snapped.

"Well, I need one," he said, making his way over to the bar.

"She's going to be with Wes, not you, Ben. The sooner you face it, the better off you're going to be."

"Don't tell me what I need to face. You look good tonight. What did you do to yourself?" he said, eyeing her.

"I thought you would never notice. I got dressed up for you," she said, taking his hand, modeling for him.

"Well, darling, you clean up real well."

"Why, thank you, darling. Let's go join the festivities."

"I'm right behind you."

Mandy and Wes were dancing to the music; people from the other yachts were beginning to arrive. Before long the large deck of the *Katie I* was full of people. Everyone was having such a good time. The music, the food, the décor; laughter filled the air as more people joined them on the dance floor.

Judy watched Mandy. *What is it about this woman that makes men crazy? I'm just as beautiful as she is,* she thought, *but there's something more about her. Wes is crazy about her and Ben is nuts about the fact she is with Wes.*

"Come on darlin,' let's dance." Ben grabbed her arm and swirled her onto the dance floor.

She couldn't take her eyes off Mandy. She watched the way she moved, the way she interacted with others. She was a special woman; everyone she came in contact with was under her spell.

Mandy and Wes sat down; they were exhausted. "Are you hungry?" he asked, snuggling up to her.

"Starving, let's get something to eat."

"I'll get it, let me surprise you," Wes said, getting to his feet.

Mandy sat patiently for Wes to come back. Judy came over and sat beside her. "Mandy, do you mind if you and I go shopping together tomorrow?"

"That's fine with me. I'll tell Wes tomorrow is ladies' day. How's that?"

"Thanks, I really appreciate it." Judy felt better. She knew Mandy could tell her what she was doing wrong. She wanted to be a lady like Mandy, not like her mother or those other rich woman her family hung out with. She wanted to be a lady that a man—a good man—would desire. She wanted to capture Ben's heart the way Mandy had.

The party went on into the wee hours of the morning. When everyone was gone, Wes and Mandy were exhausted. They said their goodnights and went to their quarters.

Mandy was getting ready for bed when she heard a knock at the door. It was Judy. "Hey, lady, what are you up to?" Mandy asked, letting her in.

"Well, I sort of wanted to talk to you," Judy said, walking over to the couch.

"Sure, what's up?"

"All my life I've been in boarding schools, college, and the only examples I've had were stuffy old rich women. I knew I didn't want to be like them. So, I've been a spoiled little rich kid. I don't want that anymore. You, on the other hand, are so graceful and beautiful and all the guys you meet want to be with you. You seem to be like a magnet. People are so drawn to you. Could you teach me what to do to be a respectable woman?" Judy was twisting her hands in her lap. It was obvious she was nervous.

"Well, I didn't know that about myself. The only thing I can tell you is respect yourself. If you respect yourself, others will respect you. I was never rich in money, but I believe I've always been rich in love and in friendship. I don't know if I'm the one you should be asking. After my husband died I became a hermit. I lived alone for over a year. I didn't communicate with the world around me. I guess I learned something about myself. I like myself. I think you have to like yourself for others to like you. Be confident in yourself, and others will be confident in you. I've only been with one man my whole life, and I'm thirty-two years old. You, on the other hand, you give yourself to people you don't even know. Respect, my friend. Respect yourself and who you are. Don't let men fool you into thinking sex is love, because it's not. Love is much more than sex." Mandy patted Judy's leg. "I'm really tired. Can we continue this conversation tomorrow?"

"Sure." Judy was anxious to continue the conversation.

Mandy could hear Ben urging Judy to come to his quarters; she was insistent upon sleeping in her own quarters, alone. Mandy smiled as she picked Duke up and held him tight. "You're such a good boy, yes you are, and I love you."

At the breakfast table the following morning there were no hangovers to be dealt with. Ben and Judy sat in silence. Wes and Mandy came in with Duke.

"Mandy, I have to check with the captain about my new deckhand. Do you think you could do without me for a little while?" Wes asked.

"As a matter of fact, Judy and I were wanting to spend the day together."

"Great." Ben stirred his coffee. "And what am I supposed to do?"

"You can stay with me, and I'll show you the ropes of yachting," Wes suggested.

"That's fine. I have crews in my business, and maybe I can show you a thing or two."

"Then it's settled, the ladies will go ashore, and we guys will hang out." Wes took another bite of eggs.

Mandy looked at Judy and winked. "I'd like to go to the beach today, what about you, Judy?"

"That sounds great, I love the beach. Wait till you see the beaches here, Mandy. You're going to love them."

Judy was so young and reckless. She had been left to find her own way in life, without the supervision of anyone willing to take the time to show her what life was really all about. She had been shipped off to schools and left for others to teach her everything but reality.

Mandy was glad she was not born with a silver spoon in her mouth. Though things may have come easier, happiness was much harder to come by. She dressed in the new swimsuit and sarong she had purchased in Tampa Bay. She felt like a leisure lady of the islands. She packed a quick carry-along bag and met Judy on deck.

"Ready to go?" Judy asked in anticipation.

"Let's do it. Have you seen the guys? I wanted to tell Wes we were leaving."

"There're down below with the new deckhand. I told them we were leaving just as soon as you finished getting ready."

"Where are we going? I have no idea about this place."

"I do. I've been coming here all my life. Let me be your tour guide today." Judy picked up her beach bag and headed down the boarding plank.

They decided to take a horse and carriage ride to the shore. In a carriage they had a better view of the scenery than in a cab. The streets were packed with tourists, the locals catering to their every need. The people were kind and helpful. People watched them as they passed by in the carriage. The old Bahamian man driving the carriage sang a song of the island as they made their way through the narrow streets. They seemed to be traveling the old roads to the beach instead of the new roads made for cars. On the back roads there were mainly bicycles or people walking.

When they arrived at the yacht club beach. Crystal-clear blue-green water and sugar-sand beaches. Little tiki huts lined the beach, each one serving a different purpose. Some were beachside bars, others carried food, while others were souvenir shops. Everything they needed was at their fingertips.

The beach had padded lounge chairs and umbrellas for your convenience. The sound of laughter and music filled the air, the warm breeze blew, and children ran up and down flying their kites. Seagulls hovering around, squawking, waiting for someone to throw them a piece of something to eat. Waiters from the tiki huts catered to the people on the beach.

The sand was hot. Mandy was glad she wore her sandals. Indeed, this was the life. The warmth of the sun was soothing to the soul; she basked in its intoxicating appeal.

Judy's anticipation to continue their conversation from the night before overcame her. "I notice you don't drink. Is that part of being a lady, not drinking?"

"Well, I don't know if that's part of being a lady or not. The only time I ever drank, I overdid it and made an idiot of myself. Clay, that's my late husband, told me maybe I shouldn't drink if I couldn't hold it. It was just not something that was a part of our life. We really never needed anything external to bring us joy. We brought each other joy."

"Man, that's cool. What do you do for fun?"

"We're having fun right now. Don't you think? And you remember what you did—no hangover effects. You can enjoy life looking it right in the face. If we distort the truth by covering up the true feeling of an adventure, how do you know whether you really enjoyed it or whether it was the intoxication you enjoyed?"

"Wow, Mandy, you should have been a head doctor," Judy said in amazement.

Mandy realized no one had ever just sat down and talked to Judy. Perhaps they saw her beauty and didn't think she had a mind. She had a mind. She wanted to express herself. She just didn't know how. "What was your major in college?"

"Marine biology. I love sea life. I love finding out the correlation between land and sea. There are so many similarities; we just think that they are two different worlds, and in a sense that is true. But by exploring the ocean we have found that there are many healing factors we can utilize for diseases and even skincare. The science community in the United States is just now tapping into that. The ancient countries have already found that correlation."

"Judy, you're a bright young woman. You need to tap into that. Instead of letting men tap into your body, let them see you have a good head on your shoulders."

"I tried that. They just want a dumb play toy."

"That's not who you are. You're intelligent. You just haven't found the right man. Take Ben, for instance. I see the way you look at him, and it's a little more than a quick roll in the hay for you, right?"

"Yeah, I really like him. I hate the way he looks at you. I thought at first I just wouldn't like you, but then I thought, why not find out what it is about you he likes and try to perfect that in myself?"

"You don't want to be like me. You just need to find that part of yourself in you. It's there, you've just never tapped into it," Mandy said watching Judy soaking it all in. "I have a deep faith in God. I lost that for a long time after Clay died. I was so angry with God for taking him away from me. I started to rot inside. Then I met Grace, that's Ben's mom. She showed me that God had never left me. That he felt my pain and he wanted to heal me so that I could go on and show others how good he is. He introduced me to Wes, who has shown me courage and perseverance. If Clay had not died, I would have never met Wes or Ben or even you."

"I've never had anything to do with God. I mean, I don't want to be one of those holy rollers, you know." Judy wrinkled her nose.

"Do I seem to be a holy roller to you?"

"No, no, you don't. There's just something about you that makes women mad and men glad." They both laughed.

"Let's have some lunch, I'm starving." Mandy got up from her chair.

"We don't have to get up, just mash that button on your chair and a waiter will be here promptly," Judy instructed her, showing her the button under her towel. "My treat."

"Thank you, Judy. I'm going to get spoiled."

"That's what they want, so you'll come back."

Lunch was wonderful; they both had shrimp pockets with conch fritters, and a glass of ice-cold lemonade, Bahamian style. Mandy noticed she was getting a little red. "Are you ready to go back and find out what the guys are doing?"

"Sure. There's one little shop I want to stop by on our way back to the yacht, if you don't mind?"

"That sounds good to me. What kind of shop is it?"

"It's a ladies' apparel shop, the dress of the islands," Judy said, winking at Mandy. "I thought we could buy us some island clothes and wear them back to the yacht. You know, surprise the guys."

"I don't know. It sounds like trouble to me." They both laughed.

The "She Shack" was a very unique shop. It had beautiful Bahamian women's apparel. The dresses were gorgeous—different, yet they looked like regular sun dresses. They just made you feel like an island woman. Mandy picked out a blue one that was hand-painted. Judy picked out a little short sarong and top to match. They changed in the dressing rooms.

"See, even the clothes we pick out is so different," Judy said in disappointment as she compared the skimpy suit she picked out to the long flowing dress Mandy picked out. "Help me pick out something, Mandy. I want to change, I do."

"Okay, let's see. What colors do you like? Look at this emerald green dress. It will really accent your eyes. Try this one."

Judy took the dress. It was shorter than the one Mandy had picked out, but it left a little to the imagination too. "I like this one. Let's get matching shoes, and we can get our hair braded in the back."

"That dress really looks good on you, Judy. You look like a real lady," Mandy said in approval.

"Want to get your hair braided? It's an island custom." Judy ushered Mandy in the back of the store where there were two Bahamian women.

"Sure, let's do it." They both sat down on the straw stools and let the women braid their hair. Both of them had long hair, so it took an hour to get it braided.

"I look like Bo Derek in the movie *Ten*," Mandy said, admiring her hair in the mirror.

"That's a compliment, don't you think?" Judy winked at the two ladies and paid them for their hard work.

On the way back to the yacht, they joked and laughed about the way they looked. It had been a wonderful day. Mandy was glad she and Judy had taken the day for themselves.

She was tired; the sun had drained her energy, and all she really wanted was a nap. It was about five o'clock in the afternoon. She knew she would have time before dinner.

Back at the docks she saw Wes and Ben carrying a cooler to the yacht. They appeared to be having a good time. Mandy smiled. *Wes is so easygoing*, she thought. *He can put up with anyone if he can put up with Ben.*

They were looking inside the ice chest talking away. When she and Judy boarded the yacht, they both stood up and stared.

"Looks like you ladies had a productive day." Wes kissed Mandy on the forehead. He took her hand and showed her what was in the ice chest. "Ben and I went fishing today," he said in excitement. "Look at all the fish we caught."

"Looks like you guys had a productive day too," Mandy replied, squeezing Wes' hand.

"Look, honey," Ben said to Judy. "I out-fished ole Wes here, though. You really look good. Who does your hair?" They all laughed.

"Truthfully, he did out-fish me. See that big one right there? I caught that one. He may have caught more, but I caught the biggest one," Wes said, proud of himself.

"Ew, you guys smell bad." Judy wrinkled her nose.

"It's the smell of true fishermen, my love." Ben was proud of himself.

"You fishermen really need a bath. We bathing beauties really need a nap," Mandy said as she made her way down to her quarters. Duke followed her; he too smelled like fish. "Wes, did you take Duke with you today?" she yelled up to Wes.

"Yes, I did, dear. Bo will wash him and bring him down to you. Come on, Duke, we're bad boys, come on, boy." Wes ushered Duke up the stairs.

Mandy soaked in a cool tub of water; she noticed she had gotten a little burned. She was surprised because she was already dark. As she wrapped up in a plush bathrobe, Bo brought Duke back nice and clean. Then Mandy and her small companion climbed up on the bed and slept.

Judy was excited Ben had noticed her right off. He really liked her new look. She watched herself move around in the dress in the mirror. She took it off and placed in on the back of the chair before she showered. She lay down on the cool sheets and fell asleep.

Wes showered and put on clean shorts and shirt; he was tired but he was too excited to sleep. He wanted the chef to prepare their catch of the day. He looked in on Mandy and Duke, and they were sound asleep. He closed the door and went up to the entertainment deck.

Ben was already on deck. "Are we having our catch for dinner?"

"Sure thing, my friend. What would you like to go with them?"

"Would you mind if I instructed the chef on dinner? I want it to be a surprise for everyone."

"Sure, take charge, mate." Wes patted his shoulder.

When Ben returned to the open deck, he saw Wes staring at the horizon. "All done. Wes, how did you and Mandy meet?"

"Well, I can thank you for that. I was driving down the Cove road when I saw a hysterical woman in the middle of the road. She was crying. I tried to get her to move and she screamed at me. I could tell she was having an anxiety attack, so I assisted, being the good doctor I am." He laughed. "It was the day you left her. I happened to be in the right place at the right time."

"It was a difficult decision, leaving her that day. I knew if I didn't get away from her, I would have fallen madly in love with her. We come from different worlds. I didn't want mine to change, and I didn't want hers to change either."

"Change is inevitable, Ben. Life changes every day. No two days are the same. Something different comes in our path every day, even if we do the same thing every day. New people, a new contract, new street sign. Each day is unique. If we become creatures of habit, we become stale and life grows dull. That's where depression comes in. We get tired of the same ole thing day after day, and we feel we don't have the means to change things. I think God intended for us to have a fresh new adventure every day. It's what keeps life exciting."

"I made the biggest mistake of my life that day. I was too proud to admit it. So I left things the way they were. I didn't contact her again until that day you saw me at her house. By then I was ready for change. I got it all right—she had met you."

"Your loss, my gain, my friend. We can't beat ourselves up over our mistakes, we must learn from them. Take Judy, for instance. If I had not met Mandy, you would not have met her, or me. That would have been a big mistake. I'm glad we met. You're a good mate." Wes patted Ben on the shoulder and they both stared at the horizon.

"Judy is a beautiful woman. She's kind, and she's also crazy." They both laughed.

"Ben, Judy is running from a life she doesn't want. She wants to be a marine biologist. She's very intelligent. She just doesn't let men see that. Her father was always gone on business, family fortune type thing, you know. All Judy wanted was a father. She couldn't care less about the cars, houses, and finding her place in the rich society."

"Judy studied to be a marine biologist?"

"She sure did, my friend."

"But she worked on your yacht."

"No, she escaped from her family on my yacht."

"Judy isn't a deckhand. You let her off for good behavior because of me?" Ben asked in shock. "She's never said a thing to let me know things were any different than they seemed. I really like her. I just didn't want to get involved with a deckhand."

"She didn't want you to like her for her money, but for her—who she is to you. She thought you wanted an easy, partying woman, so she became that for you. She's starved for good male attention. She has just never found it. I think she's found it now … look at the changes she's made since we've been here."

"Mandy's good for anyone. She could help a cripple walk. I was crippled when I met her. Her zest for life helped me walk again. My employees actually say good morning to me now, instead of ducking into their offices or pretending they are busy when I come around."

"Mandy may be a good influence, but the change is from Judy," Wes assured him.

"You're a lucky man, Wes Young."

"So are you, Ben Howard. Judy is a very special person. If you two would lay off the spirits, you'd see that."

"Something has changed. She won't sleep with me anymore," Ben said, discouraged.

"Now, that could be Mandy. She doesn't—"

"I know, believe in premarital sex. Did you know the only man she has ever been with was her late husband?" Ben said, giggling.

"Really?'

"Yes, really. You're going to have a wild cat on your hands, my friend." Ben poked Wes and laughed.

Wes didn't see the humor in such a crude statement.

The sun was beginning to set over the horizon. They both watched the huge fireball; the orange and red ring around it was enormous on the calm water. You could almost see the smoke as it appeared to disappear into the ocean.

Judy got up from her nap; she washed her face and checked her hair, and she put on the new dress and sandals she and Mandy had bought that day. She was pleased with the way she looked. Her golden hair hung on her dark brown back. The dress made her eyes stand out; they sparkled in the light. She was ready for the first day of the rest of her life. She had thought long and hard about the talk she and Mandy had had, and she was ready to let the world see she wasn't a dumb blond.

Mandy woke up and noticed Duke lying on her arm asleep. She smiled at her newfound friend and rubbed his head. He licked her on the face. She went into the bathroom and washed her face, checked her hair, and put on her new dress. She was a little burned, so the thin straps were a little uncomfortable. She looked in the cabinet and found something for her sunburn. She rubbed it in and put the straps back on her shoulders. *That is much better,* she thought. She called Duke, and they headed for the upper deck.

She saw Judy was already up; she was watching the guys watching the sunset. "Don't they look cute?" She wrinkled her nose.

"Yes, love at first sight, don't you think?" Mandy laughed.

When the guys heard the girls laughing at them, they turned, embraced each other, and started to dance toward them. A couple of people on the dock started to stare. They all laughed.

"Who are these two strange women? What did you do with our

women?" Wes said, giving both of them a hug. "You look great, ladies. Now if I may, Ben has had the chef prepare dinner for us. Let's go in and see what we're in for."

"Good, I'm starving," Mandy said. Everyone agreed as they went into the dining area to find a luscious dinner awaiting their arrival. It was set up buffet-style; the smell was wonderful. "What do we have here?"

"We have black grouper, caught by Captain Wes and myself. Cheese grits, a delicacy in the South. Tomato hush puppies. And last but not least, we have coleslaw, a Southern delight. Chef Maximo, Max for short, knows how to cook down-home Southern food too." Ben handed everyone a plate. "Dig in."

Dinner was excellent. Wes and Ben had outdone themselves on the fish. Mandy watched Ben look at Judy; she smiled. He looked at her like she was a lady instead of a drinking buddy.

"I must say, Ms. Judy, you are beautiful tonight. I think I'd like to dance with you in the moonlight after dinner."

"Why that would be grand, Sir Ben." She smiled at Mandy and wrinkled her nose.

Wes reached under the table and squeezed Mandy's hand; they both smiled.

"I think I'd like to take Ms. Mandy for a walk on the beach in the moonlight, so you guys will have the yacht to yourselves." Wes pulled Mandy's chair back.

Ben was so absorbed with Judy he didn't seem to hear Wes. Mandy and Wes put Duke on a leash and walked down to the beach. They sat on the cool sand and watched the stars. Duke lay down beside them.

"I had a long talk with Ben today. He really cared for you, you know?" Wes stared at her, hoping he could read her face.

"I really don't want to talk about Ben. I feel so foolish when it comes to that part of my life." She squirmed.

"You shouldn't. You really helped him."

"And how did I really help him?"

"You taught him how to trust again, how to live again. He's very grateful to you. I hope you can find it in your heart one day to not be so angry with him." Wes pleaded Ben's case to Mandy. "He's really a nice guy, and we've become pretty good friends. I think he will look at

Judy differently. Judy seems to be looking at herself differently, probably thanks to you."

"We talked today. She's brilliant. She loves marine biology. I told her she needed to act like one. She seemed to be looking at life kind of warped, you know?"

"Yes, I do. I've been trying to get her to work in her field for years. She just shrugged me off. She looks very ladylike today."

"We did a little talking about her looks too. She's a beautiful woman who leaves nothing to the imagination. We talked a little about the mystery of women. She's got to leave something to the imagination."

"She looks great. I love you, woman."

"I love you too. You're not jealous of Ben?"

"Why should I be jealous of Ben? His loss was my gain. I'm grateful to Ben. If it wasn't for what he did, I wouldn't have ever met you." Wes caressed her. "The braids are nice, but do you mind if we take them down? I love your hair the way it was."

"You take them down for me."

"Sit up a minute. Let's see what a surgeon's hands can do."

"You're not a surgeon."

"I know, but you'll need a surgeon's hands to take these things down." They both laughed.

Wes started the tedious job of taking each braid apart. It took an hour. Mandy's head was sore at the roots. She shook out the remaining beads and rubbed her head. "Boy, those things were tight. Judy paid for me to get it braided, think she'll be mad?"

"No, she'll understand. She used to wear her hair braided, and I would rag her about it. She never stopped braiding it, though." He chuckled.

The silence was broken by the sound of thunder. The night sky lit up with lightning. "We'd better get back, looks like a storm," Wes suggested, helping Mandy to her feet. Duke stuck close to them, obviously uncomfortable with the lighting.

Back at the yacht Ben and Judy had already gone inside. Ben met Wes at the door. "Better come with me," he said as he ushered Wes to the captain's bridge. "Looks like we have a tropical storm about seventy-five miles out, with sixty-five-mile-an-hour winds and gusts up to eighty. She was headed out to sea when she changed directions about an hour ago."

"That's not a tropical storm, that's a hurricane, my friend. We'd better try and get rooms at the hotel." Wes called for Bo. "Call the Yacht Club's Hotel and get us two rooms. Ben, you can stay with me, and the ladies can stay in the other room—better for them to be together than alone. Better yet, Bo, get a two-bedroom suite with double beds. That way we can stay together. Gather the crew. Get the yacht tied down and put all the furniture inside. Get rooms for the crew also. Come on, let's get moving. Ben, you tell the women to get some things together. We need to leave before the weather gets too bad."

Ben told the women, and they hurried to get things together for the hotel. Judy called a taxi to carry them. They gathered up Duke and his things and headed for the taxi. The wind had picked up, and it was beginning to rain. They hurried into the taxi.

They noticed other boaters bolting down the hatches to ride out the storm. Wes knew better; he had been in a hurricane in a yacht before. He didn't need a repeat performance. He hurried everyone inside. Duke was getting big and took up a lot of space in the taxi. Wes tried to hold him in his lap, but the dog was too scared. Mandy put him between her feet and consoled him as they headed for the hotel.

The wind was picking up; it pushed against the taxi. It was a relief when they reached the hotel and were safely inside. They had a suite on the eleventh floor. They went up to their room and settled in for a rough night. It was estimated the storm would hit right after daybreak, but they would be in for rough weather all night.

"Close the drapes and stay away from the windows. The wind can send debris flying a long way. Just because we're up high doesn't mean we won't feel the effects of the hurricane," Wes instructed.

They turned on the news to get an update on the storm. The storm's name was Earleen; its projected path would take it over the Bahamas early in the morning, across the tip of Florida, and into the Gulf of Mexico.

"We need to call Grace and let her know. It may not come in at the Cove, but I want her to be aware of it. She doesn't watch much TV, and she needs to keep up with its projected path," Mandy demanded.

Ben tried to call his mom; she wasn't at home. "I'll try later."

"We may not have phone service later, so call the local police and have them locate her for you," Wes recommended.

Ben made the call. You could feel the hotel swaying in the wind.

The rain pounded against the large glass windows. Thunder rumbled the floors, and lightning lit up the night sky.

The women went to their room; Mandy bedded Duke down next to her bed. He wanted on the bed with her, and she let him. Judy didn't seem to be nervous at all. "You seem awfully calm." Mandy tried to calm Duke.

"I'm used to the sea, remember? It's not a bad hurricane, just a category one. We'll get bad weather, but the people in Florida will get the worst of it. When it gets into the Gulf, it'll strengthen in the warm water. The water in the ocean is cooler than the water in the Gulf. The warm water, that's where she'll get her fury," Judy informed Mandy. "Oh, by the way, thanks for talking to me today. I really think it helped. Ben had a totally different attitude toward me. We had the most wonderful romantic evening. We danced in the moonlight until the clouds started rolling in, then we danced inside. It was wonderful. He whispered such sweet things in my ear."

"See, you have to have a little mystery to hold a man. I was married ten years. We loved each other more when Clay died than when we first got married. I didn't think that was possible, but it's true. Mystery, that's a woman's best asset."

"He loved my new clothes. Wait. Your hair, it's not braided anymore."

"Wes didn't like it all that much, so he took it down."

"Wes never did like braided hair. He used to rag me all the time about mine. I would braid it just to aggravate him. You do look better with yours down."

The weather was getting worse; there was a knock at the door. Mandy left her room to join Ben and Wes in the joint sitting area.

"Dr. Young, we've got the *Katie I* secure, as secure as she can be," Bo said, water dripping from his rain coat onto the floor. "The staff has got rooms and they are all accounted for. Chef Maximo wanted to stay with his family instead of staying at the hotel. Is there anything else you need, sir?"

"No, Bo. I appreciate all you've done. Go have a restful night. Put anything you need on your room, and I'll take care of it. You know the limits on the bar bills; inform Patrick."

"Yes, sir. He's bunking with me tonight. We got a double room. I'll take care of it," Bo said and excused himself.

"Good staff is hard to find. I hope Patrick is as good of a deckhand as Bo. If so, I will have done well, wouldn't you think?" Wes asked Ben.

"Patrick seems to be a really dependable man. His résumé was excellent," Ben replied.

"I thought so too."

Mandy was worried about Grace after she talked with Judy. "Did you ever get in touch with your mom, Ben? I'm worried about her."

"Yes, I did. She said she was at Pastor Johnny's house and heard the news. They're going over to help her secure her place, and she's going to secure your place too. She noticed you left your clay barrels out so they are going to put them in the barn for you. She's going to her sister's in Spring Hill and stay."

"Good."

"You worry more about my mom than I do."

"I love that old woman. You should pay more attention to her yourself." She caught a look of disapproval on Wes' face out of the corner of her eye. "I'm sorry. I didn't mean to be so callous," Mandy apologized.

Judy joined them in the living room. "What's all the fuss in here? Mandy, you're not giving Ben a hard time again, are you?"

"Yes, I was. I apologized. I'll get better."

"What's this, everyone taking up for poor ole Ben?" Ben laughed. "I need help when it comes to that woman. She brings new meaning to a woman scorned."

"Now, you look here—"

"Would anyone like refreshments? I can call room service." Wes squeezed Mandy's hand.

"I would. All of this excitement has made me hungry," Judy said, looking at the room service menu.

"There's a basket of goodies on the table, it's fruit and nuts." Mandy brought the basket to the table.

"I want real food, Wes," Judy insisted. "Call room service and get one of those party trays with wine. It's going to be a long night. You two can have a little wine, can't you?"

"A little wine would be nice. It'll help take the edge off."

The wind was picking up outside; the rain was coming down in sheets now. You could see the glass in the windows flexing under the pressure of the storm.

Ben turned on the weather channel on the TV. The storm was only fifty miles away now. The winds were up to eighty-five miles an hour with gusts up to one hundred. They were feeling the outward bands of the storm. The weather channel was giving instructions and precautions to be taken by people in Earleen's path. She was classified a category-two storm now.

Room service brought the food and wine. They also brought a brochure on precautions to take in a hurricane with a hurricane map, so that guests could track the storm.

"This is exciting. This is my first hurricane, and it had to be named Earleen. Earleen was the name of the girl who sat behind me in horticulture class in college. Boy, she looked like a storm had hit her. She was a modern-day hippie. Long straight hair, bellbottom pants, flower child shirt, and those high steppin' clogs. She said she was going to help save the environment with her new invention on growing vegetables. She probably will too," Ben reflected.

Judy fixed her plate, poured a glass of wine, and sat beside Ben. Ben watched the windows; he was feeling a little nervous. He didn't want the others to know. He sat beside Judy and helped her eat her food. He watched everyone else in the room. They didn't seem to be affected by the storm; they were watching TV and acting as if nothing was going on outside. Every time there was a wind gust, it shook the windowpanes; he could feel his heart jump. He wanted the storm to be over; he didn't know how much longer he could keep calm. The closer the storm got, the more fragile his nerves got.

Duke didn't like the storm either. When the wind would howl he would whine. Mandy got on the floor to play with him to keep him calm. *At least he isn't the only one who feels uncomfortable*, Ben thought.

Judy got up and put her dishes on the room service cart. "I'm going to bed. It's been a long day. The storm is coming whether I'm awake or asleep. Call me if the hotel crumbles." She laughed.

Ben didn't think it was funny. "I don't think we should joke at a time like this."

"What else can we do? What's going to happen is going to happen whether we are funny or scared. Fear is just a heart-workout emotion. Fear doesn't stop the inevitable, nor does it change anything but your heart rate, right, Wes?" Judy remarked.

"Right," Wes answered.

"I'm going to bed too," Mandy announced. "Come on, Duke, you can sleep with me."

"Goodnight, my love, sleep tight. You know, the women are right, we should get some rest. The storm won't hit until in the morning. We're going to need our rest. There's no telling what we'll find when we get back to the yacht," Wes said, getting up and heading for his room.

"I'll be there in a little while. I want to watch the weather one more time." Ben knew he wouldn't be able to sleep even if he did go to bed. He watched the weather reports over and over, hoping the storm would change course. It didn't; it just got closer and closer. The windspeed and gusts were picking up; the rain was awful. He pulled the drapes back just enough to see what was going on outside. People were still out in the streets. They were putting up plywood and chaining down sports equipment. They acted as if this was an everyday occurrence.

You could see news crews down on the street covering the storm. They were still filming in the wind and rain. He couldn't understand why people were so interested in bad weather and tragedy. He looked down on the street again; debris was flying everywhere. He wanted to rest; he knew Wes was right, but he was terrified.

He thought about his mom; she would be telling him to get on his knees and pray. He didn't know how to pray. He had never learned; when he was supposed to be paying attention in church when he was little, he was playing. He had always been a player. Maybe now was the time for him to change. "God, I hope you can hear me. Make us safe. Amen." He remembered Mandy's prayer on the beach that night; she was so sincere. He tried again. "God, I'll make a deal with you if you'll keep us safe through this storm. I'll be a better person, I promise. You keep your end of the deal, I'll keep mine." He felt a sense of peace come over him like warm water poured over his head. For the first time in his life he knew everything would be all right. "Thanks, God. Amen." He turned the TV off and went to bed.

The morning brought the storm's full fury. The winds had picked to a hundred twenty miles per hour, with gusts up to one hundred thirty; it was a category-three hurricane. The hotel was swaying, the rain pounding against the windows. You could hear debris flying around below, striking whatever was in its path. The mood was intense in the suite.

Judy dragged herself into the living room. "I'm hungry. Does anyone want breakfast? Turn on the lights, it's dark in here."

Everyone, up for at least thirty minutes already, looked at her in disbelief. Earleen was right on top of them. The power was out. They couldn't open the drapes as they served as a net in case the windows shattered.

The dark clouds outside didn't offer any light; they were in total darkness. Duke whined; he needed to go outside for his morning bathroom run. Mandy held him close to her. Wes and Ben sat on the couch waiting for the worst to pass. They sat in the dark for an hour, and the wind and rain stopped; the sun was coming out from behind the clouds, a small ray of light shined through the part in the drapes.

"Great, it's over." Ben jumped out of the chair and ran over to the window. "We can get out of this tomb now."

"It's not over, Ben. We're just in the eye of the storm. In a few minutes the wind will start blowing from the opposite direction, and we'll feel her fury again. Be patient. It's almost over. The biggest mistake people make in a hurricane is they think it's over when the eye of the storm is passing over, and they will leave their shelter. That's when most people get killed, when the backside of the storm passes," Wes instructed.

They opened the drapes to see the damage that had been done. The streets were flooded, and debris was strung everywhere. You couldn't quite see the docks, but there were boats that had been pushed across the highway by the tidal surge. Parts of the dock were beside the hotel. People were coming out of the hotel looking.

Hotel staff went out to try and get them to come back inside. The people were laughing at them. Suddenly the wind changed, and with her full fury Earleen's backside started crossing the island. Ben closed the drapes and backed away from the window.

"Did you see that, Wes? The docks are no longer in place. There's a yacht sitting beside the hotel. What about the *Katie I*?"

"We can't worry about the *Katie I* right now. Let's just get through this storm," Wes replied.

Mandy came over and sat beside Wes. "I hope this is over soon. Duke can't wait much longer."

Wes patted Duke's head compassionately. "Mandy, you know the

Katie I may not be there when this is over. We may have to stay in the hotel until we can arrange for transportation back to the Cove. Let's not tell the others. I think Judy probably already knows. Ben is a little tense about the storm, so let's not say anything just yet, okay?"

"Okay. Are you all right?"

"I'm fine."

"I know that is the last thing you have left of Kay's. It may be gone."

"Then it will have been God's will. We'll get another one. It's insured." Wes got up and paced the floor. Mandy looked at Wes, puzzled at his response.

The wind was dying down and the rain had stopped. The storm had finally passed. The sun was beginning to peek out from behind the fast-moving clouds. Wes looked at Ben. "Let's go see what we have left."

Judy and Mandy got their clothes on and put Duke on a leash. "Where do you think the two of you are going?" Wes asked.

"We're going with you," Judy replied.

"Oh no you're not. You're going to stay right here until we get back."

"I don't think so. I'm going," Judy insisted.

Mandy was right behind Judy. Wes shook his head in submission. "Come on, let's get it over with."

They started the long walk down eleven flights of stairs. Duke didn't like the narrow stairwell, but he needed to go, so he led the way. Other guests were beginning to come into the stairwell. Everyone wanted to get outside. No one talked; they just made their way to the bottom as quickly as they could. In the lobby were pieces of debris. The large plate-glass windows were shattered; glass covered the floor.

Mandy tried to make her way around the glass. Wes reached down and picked Duke up so that he wouldn't cut his feet. The others followed. Out on the street, everything was covered with trash and debris—signs, pieces of dock, boats, and furniture. Off to the left Wes spotted a body; he tried to steer the others away, but they had already seen it. He walked over and checked to see if there was any sign off life. There wasn't. Wes took a piece of linen laying on the sidewalk and covered the body with it. He recognized the man as the one who ran the desk at the marina.

They walked in silence looking at the devastation; it was everywhere. They had to walk over piles of debris from the marina. People had tried to prepare, but the storm came too quickly.

The docks were ripped off their poles and were scattered; boats were up on dry land; some were sunk; others were listing to one side. They were all looking for the *Katie I*, which they spotted floating in the middle of the lagoon. She was listing to one side. The dock where she was tied was gone. She had run aground on the reef and was hung there.

Wes knew he needed to get her moved before the water went down. The marina was partially destroyed. People were backed up at the counter. They were all yelling they needed help with this or that. Wes looked around to see if there was a tugboat docked at the marina. Perhaps he could use it to pull the *Katie I* off the reef.

"Wes, come out here and look at this," Mandy said, out of breath.

Wes ran over to where the dock used to be with Mandy. A tugboat had attached lines to the *Katie I* and was pulling her off the reef. She was floating, but she was damaged. The anchor was gone, leaving a gaping hole in the bow. The railings were hanging off the side; the captain's bridge was torn off. When the tugboat got her off the reef, she floated upright.

Everyone let out a sign of relief. "At least she floats," Ben said in excitement.

"We don't know what the side that was hung on the reef looks like," Wes said, discouraged as he looked at his beautiful yacht. He didn't want his disappointment to show to the others. He tried to muster up a smile. He didn't realize the *Katie I* meant so much to him until he saw her.

Ben hollered at the tugboat captain when he got close to the shore, "Ahoy there."

The captain came out to see what he wanted "Yes sir, can I help you."

"That's our boat you have there, Captain. You can drag her over here," Ben yelled.

"She's pretty beat up. I was going to pull her to the boat yard," the captain instructed.

"Pull her over to the boat yard, Captain," Wes yelled.

The engine on the tugboat was loud; yelling was the only way to talk to the captain. When the yacht was turned, you could see where the reef had ripped long scraping holes in the side, caused by dragging on the reef. Wes felt sick to his stomach. He sat on the shoreline with his head between his knees.

"Are you okay?" Mandy reached over and gently touched his shoulder.

"I thought I was, but now I realize that I really like that yacht. Seeing her all beat up seems to have knocked the wind out of my sail. I'm going over to the boat yard to check out the damage. Want to go?" Wes asked, squeezing Mandy's hand.

"Yes, I do. Can we drop Duke off at the hotel first?"

"Yeah, let's do that. Hey guys, we're going to drop Duke off at the hotel then go over to the boat yard to check on the *Katie I.*"

"We're going to hang out here and help if we can," Ben replied. He looked over at Judy. "I think they need to be alone. I think this is much harder on Wes than he let on."

"See you guys," Judy said, hugging Wes' neck. "It'll be all right, my friend."

"I know."

The power was back on at the hotel; they had huge generators that provided electricity when the weather was bad. The hotel staff took Duke up to their room for Mandy. She and Wes walked the long road covered with debris to the boat yard. Clean-up crews were already busy cleaning up the debris.

An ambulance served as a vehicle to transport the bodies to the hospital for identification. Mandy noticed there were several bodies in the ambulance; they were putting another one in a body bag. She started to weep. "I know this isn't a good time for this, but there are so many bodies. All the families affected by this storm."

"People think it's exciting. They don't realize the danger until it's too late. These are bodies of people who chose to stay on their boats and ride out the storm. See, that was the man who was docked next to us. He told us where to get a boat to go fishing yesterday. Now he's gone."

They walked in silence the rest of the way. He could see the *Katie I* tied to the dock ready to be pulled out.

"Who owns this boat? Are the owners still alive?" the boat yard supervisor yelled.

"Yes, that's my boat," Wes yelled to the man.

"She's pretty bad on the port side—looks like she got hung up on the reef," he said, assessing the damage. "She's going to have to be pulled out, or she will eventually sink. Your call, it's your baby."

"Pull her out. I need to know whom I can see about getting her repaired," Wes said, realizing they would have to get back to Florida another way. The *Katie I* was not going to take them.

"Dr. Young, Dr. Young!" Wes heard someone calling behind him. It was the captain of *Katie I*, Captain Berney Barnes. "Dr. Young, I can take care of her if you like."

"I would like for you to take care of her. First, I want to see what damage she has."

"I looked at her this morning, sir. She's pretty bad on the port side. I'm afraid she's going to need major repairs. Your father called to check on you and your guests. You must not have your cell phone," Captain Barnes said. "You might want to call him, sir. He's pretty upset."

"I will, Captain Barnes. I guess I left my phone on the yacht. Could I borrow yours?"

"Indeed, sir, here it is. I'll follow the *Katie I*."

"Thank you, Captain." Wes dialed his father's number; his father answered.

"Father, this is Wes. I can barely hear you. Yes, yes, we're all okay. It was a bad one. Yes, yes, I will. Thanks, Father, I appreciate it. She's fine too, we will. Thanks again." Wes hung up the phone. "Father wants us to leave the yacht here with Captain Barnes. He'll take care of the repairs. He's going to send the man down who built her to assess her and see if she can be repaired. Come on, let's go see how she is." Wes took Mandy's arm and they headed over to the dry dock area.

They had finished pulling her out and she was being lifted to a more stable setting. Wes looked at the scrapes and cuts in the hull on the port side. There were gashes that went all the way through; the master bedroom quarters were visible from the outside. The anchors were gone, both front and back, leaving large gaping holes where they had hung. The guardrails were torn off and hanging from the sides. The captain's bridge was almost torn off.

"She's in bad shape. I don't know if she can be repaired," Wes said, walking alongside of her, looking at all the damage.

"She floats." Mandy tried to encourage him as he rubbed his hands alongside her hull, feeling the gashes in the fiberglass.

"Not for long she wouldn't. Oh, Mandy, this is bad," Wes said, trying to hold back the tears. "She'll never be the same."

"You don't know that. Didn't your dad say he was sending the builder over here to look at her? He built her once. He can do it again." She tried to encourage him.

"I'm going aboard, do you want to come?"

"Sure."

They climbed the ladder to the deck; it looked pretty good. They went inside, everything was thrown down on the floor, but it was intact. They went below to the sleeping quarters; the guest quarters were intact, but the master quarters were destroyed. Gaping holes revealed the outside world to anyone standing in the master quarters. It was full of salt water, seaweed, and debris. Wes noticed something sticking out of the closet; it was a hand. He opened the door; it was Patrick, the new deckhand he had just hired. He had a bag with the silverware and some electronics in it.

"Don't come in here, Mandy. Get the harbormaster. He's the guy logging in the boat they are pulling out."

Mandy did as Wes requested. The harbormaster wanted to know what she wanted; she couldn't tell him. She asked him to "please come," as it seemed important. The harbormaster boarded the *Katie I*. Mandy directed him to Wes. Once inside the room, Wes showed the harbormaster the body.

"Looks like this fellow's line of work killed him." The harbormaster bent down to check the body out.

"He was my new deckhand. I just hired him yesterday," Wes told him.

"We'll need to rope this boat off. It's a crime scene now. Don't take anything or move anything. I'll have to ask you to leave it with me. I'll let you know what we find in our investigation."

Wes led Mandy off the yacht. "I thought we were going to be able to get a few things we might need," Mandy protested.

"Mandy, Patrick is dead in there. Looks like he tried to rob the yacht while we were all at the hotel. Speaking of hotel, have you seen Bo?"

"No, just the captain."

"Let's find Bo. I hope he's all right."

At the hotel Wes found out what room Bo was in. When they got to the room, no one answered the door. They could hear moaning inside. Wes asked the bellboy to open the door. Once inside, they found Bo on the floor tied up with blood on his head.

"Are you okay, Bo?" Wes checked him while he untied his hands and feet.

"Yes, sir, I think so. That Patrick is a crook. He put something in my wine. When it didn't work, he knocked me out and tied me up."

"Well, you don't have to worry about him anymore. He's dead. Looks like he was robbing the yacht when she tore loose from the dock. I don't know what the cause of death is, but he's dead. The police are investigating now."

"The *Katie I*, sir, is she all right?"

"I'm afraid not, Bo. She sustained a lot of damage in the storm. She tore loose from the dock and got hung up on the reef. I want you and Captain Barnes to stay here in the islands with the yacht. I'll arrange for you to stay here so that you can keep me posted, full salary of course."

"Yes, sir, whatever you say. I'm sorry, Dr. Young."

"It's not your fault, Bo. Patrick was the bad guy, not you. Let me check your head."

Wes doctored Bo's head and bandaged it up. He told Bo where to find the yacht, and he and Mandy left.

Up in their suite, Wes wanted to be alone; you could tell all of this had been a strain on him. He just wanted to rest a while; then they would worry about getting home.

Mandy went into her room and lay across the bed with Duke. She pondered what Wes must have been going through. *The Katie I felt like the only part of Kay he had left. He is having to let go of it and her all at the same time. It was Kay who had wanted the yacht. It was Kay who awakened this part of Wes that loved the ocean. It was Kay who had held the strings of his heart. It is like she is dying all over again.* Mandy could see it in his eyes as he looked at the destroyed yacht. *He feels just as broken as his yacht is. He is mourning the loss of an era in his life. One he held onto for the past six years.*

The pottery shop was her tie to Clay. She still had him as long as she had the shop. She could still feel his presence there. She could still see him sitting at the wheel covered in clay, smiling, laughing; each day was a whole new adventure for him. He never longed for that which he didn't have; he just loved and cherished what he did have. She loved him still. She was indeed a potter's wife. She wept for Wes and for herself.

Duke started to whine. She realized no one had eaten, not even Duke. She called down for sandwiches and sodas; she ordered Duke a hamburger.

By the time the food had arrived, Judy and Ben were back. They were chatting about all the damage that had been done by the storm. Wes and Mandy sat quietly listening to them ramble on.

"We need to decide how we're going to get back to Florida, whether we want to fly or take a cruise ship back. If we fly, we can fly right into Spring Hill and take a rental car back to the Cove. If we went on a cruise ship, we would have to take a car from Miami—"

Wes interrupted their rambling. "I'm for flying home. We'll get there quicker, and the ride from the airport won't be as long." Mandy took a bite from her sandwich with a nod, solidifying her decision.

"That sounds good to us," Judy and Ben agreed.

I'll make the arrangements," Wes said, getting up from his chair. You could tell the wind had been knocked out of his sail.

"I'll make the arrangements," Mandy said, patting his shoulder.

"Thanks, I really appreciate it." Wes smiled at her.

"I know you do." She smiled back.

feel better about them. She was so tired she fell asleep in his arms. He watched her as she slept in his arms. He pushed her long hair away from her face and kissed her forehead. "You will never know, Ms. Bowls, how much I love you, and I do love you. So much my heart hurts when I think of life without you."

She wiggled a little, and he held her tighter. It began to sprinkle rain. He knew he should wake her, but he didn't want this moment to end. Duke had his head laid on Wes' lap. "You're a lucky boy. You get to sleep with my woman," he said, rubbing Dukes side.

The sprinkles turned into drops. Mandy woke up. "It's raining? We'd better go inside. I'm sorry. I guess I'm more worn out than I thought."

They hurried inside the house. "I'd better be going before the rain gets too bad."

"Could you stay? I want you to stay," she said, holding his hands in hers.

"Do you mean it?"

"Yes, I do."

They fell asleep in each other's arms.

The morning brought rain and strong winds. The tropical storm was upon them. She looked over at Wes and Duke. They looked so cute. Mandy got up as not to disturb them and put on coffee. She made breakfast, and the smell of bacon brought Duke running into the kitchen. She fed him and fixed Wes a tray. She tiptoed into the bedroom, set the tray on the side table, and reached over to kiss him. "Good morning, Prince Charming, it's time to rise and shine."

"I was having the most wonderful dream. I dreamed I held you all night. It wasn't a dream, was it?"

"No, it wasn't. I made you breakfast."

"You're going to spoil me."

"I hope so."

She sat on the bed while he ate. "This is wonderful: beautiful and can cook. Are you looking for a job?" he said, squeezing her hand.

"No, thank you. I have one. In case you didn't know, I own the pottery shop. I'm a very busy woman."

"I'm a very busy man." He reached over and pulled her into bed with him. "You are a dream come true, my love."

"I'll bet you say that to all the girls."

"How did you know?" They both laughed.

"Looks like we're in for rough weather today. What can one do on a rainy day like this?" she asked.

"Let me show you," he said, pulling her close to him.

"Now, now, let's not let things get out of hand."

"They already are. Mandy, I want to marry you. You don't have to say anything now. I know you need to think about it. We haven't known each other that long, but I've known you long enough to know what I want, and that's you."

She was shocked. She hadn't known what he was going to say, but she didn't expect this. She didn't know what to say. They had only known each other a few months. She knew she loved him. She wanted to be with him, but marriage was a big step. She didn't take marriage lightly; it was a lifelong commitment to her.

"I can tell by your expression you weren't expecting me to pop the question. I picked this up in the Bahamas. Ben helped me pick it out." He reached over and took a black box from his pants pocket. "Here, this is for you."

She took the box and opened it; it was an engagement ring full of diamonds bigger than she had ever worn. She was speechless.

"If you want a long engagement, I understand." He searched her face for some sigh of reaction. He watched her, looking at the ring in the box. "It would be much prettier on your finger. Will you let me place it on your finger?"

Tears filled her eyes; she had wanted this. Now it was happening and she had no words to respond.

"Here, let me have it. Mandy Bowls, would you marry me?" He took her hand and removed the golden band Clay had placed there so many years ago and placed the engagement ring on her finger.

"Yes, I will." She cried, unable to take her eyes off the beautiful ring. She had never had anything so beautiful before.

He took her gently in his arms and held her. "You've made me the happiest man on earth."

"Ben helped you pick it out?"

"The day you and Judy took a nap, we went out and picked it out."

"He knew you were going to ask me to marry you?"

"Yes. Everyone knew, including Judy."

"She never said a word."

"I know, Ben swore her to secrecy."

"I don't know what to say."

"You've already said it. You said yes."

"My home, my shop, my life…" Mandy realized her whole world had just changed.

"I know how you feel about the pottery shop. I wouldn't interfere with that. I would want you to move in with me, when we're married, of course. It would be a little hard, you living here and me living up the road." He joked. "But my new home would be a fresh start for both of us."

"Yes." She smiled. "It would be a little hard. I love you, Westbrook Young, I guess you know this means you'll be stuck with me the rest of your life."

"I know. I don't know anyone else I'd rather be stuck with."

She laughed, still staring at the ring.

"I'm glad you said yes. Grace has planned a beautiful engagement party for us tomorrow night. If you would have said no, well, it would be like having a victory party ready and you lost the game."

"Everyone knows? What if I had said no?"

"I was banking on you saying yes. If you'd said no, I would have walked around embarrassed the rest of my life."

The rain was getting harder, and the wind was picking up. "I guess I have Earleen to thank for this." They both laughed.

"Let me get a shower and we can check on the weather."

"You didn't expect me to make love to you last night. You never even asked why?"

"I know that you don't believe in premarital sex, so I wanted to respect your wishes. You think I was going to pounce on you last night when I had the big question to pop today? No way. We'll wait. Besides, just being here with you last night was enough. When you're ready, then it'll be right." He kissed her on the forehead and went into the bathroom.

She couldn't take her eyes off the ring. *It is huge; I will have to take it off when I am working with the clay,* she thought. She didn't want to ruin it. She took the dishes back into the kitchen and washed them. She walked into the pottery shop and looked around. Even though it was Friday, she didn't think she would have very many customers in this weather.

"I've got to go to work, my love. You have a wonderful day, and I'll see you tonight," Wes said, getting his things together.

"The weather is too bad to be out in it," she warned.

"I'm a doctor, my love. I have to go. People depend on me to be there. The children in the cancer ward depend on me to be there for them."

"I know, it's just—"

"I'll be all right. Oh wait, I don't have a vehicle here, could you run me to my house?"

"Sure." She got the keys to the truck; they got drenched as they ran to the truck. They laughed.

"You be careful now," she warned when she dropped him off. She looked at the big old house he lived in. It was a beautiful two-story, old southern-style seaside mansion with large pillars and a wrap-around porch—. She couldn't imagine herself living in a house like that with servants. She hadn't been inside since Wes moved in. It had been years since she had been inside. She tried to remember what it looked like. She couldn't.

She decided since she was out, she would run by Grace's. She missed her friend and wanted to show off the ring. She ran up to the door, getting drenched again. She was shaking the water off when the door opened. It was Judy. "Come on in, my friend. We were hoping you would come by. Let me see that rock."

Mandy lifted her hand and showed Judy her ring.

"Woman, what a ring. That man has lost his mind over you. Come on in. Grace wants to see it too."

"Grace! I've missed you, old woman," she said, hugging Grace.

"I missed you too, little lady. I hear congratulations are in order. Let me see your ring. My, that's a big one. It's lovely. I'm so happy for you. Sorry it wasn't my son, no offense, honey," she said to Judy.

"None taken. I'm glad they're like oil and vinegar. That gives me a chance." Judy laughed.

"He better know he's got a good one this time. This young lady is a wonderful person. I'm glad Ben met her," Grace added.

"Me too." Judy hugged Grace.

"Everyone knew about this but me. Judy, you didn't say a word."

"Ben told me the night we were dancing on the deck of the *Katie I* in the Bahamas. He swore me to secrecy. My lips were zipped. This is so wonderful. I'm so happy for you. Can I be the maid of honor? You don't have a sister, and I *am* your best friend," Judy rambled on.

"Actually, I want Grace to be my maid of honor. She's my best friend. The best one I've ever had. Will you, Grace?" Mandy asked.

"I wouldn't miss it for the world." Grace hugged Mandy.

"I would like you to be my bridesmaid, cause you're my second-best friend," Mandy said, hugging Judy.

"I accept," Judy squealed.

"I told Wes I wanted to do the flowers," Ben said, walking in the room.

"You? Flowers?" Mandy was stunned.

"Yes, my feminine side comes out when I'm alone with flowers." He laughed. "Wes wanted to have the wedding on the *Katie I*. He was going to rename it on your wedding day. But you know what happened, so I guess it's okay to tell you that. That's why he was so upset when she got destroyed—not because of Kay. It kind of ruined his plans."

"He made all of these plans before he even asked me? You guys probably thought I was the dumbest person, not knowing something was going on."

"Actually, I was the only one who knew. I told Judy, Wes didn't. Then came Earleen, who changed everything—well, almost everything, you're still getting married. Congratulations. I'm happy for you." Ben hugged Mandy's neck.

"Now you can pray for me," Judy instructed.

"Boy...does she need prayer." Ben laughed and gave her a hug. "Nah, I think we're going to get along just fine. Looks like I'm going to have to find a place near water. Put this woman to work. She says she needs water and fish and all that stuff to work."

"This is so wonderful. I'm happy for both of you," Mandy said.

"Enough of this fuss. I've got lunch made. Bad storm outside. We'll sit in the dining room to eat. Open the blinds. It'll look like we're outside. Come on, this old woman is hungry." Grace ushered everyone into the dining room.

"See what you're in for, Judy?" Mandy laughed.

"I know. I love it. Isn't she a trip?" Judy laughed, and they all went into the dining room.

. . . . .

Wes knocked at Mandy's door at five-thirty that afternoon. The rain had stopped and Mandy was out back picking up tree limbs and debris that had gotten blown around. The water was still high; it was up to the rock walkway near the back porch. Duke was chasing the seagulls, barking.

He went around back where he heard the commotion. He watched Mandy as she dragged the last limb over to a pile she had made. She had mud on her face and on her legs up to her knees. Her hair was tied in a knot; her clothes were muddy. She looked up to find him standing there. He was all dressed up in a suit, looking handsome with his dark tan.

"You might as well get used to seeing me like this. I look like this all the time. If it's not mud, it's clay. You look so handsome. You clean up real well," she joked.

"You look fine to me, my love. Clay, mud, it doesn't matter. You're a fine woman. Come over here and give your fiancé a kiss," he said, holding out his arms.

"I'm too dirty to get next to that suit," she said trying to dust off some of the mud.

He reached down and picked up a handful of mud, wiping it on his suit. "Now come over here and give me a kiss."

"You're crazy. Look at your suit now. I'm not washing your clothes."

"You don't have to. You'll have a maid for that," he said, grabbing her and giving her a big kiss.

"Well," she said, brushing her hair back, "let me get a little muddier and let's do that again." She kissed him back.

"Let's go get a shower and pick up Grace, Ben, and Judy. We'll all go to the island for dinner, my treat," he suggested, walking up to the back porch with her.

"That sounds good to me. I like a bath, though, not a shower."

"Whatever you want is fine." He kissed her again and again.

"Let me go, you beast. Go home and change. I'll bathe and call you when I'm ready."

"Wear something real pretty."

"I'll wear what I have, I don't know if it's pretty or not, but—"

"I thought you would say that, so I brought you something. Let me get it." He walked out to the Hummer and took out a big box. "Here, wear this."

"You're going to spoil me." She was stunned.

"You haven't seen anything yet, my love," he said, getting back in the Hummer.

Mandy went inside and climbed into a bath. It felt so good to be back in her little house, in her own worn bathtub. It was an antique tub with lion's feet. She loved it; it cupped around her body. She fixed her hair and face; she opened the box on the bed. It was a beautiful red summer dress with matching jewelry and shoes. She put the dress on; she loved the way she looked in red.

She heard the Hummer pull up out front; Duke started barking and jumping at the door. He loved Wes, she could tell.

She yelled, "Come in, I'll be done in a minute."

Wes waited in the living room, playing with Duke. He couldn't wait to see her in that red dress. He loved her in red. He remembered the night they had danced on the deck of the *Katie I*. She was stunning; he squirmed with anticipation.

When she walked out he thought his heart would burst. "You look lovely tonight, my love." He tried to contain himself. He kissed her on the lips ever so gently. "Are you ready to go?"

"Ready as I'll ever be. No, Duke, you can't go. Sit."

They ran to the Hummer. Grace, Ben, and Judy were all waiting. "I'm sorry to keep you waiting," she said to everyone.

Ben looked at Mandy; she was beautiful. He was sorry he had made fun of her that day she tried to impress him. He was sorry he let her get away. He reached over, patted Judy's leg, and smiled at her.

"Everyone looks so good tonight. What's the occasion?" Mandy joked.

"Have you two set the date?" Judy asked in anticipation.

"I've only been engaged one day, and already they want a date. Wes, did you put her up to this?"

"I'm innocent. I worked all day," Wes defended himself.

"It's me. I'm really a big romantic, and this is so exciting. Wes is like my big brother. He's waited such a long time to find you, Mandy. I'm excited for him." She looked over at Ben and noticed he was staring at Mandy. She reached over and slapped his leg. "Isn't that right, my man?"

"Isn't what right?" Ben reacted to the slap.

Grace watched her son. She knew what he was thinking. She felt sorry for him, but she had tried to tell him and he wouldn't listen. She had tried to tell him someone would come along and snatch Mandy up. He couldn't wait forever; now it was done. She was no longer within his reach. She loved Wes; he was a good man and would take care of her the way she deserved. Now Ben wanted to move away from Boston, but it was too late.

When they reached the island, the restaurant was hopping. People were trying to get in the last bit of summer. They were laughing and dancing, walking on the beach; some were sitting on the deck waiting for the sun to set. The sunset was beautiful here. You could see the entire scene from the deck; the restaurant's logo was, "Come Experience Beautiful Sunsets."

They opted to sit on the deck; after all, this was a special occasion. It wasn't every day a friend gets engaged. Mandy was radiant, her happiness glowing on her face. This time last year she was alone and separated from the human race. Today she was celebrating a new beginning. Grace smiled, watching her dear friend. She deserved happiness.

Ben was trying to be happy for his new friend. But how could he? Wes had taken the thing he wanted most in life. She had been his; how could he have been so naïve, thinking she would be in that potter's shop forever waiting for him to return and sweep her off her feet?

Why did he go with Judy that night on the boat? He was drunk, and his heart was sick over seeing Mandy with Wes. He had thought perhaps it would make her jealous, but it had only made her hate him all the more.

Wes wanted to toast the evening. "This is to meeting the love of my life, to Mandy, the woman who has made me the happiest man on earth." Everyone lifted their glass and joined the toast except for Ben.

"Here, here." They all laughed.

Judy watched Ben; she knew something wasn't right. She wanted to talk to him alone. "Ben, would you like to take a walk on the beach before dinner gets here?"

"That sounds like a good idea. Excuse us," Ben said, sliding his chair back, joining Judy.

They walked for a while before she spoke. "Ben, I know something is wrong. I see the way you look at Mandy. Is there anything I can do to help?"

He could no longer contain his emotions. Tears began to roll down his cheeks. "Judy, you're a wonderful person, a good friend, but I really love Mandy. It's my fault she's with Wes. I was so stupid. I thought she was a little ole nobody from Nowhere, U.S.A. Then I saw her with Wes and my heart broke. I met you and you've been a good friend. But that's all I can offer right now. Can you understand that?"

"I understand. I've loved Wes since I was thirteen years old. I always thought we would be together, and then he met Kay. I hated her. I turned his family against her. I told them she was a gold digger and was after the family fortune. Wes has never looked at me as a woman, just his little sister. When Kay died I thought, 'This is our time. I'm all grown up now. He'll have to see me as a woman.' But he was so overtaken with grief, he didn't even look at me. When he gave me the job on the yacht, I though, 'Okay, he sees me as a woman.' But he didn't, and he probably never will. Now he's engaged to Mandy. He'll never be mine. So you see, my friend, I understand exactly what you are going through. I've just been going through it longer. I came to the point if I couldn't have him, I at least wanted him happy with whomever he chose."

Ben looked at Judy through tear-filled eyes; they both laughed. He reached out and hugged her tight. "You're a good friend. Wes is stupid for not seeing you for the woman are, because you're a beautiful lady." They danced around in the sand and laughed.

"We'd better get back, they might think something's wrong," Judy suggested.

Ben reached over, took her hand, and kissed it. "Any time you need someone to talk to, just whistle. You know, just put your lips together and blow."

Back at the table, the waiter was serving dinner. Grace watched Ben and Judy as they returned. She could tell Ben had been crying. She loved her son and hated to see him in pain, but there was nothing she could do to take the pain away. He had to find happiness for himself. She had tried to direct him in Mandy's path and had failed.

"If you don't mind, I'd like to dance with my fiancée," Wes said, taking Mandy's hand.

away at a cancer research convention, and she and Duke were running the pottery shop. Business was good; she had made a name for herself, thanks to Wes' mother and her rich friends. She had been able to build a storefront to display her pottery separate from her workroom.

Things have changed so much this last year, she thought. She no longer was that backwoods woman who had shut herself away from the world. She was a successful businesswoman that rubbed elbows with the elite. Her pieces had found themselves all over the world. She had a showing at the Boston Markets and had sold all of her pieces. She had been on the cover of several pottery magazines and was giving classes at the college in Spring Hill once a week.

Life had gotten complicated; sometimes she wished for that little pottery shop and she and Grace having coffee on the back porch. Those days were gone. She was on the rollercoaster of life; she didn't know how things had evolved into this. She turned on the kiln and sat at the table where she had clay rolled up. She needed to form the clay before it got too hard to work with. She wanted to make custom wind chimes. She began to make small shapes of birds, fish, and shells. She formed bowled shapes that she would paint along with the birds, fish, and shells.

She was into her work when the phone rang. It was Ben. "What are you doing?"

"I'm making wind chimes."

"Want some company?"

"Sure, I'll put you to work." She and Ben had become friends; he was forever helping her lift heavy barrels and would even send a crew out to do her yard and walkways. He was a big help to her.

He walked into the pottery shop and sat down beside Mandy. "Can I make one of those?"

"Sure, I have molds if you need them."

"I need them." He chuckled.

"There're on that shelf right over there," she said, pointing to a shelf that was covered in molds. "If you look through those little molds in that basket, I think that's where I put them." They were molds her students used in her classes.

"I found them. It's getting cold outside. That wind will cut right through you."

"Well, you see what I'm wearing." She had on a granny gown and fluffy slippers.

"Yeah, you really look like a world-renowned potter." They both laughed.

"I don't feel like a world-renowned potter. I feel like Mandy Bowls. Right here in the Cove working on my pieces for those little ole ladies that come down from the north, snowbirds, they call them. That looks good, ever thought about changing professions? Speaking of professions, how's business?"

"Business is good. The people of Spring Hill act like they have never had a professional landscaper. So I'm raking in the dough. I was glad most of my staff was willing to relocate. When they found out I was moving to Florida, well, that's all some of them needed to hear. Ever spent a winter in Boston? I think that's where cold was invented."

"I've always lived in the South. When I have to travel, I don't like it. I just want to be a potter, not a celebrity. It's nice, all of the attention, but it's not really me, you know?"

Duke came in and lay down at Mandy's feet. He watched her and Ben play in the clay.

"I know, but you're good at it. I watched you on the Learning Channel. That special you did last month. You wouldn't know you were a Southern belle." They laughed again.

"How's Grace tonight? She acted like she was trying to get a cold. Has she been to the doctor?"

"No, there's only one doctor she goes to, and we both know who that is. Have you heard from the boy since he's been gone?"

"Yes, he calls me three or four times a day. How's Judy?"

"She fine, they're giving her some kind of award for some type of seaweed she found that they're making a vaccine out of."

"Really?"

"Yeah."

"Boy, I've really been out of the loop. I'm home now, and I'm staying. The world can do without Mandy Bowls for awhile." She laughed. "Ben, when are you going to make an honest woman out of Judy?"

"Mandy, don't start that again. Judy and I are really good friends. We spend a lot of time together and we enjoy each other's company, but she's not the love of my life. And neither am I the love of her life. Why can't you understand that?"

"Because you make such a cute couple."

"You know as well as I do being a cute couple doesn't make a marriage."

"It's a start."

"Mandy, you're hopeless."

"Yes, I am. Would you like some homemade hot chocolate?"

"I've been waiting," he looked at his watch, "an hour for you to offer me some."

"Sorry for being such a bad hostess." She laughed as she went into the kitchen to start warming the milk.

The phone rang. "It's Wes, you wait and see," she said, smiling at Ben.

"Hello, I'm fine, how's the weather in California? Good…I see, so when are you coming home? Really…I love you too…Duke's fine…Yes, he's taking good care of me…I really don't want to go, I just got home…you have a safe trip…I love you too, bye." She smiled at Ben. "Told you."

"How's the old boy doing?" Ben asked, though he really didn't care.

"He's fine. He's flying to Washington to meet his parents for a family meeting. He'll be back in a week. I miss him when he's gone. I wish he didn't have to travel, especially abroad."

"He just leaves you here alone."

"I've got Duke, and I don't like all that traveling. Why don't you and Judy try sharing a house and see if it works out?" Mandy continued on her matchmaking quest.

"If you don't stop I'm going home. Besides it's been nice spending time with Mom. She's not getting any younger."

Mandy was totally confused; she thought Ben and Judy would have already been together. They didn't seem to have any plans at all. They just hung out together.

They sat and drank their hot chocolate together. It was medicinal on a cold night. She watched him as he talked about the rich people in Spring Hill laughing at their strange ways. She noticed when he looked at her it was with such respect and…no, it couldn't be. Did he still have feelings for her that went beyond friendship? She shuddered at the thought.

"Are you cold?"

"No, no, I'm fine. You were saying?"

He rattled on, and she watched him intensely. He was ever so careful not to let his eyes reflect his true feelings, but he wasn't successful.

"Stop, stop right there. Tell me why you and Judy aren't making future plans." She got up from the table and paced the floor.

"I told you, we're friends."

"Judy is a beautiful, intelligent woman. Any man would grab her in a heartbeat. But not you. Something's wrong here, Ben. I want you to be honest with me. We decided no more deception, remember?"

"No, you don't want me to be honest. I told you if you persisted, I was going home, so have a good night."

She grabbed his arm as he walked away. "No, you're not going anywhere. You tell me the truth. I want to know what's up. Judy doesn't date anyone else, does she?"

"Well no, but—"

"I need to know the truth, Ben, and I need to know it now." She started to cry. "Something's wrong here, I can feel it. Is the reason Judy doesn't date because she has feelings for Wes? And you, you have feelings for me? Are you two playing games with Wes and I? Tell me. Tell me now."

"I don't want to continue this conversation. I'll see myself out," Ben said, pulling his arm away from her.

"Please, Ben, I beg of you, I need to know the truth … please, Ben, don't leave," she cried as he walked out the door.

She sat on the floor and cried. Had she been in outer space or was she so involved she couldn't see the forest for the trees? She felt sick to her stomach. She went into the bathroom and washed her face. She wept uncontrollably. She was confused. Something was going on, and she needed to know what it was.

Where was Wes when she needed him? He was always off somewhere doing something. She hurried over to the phone; she dialed Grace's number. Grace picked up the phone. "Hello?"

"Is Ben there?"

"Yes, Mandy, is that you?"

"Yes, it is. I really need to talk to him. Could you put him on the phone?"

"Sure, little lady," Grace said. "Ben, the phone's for you."

"If it's Mandy, I don't want to talk to her."

Mandy dropped the phone. She ran down the beach to Grace's house. By the time Grace realized she wasn't on the phone, she was knocking on the back door.

"Where's Ben's room?"

"Up the stairs—"

She ran up the stairs and opened his door. "You can't walk out on me now."

"Mandy, please, we don't need to be talking about this. Please, I beg you, go home and wait for Wes to get home. Marry him, live happily ever after." Ben sat on his bed.

"Please, Ben, if you care anything about me, you'll tell me the truth."

Grace looked in the door. "Is everything all right?"

"Everything's fine, Mom. Mandy is just a little upset."

"Is there anything I can help with?"

"No, Mom, I'll take care of it."

"Mandy, what's wrong?"

"Ben needs to tell me something. We'll work it out."

"Okay, if you need me, little lady, you just call."

"I will, Grace, thanks. Could you shut the door?"

Grace walked out and shut the door. She could feel the tension in the air. She knew something was wrong. All she knew to do was pray. "Lord, I don't know what's going on, but you do. I ask you to heal the brokenness and bring peace. Thank you, Lord."

"Mandy, what do you want me to say?"

"I want you to tell me the truth."

"You don't want the truth. You have what you want. Go for it."

"How do you know I have what I want?"

He looked up at her. "You love Wes, don't you? After all, you said you would marry him."

"Yes, I love Wes, but I thought that was what everybody else wanted for me. Nobody has asked me what I want. I want a simple life. I don't want to rub elbows with the elite. I want my little pottery shop and living by Grace and Duke and—"

"And what?"

"And—"

"What, Mandy?"

"I don't know. I'm so confused. Wes is always gone. If we get married, I'll still be alone. I get so lonely. I have Duke, but sometimes I want human companionship."

"I try to take up the slack."

"You're the one who's always there for me."

"You're my friend. I'll always be there for you, Mandy. Don't you know that by now?"

"Men think they can shower you with gifts, then leave you and everything will be all right. Well, it's not all right."

"Mandy, you just miss Wes. He'll be back in a week."

"Don't patronize me, Ben, I'm not a little girl, I'm a woman," she cried.

"I know you're a woman," he whispered to himself.

"What did you say?"

"Nothing."

"I'm going to stay here all night if that's what it takes."

"Let me make one phone call, and you go downstairs with Mother. I'll meet you down there in a minute. I promise."

Mandy went down to sit with Grace. Ben called Judy. "We have a situation here. I need your help."

"What's going on, Ben?"

"It's Mandy. She's demanding me to tell her the truth."

"The truth about what? Oh no, Ben. What are you going to do?"

"Could you run over here? I'll wait for you. She says she's going to stay here all night until she gets the truth."

"I'll come right over." Judy, staying at Wes' house while hers was being renovated, arrived quickly. She walked into Grace's living room. The tension was so thick you could cut it with a knife. "Evening, everyone." Judy hugged Grace's neck.

"What's going on?"

"You tell me," Mandy snapped.

Grace reached over and patted Mandy's hand. "Let's not let our tempers flare."

"I'm sorry, Judy. I didn't mean to snap at you. I just need the truth, and Ben won't tell me."

"The truth about what, my friend?" Judy asked, looking at Ben.

"Do you have feelings for Wes or not?"

"Wow, that's a hard one. Of course I do, he's been like a brother to me all my life."

"That's not what I'm talking about. I mean man-woman feelings."

"Ben, you want to handle this?" Judy asked, getting up to pour herself a cup of coffee.

"I wish Wes were here," he said, looking at his mom.

"Well he's not, so—" Mandy protested.

"I like those shoes, Mandy, they're killer." Judy laughed. "Listen, Mandy, Wes has been gone for three weeks. I think you really miss him. He needs to get his butt home. I think you're lonely and you're reaching for things that just aren't there. Go home. Get a good night's sleep. Call me tomorrow, and we'll talk when you're not so upset. I can't talk to you like this."

"I won't be able to sleep. I'm sorry I'm upset. I'll calm down. Then we can talk."

"In the morning, Mandy. I'm really tired tonight. Have mercy on a working girl." Judy patted her on the shoulder. "Look at you, woman, you're a wreck. Go home get some rest. All of this will look brighter in the light of day."

"I'll let it rest tonight but—"

"First thing in the morning, I'll be over."

Mandy got up from her chair. She looked at all of them. She felt stupid. Had she made this entire thing up in her mind? She excused herself and walked back up the beach to her house. Duke was waiting at the door for her, wagging his tail. She gave him a quick pat and went to bed.

Grace looked at Ben and Judy. "I'm with Mandy. I think something is not right here. Are you two deceiving her?"

"Yes, we are, Mom, but it's for her own good."

"How can deception be good?"

"Do you really want to know?"

"Ben, I don't think we should—"

"You be still, Judy. Ben, you tell me what's going on here, son."

"Mom, I love Mandy. I always have. I probably always will."

"You messed that up yourself, son," Grace said, making another pot of coffee.

"Mom, do you want to hear the truth or not?

"Yes, I do."

"I'm not glad Mandy's getting married, neither is Judy. We think they are making a big mistake. Judy has loved Wes since she was thirteen. She's waited for him to notice her. We think that I should be with Mandy and Judy should be with Wes, but things have gotten so complicated, so out of hand. The closer it gets to the wedding, the worse it is on both of us."

"Judy, have you ever told Wes how you feel?"

"No, ma'am, I haven't."

"Ben, have you told Mandy how you feel?"

"No, I haven't."

"Then the problem is you two, not Wes and Mandy. They are honest about their feelings. You two have been deceptive. No good ever comes out of deception. The Good Lord says the truth will set you free. Both of you are in bondage to your lies. Tell the truth; you'll feel better. Mandy and Wes will know the truth and can make an honest decision based on the truth, not a lie."

"I wish it were that simple," Ben said, looking at Judy.

"It is that simple. You two are making it harder, and the truth will come out, mark my words. I don't think that little lady will rest until she has the truth. She knows something isn't right. She's a smart woman."

"Ben, maybe your mom is right. I have carried this around in my heart for fifteen years. I'm so tired of playing games. What could it hurt to tell the truth?"

"Wes and Mandy, that's who it will hurt." Ben got up and went up stairs.

Judy went home and called Wes. "Wes, this is Judy."

"How are things going, Judy? It's good to hear your voice."

"Things are not going so good. Wes, you need to come home now."

"What's wrong? Is Mandy okay?"

"No, she's not. You need to come home now."

"I just talked to her tonight, she sounded fine."

"She's not fine. You need to come home now."

"What is it? I'm supposed to fly out to Washington tomorrow and meet Mother and Father."

"Wes, all I can say is you need to come home *now*!"

"I'll call the airport and see if I can get a flight. I'll be home as soon as I can."

"Good, we'll be waiting." Judy hung up the phone. She looked around at the old Southern beach house. This is what she had dreamed of, but now that it was time to tell the truth, she was scared. She had lived a lie so long. Grace was right. Only the truth would set them all free.

Ben couldn't sleep; how could he ever tell Mandy the truth? After all, it was he who had made things the way they were. Mandy would have been his if only he had said goodbye that day. "God, I made a deal with you this past summer. You held up your end of the bargain, now I'm going to hold my end up. I don't know what to say or what to do, but if you could help just a little, I sure would appreciate it." He lay down and slept.

The next morning, pounding on the door awakened Mandy. She hurried to see who it was this early in the morning. To her surprise Wes was standing at her door. He looked haggard, as if he had not slept all night. When Mandy opened the door he grabbed her in his arms.

"What's wrong?" she said with a yawn.

"What's wrong? I got a call from Judy last night. She sounded so upset. She said something was wrong with you. Are you okay?"

"Let me wake up. Please come in and have a seat. I'll make coffee. I'm glad you're home. I've missed you. What did she say on the phone?"

"She said that something was wrong with you, and I needed to come home now. I traveled all night to get here, trying to sleep in airports and on the plane. What's going on? When I called you last night you seemed fine."

"Something is wrong, Wes. I saw it in Ben's eyes."

"Ben's been here?"

"Yes, he comes over every night to help me with heavy stuff I can't do by myself. Last night we were making wind chimes."

"You two were making wind chimes together?"

"Yes, what do you want me to do while you're gone? Sit here and cry in my coffee? Do you want to hear this or not?"

"You don't have to be so cold."

"I'm lonely, Wes. Before I was used to it. Now I'm supposed to have a mate, I expect you to be here for me. But you're always gone. You haven't been home a whole week since we've been engaged."

146

"I want you to have the best—"

"Do you know what the best is for me? It's not fancy gifts, it's not a big house or a new truck. It's family and friends and home…being together," she said, giving him his cup of coffee. "Here, drink this."

"Mandy, I don't drink coffee, never touch the stuff. A glass of water would be fine. I'm sorry, I didn't know. You never let on that you were so unhappy."

"Do I have to tell you? You can't see it? Do you even look at me when you're here? Am I real to you, or am I just someone to hang off your arm so you can show off?"

"I'm sorry—"

"You keep saying I'm sorry, but I'm sorry doesn't change things. I want a companion, a mate, someone who's going to be here for me."

"Is that Ben?"

"What?"

"Is that mate, companion, Ben?"

"Well, no. It's not Ben, it's you." She stopped and looked at him. Tears were streaming down his face. "Why are you crying?"

"The love of my life just told me she's not happy. I've traveled all night to be screamed at. I am a little confused, hurt. I don't even know what I am. Do you want me to give up my research? Is that what you want?"

She didn't know what to say. There was a knock at the door. Mandy walked over to find Ben and Judy standing there. "Please, come in."

When they came in, Wes was slumped on the couch. You could tell he was upset. Mandy stood looking at all of them. She felt like a villain; she hadn't meant to hurt anyone. She just wanted her life back. She felt like an animal trapped in a cage.

"Morning, everyone. Did we come at a bad time?" Ben asked, sitting in the chair next to the fireplace. Duke came over and smelled each of them. He was unsure; he knew his master was upset and he didn't like that.

"Could we all just sit down and talk about all of this rationally?" Judy suggested. "We could hear your argument outside, and I think if we just calm down, we can work all of this out peaceably."

"Do you and Ben have something to do with all of this?" Wes was even more confused. "What happened while I was gone?"

"I got dragged into this last night. It seems Mandy thinks I have feelings for you, feelings that go beyond brother-sister love. And she's right, I do. I always have. I've loved you, Wes, all my life. That was a fantasy. He chose you, Mandy, not me. It doesn't matter what I feel, what matters is what he feels. I've thought about this all night. I didn't get much sleep. I love you, Wes. I'm a woman, not a little girl anymore. My feelings are those of a woman. What I feel is real. I've learned to live with it." She took a deep breath, unsure whether she could continue. Ben patted her shoulder in support.

"I was the one who turned your parents against Kay. I was jealous. So I tried to get her away from you. When she died, I felt so guilty. I feel guilty now that all of this has to come out."

Wes was speechless; he looked over at Ben, waiting for some sort of reaction. Ben dropped his head. He couldn't say the words; he couldn't make himself look at Mandy and say those words. He looked up at Wes. "The best man has won. You take real good care of Mandy, you hear. Don't ever let me find out she has spent one night crying over you." He got up and left.

The three of them sat speechless. "I don't think I should leave again. When I left we were all friends. Now Ben is hurt. Judy is hurt. Mandy, you're hurt. And it's all because of me?" Wes finally said. "What do you want me to do, Judy? How can I make your pain go away? I love Mandy with all my heart. Judy, I'm sorry for your pain, but I can't deny my feelings for Mandy. She's the best thing that has happened to me in six years. I won't just throw that away." He looked deep into Mandy's eyes. "I love you. Do you understand that? To lose you would be life shattering to me."

Judy hugged both of them. "I understand, I really do. I'll leave the two of you alone now." She walked out the door.

The tears could not be held back. She walked up the road knowing Wes would never be hers. Mandy would hold his heart forever. She knew Wes; she knew that unless she could accept that his love was platonic, she would not even be a part of their lives. She loved Mandy too, and she was not willing to lose that friendship, not even over feelings that she had had ever since she could remember. She walked away from the tears; she walked away from the fantasy; she walked away from her own true love.

Mandy looked at Wes; she didn't quite know what to say. She knelt down at his feet and laid her head in his lap. He reached down and stroked her hair. She cried; he let her. He knew she felt he had deserted her. He had promised her a quieter life, and he hadn't given it to her. He had made her life complicated. He knew life had just changed for the both of them. The decision was his. He could continue as things were and lose her or commit to her and lose his work.

Chapter 9

The cold wind howled around the house. Winter had arrived with a vengeance. The cold cut though to the bone. The barren trees rocked with the wind. Leaves swirled in the yard, like small tornadoes. Mandy watched as Duke played with Wes on the floor. She was content, she was happy; this was the way things were supposed to be.

Wes had resigned as the lead researcher for the Cancer Society. He kept his practice and stayed at the Cove. He hadn't traveled anymore in the several weeks since that morning. He was afraid to leave Mandy alone. He knew loneliness was a death sentence for her. She needed him to be near. He had resolved she was more important than all those people out there who needed him to be diligent in his research. He thought about Kay; *Had she died of loneliness? Had she withered away in my absence? When she needed me most, I was not there for her. I will be here for Mandy.* For the first time in his life he realized how frail this woman was. She needed attention, not more things. Things passed away, but presence of body mind and spirit lasted a lifetime. He smiled when he looked up and caught her looking at him. How he loved her, his heart hurt.

She lay beside him on the floor stroking his face. "I want you."

He was shocked. "Now?"

"Yes, now."

He drew her near and loved her. With the sound of the fire crackling, the wind howling, they became one. He held her close, lying on the floor in front of the blazing fire. He didn't ever want this moment to end. She was his; finally, she was totally his. She had given herself to him completely, no holding back; they had become one.

She rested in his arms. She was complete; he had made her that way. She was sure now that they would always be together. They had crossed that line from maybe to certain. She looked into his beautiful brown eyes. She saw complete bliss; she smiled.

He cradled her head in his hand and held her close to his chest. She could hear his heart pounding. They fell asleep in complete harmony.

The morning was cold outside, the fire had died down, but the house was nice and warm. Mandy got up and realized Wes was gone; his morning started before daylight. She found a note he had left her on the table. "Miss you already. It was hard to leave you as I watched you sleep in my arms. Until tonight. All my love, Wes." She smiled as she remembered the way it felt to be completely his. They had reached intensity; they now knew each other in a way they had not known each other before. She was glad they had joined their souls together forever. She had a lot of work to do today. It would be a long day; she had class tonight with the college students from Spring Hill. She had to get the shop open and prepare the clay for her students. *One day I should give a class on clay preparation*, she thought. You could buy clay that was ready for molding, but she preferred to use Clay's special blend. Her pottery had its own unique color by using a unique blend of clay and sand. Each potter was different; they all had their own preferences on the type of clay used for their pieces.

She was proud of her shop. She had come a long way from that morning when she sat at the pottery wheel looking at the dusty shelves. She worked long hot hours in the shop making the best handmade pottery. She no longer used the molds for her specialty pieces. She had learned to create the art herself. She had learned the feel of the clay in her hands. She could tell if the clay was of the right consistency, texture, and color. She could tell by her hands becoming one with the clay. She kneaded the clumps of clay into large balls, placing them on the worktable under damp clothes to settle for the class.

She noticed the store had several customers. She had learned it was best to allow the customer to shop around and inspect each piece; if they had a question or wanted to purchase a piece, they would call her. She had left a large opening between the store and the workshop so customers could watch the preparation and molding of the pottery. Some customers would watch for a long time.

It brought her joy to watch them as they concentrated on the process she used. They would watch as she painted each intricate detail of her seascapes. It was like being on display as you worked every day. It set her store apart from other pottery shops.

She continued to create the unusual Bahamian pieces the potter in the Bahamas had taught her. They were good sellers. Each piece was detailed and took a lot of dedication.

She saw Grace come into the shop; she beckoned her to the workroom where she was molding a new fountain.

"Good morning, little lady. My, you sure are glowing this morning."

"Good morning to you, old woman. How are you this frosty November morning?"

"Cold. It's just downright cold out there. You have it nice and warm in here."

"The kiln is responsible for all the warmth. I started firing in the daytime to heat the shop. Smart, huh?"

"I would say so. Looks like you're busy this morning, every morning lately."

"Yeah, the pottery business is picking up. People are fascinated with it. It's a good thing for me. You taught me that. What's going on with you this morning?"

"Well, I really need to talk to you if you have time."

"Sure, go right ahead. I can talk and work at the same time."

"I want to talk to you about Wes. I've noticed that since the first of October that he doesn't work with the Cancer Society anymore. Is something wrong?" Grace asked with a concerned look on her face.

"He quit so that he could stay at home. Let someone else be the hero."

"My dear, cancer research was a big part of Wes' life before he met you. It's needed. He's blessed with a gift for helping other people. How can you ask him to give that up?"

"He made that choice, not me."

"Did you have anything to do with it?"

"Grace, you're supposed to be my friend." Mandy smiled. "Besides there are enough researchers in the world. The world doesn't need Wes, I do. He's staying home with his family."

"And his family is you?"

"Grace, what are you trying to say?"

"Mandy, I'm not trying to say anything. I'm saying it. You should encourage him to do his research. If you don't, one day he'll resent you for taking that away from him. He's one of the top researchers in the country, dear. That's who he is. You're trying to make him something he's not. Now you expect him to accept you the way you are. How can you not accept him the way he is? It just doesn't make good sense."

"Grace, I want Wes to be all he can be."

"Then encourage him to return to his research. Be woman enough to let him be who he is without you being threatened by it."

"I'm not threatened by his work."

"Good. Then encourage him to resume his work. Wes is not Clay. He can't just stay here and be your man. He's a world-renowned doctor, for Pete's sake. The people of this world need his skills. You're depriving people who have cancer of a fighting chance."

"It's not that important. He's a good doctor. The people here love him."

"Let him go, Mandy. Let him go. I tell you if you don't let him go, you'll regret it one day. No matter how much he loves you right now, one day he'll resent the fact you took his life's work from him. Let him go."

Mandy sat and stared at Grace. She had never seen Grace so passionate about anything. She was serious; this was not her average morning conversation. She had thought long and hard before she had come over to plead Wes' case. "Did Wes put you up to this?"

"Wes is too kind of a man to let anyone do his talking for him. But he doesn't want to hurt you, so he's doing what he thinks you want him to do. I beg you, little lady. Don't wait too late."

"Grace, you really think he'll resent me one day?"

"Honey, I don't think it, I know it. Your happy marriage will turn stale, and he will become bitter toward you. His first wife's death sparked in him a fire to find a cure for cancer. Now you want to snuff out that fire. What if it were you that had cancer? Would you want someone like Wes working on your team?"

"Of course I would."

"Then let him go. Release him to his work. He'll love you eternally if you do." Grace patted her on the shoulder. "I hate to lecture and run, but I have an appointment with Wes. I've been feeling poorly these past few days. So you think about what we talked about, you hear? Listen to an old woman who's been around the block a time or two. I hate to rush, but I got to go." Grace leaned over and hugged Mandy.

Mandy noticed Grace didn't have the same strength behind her hug as usual. She watched her as she made her way to the door. She was moving a little slow today. Mandy went back to her work.

Grace climbed into Ben's truck. "We can go now, son," Grace said, shutting the truck door.

"Did you tell her, Mom?"

"I told her enough."

"Did you tell her you have cancer?"

"No need to worry her just yet. Let's see what she does with our little talk." Grace lay back in the seat. She could tell her energy was draining from her. She prayed a silent prayer for Mandy.

Wes welcomed Grace and Ben with a hug. He was glad to see them. His concern for Grace and her condition had led him to do some tests in his lab. He had come to the conclusion that with proper treatment, Grace would have a fighting chance. He wanted her to start on some new drugs the Cancer Society had been testing. Grace was a strong vivacious woman and should be able to withstand the rigorous treatment. He was hopeful.

"Ben, you take care of this one. She's special. If you need anything please don't hesitate to ask, anytime day or night."

"Wes, I don't know what we'd do without you. You have been so helpful. I sleep a lot better knowing you're on my mom's side."

Wes smiled and gave Grace her medicine. "This is going to make you feel bad at first. Just go home and go to bed. Let Ben take care of the house. He knows how to cook. You just let your body rest so that it can fix itself. Have you told Mandy yet?"

"No, and I don't want you to either. She's got big decisions to make. Let her make her decisions, then I'll tell her," Grace said, patting his shoulder.

"She's hopeless." Ben took his mom back out to the truck.

Wes watched his two friends. He knew the struggle they had in front of them. He went into his office and closed the door. "Dear Lord, you have given me so much in my life, but I would trade it all right now for the knowledge of how to heal Grace. She's one of your dear ones, Lord, and you've placed her in my hands. Help me to be your hands and your heart." Wes went in to see his next patient.

Mandy worked hard all day, but she couldn't get the words Grace said out of her head. *What if it were you who had cancer?* She would want Wes on her side. She knew she had to encourage him to return to his research. But she wanted him all to herself. "God, I don't mean to be selfish, but I don't want Wes traveling all over the world. I want him here with me. Can you do both, let him do his work and stay with me? Help me make the right decision."

Her community workshop class had gathered in the pottery shop. She went in and taught them how to make abstract water fountains. When class was over she cleaned her shop and went in to stoke the fire.

Duke was lying in front of the fireplace; she had to make him move to put more wood on the fire. She thought about the night before, how she and Wes had consummated their relationship. She loved him so much; how could she live with herself if she placed shackles on him? She knew Grace was right. But it didn't make it any easier to release Wes. She wept in the same place they had loved each other the night before.

She heard Wes drive up; she brushed the tears back. She knew she had to let him go to be what he was born to be, a healer.

Wes walked in and greeted Duke at the door. Mandy pulled herself up off the floor; she walked over and gave him a big hug. "You look like you needed a hug."

"I do. It's been a hard day. Sharon has fixed a really nice dinner. Let's go to my house tonight. Duke can fend for himself. I have a patient who is seriously ill, and I need to review some data I need to help her. Besides, you've never been in my house. Don't you think it's time?" He gave her a big kiss.

"That would be wonderful. I need to talk to you about something anyway. Let's go." She closed the door behind them.

They pulled up to the old Southern beach mansion. Mandy was awed by its size. Ben had done the landscaping and everything was so beautiful. The house had been built in the early 1920s by an oil tycoon, a beach getaway for his family. There was the main house, a guesthouse, and servants' quarters. The historical society had wanted to purchase the house from Mr. Harris, but he loved the old house and kept it for his family. The house had been restored to its original splendor in the mid 1980s by the Harrises. The Harris brothers had purchased a lot of land in the Cove in the eighties. They loved the quaint sleepy environment the Cove portrayed at that time. Then the tourists found it, and it started to grow and before you knew it, it was a tourist attraction. A lot of wealthy people had moved in and built large houses on the shore. Now the only public beach was at the end of the island.

They were met at the door by a gentleman, whom Wes introduced as George. George took their coats and brought them refreshments in the living room. "Let me show you the rest of the house," Wes said, leading Mandy.

The foyer led to a huge spiral staircase; off to the right was the den, to the left was his study; as they made their way through to the back of the house there was a large living room that covered the back of the house. The entire wall was glass; there was a beautiful view of the bay with the lighthouse in the background. Lovely gardens surrounded the back of the house. Walkways wove around through beautiful tropical foliage; a fountain sat in the middle of the luscious gardens. Upstairs at the end of the staircase was huge double doors; inside was the master suite. A large king-size four-poster bed was draped with shear beige curtains to the floor. A large deck was just outside the glass wall that faced the bay. Tropical plants and lounging furniture made a place of solitude and relaxation while enjoying the view of the bay. The master bathroom had his and hers dressing rooms. The Jacuzzi tub had skylights straight overhead. The other bedrooms were just as plush, providing comfort for visiting guests.

She was impressed. Wes led her downstairs to the kitchen. Sharon greeted them; the kitchen had a huge island bar in the middle with chefs' pots hanging from the ceiling. An innovative twenty-first century kitchen had replaced the old kitchen originally built in the house.

Wes took Mandy back into the living room. She walked around

the big plush room while Wes went into his study. Mandy knew now was the time for their talk. If she didn't do it now, she knew she never would. Wes brought back a large envelope and sat it on the table.

"Well, what do you think of our new house? I've had renovations made to update the house for comfort. Mother helped me."

"I can tell. Wes, I need to talk to you about something," Mandy started.

"Wait, I have good news. The Cancer Society has set up a lab for me here to do my research. They'll fund the lab. They were so impressed with the work Judy and I have been doing on sea plants and vaccines, they'll fund us to continue our work here. I won't have to travel. Won't that be great?"

"You and Judy have been working together?"

"Well, yes." He was stunned by her tone. "Yes, Judy has made great progress in sea plants and cancer-fighting agents."

"That's great."

"Is something wrong?"

"I think you picked the wrong woman. I know nothing about cancer. Judy has decided to make it her life's work, and so have you. You two could sit around at dinner and talk about your great accomplishments. Actually, I wanted to talk to you about your research anyway. I want you to go back to your research. That's what you were made for. I see you and Judy have been doing that all along. Wonderful. If you don't mind, I'm not really hungry. Please don't bother to take me home. I can walk." Mandy made her way out the door.

Judy walked in. "Was that Mandy I heard?"

"Yes, it was."

"Where did she go?"

"Home."

"Why?"

"She found out you and I had been working together on the cancer research. You living here and all, I guess it looked really bad."

"You haven't told her you and I were working together? Oh, Wes, that's a big no no. You shouldn't keep things from her. That drives a woman crazy. Don't make the same big mistake Ben made. Both of you will be left out in the cold." She chuckled.

Wes shot a non-approving look at her. She laughed. "You think I'm going to be upset? Let her go. See if she comes around." She started for the kitchen, and then stopped. "No, you need to go after her. I'll look at the data for Grace. If it hadn't of been for her, I would have never pursued my career. I owe her that."

Wes ran down the beach to Mandy's house; it was dark. *Where is she?* he thought, then he heard sobs coming from the darkness. He walked closer to see her standing in the water crying. The temperature was thirty-one degrees; the water was cold. She would catch her death of pneumonia. He grabbed her and pulled her out of the water.

"I wish I had died instead of Clay. He knew how to face life head-on. I seem to mess everything up. Please, go home and leave me alone."

"I won't. You'll catch your death out here. Come on, let's get you dried off and warm. Come on, Mandy, I'm too tired to carry you."

She looked at him. He did look tired. He looked lost. What had she done to this wonderful man? "Wes, I'm no good for you. We live in two different worlds. I can't pretend to be something I'm not, and you can't either. Love isn't enough to carry us through this. There has to be something we have in common. But for the life of me, I can't find it."

He looked at her in utter disbelief. "How can you say these things after last night? How can you say these things to me?" he shouted. "What do you want? Lady, you're crazy if you think I'm going to say okay and walk off. It's not going to happen. I have invested the most important part of my life in you. That's my heart, do you hear me? Stop all of this nonsense. I'm too tired for this. Look around you, my love. There's a whole big world going on around you. You shut yourself away. I'm not Clay. *I'm not Clay.*" He sat on the wet sand and wept.

She reached down to comfort him; he pushed her away. "Just go, I can't talk to you right now. I'll say things I don't mean. I don't want to hurt you. And I will if you stay. Please go."

Mandy ran into her house and closed the door behind her. What had she done? Why was she so insecure? She looked at Duke; he walked away and lay by the fireplace. He lifted his head when he heard Wes. He ran to the back door and started scratching and barking at the door. She opened the door and let him out. He ran to Wes and tried to comfort him. She watched in amazement. He licked him and rubbed on him, and then he sat beside him while he cried.

She walked back down to the beach where Wes was sitting. He

looked up at her. "Well, at least Duke loves me the way I am." He chuckled, rubbing Duke's head.

Duke licked him again. She wanted to reassure him. She didn't know how. She walked toward his house; he watched her. He was confused, what was she doing? She turned and looked at him. "Are you coming?"

He got up and joined her.

"I can't say that everything will be all right or that we'll live happily ever after, but I'm willing to try. How about you? Are you willing to gamble on a crazy woman?"

"I'm willing to die trying." He put his arm around her. All three of them headed up the beach to Wes' house.

"You need to put on dry clothes." He drew her closer.

"So do you. Do you have something I could wear?"

They went up the back stairway to the master suite. Wes dug through some jogging clothes and gave them to her. He grabbed a suit for himself. "You can use the Jacuzzi tub. I'll take a hot shower."

She smiled and took the clothes and went into the bathroom. She ran the tub full of hot water and climbed in. The hot water was so welcoming; her body was freezing. She knew she was going to have to learn to sacrifice her feelings. Clay had indeed spoiled her. He made her feel like she was the only thing on earth for him. They had worked together in the pottery shop and were always together. This relationship was so different. She had to share him with so many other people. She would learn to fit into his world. Just as she and Clay had made a world for themselves, so would she and Wes.

He was sitting on the bed waiting for her when she got out of the tub. He smiled to see her in his clothes. "Come, sit right here for just a minute, then we'll go down for dinner. I've told you this before, and I want to tell you again. I love you with all of my heart. I can't see my life without you. Please don't think I would jeopardize that for anything. Thank you for understanding about my research. I'm sorry I was dishonest about my work with Judy. But I thought you would react the way you did. You have to trust me, just as I trust you. Trust is the basis for a lifelong relationship. We won't make it without it. I'm sorry I broke your trust. I won't do it again." He kissed her on the forehead; they went down to dinner.

"What do we have here?" Judy said, getting up to give Mandy a hug. "Your man is safe with me, my friend. He locks his door at night so I won't sneak in. He's yours. Accept it. As you would tell me, 'Get over it, woman.'"

Mandy smiled. "Thanks, I think. Have you been trying to sneak into his bedroom?"

"No, just said that in case you thought I was." They both laughed.

Wes smiled at the two of them going on about him. He was glad he had a say in the matter. He seated Mandy close to him. Judy sat across the table. They laughed and talked through dinner; Wes felt much better. He hoped he would be able to help Mandy with her insecurities. He wanted to know why she had them. What had caused her to be so afraid of losing love? Sure, she had lost her husband, but he felt the real reason was much deeper.

After dinner Judy went into the study; Mandy and Wes walked outside on the porch. "I have a surprise for you. I was going to wait but after tonight. I don't want to wait anymore. The *Katie I* couldn't be repaired. They sunk her off the Bahamas to make a new reef. Come on, I want to show you something."

They climbed into the Hummer and headed for the marina. Wes made her close her eyes as he led her over to the dry dock storage. Once inside he told her she could open her eyes. There sat a blue fifty-foot houseboat. The name of it was *The Eyes of Mandy*. The houseboat was the color of her eyes.

"That's why I was going to Washington. My dad knew the owner and wanted to get you something special, because you're a special woman. 'A poor man's yacht,' he said. He wanted to show it to me before she was shipped I didn't get to see her until she docked here."

Mandy was speechless. She walked over to the old houseboat and rubbed her hand down its side. It looked so long sitting there in storage. "She's beautiful. I don't know what to say."

"Let's go inside, I think you'll like it." They walked up the ladder to the deck. It was a pale blue. The inside was luxurious. "My father and mother love you so much. They wanted us to have this as a wedding gift from them, if it's all right with you. I know you really didn't like the yacht."

There was a living room area and a kitchen. He led her down into the bow where there was a bedroom. It was beautiful, with all the luxuries of home. It had a bathtub; there was a sign over it that read "Mandy's Relief." She laughed. She fell back on the bed and laughed. Wes fell beside her. "This is ours, my love, all ours." They hugged each other and kissed.

"This is more our style. Tell me about her." Mandy surveyed the teak wood on the walls.

"She's a 1957 Craftsman houseboat. She was restored several years ago by the owner. As you can see, she's straight-through living. We can cruise to the barrier islands around here and anchor out. No crew, just you and me. I'll be the captain, and you're the first mate."

"Oh, Wes, she's beautiful."

"How do you feel about accepting this gift from my parents?"

"It's kind of an expensive gift, don't you think?"

"We can pay him back for her if it makes you feel better. The only reason I accepted the *Katie I* was for Kay. She was dying and wanted to sail the ocean. Father wanted her to be comfortable, so he got her the yacht. As I told you before, it stayed in dry storage until the week-end we met. But I've always wanted a houseboat, and this is a 1957 Craftsman." Wes was so excited as he rubbed the teak wood dresser. "Doesn't she look like something out of an old movie?"

"She's beautiful."

Wes' cell phone rang. Wes answered it. It was Sharon. "Dr. Young, I have this large creature here staring at me. What should I do?"

Wes laughed. "Feed him, and he'll be yours forever."

"But I don't want him to be mine forever."

"His name is Duke, and you'd better get used to those big brown eyes. You'll be seeing them from now on."

"Yes, sir. He won't bite, will he, sir?"

"Not to worry, Sharon, the only thing he bites is his food. If you'll feed him, he'll follow you around like a puppy."

"Yes, sir."

Mandy laughed. "Don't tell me, we left Duke at your house."

"It's our house. I want you to move in with me today so we can start our lives together now."

"What about my house?"

"Judy could move into your house and that would solve the whole thing."

"My pottery shop—"

"Will be right there. You can go work there every day. What do you say?"

"Can I have time to think about it?"

"No. Your biggest problem is that you think too much."

"What if we just move on to the houseboat ?" They both laughed.

Mandy and Wes drove to Wes' house to pick up Duke. Mandy was off for the day and had a lot of things to do. Wes was going to go over the data Judy had collected. They would meet for dinner.

It was a beautiful day. The sun was out and the breeze blew off the bay. Mandy walked around her little house. She had lived here for over eleven years. It was the only home she and Clay had ever shared together. Life was changing; she knew she had to change with it, but letting go was harder than she thought.

She walked over to Grace's. She wanted to tell Grace about her decision and to see how she was doing.

"Grace," Mandy yelled through the door. She opened it and went inside. She didn't hear Grace humming that familiar old gospel tune. She looked through the living room, the kitchen and even outside, she couldn't find her. She started up the stairs when she heard a faint moan. She hurried up the stairs and found Grace on the bathroom floor. She had been sick and couldn't get up. "Grace, let me help you." She helped her back into bed. "Does Ben know you're sick?"

"Yes, he's gone to find Wes." She struggled to get the words out.

"I just left Wes, he's at home. I'll call him."

"No, no, little lady, Ben has gone to his house. He'll bring him back."

"Grace, what's wrong, how can you be this sick so quickly?

"It's the medicine. I'll be all right in a minute."

"I don't think so. Grace, what's going on? How long have you been this sick?"

"Not long, let's just wait for Wes. He'll be here soon."

She heard the door open and footsteps running up the stairs. It was Ben and Wes. "Excuse me, love, could you move aside a moment and let me look at her. Grace, tell me what you're feeling."

"I'm so sick to my stomach, Wes. I can't keep anything down, and I'm so weak I can't stand up," she uttered.

"Okay, if you two would leave me alone with Grace for a minute we're going to make her feel better," Wes instructed.

Ben and Mandy stepped outside the door. Ben ushered Mandy down the stairs.

"Ben, what's going on? What's wrong with Grace?"

"She's sick, Mandy. Can't you tell?"

"Please, I beg you. Please tell me what's wrong."

"If I could, I would, but I can't."

"Why can't you?"

"Because Mom doesn't want you to know."

"What? Are you crazy? She's my best friend, why wouldn't she want me to know?"

"Because you made Wes stop his cancer research."

"I came over here to tell her that we talked and he's continuing his research. Ben, for the love of God, please tell me what's happening?"

"Mom has cancer, a very rare kind. Judy and Wes have been working night and day to find a drug that would help her."

Mandy's blood ran cold. "She came by the shop yesterday. She told me that I was hurting so many people by not letting Wes do his research. I didn't know she was talking about herself. Oh God, please help her. Please don't let her die. I could never forgive myself."

"Calm down, Mandy, the dose of medicine she took made her sick. Wes is adjusting it now. The vaccine Judy and Wes came up with attacks the cancer cells. I guess they're mad—the cancer cells, I mean."

"How long has she known?"

"Since October."

"That's when I asked Wes to stop his research. Then yesterday, I was so mad when I found out he and Judy had been working together behind my back. I'm so naïve, so selfish."

"He only started back on his research because of Mom. That was the reason. I went to Judy, Judy went to Wes."

"And everyone left me out."

"No one wanted you to feel bad. You were going through your own head trip."

Wes came into the kitchen. "She'll rest now, Ben. I adjusted the drip. If there are any more complications call me on my cell phone.

Here's the number. The quicker I can get here and adjust the dose, the better she'll feel."

Wes didn't look at Mandy; he kept his eyes on Ben. "It's okay, my friend, I told her. She dragged it out of me."

Wes looked over at Mandy. "I couldn't tell you, Grace swore me to secrecy. Doctor-patient privilege, you know."

"It's all right. I understand I've been a jerk. If I hadn't been, you all could have trusted me. I'm so sorry. Can you ever forgive me?"

"We all forgive you, Mandy. We understand, really we do. We dropped some heavy stuff on you in October," Ben said, taking her hands.

Wes walked over to the sink and got a glass of water. He felt so bad keeping news about her best friend a secret. It was times like this that he didn't like being a doctor. Because of all the confusion after their engagement, he had tried to be totally honest with her. This was one thing he couldn't help. He turned and took Mandy's arm. "We have a lot of work to do. Mandy's moving in today. Judy's moving into Mandy's house. Come, my love. Let's let these good people get some rest. Remember, Ben. Call me as soon as the symptoms start, don't wait."

"I'll do it, Doc. Thanks for coming so fast."

"No problem, my friend." Wes hugged Ben.

They rode in silence; she couldn't believe everyone was tiptoeing around her like she was a china doll. How selfish could she be? She was only concerned with her feelings. She hadn't cared what anyone else felt. She didn't recall that being her nature. Had she changed so much? She used to be sensitive to the feelings of others. Had she wanted Wes so bad she would shut her friends out? "Oh God, help me to be sensitive to others. Take this selfish attitude away from me," she prayed.

Wes had been talking to her and she hadn't heard a word he had said. He was waiting for a response.

"I'm sorry, I was so deep in thought I didn't hear you."

"I was asking you if it was all right to move today, or did you want to wait?"

"Moving today is fine, but can I move into a guest room for a little while? I have already gone beyond my morals. I just had to have you all to myself. I just need to be me, Wes. I can't be someone else. I tried, but it doesn't work for me."

"That's fine, my love. Let's make a pact—no more intimacy until the wedding. Having you in our home, though, will make all the difference in the world to me."

"See, that's why I love you so much. You spoil me."

"You ain't seen nothing yet, honey." He smiled and squeezed her leg.

They packed some of her clothes and personal items and left the rest until later.

Wes insisted she stay in the master suite. He would take a guest room until the wedding. He wanted her to get used to living in the house. To make sure it was all right; if not she could change whatever she liked. It was her home now.

The master suite was almost as big as her whole house. She placed her clothes in the closet. You could hardly tell she had anything in it. She had never been one to buy a lot of clothes. She wore her same old frocks and shorts year after year until she needed to replace them. She couldn't image having enough clothes to fill up that closet.

Judy didn't mind the move. She would be closer to Ben. She would be lady of the house. She loved Mandy's little beach cottage. It had such character; Mandy had decorated it in seascapes. Judy loved it. She flung her things on the floor and fell into the chair by the fireplace. "Wow, what a fireplace, throw a rug on the floor and—"

A knock at the door interrupted her thoughts. It was Ben. "Hi, neighbor."

"Hi yourself, big boy. How's Mom feeling?"

"She's resting well now, thanks to Wes. The man is gifted."

"He sure is. It's wild watching him work," Judy replied. "Come into my little house, cool, huh?"

"It sure is. It won't be as far to come see you now."

"I know."

"Look at this fireplace." Ben raised his brows at her.

"Now, now, calm down. We don't want to get caught."

"Who's going to catch us?" Ben asked, discouraged.

"What if they come back for something?"

"Wes is in hog heaven now. They're not coming back over here tonight, I can tell you that. Mandy's got to get used to being the lady of the manor."

"You're bad, Ben Howard."

"That's why you love me so much." He smiled. "Let's build a fire. I'll show you how so when I come over, you can already have it built."

Chapter 10

Mandy looked around the room; it wasn't her. She liked the bed and the curtains, but everything else was so stuffy. Wes had said she could change whatever she liked. She would start in the bedroom. She didn't want to hurt Wes' mother's feeling, but things were going to have to change. He said it was her home now. She wanted it to be a home, not just a house.

Wes came up to see if she had everything she needed. She was lying across the bed when he came in. She couldn't get Grace off her mind. How sick she had been. She was worried about her. Cancer was big, even if she did have Wes for her doctor. "Lord, when my parents died I was so lost. Then there was Clay. He was ever so gentle with me. He understood the wounds in my heart. He spent our life together helping me to overcome them. Now here I am again, Lord. The same old insecurities coming up, hurting people I love. God, Grace is like a second chance at having a mother. Now she's sick. What will I do if she dies? Help me, Lord. Give me strength not to mess up this relationship," Mandy prayed, tears streaming down her cheeks.

Wes stood at the door; his heart went out to this wonderful woman who seemed so lost inside of herself. How he loved her. If he could get her to open up to him the way she had done with Clay, he too could help her overcome the pain she tried to hide. "She's not going to die."

"How do you know that? She's so sick."

"Because we caught it in the first stage. She's healthy in every other aspect of her body, and she's a fighter. What you saw was the effects of the drugs killing the cells. It makes her sick, but she's going to be fine when this is all over. Mandy, there is a deep hurt inside of you. Every once in a while it comes out in the form of insecurity. You have the need to be secure in relationships. You have the need to know things that are impossible to guarantee. Could you talk to me about it?"

"You won't love me anymore if I tell you."

"There is nothing you could say that would keep me from loving you. But I understood what makes you not love yourself."

She looked up at him. "What makes you think I don't love myself?"

"Because you drain the life out of the people who love you, and it's still not enough. Could you share that with me the way you did Clay?"

"Clay understood me."

"I know, and I want to understand you too."

Tears filled her eyes. "This is hard … my dad was an alcoholic. I was his only child. My mother worked all the time to provide for the family, as it were. My dad hung out at the marina and drank with all of his buddies. When I would get home from school, I would be alone until he came home from his daily routine. I don't know if I can do this." She began to cry.

"It's okay, take your time." He wrapped his arms around her.

"Everyone thought I was the prettiest girl in school. I didn't want to be pretty, because my dad thought I was the prettiest thing he had ever seen. He would come into the house and look for me."

"Why did he have to look for you if you were in the house?"

"Because I would hide from him. He always wanted to put his hands on my body. One day he found me hiding under the bed. He reached under the bed and pulled me out. He laughed, he said he was going to teach me how to be a woman, because every man wants a woman to be prepared for her lover. He acted like it was some sort of game. He, he … he did that thing to me every day until he was killed. I was glad he was dead. I know that's bad, but I laughed when they told me he had died. I knew then that I was free, but my mother died with him. I was out with Clay that night. I was sixteen years old. My dad had come home in a drunken stupor. He was looking for me. I wasn't there, so he beat my mom and set the house on fire. Then he passed out. They both died in the fire."

Wes, utterly shocked by her confession, held her close while she cried. After a while, she sniffed back the tears and continued. "I could never tell my mom what had happened to me. I could tell Clay. He didn't think I was dirty. He loved me. He thought I was strong for putting up with it all those years. He loved me the way I was. He always told me how beautiful I was, but when I looked in the mirror that's not what I saw. I saw an ugly girl with long curly hair and bags under her eyes. Then Clay died, and so did I."

"No, you didn't, Mandy. You're very much alive, and God has great plans for you. You are so compassionate, until your wellbeing is threatened, and then you become very dominant and protective of yourself. You won't let people love you, and you feel insecure in that love."

"That's because everything I love dies. Why is God doing this to me?"

"He's not, Mandy. Life does that to us. God is there to love us through our trials. You have become strong and self-sufficient. That's a lot. Look at how you built the pottery business. Look at how you stole my heart, Ben's heart, Judy's heart, and Grace's heart. We're not all blind. We see the love inside of you, but it's almost like you have a glass shield around you."

"I thought if I didn't make love to you, you would leave me. Then I felt bad about it. Because I knew my daddy was wrong. He shouldn't have done those things to me. He ruined my life," she cried.

"No, he didn't. You're right, he shouldn't have done those things to you. But here we are, making a life together. You have so much love to give. Don't ever hold back. This world needs love like you have, release it and let it go. Love isn't sex. Don't confuse the two. Just because your daddy told you it was doesn't make it so."

"It's not?"

"No, my love, it's not. I want you to feel secure. Don't worry about Judy, don't worry about my love, and don't worry about Grace. God has her in his hands. He's not going to take her from you just yet. She has too much fight in her still. So do you." He kissed her gently on the forehead. She leaned over on his chest.

It made Wes angry that a man could do that to his own child. The scars were deep. It made him love her all the more. For the first time, he understood how she would be so possessive about those things that were hers. So much had been stolen from her when she was a child. He held her tight. "I'll be here for you always."

"That's what Clay told me, and he died. He left me here to live by myself. It was so hard until Grace came. Oh, how I love Grace. She made me live again. I was dead inside when she moved in. She wouldn't let me die in that house. I love you too. I'm sorry I've caused you so much grief. I don't mean to, I really don't. I get so mad at myself when those feelings come up. Will they ever go away, Wes?"

"Yes, my love, one day they will be gone. You and I are going to run them away every time they try to come haunt you. You just tell me, and we'll do this together. Clay died trying to save you. He loved you, Mandy. He gave his life for yours. He saw you had so much to offer. He didn't leave you because he wanted too. I'll bet he's up there in heaven right now, smiling at you, saying, 'Go girl, you can do this, do it for both of us.'"

"I'm so glad we had this talk. I'm so glad God sent you to me that day on the road. I'm glad we're here together, and I'm glad you're going to help Grace."

He held her for the longest time; they lay together on the bed until she was sound asleep. He slipped his arm out from underneath her head and went to his room.

"Oh God, help me to help this woman of mine. I love her Lord, and I don't want to lose her." He cried for her and all the children like her.

• • • • •

When Mandy woke up, it was dark outside. She looked around the room for Wes, but he was gone. She took a long hot bath and went downstairs to find him. George said he had gone over to check on Grace and would be home soon. He also informed her that Wes had left some books for her in the study on his desk.

She opened the door to the study; it looked like Wes, everything arranged and in order. The room smelled of his sweet presence. She found the books lying on his desk. One was a beach-house decor book; the other one was a ministry book named *Tell Your Heart to Beat Again*. She opened the book, thumbing through the pages. A note fell out on the floor. "This book really helped me after Kay died, see if it helps you." She tucked it under her arm and started looking through the beach-house book. Sharon told her dinner would be ready in an hour. She took her books upstairs. She thumbed through the décor book; it had wonderful ideas in it.

Wes walked in. "Look, it's sleeping beauty."

"Hey there, yourself. Thanks for the books. Does this mean you know this house isn't my style and I want to change it?"

"Yes, ma'am, it does. You change whatever you like. You have an account. It's all set up at the bank. Just get what you want. You'll be Mrs. Wes Young soon, I hope, and I want you to be comfortable in our home. Grace is much better. She's eating now. She said to tell you she loved you."

"Wes?"

"Yes, my love?"

"You wouldn't tell anyone what we talked about, would you?"

"No, that's between you, me, and the Good Lord."

"Good. I don't want people to know. You know?"

"Yes, I do know. Now, let's go eat, I'm starving," he said taking her hand and pulling her off the bed. He grabbed her and kissed her. "That's in case I forget later."

She laughed and hugged him tight. Her fears had been resolved. He knew the dirty truth about her, yet he still loved her. She could trust him; he would be there for her. She was thankful they had had their talk earlier that day. She didn't have to hide the scars anymore. She could go to him, and he would love her, just as Clay had.

Sharon prepared a good dinner; Mandy and Wes sat side by side at the large dining room table. George would pop in and out to check on Wes to make sure he didn't need anything. It was all so strange to her. She wasn't used to people wanting to serve her. She was proud to be there with Wes. He was a good, kind soul. He treated his staff like they were family, and they treated him with the utmost respect.

After dinner, they sat in the living room watching the tide go out. "Wes, why did you always want to come to my house? Why didn't you ever bring me here?" Mandy asked, watching Duke lying beside the fireplace.

"Because your house is a home. This one was just a house until you moved in. I want you to make this house a home too. It's so big and stuffy. I have always liked your little beach cottage. It's so comfortable, so cozy. I noticed you looking at our bedroom and you had a frown on your face. So Judy found those books, and I asked her to let me use them for a while."

"I wonder what Judy is doing right now?"

"You probably don't want to know." Wes chuckled.

"I hope she found everything all right. Wes, why didn't you ever want to go out with her? She's really a beautiful woman."

"She's a little wild for me. I need someone who is a little more settled than she is. We grew up together. We were never lovers in any way. She was just like the little sister I never had who followed me around everywhere. My friends all wanted to go out with her, but I never did. To this day, I still look at her as my little sister. So you see, my love, you'll never have to worry about Judy and me."

· · · · ·

Judy and Ben were having the time of their lives. Alone for the first time since the trip to the Bahamas, they played their music loud and danced in front of the fire Ben had built. They ordered in dinner and were enjoying their privacy. Ben reminded Judy that Mandy kept everything in its place and they were making a mess of things. Judy laughed. "I'll get me a maid, honey. I don't clean house."

Ben was surprised by her response. He thought she would respect Mandy's things more.

"Look, Ben, Mandy has more stuff now that she knows what to do with. This old stuff won't mean a thing to her."

"I think you're wrong. Some of these things were Clay's. She really treasures them."

"Clay's dead, man. She's got Wes and all of his money now. What would she need with things like this?" She picked up a conch shell that had been polished and sealed.

"I think we should respect her things. That could be a special occasion piece, from one of her and Clay's adventures. Please put it down, before something happens to it," Ben asked.

Judy dropped the shell and broke the end off. "Hey, look at that, we'd better hide it."

"Hiding it's not going to do any good. She'll miss it. You watch and see if she doesn't ask you about it."

"The woman is obsessive or something, don't you think?"

"I think she's been through a lot, and what she has means a lot to her. Besides, what has she ever done to you for you to be so mean-spirited to her?"

"You're kidding, right? Because you know what she's done? She's over there with Wes right now, he's my man." Judy, drunk, was yelling. "That should be me over there in that house instead of her. Her and her sweet little innocent self."

"Wes chose her, she didn't choose him." Ben defended Mandy.

"You should be mad too. You love her. You're a coward and won't admit it, but buddy, you can see it in your eyes every time you look at her. She makes me sick."

"Judy, how can you say that?"

"I took her advice, it didn't help. She still has my man."

"Why am I here, Judy, for your pleasure? I don't think so. Her advice did help, and it helped me love you the way that I do." Ben got up to walk out.

Judy grabbed his arm, "Wait a minute, you said you love me?"

"I did, but I don't like you very much right now. You shouldn't drink, it makes you ugly."

"Mandy told me the same thing. I shouldn't drink. Do you really love me?"

"I said so, didn't I? Here I am trying to impress you and all you can do is talk about Wes, calling him your man. I'm leaving. You don't know what a man is. You're used to boys. You wouldn't know what to do with a man."

"Show me!"

He grabbed her and held her. He just wanted her to calm down enough to just be with her. "You're going to tell Mandy what you did to her shell."

"Who says?"

"I say. Do you hear me? If you want to be treated like a woman, you've got to act like one. It's time you started."

She smiled. "You do love me, don't you Ben? Teach me how to be a woman."

"I will, but it's not going to be tonight. You go to bed and sleep it off. I'll see you when you're sober." He gave her a quick kiss and helped her into bed. He looked around the room and saw the mess; he straightened up the room, locked the door, and left.

• • • • •

Wes came into the bedroom to let Mandy know he was leaving for the office. "Morning, sunshine. You know you don't have to stay in this room all the time. The whole house is here at your command. You're the lady of the manor now. Make yourself at home. It is your home, you know. Everyone on the staff is aware of who you are. They will be looking to you for their instructions."

"Wes, I've never had servants. I don't know how to give them their instructions. They know what they do better than me."

"You didn't know anything about making pottery a year ago, but look what you can do now. Got to go. If you need me just call. I love you." He kissed her forehead and was gone.

She sat in the huge bed wondering what she was supposed to do. She'd talk to Grace; Grace would know what to do. She hurried and got ready; when she turned around there was a lady standing there with a breakfast tray. "Good morning, ma'am. Here's your breakfast tray. My name is Rachel. Anything you need please let me know, and I will make sure it's taken care of."

Mandy stood looking at Rachel with her mouth open. "Good morning, Rachel, nice to meet you. Please call me Mandy. Thank you for the breakfast tray. What exactly do you do for me?"

"I turn down your bed, draw your bath, lay out your clothes, and bring you breakfast and any other meal you choose to take in your room. I take care of any other personal needs you might have. We will become very close, ma'am—"

"Mandy."

"Mandy, sorry. If you need anything just let me know."

"Everything we talk about, do you tell anyone?"

"Oh no, Ms. Mandy. Dr. Young hired me just for your needs."

"He did, did he? I'm supposed to be the lady of the manor. Do you know what that means?"

Rachel chucked with her hand over her mouth. "Yes, ma'am. What you say goes. All of the staff is at your beck and call."

"That's what Wes said, but I don't know what each person does."

"Should I call a staff meeting in the dining room?"

"Yes, if you don't mind. That way we can all introduce ourselves, and I can find out what each person does."

"Very good, ma'am. Will an hour be enough time for you to be ready?"

"An hour is fine."

"Now, what would you like to wear today?" Rachel looked in the closet and saw the little bit of clothes Mandy had. "Where are all of your clothes, Ms. Mandy?"

"That's all I have. Should there be more?"

"Why, Ms. Mandy, you don't have enough clothes for anything."

"Would you like to go shopping with me later?"

"Shopping would be nice. Dr. Young left the Volvo for you to drive. I'll have George get it ready for you. Will this dress be okay, Ms. Mandy?'

"That one will be fine. Thank you, Rachel."

"Yes, ma'am." Rachel left Mandy to dress and have breakfast.

Mandy went into the dining room to see the house staff waiting for her. Everyone stood up when she walked in the room.

"Please have a seat. My name is Mandy, and Dr. Young said I should let you all know what I want from each of you, but I don't know who you are and what you do, so I thought we should get acquainted." She smiled that beautiful smile she had. "So, if we could go around the table and tell who you are and what you do."

"My name is Sharon. I'm the house chef."

"My name is George. I take care of Dr. Young and I also take care of the cars."

"My name is Sally and I'm a housekeeper."

"My name is Rachel, and I take care of you."

"Thank you all very much. I'm not that good with names, so if you will bear with me until I learn each of yours, I'd appreciate it. This is a first for me, so any help you may give me would be appreciated. I'm sure Rachel will keep me straight. The house looks great, so all of you are doing a good job. I do like a very tidy house, so please keep that in mind. Thank you all for all you do. If you need me, please don't hesitate to come to me. I'm a very easy person to get along with, so I think we'll all do just fine. Thanks again for coming in and helping me. Have a good day."

Everyone got up and went about their daily duties. Mandy was glad that the meeting was over. The staff seemed to be attentive and kindhearted. She was glad of that too.

Rachel showed her where to pick up her car. The Volvo was sitting out front ready for her to use. It was clean inside and out; it was a far cry from what she was used to, the old beat-up '73 Ford truck. It was nice to have a car to drive around in. She and Rachel stopped by Grace's house first.

"I'll wait in the car, Ms. Mandy."

"Oh no, you won't, you come right in with me." She smiled. "Where I go, you go."

Grace was in the kitchen; she was feeling much better. Mandy introduced Rachel to Grace. They both laughed at the thought of Mandy having an attendant.

"Are you going to learn the pottery business too, young lady?" Grace asked Rachel.

"Oh no, ma'am, I'll be taking care of Ms. Mandy's personal affairs at the house. When she gets home, everything will be taken care of. I do think we need to buy her some clothes. Don't you think, Ms. Grace?"

"I sure do, it's about time she learned to dress proper." Grace laughed.

"Yes, ma'am, I think so too," Rachel replied, very serious.

Ben walked in as the ladies were laughing. "What's so funny? Good morning, Mandy."

"Mandy has an attendant. This is Rachel." Grace laughed.

"Nice to meet you Rachel. It's nice to see you laugh, Mom. Mandy, how was your first night in the big house?"

"Different. I'm used to my beach cottage. My bedroom now is almost as big as my whole house was."

"You'll get used to it. Mom, what are you going to do today?"

"I think I'll go into Spring Hill with Mandy and Rachel to buy Mandy some new clothes."

"Do you think you're up to it?"

"I do indeed. It'll be nice to get out of the house for a while. I've got to see what Mandy considers new clothes."

"Now, Grace, I've been picking out my clothes all my life. I think I do pretty well."

"If I may say something, Ms. Mandy, your clothes looks like the help's clothes when they're off. You're the lady now. You've got to dress like it. You might think about cutting that hair too."

"Oh no, I'm not cutting my hair for anyone. It took me all my life to grow this hair, and I'm not cutting it now. Not to cut you short or anything, but the hair stays," Mandy said, tucking her hair behind her back.

"Mandy, will you call Wes to see if it's okay for Mom to go with you guys?"

Mandy dialed Wes' cell number. He answered, "Dr. Young."

"Wes, this is Mandy."

"I know who this is."

"Oh, Rachel and I are going into Spring Hill to buy me appropriate clothes, according to Rachel." She laughed. "Would it be okay if Grace rode with us?"

"I'm glad you're going shopping. It will do you good. How do you like Rachel?"

"Rachel is great. What about Grace?"

"Put her on the phone."

"Here, Grace, he wants to talk to you."

"Wes, I'm going into town for a few hours with the love of your life."

"How are you feeling?"

"I feel better today than I have in along time."

"Okay, let me speak to Mandy. ... Mandy, just watch her. I think it would do her good to get out. You ladies be careful. I love you."

"I love you too," Mandy replied, hanging up.

"Dr. Young is happier now than I have ever seen him, Ms. Mandy." Rachel smiled.

"Have you known him long?"

"Yes, ma'am, I've known him for about ten years. I worked for Dr. Young before he moved, and he brought me down here with him."

"I feel honored. Ben, you did a wonderful job on the gardens and patio. You are so gifted."

"That's what I like, satisfied customers. Take good care of my mom today, she's the only one I've got." Ben reached down and kissed Grace on the cheek. "I love you, Mom. Mandy, call me when you get near the house, and I'll come home."

"There's no need for that. I'll take her home with me and you can pick her up when you're done."

"Thanks, Mandy. I really do need to work."

Mandy gathered up Grace's coat and purse and they set out for Spring Hill. "What do you think about my car, Grace?"

"It's rather nice. It fits you better than that old truck."

"Grace, I don't know what kind of clothes to buy, do you?"

"Little lady, this young woman here will help you do anything you need to do. She'll help you, and I'll watch. This should be good." Grace laughed.

Rachel said they should go to the mall. They rented a wheelchair from the information desk and let Grace ride instead of walk. She protested, but Mandy wouldn't have it any other way.

Rachel showed Mandy the type of clothes she may consider buying. Mandy was not impressed with her selection. Mandy picked out a couple of pieces and showed them to Grace and Rachel. Grace really liked them; Rachel said they would do. Mandy bought the clothes and they moved on to another store. She purchased several suits. They were all tired and decided to call it a day.

When they pulled up in the driveway at Mandy and Wes' house, Grace was awed. "So this is where you live now, little lady?"

"Yes. It's big, isn't it?"

"I'll say. You could get lost inside that house."

"I know. I almost did this morning."

Mandy started to unload her new clothes when Rachel ran around screaming, "Oh no, Ms. Mandy. George will get these, and I'll put them away for you."

Mandy looked at Grace. "That's fine, thank you, Rachel."

George came out to retrieve her packages. "Will you need your car anymore this afternoon, Ms. Mandy?"

"No, George, thank you."

"I'll put it in the garage after I take your packages in."

"That would be nice, thanks again." Mandy and Grace looked at each other and laughed. "I don't know if I'll get used to this or not."

Mandy helped Grace into the living room onto the sofa. She covered Grace with a blanket and turned the gas fireplace up. "How's that, Grace? Are you comfy? Isn't this place amazing?"

"It sure is, little lady. What have you gotten yourself into?"

"I don't know, old woman, but it's been an adventure. This morning, Wes told me to instruct the staff. I didn't even know who the staff was. So we all got together and introduced ourselves. They won't let me do anything. We're going to have to change the rules a little. I like to cook and clean, but they do it all. Of course, I don't know about cleaning this big house all the time."

"God has blessed you, Mandy. This is not a curse. It's a blessing. God has seen that you were able to touch these people for him, and look where you get to live while you're a doing it. Little lady, the Good Lord has indeed looked good on you."

"Do you think that's what it is? Because I feel like Cinderella, and Wes is my Prince Charming."

"You've wanted a family of your own for so long, and the Good Lord has given you one."

"Oh, Grace, you're my family, you and Ben and Wes. I feel I already have a family."

"Well, little lady, Wes' parents, they really like you. You can touch their hearts. Let them see the Glory of God shining through you. He does, you know. You have this kind of magnetism. It draws people to you. They don't look down on you, they look up to you."

"No, Grace, you're making that up. I'm just me, and sometimes it's hard to be me. I have a hard time loving a man. I'm scared all the time—except with Clay. He made me feel special."

"Well, look around you. Wes thinks you're special too."

"He's a good man. I'm just afraid I'm going to wake up and it's all going to be a dream. I mean, this is from pauper to rich woman."

"God measures wealth different from us. We look at money and things. God looks at love and integrity. You have both of those, little lady. I've been proud to know you. From the first day I met you, I knew you were a special one and that God wasn't going to let you dry up and die in that little old cottage."

"Grace, you're the best mom anyone could ever have. I've never had a mom like you, my mom never paid any attention to me, and she left me to my daddy's rule. I'm so glad God introduced us. I really think he did. He knew I needed a woman's guidance. You've been such a blessing," Mandy said, sitting on the floor in front of Grace, laying her head on Grace's chest.

Grace reached down and stoked her hair. "Well, little lady, the Lord sure works in mysterious ways. I always wanted a daughter, and now I have one."

"Really, Grace? Because I'd be proud to be your daughter."

Ben stood at the door of the living room, tears streaming down his cheeks. Wes walked up behind him; Ben stuck his hand out to stop Wes and pointed into the living room. The scene he was witnessing in their house moved Wes. *She's already making it a home*, he thought.

Wes and Ben went back into the kitchen where Sharon was making dinner. "Dr. Young, Ms. Mandy met the entire staff today. She's a wonderful lady, I really like her. She has a very kind heart. It's a pleasure to know her."

"Why, thank you, Sharon. I kind of like her myself. Ben, since you and your mom are here already, why not stay and have dinner? I know Mandy would love it. Call Judy at work and ask her over also. You can handle that, right, Sharon?"

"Not a problem, Dr. Young." Sharon smiled. She loved seeing her employer so happy. It had been many years since she had seen him glow like this.

"That sounds great. I'll call Judy now. Where's your phone?" Ben welcomed the company of everyone tonight; he was not looking forward to facing Judy alone, not just yet any way.

"Right this way, my friend." Wes showed Ben into the study.

Mandy met them in the hall. "Grace is asleep."

"Good evening, my love." Wes greeted Mandy with a kiss. "How was your day? Did Grace do all right on your day adventure?"

"Yes, she did fine. We had the best time. I don't know about this clothes business. Rachel thinks I should dress like your mom."

"Tell her I don't want you to be my mother. I want you to be you."

"She seems nice enough. But, is it necessary to have a personal attendant? Couldn't I just do things for myself?" Mandy whispered.

"If you ever get used to it, it's wonderful. Try it for a while, and if it's bothersome, we'll do something else," Wes said, throwing his hands up, laughing.

Ben snickered watching them together. If he couldn't have Mandy, there was no one else he would rather give her up to than Wes. Ben liked Wes a lot. They had grown close during the last months. It was nice having a good friend. He had lost all of his friends when his wife died. He'd started drinking a lot, and his friends just got to where they didn't come around anymore.

"Did I tell you I invited Ben, Grace, and Judy to dinner?"

"No, that's fine. Did you tell Sharon?"

"Yes, I did, my love."

"See, I'm here one day and already I'm the last person to know anything." She laughed.

Ben envied Wes; Wes had done what he was not able to do, make Mandy happy. She glowed with the happiness that had finally come her way. He watched as her eyes sparkled when she looked at him. It wasn't the wealth; he could tell that now. It was the peace she had found in Wes. He had touched a part of her that made her radiant when he entered the room. She was content to learn new ways of life; she was willing to change everything in her life for him. How had he reached her inner most being to rectify the brokenness she had once known? How had he erased her memory of Clay to the point she was content to live again? His train of thought was broken when Judy came bouncing in the door.

"Hey, darling, how was your day? I'm tired. Boy, it was a long day today. How's Mom doing?"

Grace woke up and heard them talking in the other room. "Mom is fine, dear, glad to see you all here together again. Things have been tense since the last little meeting we all had together. Good to see you have worked it all out. Ben, I guess we should be going, son. I'm kind of hungry."

"We've taken care of that, Grace, everyone is staying for dinner. Sharon has prepared a fine healthy meal for you," Wes said, putting his arm around Grace and leading her into the dining room.

"I'm starved. I really miss Sharon fixing my dinner every night. I have to fend for myself now," Judy said, making her way into the dining room.

Wes shot a look of disapproval at her; she smiled and wrinkled her nose at him.

"Mandy, you sit next to me, and Grace you sit here. I want both of my ladies close to me tonight. It's not every day a man gets two beautiful ladies to sit next to him at one time."

"Hey, what about me?" Judy broke in.

"Well, honey, you'll have to settle for Ben." Wes winked at Ben.

Ben rolled his eyes as he looked over at her next to him. *Give me strength, Lord. I can't decide if this woman is a blessing or punishment*, he thought.

"That's okay, Ben loves me." Judy smirked.

Wes looked over at Ben, who was watching Mandy place her napkin in her lap. He didn't even hear what Judy had said. Judy poked him in the ribs. "What?" He jumped.

"I said, you love me, don't you?" she said, holding his arm and laying her head on his shoulder.

"Sure." Ben wondered what he saw in her. *Sure she looks beautiful, but she is rough around the edges. Her personality leaves something to be desired. She would be fine if she wouldn't open her mouth*, he thought.

Mandy, on the other hand, was a lady, the way she moved, the way she talked, everything about her stood out. Her beauty entranced him; it seemed to illuminate from the inside out. She was a catch indeed, and he could have had her first.

After dinner, they all retired to the living room. The moon was full, and it illuminated the night. It was a wonder to behold on the bay and its reflection on the still water. Wes and Mandy sat on the couch near the fireplace; Grace sat in the easy chair next to them. Ben sat near the window with Judy at his feet. Sally brought in coffee and water for them to drink. Judy didn't want that; she walked over to the bar. Ben cleared his throat really loud; she turned to look at him and put the top back on the bottle. She poured herself a cup of coffee and sat down again. Ben smiled at her; she smiled back, holding up the cup of coffee to him.

Grace watched her son. Judy seemed to be a nuisance. Her heart went out to him. She knew he had kicked himself a hundred times for letting Mandy get away, but what was done was done. There was no going back. Time would not stand still for him to change what he had done. She was proud of him, the way he was a graceful loser to Wes. It never seemed to affect the way he felt about Wes. He just couldn't keep his eyes off Mandy. She also noticed Wes watching him. Ben had not seen Wes looking at him; he could only look at Mandy.

Wes put his arm around Mandy and drew her close. She leaned her head over and lay in on his shoulder. Ben snapped out of his trance. He looked at Wes with an apologetic look. Wes smiled at him; Judy poked Ben again. "Let's go. I'm tired, and your mom probably is too."

"Yeah, I think it's time for us to be getting on home. Thanks so much for the shopping and for dinner. Mandy, stop by tomorrow, and we can visit," Grace said, getting up from her chair.

"That sounds good, Grace. I love you, old woman," Mandy said, hugging her friend.

"I love you too, little lady."

When everyone else was gone, Wes wanted to see what Mandy had bought.

"Come into my den." Mandy motioned for Wes to come into the bedroom.

He went in and fell on the bed. "Boy, I miss this bed. Show me what you bought. Better yet, model it for me," he said, laying up against the pillows with his hands behind his head. "Come on, baby, let me see what you got." They laughed.

Mandy modeled each piece for him. She came out of the dressing room prancing and spinning like a model. Wes loved it; he would whistle and clap for each piece. She saved the best for last. She went in and stayed about ten minutes. Wes started to boo and holler. She stuck her bare leg out of the dressing room and pulled it back. She stuck it out again with bunny slippers on. He started to hoot and holler. She stuck out an arm then a shoulder, and then she popped out of the dressing room with a granny nightgown on.

Wes fell over laughing. "Woman, you're too much. Come over here in that sexy granny gown."

She ran over, jumped on the bed, and fell over against him. He grabbed her and held her close. "Hey, this is my bed, don't get too comfortable." She laughed. He didn't respond; she looked up and he was sound asleep. She eased over and pulled the covers over him. "You'll do anything to get into my bed." She laughed and rubbed her hand down his cheek. He was so handsome; he was her foundation. She reflected on the conversation she and Grace had had earlier that day. "Truly I have been blessed, Lord." She cuddled up next to him and went to sleep.

· · · · ·

Sharon and Sally were in the kitchen finishing up the last of the dinner dishes. "Did you hear all the commotion upstairs?" Sally said, laughing into her hand.

"Yes, Dr. Young is so happy. It's been so long since I've seen him this happy. He radiates in her presence, don't you think?" Sharon replied.

"She's such a nice person, so down-to-earth, like us. She's not like the snobs that I normally work for," Sally said, sitting at the table.

"No indeed. She isn't. She came from a poor family, you know. She's made her way in the world with her pottery and art. I went to her shop one day. She didn't know who I was. We had never met. But that's all Dr. Young talked about was her. I had to meet her. Her work is exquisite, so original. Ms. Catherine raves about her work. I've never heard Ms. Catherine rave about anything. She's so kind and helpful when you go into her shop. I had to buy a piece of her pottery," Sharon said, looking into the air.

"I'm glad Dr. Young has found someone like her."

"Me too," Sharon said, sitting at the kitchen table with a cup of coffee.

"What are you women going on about?" George came in, poured himself a cup of coffee, and sat at the table with Sharon.

"We're talking about Ms. Mandy, what a delightful person she is. She is a welcome sight to this household," Sharon responded.

"Yeah, I'm glad that Ms. Judy moved out. She was impossible. She wanted to be waited on hand and foot. Ms. Mandy hasn't asked me for one thing. She just praises me for a job well done. I like her," Sally said, joining the others at the table.

"Indeed, she is a welcome party to this household. I brought the Volvo around this morning for her to use. She smiled and thanked me for all I do for Dr. Young. She brushed her feet off before she got in. Imagine that," George said, sipping his coffee.

"I think our new mistress of the house is going to work out just fine," Sharon said, eating a freshly baked cookie. "Did you hear all of that laughter and whistling going on upstairs?"

"Yes, I did. I think I would make a fool of myself too if I had such a woman as Ms. Mandy. She's quite lovely, in a natural kind of way. Her beauty actually seems to radiate from within her. But the outside is a pleasure to look at as well," George said, leaning back in his chair.

"Sharon has been to her shop. She bought one of her pieces. She has it in her room," Sally remarked, grabbing a cookie.

"Is that so, Sharon? Do you think she'd mind if I went to her shop now that she knows who we all are?" George asked.

"I wouldn't think so. She doesn't seem like the type. You must go, George. She has handmade fountains. I know you like those. She hand paints each and every detail, marvelous," Sharon remarked.

"Well, I'm tired, I'm going to bed. Dr. Young leaves so early in the morning, I have to be up and have his breakfast ready at five-thirty. See you later, sleep well." Sharon pushed her chair back.

"Wait for me, Sharon, and I'll walk with you."

"I've got to lock down the house and turn in myself. Goodnight, ladies."

• • • • •

The morning was bright; the wind was blowing a gale. The skies looked heavy with rain. Wes eased out of the bed and showered. He dressed and watched Mandy sleep. He hated to wake her, but he couldn't bear leaving without telling her. He sat on the side of the bed where Mandy was still wearing the granny gown and bunny slippers. Her hair was lying long and wavy on the pillow. Her smooth skin was flawless. Her chest rose and fell with each breath she took. He could sit and watch her all day. But he knew the day held difficulties for him at the office. He had to leave her. He ever so gently reached down and kissed her forehead. She reached up and put her arms around his neck. "You sleep in your own bed tonight, Dr. Young." She smiled through her sleepy eyes.

"I have to go, my love. Have a wonderful day. Make beautiful things to bring people pleasure." He whispered in her ear.

"You save lives, my sweet one. I love you."

"And I love you. Please take the car. Your old truck needs repairs. I don't want you breaking down on the road."

"Whatever you say. I need to get up too."

"No, no, it's early, it's only five o'clock. You sleep. Rachel will wake you at seven."

Mandy rolled over and held the pillow up next to her and went back to sleep. Wes pushed her hair back and kissed her again.

In the kitchen Sharon had his breakfast waiting for him. "Good morning, Dr. Young, your breakfast is ready. Have a seat. I'll get your orange juice."

"Thank you, Sharon. I'm sorry for all the noise last night, we—"

"No need to explain, Dr. Young. It's a pleasure to hear laughter in this house. Ms. Mandy is a fine lady. I'm pleased to serve her."

"She is, isn't she? The Good Lord has sure shined down on me, Sharon," Wes said, sipping his orange juice.

"Indeed he has, sir. I think she brings sunshine to this house. I love what she's done for you. I haven't seen you like this—"

"I don't think I have ever felt like this before in my whole life. She brings sunshine to my life," Wes said, getting up from the table.

"Good morning, sir."

"Good morning, George."

"Looks like rain, sir. I brought the Hummer around for you to drive today."

"Thanks, George. You take such good care of me. Would you make sure Mandy takes the Volvo today? Her old truck leaves much to be desired. I don't want her driving that old thing anymore."

"Yes sir, I'll make sure of it, sir," George said, helping Wes with his coat. He handed him his briefcase, and Wes was out the door.

He pulled his coat around him. The wind was strong and cold. He looked at the skies; they were dark and angry. He missed Mandy already. He wished he didn't have to go to work, but there were people who needed him to be there for them.

Rachel walked into Mandy's room and pulled the drapes back. "Time to rise and shine, Ms. Mandy. Work waits." Rachel went into the bathroom and started drawing a hot bath for her. She was humming an old gospel hymn. It was the same one Grace hummed. Mandy wished she could remember the name of the hymn. She rolled out of bed. Rachel came back into the bedroom and looked at the gown and shoes. "Ms. Mandy, I just love your bed clothes."

Mandy laughed. "So does Dr. Young." She sat on the side of the bed trying to make her eyes stay open.

"Late night?"

"No, just good sleep. That bed sleeps so good."

"It should. Dr. Young had it made especially for him. NASA made the mattress. Some new innovative foam, it's supposed to surround your body or something," she said, busying herself picking up the room. "He had one made for each of us on the staff. He wanted to make sure we slept healthy. You know how doctors are."

"I'm going to take my bath now," Mandy informed Rachel.

She slid into the nice hot bath; it was just right. *How did she know how I like my bath?* She soaked for a half hour. When she went back into the bedroom her clothes were all laid out on the freshly made bed. The room had been straightened up. "Rachel?"

"Yes, ma'am?"

"How would you like to go to work with me today?"

"Anything you need, Ms. Mandy."

"Not because I need it, but because you want to go with me?"

"I would like that. I've never been to a pottery shop before."

"Then it's settled."

"Yes, ma'am," Rachel said, smiling at Mandy. "Your breakfast is on the table in front of the couch. Do you need me for anything else right now?"

"No, I'll be down in a minute."

Rachel went into the kitchen for a second cup of coffee. "I get to go with Ms. Mandy today to see her shop."

"Oh, you'll love it, Rachel. I've been myself a couple of weeks ago, bought myself one of her vases. It has the most realistic seascape on it I've ever seen."

"Good morning, ladies."

"Good morning, Ms. Mandy, did you sleep well?"

"Wonderful, I'm sorry we were a little loud last night."

"Not to worry, it's good to have laughter in this house," Sharon said, cleaning up the kitchen.

"Sharon, I would like a special candlelight dinner for me and Dr. Young tonight. I don't know what his favorite dishes are. Could you do that and make his favorite?"

"It would be a pleasure, Ms. Mandy."

"Thanks, I really appreciate it. Rachel, are you ready to go?"

"Yes, Ms. Mandy." She smiled back at Sharon and winked.

Mandy unlocked the door to the pottery shop; she noticed right away someone had been inside. The lights were on, and several pieces were knocked onto the floor. She picked up the pieces and inspected them for breaks or cracks. She put her things away and turned on the kiln. She unlocked the door that led to the house and opened it. She was shocked at what she found. The house had been torn to pieces. Food in the sink; clothes on the floor. Her what-knots were turned over. The bed was unmade, and the bathroom had a strange odor. She began cleaning up; Rachel stopped her.

"I'll do this, Ms. Mandy. You just leave it to me." Rachel began cleaning up the mess. Mandy was furious, she went back into the shop and sat at the potter's wheel. She ran her fingers through her hair and picked up the phone. She dialed Judy's work number.

"Hello, this is Dr. Bearden."

"Judy, this is Mandy—"

"I was wondering how long it would take you to call."

"Judy, did someone break in and ransack the house?"

"No, I had a little private party last night."

"Why did you go into the pottery shop?"

"One of the guys went in to take a peek."

"You let strangers into my house, into my shop?" Mandy's voice got louder.

"They weren't strangers. I knew every one of them. Ben said you would be mad—"

"Ben was here while this was going on?"

"He left, he said you—"

"Judy, I don't think this is going to work out, you living here. Perhaps you should find another place to live."

"I had a place to live, and Wes kicked me out because of you."

Wes listened as he heard Judy talking to Mandy. He excused himself from the nurse, went into the office, and closed the door. He stood and listened; Judy didn't know he was listening.

"You spoiled everything. I don't have to find another place to live. You find another place to live."

Wes took the phone out of Judy's hand. "Mandy, I'll take care of this. She won't be coming back to your house. I love you." He hung up and stared at Judy. "Judy, I've tried to help you. I've over looked so many things in the past, but I refuse to overlook this. Take the rest of the day and find yourself a place to live, starting today." Wes went to walk away.

Judy grabbed him, turned him around, and kissed him. He took her arms and pushed her away. "You're fired."

"You can't fire me. I work for the Foundation, not you," she screamed.

"I run the Foundation, or have you forgotten? I don't know what's gotten into to you lately, but I don't need all the drama." He walked out, leaving her alone.

She sat back in her chair and cried. She just couldn't be like Ben and watch the two of them live happily ever after. She would fix Mandy; she'd done it before. She'd tell Catherine what she had done. Catherine would take care of it for her. She packed her things and left.

Rachel came back into the shop where Mandy was working at the potter's wheel. She watched as Mandy let the clay glide through her hands as she caressed it. She moved her thumb ever so slightly and a pattern started to form on the side of the bowl. She took her sponge and dripped a little water inside to smooth the edges. She used the sponge in one hand while the other hand held the bowl steady as the wheel turned. It seemed so easy to watch her. Mandy removed the bowl from the wheel by cutting around the bottom with a piece of wire and slipping it onto a thin board.

"Put on that apron over there and come here," Mandy instructed. "Sit right here, allow the wheel to be between your legs like this," she said, showing her how to sit. "Now, take this ball and put one hand on the outside and one hand on the top, thumb down. I'm going to turn the wheel on slow. Keep your hands in place. Good. Now as the wheel turns let your thumb put pressure on the top, there you go. See how it makes the inside of the bowl?"

Rachel laughed with joy; she was doing it. The clay was cool and wet in her hands.

Mandy smiled. "Now let your thumb come closer to your hand on the outside, slowly, slowly. Now, take your fingers one on the inside and the other one on the outside and pull upward real slow. That's it. See how the bowl is getting taller? Good. Now, pull your hands away from the clay real slow."

Rachel watched in amazement as the ball of clay turned into a hollow bowl. She gently allowed the clay to succumb to her touch.

"That's it. You've made yourself a bowl." Mandy patted her on the shoulder. "Take this wire and run it flatways on the bottom. That cuts the clay away from the wheel."

Rachel took the wire and gently slid it under the freshly molded piece of clay.

"Good. Take this piece of wood and slide the bowl over on it real slow." She eased the bowl on to the thin piece of wood.

"You're done with step one. We'll cover the bowl with this cloth, and tomorrow you can paint it."

"Oh, Ms. Mandy, that was fun! Can I do something else?"

"Sure, I'll teach you how to make a fountain."

"George loves fountains. I'll make him one."

"How sweet. Come over here, put this clay on the press, and lift up the canvas. Lay the clay on that canvas and put the top piece back over the ball of clay. Take that handle and pull the rollers all the way down the table. Now, pull it back again. Lift the canvas."

Rachel followed each instruction carefully as Mandy gave them.

"See, you have a sheet of clay. Now go over to that shelf over there and find the mold you want to use."

Mandy went in and waited on a customer while Rachel picked out her mold. She watched Mandy; she described each detail of the vase to the lady. The lady bought several pieces.

Mandy returned to Rachel. "Oh, that's a good one for a fountain." She picked one that looked like it had fossils of shells in it. "You can make two, one for George and one for yourself."

She walked Rachel through the steps of making her tiers. She showed her how to roll the clay to make pillars to go between each tier. Rachel was so happy, she couldn't wait to get home and tell Sharon what she had done.

At the end of the day Rachel helped Mandy clean everything up and close the shop. She chatted all the way home. Mandy smiled. She was glad she was able to do something for Rachel; Rachel had done so much for her.

She dreaded seeing Wes; she didn't know what frame of mind he would be in when he got home. The incident with Judy had left her shaken. She could tell Wes was angry with Judy; she didn't want to be the one who broke up a lifelong friendship. She prayed there was a way to fix the problem.

Rachel drew her a hot bath and laid her clothes out on the bed. She soaked for a long time. She knew there would be no candlelight dinner for her and Wes tonight. She heard the door of the bedroom open.

"Mandy?" It was Wes. She got out and put her robe on; she peeked into the room and saw him sitting in a chair looking out at the rain.

"Yes," she responded.

He came over to her and held her tight. "I'm sorry about your house. I didn't know Judy would do that. Rachel told me how bad it was. I'm so sorry, my love. I fired her today. I just can't put up with any more of her games. She tires me out trying to clean up her stunts."

"Wes, please don't fire her. Please give her another chance. I know her house is finished. Couldn't she live there and still work for the Foundation? Please, Wes, for me."

He looked at her in utter amazement. How could she defend Judy after what she had done to her? This woman had a heart as big as the ocean.

"Okay, tomorrow we'll get her settled in," Wes relented. "How was your day?"

"Wonderful, and yours?"

"Long and busy. I do need Judy. Her absence was felt today. I'll go call her. You finish getting dressed. On the other hand—" He grabbed her and threw her on the bed. "You're mine now." He kissed her all over. She laughed so hard she lost her breath.

． ． ． ． ．

Sharon looked up at the ceiling, then over at Sally. "There're at it again." They both smiled.

． ． ． ． ．

Wes called Judy and told her what Mandy had asked him. He even offered for her to stay at their home that evening, on the condition that she move into her own home the next day. She was so surprised. She had thought Mandy would have him throw her out for good. She walked in the door with her head hung. Rachel passed her in the foyer. "You'd better be glad Ms. Mandy is such a fine person. She begged Dr. Young not to fire you."

Judy felt so bad. She had been so ugly to Mandy. She had taken out all of her frustrations on her. She had even tried to force herself upon Wes. She knew that Mandy was a friend you keep close to you. She couldn't wait to apologize.

Mandy came in and greeted her as if nothing had happened. It made Judy feel even worse for what she had done. Mandy hugged and welcomed her. "It's good to see you, Judy. You can have your old room, if you'd like to freshen up before dinner."

Judy stopped and tried to apologize, "Mandy, I'm—"

"Not another word. It's forgotten." Mandy smiled and went to find Rachel, whom she found with Sharon in the kitchen. "Rachel, who cared for Judy while she was living here?"

"Well, it was Sally, but she doesn't want to do it again."

"Could you ask Sally to come into the living room?"

Sally walked into the living room where Mandy was standing with Wes. "Oh good, Sally, would you please do me a favor and see if Judy could use any help? I know, it's not your favorite thing to do, but if you would do it just this one time while she's a guest here, I would consider it a personal favor."

"Yes, Ms. Mandy, anything for you," Sally said.

"You can come to the shop on your day off and I'll give you a personal pottery lesson." Mandy smiled.

"Oh, thank you, Ms. Mandy. I'll take real good care of Ms. Judy for you. She'll think she's a queen."

"That's my girl."

Wes watched in amazement at the way Mandy handled a difficult situation. When Judy was here before all of the staff members fussed about who was going to have to help Judy. Mandy had made it seem like the thing to do. He knew she was going to be just fine.

Chapter 11

Christmas Eve was upon them. The house was buzzing with decorating for the season. Mandy had called a staff meeting, and everyone was in the dining room waiting for her to come in. She thanked everyone for being there on such short notice.

"The reason I called this meeting is because I want to celebrate the real meaning of Christmas. That's the birth of Christ. I really don't go for all of the Santa stuff. Let's use angels, a nativity, "hark the herald," and that kind of stuff. I know it's different for everyone, but if you could just humor me on this one thing. ... "

"We'll do whatever you say, Ms. Mandy," George said. "Now, you know Ms. Catherine will be visiting this evening?"

"That's fine, Catherine decorates her house and we decorate ours, right?" Mandy smiled. "Can we have it done by the time they arrive?"

"Yes, ma'am."

The staff loved the way Mandy always referred to the house as their house too. She treated each of them with respect. She even sat and listened to their personal problems and would give them advice. She would bring them special gifts from her shop.

Wes was pleased with the way she ran the house. He was nervous about his parents coming, but he knew she would have everything under control. He knew that he had a jewel and didn't want his parents to ruin it for him. He knew they liked her, but she ran her house different from anyone he knew. He heard the doorbell downstairs. He knew it was his parents; he heard his father's voice. "Merry Christmas, everyone."

Wes hurried down the stairs to greet his parents. "Hello, Mother and Father. How was your trip?"

"Our trip was fine, son, where's that beautiful woman of yours?" Wes' father said, looking around.

"Now, now, Raymond, just cool your jets. She's probably getting ready, you know how women are," Catherine scolded him.

"Well, actually, she's checking on dinner, if you would like to come into the living room." Wes led his parents into the living room.

"How wonderful the house looks. I can see Mandy has already put her touch on it. Look, Raymond, a nativity scene instead of a Christmas tree. Where do you put your gifts?" Catherine said, admiring the decorations.

"Just put them right over there, Mother," Wes said, looking for Mandy to come down the hall.

"George, just put those things right over there," Catherine instructed.

Mandy walked into the room, and everyone turned to look at her. She wore a red velvet floor-length dress with green trim. "Welcome, Raymond, Catherine." She greeted them with a hug.

"I like this woman, son. If you ever get tired of her, just send her to us. We'll take really good care of her," Raymond said, eyeing Mandy as she made her way over to Wes.

"Mandy, the house looks wonderful. I like what you've done with it. I'd love to see the rest of it," Catherine said, admiring the new furniture and accessories. "Look, you have some of your pieces in here. I'd know your work anywhere. All my friends are so jealous you're going to be my daughter-in-law. They are just green with envy."

Mandy led Catherine upstairs to show her the bedrooms. She had changed the master bedroom to look like an island suite. The whole house had been done with an island theme. Mandy thought since they lived on the beach their house should reflect that. It also made her feel more at home. She missed her little cottage.

Catherine loved the theme of the islands. "This makes you feel like you're on vacation all the time. I know you just love it."

"Thanks, we like it. As long as Wes is happy then I'm happy." Mandy led the way back downstairs.

"Westbrook, how is the research coming? The foundation is very glad you came back," Raymond said, taking his drink from Sally.

"It's going fine, Father, how are things in L.A.? Still making those women beautiful?" Wes laughed.

"Look, I'm a surgeon, not a miracle worker. Now, you take Mandy, she has a natural beauty. I wouldn't touch anything about her. She's the Mona Lisa of women. How in the world did you find a woman like that in a place like this?"

"Right next door, actually. I had an encounter of road rage with her. I was on the road, she was in a rage." They both laughed.

"What are you men laughing about?" Catherine asked as they entered the room.

"Road rage, my dear."

Mandy felt her face get hot; she knew she was blushing. "I had a really bad day that day. Then Wes came along, he just happened to be in the wrong place at the wrong time."

"I'd say he was at the right place at the right time." Raymond chuckled. "Come over here, dear, and sit by me."

Mandy crossed the room and sat beside Raymond on the couch. "First thing I want to tell you is, you need to let Catherine know who your decorator is. The second thing is, you need to come live with us and let my son find him another woman."

"First of all, I decorated the house. Second, I wouldn't leave Wes if you tried to drag me away," Mandy said, laughing.

"Before Richard and Chad get here, I want to let you in on a little secret. They are wild boys. Spoiled rich kids. Wes is the only one I have that works and earns his own way. He's the best of the litter. So don't let those others sons of mine turn your head."

"Raymond, no one could make me turn my head away from Wes. He's the pick of my litter too."

Raymond roared with laughter. "Didn't I tell you I love this woman?"

The doorbell rang; George showed Richard and Chad into the living room. "Wow, Wes, I like your pad."

"Hello to you too, Chad," Wes said, hugging his brother's neck. "Chad, Richard, this is my fiancée, Mandy Bowls."

Chad and Richard stopped and stared; Mandy walked over and gave them both a hug. "How wonderful to meet you. Welcome to our home."

"Wes, you've been holding out on us. Hello, I'm Chad, and I'm bad."

"I'm Wes, and you're a mess," Wes said, taking Mandy's hand. "Let's go into dinner."

Chad was loud and outspoken; Richard, on the other hand, hardly said a word the entire evening. Both brothers were handsome men. Chad thought he was God's gift to women; Richard, on the other hand, didn't even date. Mandy watched Richard; there was something sad about him. His eyes were distant. When Rachel passed the doorway, his eyes lit up. Mandy noticed his eyes followed her until he couldn't see her anymore.

"I hope everyone is staying the night. We have rooms for everyone. Would you excuse me for a moment, please?" Mandy said, leaving the room. She found Rachel in the kitchen.

"Rachel, could I talk to you for a minute please?"

"Yes, ma'am."

"Rachel do you know Richard, Wes' brother?"

"Why yes, ma'am, I was his mother's personal attendant," she said, lowering her head.

"Uh huh, did you two have something going between you?"

Rachel looked at Mandy. She didn't want to answer. "It's okay, Rachel, this is me you're talking to, not Catherine."

"Yes, ma'am. We love each other, but he's the son of a rich man, and I'm a servant."

"You're not a servant, you know better than that. Did Catherine send you here?"

"She found out about Raymond and me. She loved me, but she loves her son more."

"Have you ever heard of Cinderella?"

"Yes, ma'am, everyone has."

"Well then, you know nothing is impossible. Come upstairs with me."

Mandy and Rachel ran up the back stairs laughing like little girls. Mandy picked out a lovely rose-colored dress. "Here, put this on."

"But Ms. Mandy—"

"Don't *but Ms. Mandy* me. I was a poor potter's wife. God sent me Wes, now look at me. So your occupation is a hazard for getting what you want. But all things are possible with God. Here, let me fix your face and hair." Rachel was a lovely young woman. She had long auburn hair, a nice figure, hazel green eyes, and flawless ivory skin. Mandy stood back and looked at her. "Now look in the mirror."

"Wow, Ms. Mandy. I don't even look like myself."

"Exactly. What is your middle name, Anne? Okay, you're my friend Anne."

"But what if they recognize me?"

"No one will recognize you but Wes, and he'll keep our secret. Stop all that ma'am stuff and talk to me and the others like you would talk to Sharon or George."

"Mandy, you're too much, do you know that?"

"What people don't know won't hurt them. Now go down the back stairs and come around to the front door. I'll tell George you're coming and how to introduce you."

Rachel scurried down the back stairs and made her way to the front door. Mandy whispered into George's ear what they were doing. His eyes got big and he smiled. "You're too much, Ms. Mandy."

"You are too, George."

The doorbell rang. George brought Rachel into the living room, "Ms. Anne for Ms. Mandy."

Mandy squeezed Wes' hand and nodded her head so that he wouldn't let the cat out of the bag. "Why, Anne, I'm so glad you could make it tonight. Please come in and meet my guests. This is my fiancé, Wes, whom you've met. This is Dr. Raymond and Catherine Young, and this is Chad and Richard Young, Wes' brothers."

Richard froze in his tracks; Catherine and Raymond shook Anne's hand and said how they were glad to meet her. Chad jumped in front of Richard and tried to put the moves on her. Mandy stepped in between them and led Anne and Richard over to the sofa.

The light came back into Richard's eyes; Mandy smiled at Wes and squeezed his hand. "Would anyone like a drink?" When Anne started to get up, Mandy stepped in front of her. "Sally, could you get everyone some eggnog? Thanks."

Richard looked at Mandy then at Wes. Wes nodded his head, giving the okay to his brother. Richard and Anne talked all evening.

"Why, Anne, I don't think I've ever heard Richard talk that much. Where did you say you worked?"

"She's my assistant at the pottery shop." Mandy interrupted.

"Wonderful, it's so nice to meet you. I think Raymond and I are going to turn in for the evening. We'll see you in the morning."

"Goodnight," Mandy and Wes said at the same time.

"I think I'm going to ride around and see what is happening in Hicksville," Chad said, getting up. "Want to go, Richard?"

"No, I think I'll stay here. Thanks anyway, Chad."

When Chad was gone, Richard looked over at Mandy. "How did you know?"

"Don't ask, brother, she knows," Wes said, shaking his head.

"I could see it in your eyes. The eyes are the windows to the soul. Yours were so empty until Anne walked by and the light returned to them. It's a woman thing. Now, Anne, here's the keys to my house. You stay there tonight and be back for Christmas dinner tomorrow. Good night, you two." Mandy took Wes' hand and led him upstairs.

"Wait!" Richard said, "I want to thank you." He hugged her tight. "Thanks, I really mean it."

"It was nothing," Mandy said and headed back upstairs.

"My love, truly you are one of the most incredible people I have ever met. Oh, by the way, Mother and Father have my room. Where am I going to sleep?"

"On the floor." She smiled and jumped into bed, dress and all.

"Oh, no, you don't." He jumped into bed with her. They lay looking at each other. "Let's not wait until February. Let's get married right now. During the Christmas season. I don't care about a big wedding. I just want to make you mine," Wes said, pushing her hair away from her face.

"Dr. Young, you've already done that," she said, kissing him. "Let's do it. Do you know a justice of the peace?"

"Do you mean it? Because I do know a notary. They can marry us. We already have our license. Can we do it now, tonight, on Christmas eve?"

"Sure, call them."

"We don't have to. It's Grace. She does notary work for me all the time."

"It's late, Wes. She's in bed."

"Let's get her up. You know her cancer is in remission. Please, Mandy."

"Let's do it."

They snuck out the back stairway, got into the Hummer, and headed to Grace's house. He looked so handsome in his tux, and she had on her red gown. They knocked on the door. A light upstairs came on and Grace answered the door. "What are you two doing out so late?"

"Grace, we want you to marry us right now."

"What better time than Christmas eve to start a new life together. I'll need a witness. Ben, Ben, come down here, son."

Ben came down the stairs in his pajamas. "What, Mom? Oh, hi, Wes. Hi, Mandy. What are you doing here so late?"

"I'm going to marry them, and I need a witness. Let me get my stuff."

Grace married them, and Ben witnessed it. They signed all of the paperwork and the two lovebirds left. As they were sneaking up the back stairway, George came out and startled them.

"Excuse me, sir, I thought someone was trying to break in."

"They were, it was us." Wes put his finger up to his month. "Don't tell my parents you caught us sneaking into the house." They both laughed and headed up the stairs. George shook his head and returned to his room.

"Now you're mine, woman. You can't run from me anymore." He grabbed her and threw her on the bed. He held her down so that she couldn't move.

"Why, Wes, I didn't know you were so strong."

"You ain't seen nothing yet, honey." They laughed and cried and loved each other. Rachel was not there to get her up, so Sally walked in and got Mandy's things ready. They were sleeping under the covers and Sally didn't see them. She drew the drapes back and started to pull the covers back when she saw a man's leg sticking out. She backed away from the bed. "Dr. Young, it's time to get up."

Wes stuck his head out from under the covers; he squinted his eyes at the bright light from the windows. "What time is it?"

"It's eight o'clock, sir. Your parents are already in the dining room. Richard seems to be missing. Your mother is frantic."

"Okay, thanks, Sally. That will be all."

"Thank you, sir."

Mandy giggled under the covers. When Sally was gone she climbed out. "Well, Mrs. Young, how do you feel this Christmas morning?"

"Sleepy. Do I have to be lady of the manor today? I just want to stay in bed and sleep."

"My parents will leave after lunch and fly back to L.A. Then it's just you and me, kid," he said, washing her back.

They both got dressed and went down to the dining room. Everyone was waiting except Richard. Catherine was crying. "Don't cry, Mother. Richard took Mandy's friend home last night." Wes said, helping Mandy with her chair.

"I have some good news, if everyone would be quiet just a minute. I would like to introduce to you the newest Mrs. Young." Wes hugged Mandy.

"When did this happen?" Catherine cried. "What about the wedding? I've sent out invitations and everything, all my friends—"

"Don't panic, Mother, we're still going to have the wedding. We just got married. You and father stayed in my room. I didn't have anywhere to stay, so I had to marry her last night, so I'd have a place to sleep."

"How wonderful, son. Welcome to the family, Mandy." Raymond got up and hugged both of them. "Did Wes show you what I got for your wedding present?"

"Yes, he did, and it's beautiful. We'll enjoy it. Thank you so much," she said, hugging him again.

"Are you serious. You really got married last night?" Catherine asked, wiping her face.

"Yes, Mother, we did."

"Congratulations to the both of you. What a wonderful thing to do on Christmas Eve. That's so romantic, isn't it, Raymond?" she cried.

Mandy started to take a drink of her orange juice when she felt sick; she had to run to the bathroom. She didn't even have time to excuse herself. Wes followed her.

"Are you okay, my love?" Wes asked her, getting a cold rag for her face.

"I don't know what came over me. All of a sudden I felt like I was going to be sick..." She started throwing up; her face was pale and her skin was clammy.

"Are you coming down with something?"

"I don't know. The smell of that food just made me so sick. Maybe it's my hormones. I was going to go to the doctor after the new year, because my cycle seems to have just stopped. I've just been so busy with the house and all. I haven't had time."

Wes looked at her and smiled. "It looks like we got married just in time."

"Just in time for what?"

"How long has it been since you've had a cycle?"

"Since November … Wes, you don't think I'm—"

"I do, my love, I sure do. I think we're going to be parents." Wes gleamed with the thought.

"We should find out for sure before we tell anyone," she said, wiping her face.

"Yes, especially since I gave my parents that speech about my room." Wes was so happy he could not contain himself. He took her hands and swung her around the bathroom.

"Careful, we don't want me to be sick again." She smiled. "Are you happy?"

"It's the best Christmas present you could ever give me."

Richard was at the table when Mandy and Wes returned. "Good morning, Richard. Sleep a little late?"

"Yeah, I did. Your friend is really a nice person. She says she is coming over for Christmas dinner."

"Yes, Mandy invited her. She doesn't have any family to speak of, and she and Mandy are so close. We thought it would be all right."

"Are you all right, dear? You're a little pale," Catherine asked Mandy.

"I'm fine. I'm just a little under the weather this morning."

"Where is Rachel? I haven't seen her since I've been here."

"She's on vacation this week. She'll be back next week I think," Mandy replied, looking at Wes, smiling.

The smile seemed to be permanently plastered on Wes' face. He wouldn't let Mandy out of his sight. He followed her around like a shadow. Anne came just in time for Christmas dinner.

"I'm sorry, ma'am. I had to wear one of your dresses. The choices were slim," Anne whispered. "Really, ma'am, you should change your wardrobe."

Dinner was lovely; they exchanged gifts, and then the Youngs excused themselves to catch their two o'clock flight. Chad was flying back to L.A. with them. Richard opted to stay a few days and catch up with Wes.

George drove them to the airport in Spring Hill. Catherine kept talking about Anne and what a wonderful person she was. She was glad Richard had met her, hoping perhaps they would get to know each other better. It was all George could do to keep his composure. He was happy for Rachel and was glad she had someone like Ms. Mandy to help her up in life. He relaxed in the seat and drove through the traffic to the airport.

• • • • •

"Ms. Mandy, I don't know how I can ever thank you for what you've done for us." Rachel cried as she held Richard's arm.

"Well, first of all, don't call me Ms. Mandy anymore. Second, you're fired as my personal attendant. I really need an assistant at the pottery shop, so you have a new job. Thirdly, you can't live here anymore. You'll have to live at the cottage. You know how I am, keep it neat and clean."

"Are you serious Ms.—I mean, Mandy?" Rachel was so shocked, tears streamed down her face.

Richard hugged Mandy tight. "You're the best sister. Wes, you've got a real winner here. Thanks for all you two have done to help us. I've loved this woman since the day I saw her walk into our house. Mother wouldn't hear of us being together. What would her friends say?"

"Looks like you're going to need a job, brother. How about being in charge of the research center's personnel? Our personnel manager had to go back to Boston. Her mother is ill. What do you say?"

"I'll take it."

"Before you say you'll take it, it's a working man's salary. It's not what Mother and Father slip you all the time. I need someone who is going to take care of my staff. No partying and not showing up for work."

"The only reason I drank and partied all the time was because I just couldn't get Rachel out of my mind."

"How would you like to start using your second name, Rachel?"

"Anne is a nice name. I like it," Richard said, rubbing her hair.

"Then Anne it is," Anne said, hugging Richard. "I never thought we would ever be together. Mandy dragged me upstairs and started talking about Cinderella. I thought she had lost her mind. You're the best person I've ever met. I will be eternally grateful to you. You said with God all things are possible. I believe you."

Mandy smiled that smile, thankful everything had worked out. She was so tired all of a sudden. "If you guys can spare me, I'm a little tired. I think I'll take a nap before dinner." Mandy yawned.

"I'll go with you. You guys make yourself at home or go home or whatever you want to do—my wife needs me. That sounds so good, my wife." Wes smiled and followed Mandy up the stairs.

Mandy went into the bedroom and fell into the bed. "No, no, Daddy, I'm taking a nap, and then we'll talk." She laughed and snuggled into her pillow.

Wes lay beside her; they both slept.

. . . . .

"Richard, you're welcome to stay with me. Wouldn't it be wonderful to live together without worrying about anyone finding out? Your new sister-in-law is a wonderful person. I have enjoyed working for her. She takes me to her shop every day and teaches me about the clay and design and firing the pottery. She didn't have to do that. She just did."

"I can't believe Mother didn't even recognize you. You do look different all prettied up. But I've always loved you just the way you were. Change is good. Don't get me wrong, you are more beautiful today and last night than I have ever seen you."

"Happiness has a way of doing that to you." Rachel smiled. "And I'm so happy, Richard."

"Let's go home. Let's let the newlyweds enjoy their privacy," Richard said.

. . . . .

The wind was raging, and its cold force ripped right through you. The tidal winds off the bay were wet and harsh in the winter. A haze of moisture hung low on the bay; you couldn't even see the lighthouse or the rock levee. Mandy sat in their bedroom looking out at the deteriorating weather. She remembered when her life had felt just like the weather. It seemed like that cold dark haze loomed over her every day.

Now she sat here watching her husband sleep in perfect bliss. She was happier than she could remember. She looked down the shoreline and saw the silhouette of her small cottage. That place was no longer her home but a memory of the past; she had come so far.

She wept; she didn't know if they were tears of times gone by or whether they were tears of happiness for the present. She tried to muster a smile, but her heart was heavy, as if something was being dug out of her spirit and being thrown into the troubled waters of the bay. The past seemed far in the distance, and the present was all too real for her. She looked at Wes, her prince in shining armor. He had rescued her from a life of dread and guilt.

She wanted better for her child. She wanted to protect it from the pain that came with life; she knew she couldn't, no more than her mother could rescue her from the pain of her childhood.

She felt queasy; her stomach felt sick. She went into the bathroom and washed her face with a cool cloth. She looked in the mirror; she no longer saw the ugly girl but a beautiful woman. Her long wavy hair shined; her skin was no longer blotched but clear and radiant. The dark circles under her eyes were no longer there. She brushed her hair back and tied it into a knot. She reached up and shook it down. She found a hair clasp on the counter and pulled her hair back with it.

She heard Wes stirring. She walked over to him and kissed him ever so gently, and he reached up and held her. He smelled her hair and drew her closer. "I love the way you smell. If I ever went blind, I would be able to tell it was you by your smell." He took another deep breath and slept again. She smiled.

Down in the kitchen, Sharon was preparing dinner. Mandy decided she would try to help her. Sharon was humming as she worked cutting, stirring, and tasting the meal she was masterminding. Mandy watched as she spun around the room as though she were dancing with someone. Mandy wondered if Sharon had ever had the desire to have a life outside of this? *Perhaps she dreams of an awaiting prince to come and sweep her off her feet.* Mandy hated to interrupt, but she wanted to do something. She was bored.

Sharon spun around and saw Mandy standing in the doorway. She seemed embarrassed to have been caught frolicking. "Oh. I'm terribly sorry, Ms. Mandy, I was just—"

"No need to explain. If I felt better I would dance with you myself." They both laughed.

"You look a little piqued, are you okay? Would you like to sit down?" Sharon asked, pulling out a chair.

"No, I sit too much as it is." Mandy started to cross the room when she fainted.

Sharon grabbed her to keep her from hitting the floor. She screamed for Dr. Young.

Wes opened his eyes when he heard the blood-curdling cry for help. He jumped up and ran down the stairs. Sharon screamed again; he ran into the kitchen to find Mandy on the floor with her head in Sharon's lap.

"She just fainted, Dr. Young," Sharon cried.

"Let me get my bag. Put a cool cloth on her forehead," Wes ordered.

Sally walked in and gasped. "What's going on?"

"Grab a cloth from the drawer, wet it with cool water, and bring it to me," Sharon shouted.

Mandy's skin was pale, sweat was pouring off her face, and she was cold and clammy.

Wes returned with his bag. He took her vital signs; they were fine. He put a vial of ammonia under her nose to bring her to. She opened her eyes; she was confused and dazed. "What happened?"

"You fainted," Sharon said.

"How silly of you to fuss over me like this."

"Just lie still for a minute. Let your head clear. Then we'll sit you up," Wes instructed.

Wes picked her up; he took her into the living room and laid her on the couch. Her color was returning, and she had stopped sweating. "Can you tell me what happened?"

"I was talking to Sharon, and then you all were hovered over me. That's it."

"Mandy, I really do think you're pregnant. That could be the reason this happened. I don't know for sure, so let's take a ride over to the office. I can better assess the situation there."

"Whatever you say, Wes."

Wes asked George to being the Hummer around for them. The weather was getting worse; you could tell there was a storm brewing in the Gulf. It had started to sprinkle rain by the time they reached Wes' office. They hurried inside to beat the rain. He helped her get up on the examination table. He took a blood sample and took it into the lab. When he returned, he had a smile on his face. "Looks like we're going to be parents after all, Mrs. Young."

"Is that so, Doctor? Is that the reason I feel so bad?"

"It sure is. I'm going to run some other tests on your blood to make sure everything is okay, but on the short run, looks like we're pregnant. Probably about six weeks along. This is the bad time of pregnancy, the first three months or so. I'm going to make you an appointment with a friend of mine who is a gynecologist tomorrow. Looks like you'll be sick for a little while. It's worse on some than on others. You're thirty-two. You're in good health; everything should go smoothly. She can give you something for the nausea and fainting," Wes said, helping her off the table. "You're not going to be able to lift those heavy barrels of clay anymore, and you're going to have to be careful about some aspects of your work, but other than that, you should be able to continue work just like things are. Let's go home before the bottom falls out of the sky."

The clouds were dark and angry, and the wind was picking up. She was chilled. He turned the heater up and gave her a blanket he kept in the backseat. She cuddled up in the blanket and then threw it off. "Boy, it's hot in here." She chuckled. "If this is the way it's going to be, I vote you have the children." They both laughed.

"Should we tell the staff? Grace? Whom should we tell?"

"We definitely should tell all of the above. They need to know. If you could have seen the look on Sharon's face when I came in the room, you'd know why!"

When they arrived home, Richard and Anne were awaiting news along with the staff; everyone was in the kitchen. When they heard the door open, they rushed to it to see if everything was okay. Everyone started talking at once. Wes put his hands up to silence them. "If you would all go into the living room, we'll tell you what it is."

Everyone took a seat and patiently waited for Wes to seat Mandy. "Looks like in about eight months, give or take a week, there will be the patter of little feet in the house."

Everyone tried to talk at once again. Wes held up his hand to silence them. "Mandy's okay, we're just pregnant. Now, Anne, I'm going to depend on you to keep an eye on Mandy at work. Don't let her lift anything heavy or overdo it. The rest of you, well, we'll just see how things progress. Sharon, you may be affected by the cravings she may have. You know how pregnant women are. I want you to move into Rachel's old room, the room upstairs next to George. There's no need in you having to run back and forth. I'll put a monitor in your room in case she needs something. She can reach you without having to run the stairs. Sally, I want you to help Mandy. She'll need that now more than ever. Sally squealed with excitement. "I'll take really good care of her, sir. You can count on me."

"I know I can. Are there any questions?" Wes asked.

"I told you, you would need a new wardrobe." Anne laughed.

"God works in mysterious ways, Anne," Mandy replied.

Anne looked over at Richard. "He sure does."

"Now, how about dinner for our little mama?" Wes asked, helping her to the dining room. "Sharon, do you have some dry toast and tomato juice? I think that will settle her stomach."

"Yes, sir, right away."

When everyone was seated, Wes wanted to say a prayer. "Lord, we thank you for this time of year, when we celebrate your son coming into the world to show us the way. We thank you for this home and these people you have blessed us to share our lives with. And Lord, we thank you for the little one that's on the way, amen."

The table was buzzing with conversation that night. The foursome seemed to have a renewed sense of joy. Christmas had brought good news for everyone. Mandy watched the guests at her table; she was pleased to see the excitement that absorbed each of them. Truly, this had been a good Christmas.

• • • • •

The morning brought sunny skies and a new outlook on life. She was going to be a mother for the first time in her life. She was excited and uncertain at the same time. Thoughts of motherhood filled her head. How would she know what to do? She didn't have an example to follow. She didn't want her child to endure the heartache and pain she had endured as a child. She wanted more for her child than she'd had.

She busied herself getting ready to open the shop. Anne stocked the shelves with the newly fired pieces from the kiln. She marveled at each piece; each one was unique. There were no two pieces alike.

Mandy couldn't wait to tell Grace the good news. She knew the news would need an explanation. She was concerned about what she would say if Grace wanted to know how this could be. She asked Ann to watch the shop while she went over to Grace's. Anne was honored that Mandy trusted her with her business.

Grace was inside humming that old gospel hymn she always hummed. Mandy decided she would just ask Grace the name of it, instead of trying to figure it out.

Grace was glad to see Mandy; she noticed right off that Mandy was pale. "Are you feeling all right, little lady? You look a little pale."

"I'm fine. I have good news for you. Wes and I are going to have a baby. I'm going to be a mother." Mandy glowed with excitement.

Grace cocked her head ever so slightly, looking at Mandy with a confused look. "Well, little lady, you sure do move fast."

Mandy smiled. "We're good, don't you think?"

Grace reached over and took Mandy's hand. "I told you the Good Lord was going to bless you. He has indeed. This is wonderful news. I know the two of you are so happy. Is that the reason you had the rush wedding Christmas Eve?"

"Actually, no, we didn't find out until yesterday. I got sick, then fainted. Wes took me to his office and ran the test, and *voilà*, instant family."

"How does Wes feel about it?"

"He's so happy, Grace, he smiles all the time. He even said grace at the table last night. God works in mysterious ways, that's what some old woman tells me all the time."

They both laughed. "How are you doing?"

"Fine, I haven't felt this good in a long time. That husband of yours knows his medicine. I'm thankful you grabbed him when you did, or there's no telling where I'd be right now."

"Good catch, huh?"

"Good catch. What are you going to do about the shop? You'll have to hire someone, too much heavy lifting."

"I have hired someone, yesterday, as a matter of fact."

"You hired someone on Christmas day?"

"Sure did, a good trusted employee, Rachel, who we now call Anne. She and Richard, Wes' oldest brother, have been in love for years. I worked it out so they can be together. Richard started to work for Wes today, and Anne started with me. They are living in my cottage. Perhaps we will hear wedding bells for them too soon."

Grace looked at Mandy. "You are indeed a special little lady, and I can see why the Good Lord loves you so much. This has been a big Christmas for all of you."

"I know. We're all becoming a family. I owe it all to you and God. I don't know where I would be without you. Still over there in that cottage drowning in grief and guilt," Mandy said, tears rolling down her cheeks.

"I'll have to come over and meet Anne. I know Rachel, but Anne I don't." They both laughed.

Ben came walking down the stairs. "Good morning, Mrs. Young. How are you this fine, sunny morning?"

"Mighty fine indeed. How is your world treating you?"

"Thanks to you, it's wonderful. I really appreciate what you did for Judy again. She is a totally different person. What you did seemed to heal something in her that caused her to be so self-centered. She's learned to look at other people and consider their feelings, even mine. She comes over and cooks for Mom and myself every day after work. She helps Mom with keeping up the house. Can you believe that, Judy cooking and cleaning? Will wonders never cease? I hate to leave good company, but I really need to get going. I'm already late," Ben, said, kissing his mom goodbye.

"I'm really glad everything is working out for the two of you. She's really a fine woman, just a little rough around the edges."

Ben nodded in appreciation as he walked out the door.

Grace poured them another cup of coffee. "What are your plans for New Year's?"

"To be the best wife and mother my family could ask for. If I can do that, I'll be satisfied. I do want to have a New Year's gathering for all of us. I would also like to invite Wes' staff. You all are invited. Tell Ben and Judy, our house New Year's Eve, whenever the notion strikes you. I need to be getting back. Today is Anne's first day, and it could be busy the day after Christmas. I love you, old woman," Mandy said, giving Grace a kiss on the cheek.

"I love you too, little lady," Grace said, hugging Mandy. "If you need any advice about the baby thing, you know I'm here for you."

"Thanks, Grace. I'll probably be calling you a lot."

Mandy walked back up the road to the pottery shop. The morning air was brisk, but the sun was warming to the soul. The birds were singing. The trees were barren; the beautiful flowers that usually lined the road were dried up. She listened to the melody the birds were singing, and she realized she'd forgotten to ask Grace about that hymn she always hums.

She noticed a lot of cars at the shop; she quickened her steps. When she arrived, Anne was busy assisting customers. She looked up at Mandy with a sign of relief. Mandy put her apron on and started to work. The shop was busy all day. Anne made them lunch while Mandy prepared a load of pottery for the kiln. When it was time to close the shop, both of them dropped in a chair and laughed at each other.

"I didn't realize running your own business was so tiring. It's hard work," Anne said, looking at Mandy.

"Yes, it is. There's a lot I need to teach you in the next eight months. I also wanted to tell you how good the cottage looks. If you want to change things around to suit you, please do. How are things with you and Richard?"

"Oh, Mandy, I owe you so much. This is a dream come true for us. We never dreamed we would be having a life together. We had both resolved to the fact that we were born in two different worlds that would never touch. Letting us use your house; you and Wes giving us jobs—it has been the most wonderful Christmas we have ever had. It's so wonderful to take care of that man. This morning he put on one of the suits Wes gave him, and he looked so handsome. His whole face was smiling, for the first time in his life he has something to call his own. Something his father didn't buy for him. He was excited about his first day at work. I think I hear him coming up now."

"I'm so glad for the both of you. I need to get going. My husband will be home soon."

"Mandy, do you think Grace would marry us too? We've decided if we get married, there's nothing his family could do to us, except disown Richard. Now we both have jobs, so it wouldn't matter. The money doesn't matter to Richard anymore."

Mandy didn't feel worthy to take credit for anything she may have done. Grace had helped her so much, changing her life so dramatically; she wanted to return the favor and help others. *If everyone did that this would be a better world to live in,* she thought.

Wes was already at home when she arrived. She was so glad to see him; she wanted to find out how the day went for Richard. "How was your day? How did it go with Richard?"

"My day was fine. Richard is a brilliant business man. I think he's going to be able to stretch our dollar a little farther. I forgot he got a degree in business management. I think he's going to do just fine. He's talking about marrying Anne, right away."

"I know, Anne told me today. I think they're serious. Anne is so excited about their new life together. She said Richard realizes his father may disown him. It doesn't seem to bother them."

"My father said he was going to disown me when I married Kay. I didn't care, but he didn't," Wes said, holding her tight. "How are my wife and little one doing today?" he asked, rubbing her stomach.

"We're both fine. I haven't been sick today at all."

"It could have been the stress of my parents, the holidays, who knows. I made an appointment with Dr. Boyd for you in the morning at ten. Do you think you can make that?"

"I think I can. It's so good to be home with you. Ben said he and Judy are doing real good. She's cooking and cleaning, can you picture that?"

"I don't know much about what the cooking must be like. Judy was beaming today. She appears to have changed since our little incident. She's not as self-serving as she was. It sure makes it easier for the rest of the staff. You're just a special person, Mandy Young," he said, giving her a big kiss. "I'm so hungry. Wonder if Sharon has dinner ready yet?"

"I'll check. You go into the living room and relax, and I'll check with Sharon. Can I get you anything?"

"No, just food. Just think—we have the whole house to ourselves tonight. We can start our honeymoon now. When we have the wedding in February we can have a real one," he said, patting her on the behind.

"Food, I'll get food." She laughed.

Sally met Mandy in the hall. "Good evening, Mrs. Young. Is there anything I can do for you?"

"No thanks, I'm checking on dinner."

"I was just on my way to tell you dinner will be served in fifteen minutes."

"Thank you, Sally."

Tonight is the perfect night for the candlelight dinner, Mandy thought. She would make sure of it. She went to tell Sharon and Sally, but when she walked into the dining room; they already had the lights dimmed, candles burning, and soft music playing. Sharon had cooked his favorite dinner, remembering Mandy had wanted the romantic dinner before, but circumstances had not permitted them to have it. She was hoping that tonight would be a good night to plan it; she was one step ahead of Mandy.

When Wes came in for dinner, he was surprised by the romantic settings. He smiled. *Sharon, I know why I keep you around*, he thought. The staff made themselves scarce. They wanted Mandy and Wes to have the time to themselves they had been denied. They watched from the kitchen as Wes seated Mandy beside him; he kissed her hand. Dinner was served one course at a time.

After dinner they walked into the living room where Sally had turned down the lights; the room was lit by candlelight, and the sound of soft romantic music was playing. The moon was full; it lit up the whole sky, casting a silhouette on the bay and the garden. They danced to the soft music. They yielded themselves to the moment, allowing their emotions to dominate their actions.

The staff watched them together. Sally sighed. "This is so romantic, George. Would you like to dance?"

"Get a hold of yourself, Sally. I think we should leave them alone now. Help Sharon with the kitchen, and I'll lock the house."

Sharon smiled at the two of them; she was so glad her employer had found the love of his life. She had been with him from the beginning. His parents had sent her to his first house to be his chef. She had witnessed the arguing, the nights Wes slept in the guest room. And the tragedy of Kay's long illness followed by her death. The way Wes had mourned over a woman who couldn't have cared less about him. But this woman loved him implicitly. She intertwined her life with his. Her desire was to make his life complete. She was truly a virtuous woman. One day her children would rise up and call her blessed. She wiped the tears from her cheeks and headed for the kitchen to finish up for the night.

·   ·   ·   ·   ·

Mandy and Wes danced in the moonlight. They caressed each other, sharing their love without words. Just the touch of her body next to his made him relent to her. He was totally and completely hers, and she was totally and completely his. He stroked her face; the soft light of the candles made her ocean-blue eyes sparkle. She smiled at him and buried her head in his chest; she could hear the sound of his heart beating next to hers.

She thought about the life that was growing inside of her, a part of each of them would one day bring to fruition the evidence of their love together. Her heart was full; she knew she had made the right choice. He truly was her man and she would spend her life making him happy.

Wes could feel the love radiating from her body. He could feel her heart beat next to his. He knew this was the way life was supposed to be. They didn't need anything to make them happy but each other. *Life will be so different with Mandy than it was with Kay. Kay wanted to impress others; she really didn't care about pleasing me. She wanted others to notice her and who she was. But this woman needs nothing more than the love I give her.* He drew her closer to him, and she sighed. They lay on the floor next to the fire; he pushed her hair away from her face. Running his fingertips over her lips, he explored every part of her face. She was so beautiful; he remembered the Songs of Solomon, how he had praised the beauty of his wife. Wes understood the text for the first time in his life. He experienced the ecstasy that Solomon wrote about so vividly.

They intertwined themselves into that world that no one else could invade. It was just the two of them, their hearts beating in unison, their souls becoming one, their lives being joined together so that no one could separate them. He loved her with his whole being. They slept together by the fire, warmed not by the fire, but by their love for one another.

Chapter 12

Mandy and the staff readied the house for New Year's Eve. She wanted everything to be perfect for Wes' employees. The house was decorated; the dinner and hors d'oeuvres were ready. She was checking for any last-minute details that may need her attention before she went upstairs to dress. Sally assured her everything was perfect, and she needed to hurry and dress.

She felt a little queasy. She went upstairs and lay on the bed for just a minute to get her head straight before she bathed and dressed. Sally came in and drew a bath for her; she laid an ocean-blue gown on the bed for her to wear. She noticed she was not stirring around. She went over to check on her, and then she saw the blood. She screamed for Dr. Young. He came running up the stairs.

"Something's wrong, Dr. Young. I can't wake her, and she's bleeding!" Sally cried.

"Call 911. Sally, do it now! Mandy, Mandy, can you hear me?"

She moaned.

"Sally, get me my bag out of the closet and call Dr. Boyd. Her number is beside the bed."

Sally hurried to carry out Wes' requests. The doorbell rang. George answered it, and he was surprised to see the Emergency Medical Technicians standing at the door.

"We got a call."

"Dr. Young must have called."

Sally ran down the stairs. "This way, hurry."

George stood, looking up the stairs. He noticed the ambulance attendants went into the master suite. He ran into the kitchen. "Something is wrong with the missis."

Sharon dropped her apron and instructed the caterers to finish up. She ran up the stairs with George to see what was wrong. Sally was crying, and Wes was sitting by Mandy's side on the bed calling her name. Dr. Boyd came in the front door without knocking; she ran up the stairs, pushing Sharon and George aside. "Let me through."

The door shut; the doorbell rang again, and it was Grace, Ben, and Judy. They were all dressed and ready for the party. They were curious about the ambulance out front. George explained to them that something was wrong with Mandy. Grace pushed George aside and made her way up the stairs. She swung the door open and walked over beside the bed where the doctor was examining Mandy.

She walked to the opposite side of the bed. She crawled onto the bed with Mandy; she took her hand and started praying. "Devil, you won't have this child. It was conceived in love, and it will live. God, we praise you for intervening right now to save the life of this child."

Silence fell over the room as they watched Grace. Wes nodded at Dr. Boyd to let her know it was all right for Grace to be there.

Mandy opened her eyes. "What's going on? Is everything all right?"

Grace wiped her forehead. "Everything is going to be just fine, little lady. You're just going to have to take it a little easier from now on." Grace held her hand as Dr. Boyd examined her.

"It looks like the bleeding has stopped. How are you feeling, Mandy?" Dr. Boyd asked, checking her vital signs.

"I'm okay. Why are all of these people here?" Mandy asked, looking at the emergency attendants and Dr. Boyd.

"You gave everyone a little scare. How do you feel now?" Dr. Boyd asked

"I feel better. I was a little faint, and I was going to lie down for just a minute before I got dressed. I think I feel asleep. Is everything all right? Is the baby all right?"

"Everything's going to be fine. You've just been overdoing it, I think. Wes, could I talk to you a moment?" Dr. Boyd said, getting up from the bed. "I think you guys can go now, she'll be fine. Let me sign your report."

Grace held Mandy as she fought back tears of confusion. Dr. Boyd signed the papers then pulled Wes into the hallway, making sure the bedroom door was securely shut before beginning.

"Wes, she seems to be a little weak right now. Perhaps it might be better if she didn't work throughout the pregnancy. She's thirty-two years old and has never had a child before. It may be a little too strenuous for her. Let's put her on bed rest until I see her day after tomorrow. If anything else comes up, just call. I'm only two blocks down the street."

"Thank you, Debra. I'm glad you got here so fast. This one scared me," Wes said, releasing the tears.

She patted his shoulder. "Let me handle this. You take care of all those cancer patients. I'll take good care of Mandy. Bleeding in early stages of pregnancy is not that unusual. We'll keep an eye on her. Make her rest. You can let her lie on the couch downstairs so that she can partake of the evening without straining herself. Make sure she gets lots of rest, and you two need to talk about her discontinuing her work. I have a dinner party at my house, so if you need me, that's where I'll be. Goodnight, and Happy New Year."

Wes reentered the room then sat on the bed a tear rolled down his cheek. Mandy reached up and hugged him. "Everything's going to be fine. Please don't worry."

"Sally, will you help her get ready?" Wes reached over and held Mandy as Sally began preparations. "You better take it easy, my love. I need you for the rest of my life."

Grace helped Sally. Mandy insisted on wearing her gown and dressing for the party as she had planned. She was a hardheaded woman. She wanted everything to be perfect; it was her first party, and she felt she had already ruined it.

Downstairs, more guests were beginning to arrive. Ben and Judy wanted to know about Mandy; Wes let them know she would be fine.

Sally fixed her a comfortable place to sit for the evening. Wes carried her down the stairs and placed her on the sofa. She was beautiful in her blue dress and matching jewelry. She was glad to be with everyone else, but she didn't want them fussing over her.

Grace sat next to her; Sally stood nearby in case she needed anything. All of the guests had arrived. The house was lovely and the hors d'oeuvres were delicious. Everyone seemed to be having such a good time. People stopped by and talk to her. She felt like she was a part, even though she had to stay seated. She was happy watching her guests enjoy themselves. There was music and dancing, party hats and favors. Wes' staff thanked her for the party; she had a special surprise for each of them at their seats at the dining room table. Sally rang for dinner; Mandy insisted on walking to the dining room herself, although Wes was close by her side.

Wes made a toast. "To the love of my life, who has made all of this possible. To our friends who never gave up on us, and to my dedicated staff—without them my research would be nothing. Now, I think my wife has something for my staff."

Mandy looked at Wes; she was so proud of him. He'd dedicated his life to the healing of others. She was thankful God had seen fit for her to meet him on the road that day. She looked around the room at her guests; they were wonderful people. "To Wes' staff, by each of your plates there is a present. I would like for you to open them now. We wanted to let you know what you mean to us."

Each one opened their presents, revealing individualized plaques thanking them for their dedication to the Foundation. The staff was amazed at how beautiful they were, each one hand inscribed. "We're the ones that should be thankful. Wes is the best boss," Glenn, one of the lab techs, said. Everyone lifted their glasses. "To the world's greatest boss and his lovely bride."

George brought in a four-foot trophy and set it beside Wes. The inscription on the trophy said, "To Westbrook Young, Ph. D. Your work and dedication has saved countless lives." Wes was overwhelmed and couldn't speak. Mandy patted him on the back.

"I don't think I can stand many more surprises this evening. May God bless you all through this New Year. Happy New Year." His voice broke.

"To Wes!" everyone said, lifting their glasses.

After everyone had left, Wes carried Mandy upstairs. "If you get any heavier, I won't be able to carry you." He laughed, laying her on the bed. "Happy New Year, my love. Thank you for this evening. You made it so special for my staff. Richard was so impressed by how smoothly your party went. He said Mother couldn't have done it better herself. That's a compliment coming from Richard. He's a mommy's boy."

"Is that why he let Rachel go?"

"I would imagine. He always wants to please Mother. She was devastated when she found out about them. I get her names confused—Rachel, Anne. I've always known her as Rachel. I guess after tonight it won't matter," Wes said, winking his eye.

"What do you mean by that?"

"They are probably getting married as we speak."

"Are you serious? Right now?

"They are as sneaky as we were. He was so happy, he could hardly contain himself tonight."

"Why didn't someone tell me? I'm always the last to know," Mandy pouted.

"I was going to tell you, but then you got sick and I forgot until just now. Sorry, my love, it wasn't as if we were keeping it from you, just that I forgot." Wes lay on the bed next to Mandy. "You looked lovely in that gown tonight. Of course, you look lovely in anything. How are you feeling?"

"A little tired. I guess I need to concentrate on the wedding now. It seems so strange to talk about a wedding since we are already married," Mandy said, taking off her clothes. "I'm going to take a hot bath. He watched her as she sunk deep into the tub. He could tell she was exhausted, though she would never let on she was. He smiled at her; she reached out her hand to him. He walked over and sat beside the tub. He saw her eyes fill with tears.

"I really want this baby. I'm going to try real hard to keep it. It's scary. I've never had a child before. I've longed for one for a very long time. I really want to make you proud—"

"I am proud of you, of us. There's nothing you could do to change that. If it's meant to be for us to have this child, we will. Don't worry. That's the worst thing for you to do, worry." He reached over and hugged her tight. "You relax; enjoy your bath. Everything is going to be just fine. We need to decide what you're going to do about work. Have you thought about it?"

"That's all I've done is think about it. I think if all I do is make the pottery and paint it, then Anne could do the rest. Don't you think? If I get tired, I can go lie down in the cottage or come home, but it's important to me to keep the pottery shop open."

"You're supposed to be on bed rest. Debra said it's important you don't over do it. What if we took the building that was built for the staff and make your shop in there? There's a lot more room, and you'd be here where everyone could keep an eye on you. We could have it all done within a week. We don't ever use it. The staff lives in the guest-house. Then when you felt like working in the evenings, you could."

"What about my customers?"

"We'll put a sign on the road that you moved, and let them know where you've moved to. It seems like the best solution. Then Richard and Anne could expand the cottage. That would give them more room."

"I guess that sounds okay. It's just—"

"My love, Clay is gone. He doesn't hang around that old place waiting for you to come in every morning. He's gone. Someday you're going to have to accept that. Perhaps the move will help you let go. Just think about it." He dropped her hand and went to take a shower.

His heart was heavy; he knew she had loved Clay, but he had never really realized how much. Now he knew. He had been her life; she still had not cut the ties that bound them together. She still lived in a fantasy world that he was still there waiting for her. Wes thought, *A pottery shop is a pottery shop. The location really doesn't matter. She's the potter now, not Clay.* He would be glad when that pottery shop was gone. It wasn't as if he wanted to take Clay's place in her life, he was just hoping what they had would be enough for her. That it was she thought about when she sat at the potter's wheel instead of Clay. He felt silly being jealous of a dead man, but he was.

Mandy got ready for bed; she buried herself in the covers. It was cold outside. The tide was changing, and the tidal winds were howling outside the window.

Wes lit the fireplace and jumped into bed. He reached for her; she didn't respond. He knew he had invaded that place she shared with Clay. Those places where in her mind they were still young playing on the beach together. He listened to her cry into her pillow, and he knew there was nothing he could do. He could only hope one day she could forget her youth with Clay and accept her future with him.

It wasn't as if she didn't love Wes, she did. But she still loved Clay. She had not asked for him to die that day. She hadn't wanted her life torn apart. She had just wanted to live with Clay the rest of her life. Here she was in a strange house with different people trying to carve out a new existence with Wes. It was unfair to call it an existence; she wanted a life, a life with Wes. Why wouldn't her heart let her let Clay go once and for all? Perhaps moving the shop would help her let go of her old life and move into her new life. She tried to sleep, but sleep was far from her.

She lay awake listening to the howling wind outside. She got up and watched the wind blowing across the gardens. The sky was angry; the moon was hidden behind the clouds. There were no stars to be seen. She was lonely; though she had a house full of people who loved her dearly, she was lonely. She had just this very moment realized that even though she appeared happy on the outside, she was unhappy on the inside. She looked over at Wes; he was so handsome. He was kind and loving and would give her the whole world, but he couldn't give her Clay back.

She walked over to the windows, and she watched as the trees were tossed to and fro. That's the way she felt, tossed into a world that she knew nothing about. She gently opened the door and stepped out onto the large patio. She walked over to the edge; she could see the light-house and the rock levee. Tears began to fill her eyes. Something was tearing at her heart. She couldn't control the sobs that rose from inside of her. She looked down the shoreline to her little cottage; she could see the lights were still on. She walked down the stairs to the garden; the grounds were so beautiful, she walked out to the beach and started walking toward her old house.

The wind was cold, and she realized she was in her nightclothes and barefooted. She didn't care, something was driving her and she had to go. She walked up to Clay's old shed, where he had kept his tools. She opened the door and turned on the light. She looked around until she saw what looked like a canvas covered by a tarp. She reached over and pulled the tarp down to find the portrait of Clay she had painted one day while they were on the beach. She dragged it out. She looked deep into his eyes. *What is it?* She thought, *It is his eyes; there is something about his eyes.* She looked deep into them. *There is sadness in his eyes.* She pulled the picture out into the light. *Yes, that is what it was; he was not happy. How could he not have been happy? How did the portrait get in here?* She looked and found a black box underneath where the painting had been sitting. *What is this?* She opened the box; it was filled with letters bound with a ribbon. She took the package of letters out and realized they were from a woman. She opened one of the letters; it was dated two days before Clay's death. She felt the sting of the tears as she began to read.

My dearest Clay: Though it has only been a week since we last met, I feel like it has been an eternity. I can feel your presence with me now. The remembrance of our last meeting has left me wanting you all the more. I know you explained to me Mandy was not well and you couldn't see hurting her with a divorce right now. I long for you to be here with me. I can't wait for your return so that we can lie on the beach and love each other again. I miss you. I know you have an obligation to Mandy, but I pray one day, she will let you go.

When you told me the story of how you met her and how you felt obligated to marry her because she was all alone, it only made me love you more. But now it's our time and she needs to move on with her life, just as we should move forward with ours.

I hope you will reconsider my invitation to come and live with me. You can move your pottery shop here and create your beautiful pieces for me instead of for her. I don't mean to be insensitive, but too much time has passed, and I just can't wait forever. You know we were meant to be together. Come home to me soon. With all my love, Sarah.

The stack of letters was high. She looked through the hundreds of letters. Some of them were five years old. All of them bid him to come to her. She put the painting up in the light again and looked at his face. She remembered the day she had painted it. They were having a picnic on the beach; she brought a canvas out and painted the portrait while he posed for her. He wasn't happy; she wasn't his princess as he had always called her. She was someone he felt sorry for.

Ten years of lies; ten years of thinking they were the only two people on earth that mattered. But he had led two separate lives, one with her and another one with this Sarah. She looked at the address; it was Spring Creek. He had spent a lot of time in Spring Creek, with Sarah.

She threw the painting on the floor. She grabbed the letters, and she noticed something shiny in the bottom of the box. It was an engagement ring. The ring was attached to a note. She opened the note.

> Dearest Clay: I know you have made your decision, so I'm returning your ring. I know Mandy needs you. So do I, but I love you enough to let you go to her. I don't know how I'll live without you. I've loved you all of my life. But I won't stand in the way of your happiness if she's what makes you happy. I pray we can be together someday. Sarah.

She sat down on a crate; she felt dizzy. Her fairy tale was just that, a fairy tale. She couldn't contain the anger, the hurt any longer. She started tearing through the boxes of Clay's things. She had not been the one to put his things away, Pastor Johnny had. *Had he known of the ten-year love affair Clay had with another woman?* She could hear her name being called in the distance. She didn't care. She had to know what else he had hidden from her. She ripped through the boxes, tossing things onto the floor. Another box fell on the floor; it contained pictures. She opened the box and started looking though them; they were not pictures of her and Clay, but of this other woman and Clay. *They were happy.* She looked into his eyes. *He was happy.*

She sat back on the floor, boxes strewn all around her. She heard her name being called. She couldn't reply; she could only cry. The day Clay died, we had been arguing about Clay spending so much time away from home. *Was I suspicious then? Yes, that's what had started the argument. I had asked him that day if there was another woman, and Clay hadn't answered. I had demanded to know, but he wouldn't say anything, he just walked away. I had been furious. I had stormed out of the house and ran onto the rock levee, waiting for him on the levee. I knew he would come for me, and he did. But he never returned.*

That day at the marina, a beautiful blonde-headed girl was weeping. Yes, she could remember now. She was weeping; she followed Clay's body to the ambulance. Wes pronounced him dead; I fainted. It was all coming back to her. The blonde-headed woman was at the hospital when I arrived to claim Clay's body. It was her that day. She had come to see the love of her life, but he was dead. I had thought the woman had come to see someone else, but it was Clay. She was at the marina when they brought his body in.

I know this woman; the three of us were in high school together. She was the one Clay's family had talked about all those years. The one he should have married. Clay's mother had never accepted me as Clay's wife—that's why the ring, the pictures, and the letters. How could I have been so blind? She understood so many things now. Why Clay would stand at the window looking so far away; he was longing for her. He would walk down the beach by himself and cry; I had seen him, though he didn't know she had.

How could I make such a perfect marriage out of all of this? The voice calling her name got closer; it was Wes. She didn't want to face him right now. There were too many things she needed to remember.

He ran into the building, out of breath. "Mandy, what are you doing? It's thirty-two degrees out here. Look, you're not even dressed. What are you doing?"

He saw the mess around her. He saw the opened letters in her hand; he saw the portrait. "Come with me, honey. Let's go home."

She didn't move; she just sat looking at the evidence of a failed marriage. She had tied Clay down; she had not held him with her love. He had been in prison; he longed for Sarah, but he had stayed with her out of pity. She lifted the letters up and showed them to Wes.

"I know, my love. I know." He hung his head as he sat next to her.

"You knew?"

"Yes, I did. I've known since that night at the restaurant when you

223

remembered I pronounced Clay dead. Sarah had come to me at the marina that day, devastated. I had thought she was Clay's wife. I told her to follow the ambulance to the hospital. I didn't find out until that night at the restaurant that you were his wife."

"You must have thought I was such a fool to hold onto him when you knew the truth about him."

"No, I didn't. I thought you were a dedicated wife. That's when I knew you were the woman for me. The rest, time would have to take care of. And it has, right now. Now you know. It's over. There's nothing any of us can do to relive the past or to change it in anyway."

"But I kept him in prison for ten years."

"No, you didn't. It was Clay's decision to stay with you. I don't think it was out of pity. I think it was out of love. He was torn between his love for the two of you, and he chose you. That's the way I look at it."

"To think you know someone so well and find out you don't know them at all. How could he have cheated on me the way he did, for ten years?"

"Some people just can't make up their minds, and they get hung between two people. That's what I think happened to him. He was a man of honor, and he stood up for the promises he made to you. He tried to, anyway."

"How can you defend him?"

"Because we have the same taste in women. He just didn't know what he had, and I do. And I'll spend the rest of my life proving it to you, if you'll let me."

She put the letters down on the box, and she looked at the ring. Wes could see the question in her eyes.

"They were engaged before he asked you to marry him."

"How do you know what happened?"

"I talked to Sarah one day in my office, after our venture down to the Bahamas. She came in, and I just had to know who she was. So I asked her. She told me the whole story. She went to school with you and Clay. She always had a crush on him. They saw each other for about six months, and he proposed to her, gave her the ring and all. You came back into his life, and he chose you instead. She was devastated; she even moved back to Spring Creek to be near him. Clay went to South Carolina for a potter's convention. She was there for a client meeting. They met again, had dinner, and, you know, old feelings came back. Their affair lasted about nine years then Clay died. End of story."

Mandy sat with her mouth open, listening to Wes tell her about her late husband's affair. She placed the ring in the box with the letters. She looked over at the portrait and stood up. She put the box under her arm and walked out the door.

Anne and Richard were standing on the back porch; they had seen the light and thought someone was robbing the shed. When they saw Wes run into the shed, they waited to make sure everything was all right. Anne knew what was in the shed; when she was moving some of Mandy's things out, she had seen the box of letters and had read a couple of them before putting them back where she had found them. She had told Richard what she had found, and they both went to Wes.

Wes had gone into the shed one night while Mandy was asleep, and he had read all of the letters; he had seen the portrait, and he had even seen the ring with the note attached. He had carefully placed everything back where he had found it. Then he prayed Mandy would find out the truth, though he would not be the one who would tell her.

Mandy looked at her friends standing on the porch looking at them. She turned and looked at Wes. "I want to give the box of letters, the ring, and the portrait to Sarah. These are her memories, not mine." She handed the box to Wes and walked up the beach to their house.

She had not even felt the cold until she started home. The tears seemed to freeze on her face. She was leaving behind a life full of lies and deception that she had mistaken for a life of love. She was glad she knew; she had been troubled since Clay's death. Now she knew. She had tried to forget, when she needed to remember. She had recreated a perfect marriage in her mind, a marriage that had never existed. She crawled into the bed and slept.

The morning brought the wind howling around the house, the rain beating on the windows like an unwelcome friend. Wes decided to go into the office later this morning; he wanted to make sure Mandy was all right; she had been asleep when he returned home. He would take her to her doctor's appointment and then to work.

He sat in the kitchen reading the paper; Sharon knew something was not right with her employer, so she didn't pry. She busied herself around him. She called Sally in to take Mandy her breakfast. He looked up from the paper but didn't say a word.

Sally took the tray up the stairs where Mandy was still in bed. The curtains were already opened, so she set the tray down and started getting Mandy's bath ready. She laid her clothes on the couch and started cleaning up. "Are you going to sleep in this morning, Ms. Mandy?" Sally asked in her usual chipper tone.

"I'm on bed rest until I see the doctor today. So I guess I should stay in bed."

"Perhaps a nice hot bath would make you feel better. Why don't you take your bath, and I'll finish cleaning the room."

Mandy dragged herself out of bed; she soaked in the hot bath. It did feel so good. She sank into the tub and let the hot water warm her body. She heard Wes in the bedroom; she called to him. He stuck his head in the door. "Please come over and sit for a minute."

He came in and sat on the side of the tub, and his eyes searched hers for some sort of evidence that everything was all right. "How are you this morning?" he whispered.

"I'm better today than yesterday. I thought I was giving up my whole life, but I found out I wasn't giving up anything. Just a lot of assuredness and pain. I had blocked out so much of the truth to believe a lie. I'm sorry I put you through all of that, crazy, huh?"

"No, sometimes the truth is too painful. We believe what we want to believe. There's nothing wrong with that. It was the way you handled your grief. You had felt like it was your fault for so long, and it wasn't. Do you really know what happened that day?"

"No, I don't think I do."

"And you may never know, but that shouldn't prevent you from having a future."

"I love you, Dr. Young," she said, kissing him on his hand.

"I love you, my love, more than you will ever know. I won't ever hurt you like that. I was hurt just like that myself. I found out after Kay died she had had an affair with Chad."

"Your younger brother?"

"Yes, is that a kicker or what? He loves women; he always has. He couldn't resist Kay. She had a way about her that let other men know she was available. That was the lie I had to live down. Everyone knew;

I knew, I just couldn't face it. That's why it took me so long to trust again. When I met you, and I saw the way you loved Clay, I said, *Wes, that's the woman for you.* See, my love, we aren't so different after all. We both need dedicated love. Perhaps we can help each other heal."

"You're the healer, not me."

"That's where you're wrong. Your love has healed so many people, including me. I knew I wanted to spend the rest of my life with you. The way you made me feel like I was the only man in the world for you."

"You are the only man in the world for me. Thank you for helping me find out the truth."

"I didn't do anything."

"Yes, you did. I know you. You prayed I would find out, didn't you?"

"Yes, I did. I knew if you found out the truth, you could let him go and love me," Wes confessed.

"Let's make it a lifelong deal, deal?"

"Deal."

"Look at my stomach. The baby's already starting to show. I'm losing my schoolgirl figure already."

"I forgot to tell you. Young babies are always big babies. So get ready to have a ten-pounder." They both laughed.

Wes wanted to be at the doctor's with Mandy. He wanted to make sure last night had not hurt her. He waited in the waiting room with all the other expectant mothers while they were getting Mandy ready in the back. Dr. Boyd came out and motioned for him to come back.

"I wanted to run an ultrasound today to make sure everything is okay after the bleeding. I thought maybe Daddy would want to be present. We may be able to tell the baby's sex today. We'll see, put on that gown right over there, and come into this room when you're ready." Dr. Boyd went into the room where Mandy was lying on a table.

Wes walked in, and Mandy started to laugh. "What?" he asked.

"You look so cute in your gown."

"Look at you, my love, we match."

Dr. Boyd started the ultrasound. She explained each step of the procedure to Wes and Mandy. She showed them the baby's toes and fingers, its head and chest, and you could see the heart beating. Everything looked good. "Let's see if we can tell the sex. Sometimes you can't this early, but let's try. There we go, see? That looks like you're probably going to have a boy."

Wes was glowing with pride. "A boy, huh? A boy. A boy's good, don't you think, Mandy? We can handle a boy."

Mandy and Dr. Boyd looked at Wes, and they both laughed. "Dr. Young, I'm not going to have to pick you up off the floor or anything, am I? Because if so, sit right over here. Take a deep breath and be still." They laughed. "Looks like everything is fine, Mandy. I still want you to take it easy. Have you discussed your work?"

"Yes, we have. Wes is going to move my shop over to the staff house on our new place. That way I'll be there in case I need something. Isn't that right, honey?"

He was glad she had made that decision. "Yes, that's right."

"I think that's much better. Okay, you can get dressed. She's all yours, Dr. Young. Mandy, I'll see you next month, unless anything comes up ... which in that case, call me."

Wes was relieved everything was all right; he had been so worried something was wrong. Though he didn't know much about obstetrics, he thought things should go smoother than they had. Perhaps Mandy's age was a factor; perhaps it was all of the stress she had been under. He was just glad mother and baby was fine. The thought of having a son made him proud; one day he would have someone to follow in his footsteps. He would have the opportunity to show his son that wealth was love of family and friends, not money.

He smiled as he led her to the Hummer, helping her climb into the truck.

He was proud of the way Mandy had handled the situation last night. He was happy; life seemed to finally be on track. Now he could relax and concentrate on his work and being a good husband. No more living with the ghost of Clay. He had destroyed his own memory, with the double life he led. Wes didn't want to tarnish the man's life, but he was glad Mandy had found the letters and the ring. That was all the proof she needed to know life would be better now, with him.

Mandy was relieved that all was well with the baby; she had been so worried. This was her first child, and she really didn't know what to expect. She could go to work knowing that her little one would be fine. The thought of a son was exciting; he would be a little Wes. She was glad she and Clay had not had children. She was glad she was having Wes' son; Wes would love them both. Wes wasn't a liar, as Clay had been. He had lied to her for nine years. She had lived the lie and was even willing to spend the rest of her life believing a lie. God was good; he had led her to the truth. She could finally let Clay rest in peace, and she could live in peace.

She smiled at her husband, who was carefully navigating the Hummer out of the parking lot.

"I really don't want you going to work today. I'll have a crew come in and move your shop starting today. If you go in, I know you'll have to help, and Anne can do what needs to be done. You should concentrate on how you want the shop laid out. Maybe that would be a good thing for you to do today. Go out into the staff house and think about how you want things set up. Have you ever been inside?"

"No, I don't believe I have. I don't want to talk about the shop. I want to talk about us."

Wes felt his blood run cold; fear crept up the back of his neck. What was it she needed to talk to him about? He thought they had said everything last night. "Okay."

"I'm really sorry for the way I've been acting. It was almost as if I was being unfaithful to Clay. What a laugh, huh? You've been so patient and caring. You've allowed me to put the past to rest. I needed that. I needed to find out about Clay's life. I thought I knew, but was I ever shocked when I found the black box in the shed. Can we act like today is the first day of the rest of our lives? Can we start over?"

"I don't know if we can start over." He looked down at her stomach. "But we can sure have fun trying."

She laughed and hit his arm. "Wes, you're so silly sometimes."

"Look, you're the one that took me seriously. We were just having fun." He laughed. "I'm a fun kind of guy, don't you think?" He relaxed; he thought she had needed something else. Some other closure ... he didn't know what he thought. He was glad it was finally over.

"You really don't want to know what I think. Can I spend money on the new shop?" Mandy asked.

"What kind of money?"

"You know, for redecorating."

"Don't you make good money?"

229

"Yes, but I'd rather use yours."

"Get out of here. You need to reinvest your money into your own business. If you need money, you know everything I have is yours. But if you just want my money, forget it." He laughed.

She hit him on the arm again, and then she reached over and gave him a big kiss. "You know you love me, and you would give me anything I asked for."

"I sure do love you, and yes, I guess I would give you anything you asked for. What do you need?"

"Nothing. I just wanted to know if I wanted it, I could have it."

"You're a mean woman, Mandy Young."

She laughed. "Where are you taking me? This isn't the way home."

"You know, you're right."

Mandy looked out the window; it looked like they were going to Spring Creek. She felt her heart skip a beat. "Wes, where are we going?"

"You said you wanted today to be the first day of the rest of our lives. If that's true, then you have one thing left undone."

"Oh, Wes, we're not going to Sarah's house, are we?"

"Yes, we are, my love. I think you two have a lot to talk about."

"How do you know where she lives?"

"I called her this morning. She's wanted to talk to you since Clay's death. She just didn't know when would be a good time. Now is as good a time as any. We can't start over until we bury this ghost that seems to be lurking in the background all of the time. I want it over, Mandy, once and for all." Wes raised his voice to her for the first time since they had met. "I'm sorry, it's just gotten to be so crazy, and I want it over, don't you?"

"Yes, I do, and you're right. Now is as good a time as any, I guess."

"I know you. If you don't talk to her, it will eat away at you. So let's just get it over with, for me if for nothing else. I think you owe me that much. I want you to return the black box of letters and the ring. It's not my place. I would do anything for you, but this is something you have to do yourself. I'm going to drop you off. I have to go over to Todd's house, and I will pick you up when you're ready. Just call me."

"Thanks, Wes. I don't think I would have the guts to do it myself. You're right. It is my responsibility."

Mandy didn't know what she would encounter. This woman had

lived without the man she loved because of her. What did she need to talk to Mandy about? She could only wait and see.

Wes stopped and opened the door for her. "We're here. She lives right there. She's waiting for you, so don't be scared. Just do what you need to do. I'll be waiting." He kissed her and hugged her tight. "You'll be fine."

Mandy walked up to the door, and she hesitated before she knocked. She heard the sound of a little girl talking to her mom. She knocked. Sarah came to the door, and she had a big smile on her face. "Good morning, please come in. I've wanted to talk to you for such a long time. I'm sorry it had to be like this. Your husband told me you found a box of my letters and my ring."

"Yes, last night, I found out everything." Mandy tried not to show anger.

"Well, you didn't find out everything, but I'm sure you found out enough for you to swallow. Come in here, Amy, there's someone I want you to meet. This is Ms. Mandy. Mandy, this is Amy, Clay's daughter."

Mandy felt the color drain out of her face; the little girl looked just like Clay. She had long dark brown curly hair and blue eyes, and she was beautiful. She climbed up in Mandy's lap and gave her a big kiss.

"My daddy taught me to do that. He died, you know," Amy said, smiling at Mandy.

"Yes, I know."

"Look, your hair looks like mine," she said, brushing Mandy's hair with her hand. "Your eyes look like mine too. Did you know my daddy? Momma says I look just like Daddy, but I think I look like you."

"You do look like your daddy. He looked a lot like me, I guess." Mandy smiled at Amy. She looked up at Sarah, shocked.

"Amy, you can go over and play with Macy now. Stay in the fence and don't eat those berries. Here, put your coat on," Sarah said, ushering little Amy out to play.

Mandy was still in shock. "How old is she?"

"She's seven years old. She's in the first grade. I kept her out of school today because I wanted you to meet her. She looks just like Clay, don't you think? She's been a godsend since his death. You, on the other hand, have not been as lucky. I had Amy. You've had no one. I wanted to come over to the pottery shop. I heard you had reopened it, but I just didn't know how you would take it until you found out the truth. Wes said you found—"

Mandy handed her the box of letters and the ring. "I found this in the shed. Pastor Johnny put them there. I didn't—"

"I know you didn't know. We were careful not to let anyone know but the people here in Spring Creek, and Pastor Johnny of course. The people here didn't know about you, so it seemed like the right thing to do. I know you have a million questions. I'm ready to answer them all. Are you all right? You look a little pale."

"Yes, I'm fine. I just left the doctor's office. She said I'm fine."

"Your husband told me about your little one on the way. I'm so glad. It makes all of this easier."

"Easier? How can any of this be easy? I was married to a man for ten years. He had an affair with you for nine of those ten years, now I find out he fathered a child. Sarah, this is anything but easy."

"But you're remarried. You're going to have your own child. I thought now would be a good time. The pain—"

"You don't know anything about my pain. I'm sorry. Please forgive me. I don't want to take my anger out on you. It's Clay I'm mad at. How did all of this happen like this?"

"I met Clay in high school. Remember, we were in the same class? We fell in love right off the bat, love at first sight, if you will. You and he had been friends since you were children. You had gone to live with your aunt, and Clay and I dated. We got engaged, and then you came back. You moved into the little duplexes down the street from Clay's house. Clay felt like he belonged to you. You two had made a pact or something when you were children. He knew you were all alone in the world—"

"He felt sorry for me is what you want to say. You said it well in your letter."

"Yeah, something like that. He came to me and told me he couldn't marry me. He had made a promise, and he had to keep it. I was devastated. It was only two weeks before the wedding. Our mothers had already planned everything. It was like getting left at the altar. I tried to honor his wishes. I really did. Then about a year later he went to a potter's convention or something. I was there on business too. When we saw each other again after so long, well, it just happened. He told me he could never see me again, that he was married, and he loved his wife. He came by my house the following week. Then he came twice a week to see me for two years, and then I got pregnant with Amy. He was so happy. He started coming to see me as often as he could. He would deliver pottery, come to see us, and go home to you. He did that for the last six years of his life. I wrote to him all the time. It seemed to help. There were times I came into the shop when you were away. We used to go fishing together, we used to—"

"What's your reason for telling me this, do you want to show me Clay loved you more?"

"Not at all. He loved you more. If not, he would have left you and come to stay with me and Amy. He chose you, Mandy. You should be proud of that."

"Proud that I lived a lie all those years? I used to catch him crying. He wanted to be with you and his child."

"Things had been so hard for you. He told me about your father. The awful things he did to you. He used to cry about it. It tore at his soul. He couldn't hurt you any more than you had been hurt."

"Don't you see? He did hurt me. He let me live a lie. I have spent the last two years believing the lie. I almost lost Wes over the lie. My God, he almost destroyed me. Now you want me to accept the fact—"

"Mandy, please, it's over. Let's not think about what could have happened. We have to live with what did happen. Amy knows all about you, and she's been anxious to meet you. She's been—"

"She's been in my shop. Last week. I remember seeing her. I gave her a—"

"A bird wind chime. She treasures it. Please come see where she keeps it." Sarah led Mandy into Amy's room; the wind chime was hung over her bed. She had lots of pottery in her room, toys Clay had made for her. "She thinks you're Clay's sister. When my mom went into the shop, she knew that was where her daddy worked. My mom told her you were her daddy's sister. She wanted to personally meet you after that. I'm sorry. My mom didn't know what to say. She didn't know Amy had been there before."

"Why did she hang it over her bed?"

"So that it would be the last thing she saw at night before she went to sleep. She thinks her daddy sent you here to watch over her for him.

She's a child, and children have vivid imaginations. You'll find out for yourself soon."

Mandy wasn't angry; she was honored. This little girl thought she was here to watch over her for her daddy. "I don't know what to say. All of this has been such a shock. I wasn't expecting this. She's a beautiful little girl. You're blessed to have her. I know it made losing Clay a little easier having Amy here. I'm glad for you."

"You will know true love with your husband. He's a wonderful person. I met him a while back at his office. Do you know what the baby is yet?"

"I think so. We found out this morning. A boy, Dr. Boyd thinks," Mandy said, rubbing her stomach.

"You'll love Dr. Boyd. She's a wonderful doctor. She delivered Amy. I date one of your husband's employees, Glenn Miller. We're supposed to be married next month. I'm so happy; so is Amy. She loves Glenn, and he loves her. I went by to see him the day I met your husband."

"Wes."

"Pardon me?"

"My husband's name is Wes. Surely you understand, all of this is a shock for me," Mandy said, tears streaming down her cheeks.

"I do realize now what this must be doing to you. I think Clay wanted the best of both worlds. He said you weren't ready to have children. He always wanted children. That's why he was so happy when Amy was born. I wanted him to get a divorce, but he wouldn't. He said he made you a promise—"

"He did. He said we would always be together. He never told me he wanted children. I always thought we had time. He lied; that's all he did, lie to me. What a fool you must think I am."

"Not at all, I was hoping we could—"

"Please don't ask me that. Not right now. Maybe later when all of this has sunk in, but not now. Wes knew about Amy?"

"I don't think he knew she was Clay's daughter, but he knew I had a daughter," Sarah said, moving next to Mandy.

Mandy felt lightheaded. How could she not have known? Sarah was so pretty; she had long blonde hair and green eyes, she was tall and slim, and she had a smile that covered her entire face. She seemed to be kind and generous; she loved her daughter; she had loved Clay. It was Mandy who had taken Clay away from Sarah; Sarah had not taken him from her. "You must have been heartbroken when he broke his engagement to you. You seem like you really loved him."

"I will always love him. He was my first love."

"Mine too. Clay told you about me and my family, everything?"

"Yes, everything. He used to sit and talk about you for hours. What a special person you were. I didn't want to hear it, but he needed to talk, and I needed him to be here for me, so … I let him talk. I used to be so jealous of you. You had everything in life I wanted. When he died we both lost out. Now we both have a second chance at life. I'm going to take mine. I hope you will too."

"It's a little late for me not to take it." Mandy laughed as she rubbed her stomach. "Thank you for talking to me. Wes was right. I needed to know the whole truth. I've wanted him to be like Clay, isn't that funny? Now I'm glad he isn't."

"I'm glad you came. If you change your mind about Amy, let me know. Remember, she thinks you're her daddy's sister," Sarah said, walking Mandy to the door.

"I'll think about it. Why didn't you come to the New Year's Eve party we gave for Wes' staff?" Mandy stood on the front porch.

"I thought that would be a little forward of me, to go to your house and all." Sarah looked away.

"Next time we have a party for his staff, please come. It would be a pleasure to have you at my home. Thank Amy for me. Take good care of that little girl. Bring her by the shop sometimes. I'll make her some more wind chimes." Mandy was glad she was outside so that she could breathe. She called Wes to come pick her up. Todd only lived two houses down. She thought about the day she got the puppy. He knew about Clay and Sarah and even about little Amy. What must he have been thinking of her?

Wes picked her up at the end of the driveway. He kept looking at her, as if she would tell him what they talked about. She looked straight ahead. He could no longer contain himself. "Well?"

"Well what?"

"Mandy, don't play games with me. Is the little girl Clay's?"

"Yes, she is."

"I knew it. I just knew it. The resemblance was too much. Actually, you could have been her mother, don't you think?"

"We do favor, yes. But I'm not her mother. She thinks I'm Clay's sister."

"What?"

"One day her grandmother brought her into the shop. Amy knew that was where her daddy worked, so her grandmother told her I was Clay's sister. She thinks I'm her long-lost aunt."

"You've got to be kidding."

Mandy shot him one of those *no-I'm-not-kidding* looks. He looked back at the road. She could not believe what she had just encountered. She knew it was the Christian thing to invite Sarah to the company parties; Glenn would want her there. Amy was a very pretty little girl. Perhaps one day Amy and their little boy would be friends. The way life was going … nothing was impossible.

"How about me taking the rest of the day off and looking at the servant's house with you today? I called a moving company. They will start moving your things tomorrow. Anne and Richard are packing up your pottery now."

"Richard?"

"I gave him the day off. It's their honeymoon today."

"What? They did get married yesterday?"

"Yes, Judy called Mother. She's jealous because Ben won't ask her to marry him. So she squealed on Anne and Richard."

"Too late now." Mandy laughed.

"I thought that would make you feel better. Boy, if you get any prettier, I don't know what I'm going to do."

"I'll bet you say that to all the women." She laughed.

"No, my love, I only say it to you. I think it about other women."

"You're mean."

"Come on. Let's see what we can do with this building," Wes said, getting out of the car.

"Let's do it." Mandy followed.

The old staff house was a very nice place. It had been restored in the eighties also. It had an old colonial-style porch that wrapped around the house. Large double doors were at the entrance, and a foyer led to several rooms off to each side. The staircase was spiral like the one in the big house but smaller. It had a kitchen, a living room, dining room, and seven bedrooms. She would need four walls to be torn out so that she could have a large display room for her finished pieces. She wanted the work area to overlook the display floor.

Wes called a contractor and asked him to come over and look at what she wanted to see if it was possible. It might require closing the shop for renovations for a couple of weeks, but it would give her something to do. She was excited about the shop being close to her. Sometimes at night she loved to go in the shop and create new pieces. During the day it was hectic to get anything done.

She looked over the house; she would even have a place for an office. At her old cottage the pottery shop was built onto the house. She had used the money Catherine's rich friends had spent at the shop to build the display area. It had served really well, and she wanted to use the same set-up here.

Ace Construction Company drove up; Wes met the man at the truck. They walked into the house together. Mandy was upstairs looking out the window. In the back of the house it was all glass. She wanted her work-shop in the back, so that she would have the view of the bay while she was working. She heard them downstairs talking about the weight-bearing walls and pillars to sustain the weight. He asked about the upstairs, and Wes told him the upstairs wouldn't need renovating.

The gentleman gave Wes an estimate and told him it would take two weeks for them to complete the work. Wes asked them to get started in the morning. Mandy ran down the stairs. "They can do it?"

"Yes, he said it would take about two weeks to complete. You shouldn't be running down those stairs. What if you tripped and fell?"

"Well, I didn't. I'll be more careful. How much is it going to cost?"

"You don't worry about cost. Let me handle the cost," he said, hugging her tight.

"But you told me this morning—"

"Never mind what I told you this morning. Your work area will be big enough to put a playpen in it, so little Wes can hang out with you," he said, rubbing her stomach.

"What is this 'little Wes' stuff? We're not going to have a 'junior,' are we? I really don't want a junior. Let's name him something like Brook. He will still have part of your name, and he's not a junior."

Chapter 13

Two weeks went by quickly. The new pottery shop was wonderful; it was spacious with seascape designs on the walls. Large pillars stood in the middle of the room, adding a touch of elegance to the storefront and display area. She had a large workroom at the back of the house. Her kilns had their own special room to block the heat from coming into the shop. Wes didn't want the baby to have access to the hot kilns.

They decorated the porch with some of her abstract pieces. They built a pond and fountain out front, demonstrating her garden pieces. She was so happy the shop was finally finished. She and Anne had finished setting up all of the shelves of pottery and the workshop out back. She had a large back porch to set her barrels of clay on while they were settling. They left the upstairs as it was; it had a bathroom and two bedrooms. The bedrooms would come in handy when the baby was born. Sally and George were in and out checking on her, making sure she wasn't overdoing it. She loved to work in her shop.

Anne and Mandy were sitting on the front porch drinking water when Wes got home from the office. He made his way over to the new shop; he saw the two of them sitting on the porch. "You're never going to make any money that way, my love," he said, sitting next to her.

"The grand opening is tomorrow. I ran ads in the newspaper and on the radio. We should be swamped," she said, leaning her head on his shoulder. "I'm tired. Take me home."

"Anne, why don't you and Richard come over for dinner tonight? Sharon is making something real good," Wes said, helping Mandy up.

"What are you having?"

"I don't know, but if I know Sharon, it will be real good."

"Wes, you're too much. Mandy, how do you put up with him? I'll talk to Richard about dinner."

"I already have. He says it's up to you."

"Any time I don't have to cook, we'll be here."

"See you around six-thirty then. Tell my brother I love him."

"Will do," she said, getting up from the porch.

Mandy and Wes went arm-in-arm to the house. She wanted a hot bath and a few minutes to wind down. Sally had her bath ready for her. She climbed in and lay back to relax. Wes came in to talk. She didn't want to talk; she just wanted to relax and soak. Duke came in and lay beside the tub. He had missed them; the past month, he had been in obedience school, as he had gotten too big to handle. Wes wanted him to go through school so that he would obey them, especially with the baby coming. Duke seemed glad to be home.

She sat and listened to him talk about his day at work. He had made a very significant discovery today, and he was rattling on about it. She didn't understand half of what he was saying. She just nodded and said, "Really?" That seemed to pacify him.

She noticed her stomach was getting bigger every day. She felt something; she sat up. It was like a butterfly in her stomach.

"What's wrong?"

"Nothing, I think I just had a quickening. I felt the baby move," she cried.

"What? Can I feel it?"

"I don't know. Put your hand right here, that's where it happened. Did you feel that?"

"No, wait, yes—I felt that. He's a kicker."

"No, he's not. They start moving about this time. Dr. Boyd said I should be feeling it any day now," Mandy explained.

"My love, he's really beginning to show. Look at your stomach."

"I look at my stomach every day. You don't ever look at me anymore." She pouted.

He jumped in the tub with her, clothes and all. He started stripping his clothes off and throwing them on Duke. His three-piece suit was soon soaking wet.

"What are you doing?"

"You said I don't ever look at you anymore. Well, baby, I'm looking at you. Slide over, Daddy's coming in." They both laughed.

Sally walked to the door. "Is everything all right, Ms. Mandy?"

"Run, Sally, while you still can." She laughed from the bathroom.

"Newlyweds."

Richard and Anne arrived about six-thirty; Anne was all excited about the grand opening tomorrow. She and Sharon were in the dining room chatting away when Mandy and Wes came down.

Sally rolled her eyes when she saw them. Wes gave her a big hug. "You're a good woman, Sally, and we really appreciate you." He laughed.

"Thank you, sir," she replied, shaking her head.

"What was that all about?" Anne asked.

Mandy and Wes laughed. "Private joke," Wes replied.

"How are you two doing? Married life treating you good?" Mandy asked, sitting at the table.

"Judy called Mother. She is furious, and she said Father refuses to talk to me," Richard said, helping Anne with her chair. "You knew that would be their reaction when you got married. Don't worry about it. They'll come around. We felt the baby move this afternoon. It was an enlightening experience. All those scientists that say life is not considered life at conception don't know what they are talking about. That little one was moving all around," Wes said proudly.

Mandy watched Anne; she was quiet. Mandy knew something was bothering her. She reached over and patted her hand. Anne smiled and sighed deeply. Mandy knew she felt bad because Richard's parents had not responded in a positive way about their marriage. Anne loved Richard, and she didn't want him to be an outcast in his family because of her.

She excused herself from the table; Mandy followed her. She was in the living room crying, and Mandy held her until she finished. "I know you think I'm crazy, but Richard has always been a mama's boy. If you could have seen the look on his face when his mother hung up on him. He tried to hide it. He even tried to make me believe it didn't bother him, but I know it did. It was written all over his face. Mandy, how do we deal with people like that? Why can't they just let Richard live his own life?"

"Richard will have to be the one that stands up to them. He'll have to show them it's his life and he'll live it the way he sees fit." She brushed Anne's hair away from her face. "I know, but I don't want him to be separated from his family."

"He's not. He's in there right now with his brother. Wes is his family too. The others will come around. It'll just take time, and you're going to have to be strong for him. Let him know he didn't make a mistake choosing you. You should feel proud, not sad. Smile, my friend, life is good. Don't cry over the happy times. There are enough bad times to cry over. Go in there and make that man of yours proud." Mandy kissed her forehead.

"I love you, Mandy. You're the best sister I could ever have. I'm glad we met. I'm glad you're my friend," Anne said, drying her tears.

"Let's go have dinner with those handsome Young brothers."

Richard and Wes favored each other a lot, their Greek heritage showing in both of them—dark wavy hair, dark eyes, and olive skin. Richard was taller than Wes, but other than that they looked remarkably alike. Richard was quieter and more reserved than Wes; Wes was sociable and never met a stranger. He always said there was no such thing as a stranger, just a friend you haven't met yet.

Mandy and Anne stood in the doorway watching them talk about this and that. They were so happy; Wes was glad he had hired Richard. Richard had been able to get the Foundation another grant and was teaching the staff how to save money by getting bids for outside labor.

"You're so right, Mandy. How could I be sad with a man like Richard?" Anne hugged Mandy, and they returned to the table with the men.

The doorbell rang. It was Grace and Ben; they had been driving around and decided to stop and see the new shop. Everyone put on their coats and walked over to the shop.

"Mandy, I can have some men come over to detail your fountain and pond. I love what you did with it," Ben said, eyeing her yard area.

"I did want you to come over and landscape, I want walkways and…well, you know what to do. I wanted to wait until the builders were finished, so they wouldn't walk all over it. Come on inside, everyone."

"She's just a little bit proud," Wes whispered to Grace.

Mandy turned the lights on. In the front was a counter and small item display. The room was totally open with the four Greek-styled beams placed around the huge room. They had categorized the pottery; she had a kid's area, a seascape area, a pond and fountain area, and she had set up a Bahamian artwork section, and typical bowl and vase area. The workroom was sectioned off with only a counter, so that customers could come sit at the counter and watch her work the clay. The back glass doors had been replaced with large antique windows she could open and look out of in the summer. She had a perfect view of the lighthouse and rock levee.

Everyone was impressed; it looked like a shop in New York or Boston, but it had an international appeal. Her seascapes were still her specialty. She also had placed some of her paintings in the shop for decoration.

"Little lady, this is what you call a pottery shop. Did you ever think a year ago you would have a shop like this?"

"A year ago I didn't even think I would have a shop, most less one like this."

"Only the best for my love. See, in the workroom we had a corner made for our little one when he's born. Mandy can put a playpen right over there, and he can stay here with her. She's not into nannies, she wants to take care of him herself." Wes proudly showed them the baby's place.

"You keep saying *him* and *he*, does that mean you know what the baby is now?" Grace inquired.

"Well, as a matter of fact, the doctor told us that we were probably going to have a boy. No 'juniors' though. Mandy won't hear of a junior. She wants to call him Brook or something."

"Congratulations, brother," Richard said, hugging his brother. "I know you're so proud. Kay never wanted children. She said it would mess up her figure. She was a ladies' man. Oh, I'm sorry, Wes. I know that is painful for you, and I wouldn't hurt you for the world."

"That's perfectly all right. That was then; this is now. I have the woman of my dreams. I figure the first one was practice."

They all laughed, but Richard saw the hurt in his brother's eyes. He knew how much Wes had loved Kay regardless of the fact she ran around on him. He was a family man, and he stood by the promises he made, even if it was painful for him.

Mandy wanted to talk to Grace about her meeting with Sarah earlier, but she wanted them to be alone. "Grace, how about coming over early tomorrow so that I can show you some of my new work? We can have orange juice or something. Wes won't let me drink coffee."

"It's bad for you," he said, rubbing her stomach. He kissed her on the forehead and drew her close with his arm. "I want this one to be around a lifetime."

Mandy smiled; she knew she had a wonderful man. He was nothing like Clay, but he was exactly what she wanted.

Ben watched the two of them together; he wanted to be proud for them, but his heart yearned for Mandy. He wished it were his son she was carrying instead of Wes.' He would have to live with that fateful day the rest of his life. He watched her laugh and touch the bulge in her stomach. She looked radiant; her beauty was more than he could handle, and she brushed his arm as she walked passed. He felt his heart miss a beat. He closed his eyes, trying to regain his composure. He wanted to move back to Boston to get away from seeing her, but he knew he needed to stay for his mom.

Grace watched her son; she could feel his pain, but there was nothing she could do to help him. She looked at Mandy and Wes together; they were the perfect couple. They were totally in love. Mandy would never be Ben's, and she knew it. Her heart ached for her son; she wished there were some magic words she could say to help his hurting heart, but there weren't. He would have to bear the cross he had made for himself.

Wes walked over and put his arm around Ben's shoulder. "Well, what do you think, my friend, have I outdone myself or what?" Wes was proud of the new shop he was able to provide for his wife. He wanted her close to him; he knew she liked to come out at night and work. He wanted her to be home instead of down the road. Now she could come out any time she wanted to work on her pottery.

• • • • •

The morning sun shining through the open curtains awoke Mandy. Wes had already gotten up and was dressing for the office. She heard him humming in the bathroom; it was the same song Grace hummed all of the time. She got out of bed and walked into his bathroom. "What's the name of that tune you're humming?" she asked, hugging him from behind.

"Oh, I don't know. It's some tune Grace hums all of the time. It's kind of catchy, and I just started humming it," he replied, turning around to give her a big hug. "You have a big day today, the grand opening and all. Don't overdo it now. I mean it. You let Anne do all of the heavy stuff. Promise me."

"I promise. What do you have up your sleeve for today?"

"I have to go into Spring Hill today to the children's ward and see three patients. Then I'll be back at the lab. If you need me, call me on my cell phone. Are you coming down for breakfast this morning?"

"Yes, I'll be right down," she said, patting his back.

She put on one of her favorite frocks and headed down the stairs. She met Sally coming up. "Really, Ms. Mandy, you should do something about the clothes you wear. That old dress looks like it's a hundred years old. It seems you could afford new clothes."

"Good morning to you too, Sally." Mandy laughed as she continued, undeterred.

"Good morning, Ms. Mandy. I just sent Sally up to your room," Sharon said, pouring her a glass of orange juice.

"I saw her on the stairs, and she didn't like my dress. It's not like I go to an office every day. I have a pottery shop, for Pete's sake. Besides, I can't wear any of my clothes now except these old frocks. The little one is getting bigger." They all laughed.

"I need to go. You have a wonderful day, my love, and make lots of money. You'll need it." He kissed her, got his coat, and left.

She finished her breakfast and hurried over to the shop. She turned on all the lights, soft music, and started preparing clay for the day's projects. She heard the door open; it was Grace with a jug of orange juice. She hurried over to greet her. "I'm so glad you could come over this morning. I have something to tell you. Come in the back and sit on the couch while I talk."

Grace sat on the couch and listened as Mandy told her the bizarre story that had unfolded to her just two weeks ago. She told her about the letters, the ring, and about Amy. Grace sat quietly and listened to every word.

"I'd love to tell you this is news to me, but I already knew. One of the ladies at church told me about Sarah and Amy almost a year ago," Grace said, drinking her juice.

"You knew, and you didn't tell me?" Mandy asked, sitting next to Grace on the couch.

"I didn't see the need. You were already having such a hard time at it. I didn't want to add to your burden. God knows when to let things come out, and he did, just at the right time. Did it change your life?"

"No. Yes. It helped me to see how much Wes truly loves me and that Clay never did."

"How can you say that? Did Clay tell you he never loved you?"

"Didn't you hear what I just said? He had a child with this woman."

"Yes, but he chose to stay with you. All the rest is—"

"That's what Wes said. Sometimes I think the two of you gang up on me." She laughed and went back to work with the clay.

Anne came into the front door singing a song; she put her things away and started arranging the toys. "Ben and his crew are outside. He said he needs you to come out and show him what you want him to do."

"I'll be right out. Grace, what is the name of that song you're always humming?"

"'What a Friend We Have in Jesus.'"

"I know, but what's the name of the song—"

"The name of the song is 'What a Friend We Have in Jesus.' I love that old hymn. It keeps me reminded that he's in control, not me. And when things get tough and I feel all alone, he's always with me. You should get the words and read them, keep them in your heart."

Grace had a strange feeling about Mandy that morning; she didn't know what it was, but she couldn't shake it. Every time she got near her, she had the premonition, the feeling. She followed Mandy outside to talk to Ben. Mandy showed Ben what she wanted done about the walkways and the pond area. She gave Ben a big hug and thanked him for helping her.

He wanted to grab her and hold her, but he knew he couldn't. She didn't belong to him; she belonged to Wes. He quickly moved away from her and started telling his crew what he needed done. He looked back over his shoulder; she was talking to his mom. Mandy gave Grace a hug, and Grace walked over to Ben.

"I'm on my way home now, son, but keep an eye on Mandy today. I have a strange feeling." Grace kissed her son on the cheek and started down the road to her house.

Ben turned and looked at Mandy; she was walking inside the shop. He went back to work.

The day was busy; the shop was full all day. The bar in front of the work area was lined up with customers watching her mold the clay into beautiful dishes. They were awed that a ball of clay in her hands came out looking like a piece of fine china.

At about four o'clock in the afternoon, Richard called; he wanted to talk to Mandy. "Hello, Richard, nice to hear from you. What is my husband doing? Is he back from Spring Hill yet?"

"That's why I'm calling. He never made it to Spring Hill. The hospital called and said he was supposed to be there this morning to see several patients in the children's ward," Richard said with concern in his voice.

"He left at seven this morning headed for Spring Hill. Oh, Richard, something's wrong. Wes is very punctual. He wouldn't just not show up. You haven't heard from him?" Mandy could feel her heart quicken its beat.

"No, that's why I'm calling you. I thought maybe he decided to stay home with you. I'll call the sheriff's department to see if there have been any accidents reported."

"Call me as soon as you know anything," she cried. She paced back and forth in the shop; she took off her apron. "Anne, could you close up the shop at five? I'll be at the main house if you need me." She ran out the door to the house.

Ben watched her run to the house; he dropped his tools and followed her. Inside he caught up with her. "What's going on? Is everything all right?"

"No one has seen Wes today. He was supposed to go into Spring Hill to see three children at the hospital, and he never made it. Something's wrong, I can feel it. This is not like Wes," she cried.

Ben remembered what his mom had said before she left this morning. He walked out on the front porch and called her on his cell. "Mom, hi, this is Ben. I think something is wrong. Wes never showed up at the hospital this morning. Mandy is all upset, could you come over here and stay with her?"

"I'll be right over." Grace climbed in her old car and drove to their house. She'd had that uneasy feeling all day. She just prayed. She knew something wasn't right this morning when she was with Mandy. She could feel tragedy around her. She hurried up to the house; Mandy was in the living room crying. Ben walked back and forth until his mother got there.

"I'm so glad you're here. I tried to calm her down, but she's so upset," Ben said, leaving the room.

"Now, now, dear, you're going to have to calm down. It's not good for the baby for you to be all in a tizzy like this. Here, dry your eyes. You've got to be strong. We don't know what's going on, so we have to wait and pray."

"Oh, Grace, I've been praying. It feels like the day Clay disappeared. What if something bad has happened?"

"We can't think like that. We've got to trust God. We've got to think positive things. Here, I brought you the words to that hymn I was telling you about this morning. You sit right here and read them. I'm going to talk to Ben for a minute. I'll be right back." Grace comforted Mandy.

"Ben, you get in your truck and backtrack the road Wes took to the city today. Do you know which way he goes?" Grace instructed her son.

"No, I don't. There's three ways he could've gone," Ben replied.

"Then you backtrack each one of them, go on now."

Ben tracked the most popular road into Spring Hill first. The traffic was terrible. It was hard for him to see the opposite side of the road. He tried to drive slow enough to see if there were fresh skid marks off the road. The traffic wouldn't allow him to drive slow enough to get a good look. He was frustrated and decided to just drive slowly in spite of the traffic flow. Cars were blowing their horns and yelling obscene things at him as he drove slowly along the road. Wes was his best friend; he had to find him, and he just had to be okay.

He noticed a car sitting on the side of the road; it looked like a BMW convertible. It was. He stopped and looked inside the car. Wes' doctor bag and cell phone were still on the seat. The car was locked. He looked around the car; he noticed footprints leading away from the car. He went back to his truck and called the police on his radio. He didn't want to disturb anything; he wanted to wait until the police arrived. Wes' father had already called a detective; he met Ben at the car. The detective called in the crime scene investigators.

"I'm Detective Norris. I was called by the Young family to find Dr. Wes Young, who seems to be missing."

"This is his car. I'm sorry, my name is Ben Harris, and Dr. Young is my best friend. The car is abandoned. His doctor bag and cell phone are still on the seat. I don't understand. It seems like if he ran out of gas or the car broke down, he would have taken his cell phone or called someone. I tried not to disturb anything. I didn't touch the car. There appears to be footprints leading away from the car down the road," Ben explained. "I want to call his wife and let her know we found the car."

"Not just yet. Dr. Young said his daughter-in-law was pregnant and was having a bad time of it. Let's look at what we have first." Detective Norris looked inside the car and looked at the footprints. "There appear to be two sets of prints here. Don't walk near them. Let's just walk on the road so that we don't add additional prints to the area. The crime scene investigators are on their way."

Ben patiently followed the detective down the road. "It appears we have another car that was stopped right here. The footprints end," Detective Norris said, squatting down to look at the prints.

It was beginning to get dark; the sun had already begun to set over the horizon. Ben was worried the darkness would hinder them from finding Wes. He looked at his watch. It was five forty-five now, and the sun was dropping fast. The detective set out flares to let oncoming traffic know to go around. A deputy had arrived and was directing the traffic away from the scene.

Ben had to call home; he slipped away from the officers who were talking and went back to his truck. He dialed Mandy's number. George answered the phone. "Young residence."

"George, this is Ben. Is my mother still there?"

"Indeed, sir, she's with Ms. Mandy. Shall I call her to the phone?"

"Yes, George, thanks." Ben waited for his mother to pick up the phone.

"Hello, Ben, have you found him?"

"Mom, where are you in the house? Is Mandy in the room with you?"

"No, son, I'm in the living room, Mandy is upstairs lying down for a spell. Did you find Wes?"

"No, Mom, but I found his car. I don't know what's going on yet. There are detectives, police officers, and crime scene investigators here. It doesn't look good, his doctor bag and cell phone are still in the car. A locksmith just pulled up."

"Richard called his parents. They are flying in right now. Dr. Young received a strange phone call yesterday, and he seems to think this has something to do with the call. He doesn't want Mandy to know about it. Richard is worried. His daddy told him what the phone call was about, but he won't tell anyone else. Son, what does it look like?"

"It looks like he had car trouble, but it seems he would have called AAA or someone to come and assist. Looks like he may have gotten in the car with someone else. They're looking at every little piece of gravel, every broken twig, and everything. There're about ten people here now. They have the road blocked off. The detective is coming my way. Let me go. I'll keep you posted." Ben hung up the phone and stepped out of the truck.

Detective Norris came over. "There seemed to be a struggle at the second car. The footprints showed that. The crime scene people are checking everything. You can go home if you want. Thanks for calling us." He shook Ben's hand and went back to the others.

Ben stood looking at Wes' car; he could feel the sting of tears in his eyes. He didn't know if he was crying over his missing friend or the pain Mandy must be feeling right now. He looked up at the sky. "God, I've kept my end of the bargain, but if I could ask you one more thing. Please let Wes be alive and safe. I do love that woman, but I love Wes too. I'd really appreciate you helping us out here." He got into his truck and headed back to the Cove.

By the time he got home, the house was full of people. Richard, Anne, Judy, his mom, Dr. Boyd, and some of Wes' staff were anxiously waiting. His parents had taken their private jet and were on their way. Sharon had set up a buffet table for the guests to eat as they wanted to. George was taking coats and sending people to the living room. Dr. Boyd and Grace were upstairs with Mandy. Ben slipped through the crowd and went upstairs. His mother was lying on the bed with Mandy, singing "What a Friend We Have in Jesus." Dr. Boyd was sitting in a chair near the windows looking out.

Ben crept into the room; Mandy looked up at him. "Did you find him? Is he all right?"

"No, honey, he didn't find him. The police are working hard to find him," Grace reassured her, pushing her hair away from her face. "You just lie back and rest. You don't need to make yourself sick. Wes would be terribly upset if you did."

Grace motioned for Ben to sit in the chair next to the bed. Dr. Boyd smiled at him and came over to introduce herself. "Hi, I'm Dr. Boyd. I don't think we've ever met."

"I'm Ben Harris, Grace's son. Nice to meet you."

"It's nice to meet you, too. I hear you're Dr. Young's best friend."

"Yes, I kind of like the ole fella." Ben smiled back.

She sat next to him near the bed. "This woman has been through some tough times. I hope this all turns out good. What do you do?"

Ben looked over at Dr. Boyd. "I'm a landscaper. I had a business in Boston, but I moved out here to be close to my mom. I do industrial and professional buildings."

"Please forgive my rudeness. My name is Debra Boyd. You can call me Debra. I'm so used to the formal name. I forget to let people know I have a real name. That sounds like a really nice thing to do. You make the world a beautiful place to live in."

"I never really thought of it like that. I take after my dad. He was a landscaper too. He loved to dig in the soil. He could make anything grow. He was a fine man. I was lucky to have him as my dad. My mom's pretty special too."

"Yes, I've found out she's the only one that could calm Mandy down. She just whispers to her, and she stops crying. Remarkable woman, she's been singing to her. So you live close to the Youngs?"

"Yes, right down the road, next to Mandy's old place." Ben looked at Debra. She was a very lovely woman; she didn't have a ring on her finger. She had dark brown eyes that seemed to look inside of your soul. She had light brown shoulder-length hair; she was tall and thin. There was nothing really special about her looks, but he noticed he just felt good in her presence. Her beauty came from the inside. She sat beside Mandy and checked her vital signs, washed her face with a cold cloth, and watched the clock.

"Do you ever do private landscaping for individual people?" she asked.

"Yes, I did all the work for Mandy and Wes, here and at the Foundation. If you'd like I could come over and see what your yard looks like, and we could go from there," he said, noticing her penetrating smile.

"Thanks, that would be nice. Are you married?"

Ben chuckled. "No, I'm afraid not."

She smiled at him and sat back in her chair. "It's so beautiful here in the Cove. I moved here to be with my mother ten years ago. After she died I just stayed. My office is in the same building with the foundation. Therefore, I see Wes a lot. They just found out the sex of the baby, you know." She noticed tears were rolling down the side of Mandy's face. She took the cool cloth and washed them away. "She's been doing that all evening. It's almost as if she's grieving inside. I gave her a sedative earlier. She hasn't said much in the last several hours. She just lies there looking at the ceiling. Poor thing, what in the world could have possibly happened to Wes?"

Ben heard voices downstairs and excused himself to go and see what was going on. When he reached the bottom of the stairs, he saw a man that looked remarkably like Wes and a woman, both of whom were in tears. He looked over at Richard. Richard stood up and greeted the new visitors as mother and father. *These must be the Youngs*, Ben thought as he entered the room. He heard his mother enter after him.

"You must be Ben Harris. Our son talks about you all the time. And this must be Grace," Catherine said, hugging Grace's neck. "I'm Catherine, Wes' mother, and this is Raymond, Wes' father."

Raymond stepped in front of Catherine. "Could I speak to you, young man? In here, please." Raymond motioned toward Wes' study.

Ben followed Richard, Catherine, and Raymond into the study. He sat in a chair near the desk. Raymond sat at Wes' desk. "I got a phone call from a man yesterday that made me feel uncomfortable. He said his wife had come into our surgery wing and had some plastic surgery done. He didn't care for the outcome of the surgery. Seems his wife left him shortly after the surgery. She wanted breast implants and a facelift. The work our center did was excellent; seems he blames us for his wife leaving him. He made threats to me that I would pay. I would see what it felt like to lose the thing you love the most. Then he hung up. I don't know how he could have found Wes, except for the fact he was in the papers last week for the new vaccine he and Judy came up with. This nut could have taken our son."

Catherine cried out, and Richard pulled her close to him to comfort her. "Raymond, find my son."

"Yes, yes, Catherine. Detective Norris said you found Wes' car this evening on the side of the road."

"I did. All of his things were still in the seat, and the car was locked. The detective told me it looked like there was a struggle at the second vehicle. Do you think this man could have taken Wes?"

"I do indeed, son. There are crazy people in this world we live in. The police are coming over to set up a call trace center here. I want Mandy kept away from all of this. She's carrying my first grandchild, and I don't want her upset by all of this, do you understand?"

"Mandy is a strong-willed person. She'll want to know what's going on. Wes is her life, and she's not one of those women you can pacify with *it'll be all right, honey*. The doctor seems to have her sedated right now. She's upstairs. But she won't let herself sleep, even with the sedation. She's just staring at the ceiling. My mom and Dr. Boyd have been with her all evening. But she's going to want to know."

"I need to go to her, Raymond," Catherine cried.

"Not until you get yourself together. I don't want her to see you crying. Go get a drink and calm down, then you can go in and see her," Raymond ordered.

Catherine left the study and went into the living room where everyone else was waiting. The police came in looking for Raymond. Catherine directed them to the study. She asked Sally to get her a stiff drink. She looked over and saw Rachel looking out the window at the gardens. She walked over and put her arm around her shoulders. They just stood there together looking at the gardens. Rachel looked up at Catherine. Catherine smiled. "Hello, my friend. I'm sorry I haven't been more supportive of you and Richard. Wes was right. Family is the greatest wealth. Isn't this ironic? He's the only one in this family with any good sense, and he's the one that's missing."

Rachel turned around and buried her head in Catherine's chest. She cried; Catherine patted her back and let her cry. "We didn't mean to deceive you. It's just—"

"Honey, you don't have to say a word. It was our fault, not yours or Richard's. After you left, he just seemed to drift away from us. Youngs, we're not that smart to be so brilliant." Catherine tried to laugh. "Have you seen Mandy?"

"No, her doctor isn't letting any of us see her. She wants her to rest. She'd been doing real well with the baby lately. Wes built her a new pottery shop, and she was so happy, and now this. You never know when life is going to throw you a curve, do you?" Rachel cried.

"No, you don't. Wes has so much wisdom for his young years. I wished I had listened to him more. He tried to tell me that breaking you and Richard up was a bad thing. I didn't listen. Richard has the right woman for him, and I dare Raymond to say a word. What better woman for him than you? You know this family inside and out. What a clever plot to change your name. Can I call you Rachel again instead of Anne? I've always loved you as Rachel."

A police officer came into the living room and instructed everyone not to answer the phone. They were running traces on all calls, and they needed to answer the phone in the study.

"Let's go up and see Mandy. I'm calmer now. Come on, she's your sister and my daughter," Catherine said, ushering Rachel to the stairs.

When they walked into the room, the lights were dim. Dr. Boyd got up from her chair. Grace let her know that was Wes' mother; pacified, Dr. Boyd returned to her chair. Catherine walked up to the bed and sat on the edge. "Mandy, I'm here for you, honey."

Mandy looked over at Catherine; tears started rolling down her cheeks. She knew if Catherine and Raymond were here, something was wrong. "Have they found Wes yet?" she whispered.

"Not yet, honey, but they have a lot of people looking for him," Catherine said, stroking her face with her hand.

Mandy turned her head to Grace. "They will find him, and he'll come home to me, won't he? He's okay, isn't he? Why are all these people here?"

"Because they all love Wes too. Wes is in the Good Lord's hands. He's as safe as he can be. You keep singing to that baby now."

Catherine looked and she could see Mandy was showing already; she was so proud of her children. How could she have let the family become divided as she had? When this was over, she would make sure her family would be one again.

The phone rang, and Mandy reached over to answer it. Catherine placed her hand on Mandy's. "Let the men answer the phone, honey."

Raymond answered the phone; he had been instructed by the police to keep the person on the phone as long as he could so that they could trace the call. "Hello."

"I want to speak to Raymond Young."

"This is he."

"Dr. Young, I have your son with me. He wasn't the one I was after. I want Chad Young. You give me Chad Young, and I'll give you this one back," the voice on the other end of the phone demanded.

"Chad's not here. Is Wes all right?"

"Wes is fine. He says he's fixin' to be a father, is that true?"

"Yes, his wife is upstairs right now, she's upset—"

"Well, so am I, big-time doctor. Your son Chad ran off with my wife, and I want that little SOB, or I'm going to kill this one."

"Let's not be hasty. Wes hasn't done anything to you. It was his brother, Chad. You say he ran off with your wife?"

"Yes, he did, in that big yacht he has. He's taken her away from me, and I'm going to take your son away from you."

"Can I talk to Wes, so I can see if he's okay?"

"He's fine. He's worried about his little missis, so I'll let him talk to her, not you."

Raymond put his hand over the phone. "He wants to talk to Mandy, get her."

Detective Norris ran up the stairs and excused himself to the ladies. "I need Mandy to come downstairs. Wes wants to talk to her on the phone."

She sat up, pushed Catherine aside, and ran down the stairs. She struggled to followed the police officer to the study. She saw Raymond had the phone. The detective updated her quickly as to what had occurred and instructed her as to what she needed to do when she got on the phone.

She took the phone from Raymond. "Wes?'

"Hold on a minute.'

"Mandy, oh Mandy, it's so good to hear your voice. Are you all right, my love?"

"Wes, where are you? Are you all right?" She fought the tears back.

"I'm fine, are you all right?"

"Yes, I want you to come home to me, Wes."

"I'm coming home, my love, I've just got to help this gentleman first, and then I'll be home. Don't worry, take care of our son."

"Wes, I want to talk to the man you're with."

"No, I don't want you to."

"Put him on the phone, Wes," she demanded. She heard a slight scuffle on the other end.

"Yep, what can I do for you?"

"I'm Wes' wife. I'm pregnant with our first child. Wes is a good man, and he has dedicated his whole life to healing others. He's never hurt anyone in his life. Please don't hurt him. He's all I've got. My first husband was killed, and I don't think I could go through that again. Please, I beg you, let my husband go. I know you're hurting. So am I. But hurting Wes won't solve the problem. Just let him go, and we'll find Chad. You can settle your score with Chad. I need my husband; our baby needs him. Please, for me, please. I promise you, if you let Wes go, you can have Chad," she pleaded.

Raymond started to take the phone from her, but the detective caught him. "Let her talk to him."

"How do I know you're telling the truth? You're trying to trick me."

"Ask my husband. I don't tell lies. What I say is the truth. I'll keep my word. I promise."

There was silence on the other end of the phone; you could hear the kidnapper and Wes talking to each other.

"Okay, you can pick your husband up at the Foundation. You come to get him alone. Just you, no one else."

"I'm pregnant, and the doctor gave me a sedative. Can I get a friend to bring me? We'll be in a silver Chevrolet truck. It'll be just the two of us. I promise."

"I'll be waiting." He hung up the phone.

Raymond started to get up to go; Mandy stopped him. "Let me tell you something. Wes is my husband. I gave the man my word. Ben and I will go and get him. You'll stay here and wait for us. I have a cell phone. If anything goes wrong, I'll call you. You had better not try to follow us, or you'll answer to me. This time you're just going to have to sit and wait. This is my responsibility."

She went into the living room. Ben was standing by the back door. "Ben, come with me, please."

Ben looked around. "What are you doing up?"

"I need you to come with me." She turned and walked out the door. George gave her her coat, and the two of them were on their way.

"Where are we going?"

"We're going to get Wes."

"What?"

"Just drive to the Foundation." She looked ahead. She was nervous, but this was no time to break down. She was not willing to lose another husband, especially Wes. She would fight for him. Her cell phone rang.

"Hello, Mrs. Young? I don't want you to go to the Foundation. Go to the marina where your boat is in dry dock. Pull up to the building where your boat is and wait." The call ended before Mandy could get a word in. She turned to Ben.

"Go to the marina, not the Foundation. I'll show you where to stop."

"Mandy, are you sure we're doing the right thing?" Ben asked, turning the truck around.

"I know that we have all prayed, and God is going to honor those prayers. Wes is alive, and the man that has him is going to let him go to me."

"How do you know?"

"I feel it," she assured him. "This time it's going to be different. I believe God answers prayers. Why shouldn't he answer mine?"

Ben thought about the prayer he prayed by the side of the road. He felt it too. They drove to the marina to the dry dock area. She directed him to the building where they needed to wait. They sat in front of the building with their headlights off.

Mandy saw a shadow of a small person at the end of the building.

"Get out of the truck, Mrs. Young," the voice instructed.

Ben reached over and took her hand; she shook loose from him, opened the truck door, and stepped out beside the truck. She slowly walked toward the small man.

"Stop right there," the voice hollered.

She saw Wes standing next to him. "Tell your friend to get out."

She looked at Ben and asked him to get out of the truck; he opened the door and walked to the front of the truck where Mandy was standing. She noticed the man doing something to Wes then push Wes toward her. Wes walked forward until he reached the truck; he grabbed Mandy and held her. Mandy looked over his shoulder to see the man, but he was gone.

"How did you talk him in to letting me go? I tried all day." Wes kissed her all over her face.

"I told him my first husband was killed, and I couldn't live though the death of another husband. I begged him let you come home to our baby and me. Are you all right? Are you hurt anywhere?" she asked, looking him over.

He had dried blood on his face, and his wrists were blood red. "I'm fine. He told me to give you this." Wes handed her an envelope. "He said you made him a promise."

"I did. I told him he could have Chad if he would let you come home."

"You told him what? What did my father say?"

"He tried to stop me, but the detective told him to leave me alone. I told him that you were my responsibility. Chad is his. He can have Chad but not you. The man was angry with your father and Chad, not us. Let them deal with their responsibility. We'll deal with ours. I don't care. He let you go. That's all that matters to me," Mandy explained as she opened the envelope.

"What is it?" Ben asked.

"It's a note. He says if I break my promise, he'll come back for me."

"He'll come back for you? Why? Why would he come after you?"

"Because I told him he could have Chad, not you."

"This man was mad, Mandy. Chad took his wife. He's ready to kill someone. I can't just give him my baby brother."

"Then the police will have to stop him. Chad should think about what he does before he just takes what he wants. That's not the way life works. There are consequences to pay for the things we do. He needs to learn that. Your father should have taught him that. Instead he just lets him run wild. We were about to have to pay for his folly. I'm not willing to do that, are you?"

"No, no I'm not, and perhaps you're right. I'm just tired and hungry, and I'm glad to see you, my love. Let's not talk about this anymore. I just want to go home." Wes climbed into the truck with Ben and Mandy.

"Thanks for bringing her, Ben. Thank you for being my friend." Wes hugged him.

"No problem, my friend. If you needed attention, all you had to do was ask. You didn't have to go through all of this." They laughed.

"We'd better call home and let them know everything is all right. We don't want them to call out the cavalry," Ben said, grabbing Mandy's phone.

On the way home Wes called his father. "Father, we're on our way home. We should be there in about ten minutes."

"Are you all right? How's that wife of yours? She's a feisty one. I like her. She put me in my place. That's the first time I have ever had a woman do that. She's a keeper, son."

"I'm fine. We need to talk when I get home," Wes said, looking over at Mandy.

Everyone was waiting for them on the front porch when they arrived. They all tried to talk at once. Detective Norris took Wes, Mandy, and Ben into the study. He had questions he needed to ask Wes about where the kidnapper had kept him all day.

"Wes, could you tell us what happened?" Detective Norris asked, turning on a tape recorder.

Wes sat next to Mandy on the couch. "I was headed for Spring Hill. I had children to visit today. My car started acting like it was out of gas. It stalled, and I pulled over to the side of the road. I looked at the gas gauge, and I was out of gas. A truck pulled over to assist me. This man got out and helped me push the car out off the way. I went back to get my cell phone, but he stopped me, telling me there was a station right up the street. Therefore, I went with him. When I started to get into the car, I saw a picture of Chad and some woman on the seat. I tried to run, but he hit me across the head with something. The next thing I knew, I was on the boat. My hands were tied, and I was bleeding. I don't know how he got me up the ladder, or if someone else was there helping him. I just don't know. I tried to reason with him, but he wouldn't listen. He kept drinking and saying he was going to kill Chad. I asked him why he was so angry at Chad. He told me Chad had run off with his wife. Your surgery center, Father, had done some reconstructive work on her. She met Chad, and they ran off together on your yacht. I think he thought our boat was yours. He kept asking me who Mandy was. I told him she was my wife. That the boat was a wedding present from my father to her. He just kept drinking and swearing at Chad and you, Father. He used the ship-to-shore line to call you."

"That's why we couldn't trace the call," Detective Norris interrupted.

"Well, you know the rest. Who is this man, and what have you and Chad done to him? I mean, he kept sticking that gun up to my head and making a sound like he shot me. He's a very disturbed man."

"My center did some work on his wife. Chad came in one day when she was there for a follow-up visit. They talked, and I think your little brother bit off more than he can chew. I'm sorry you got caught in the middle of this, son."

"Father, I have a family. You've got to do something about Chad. Mandy has a note that the man sent to her. Give them the note, my love."

Detective Norris read the note. "Looks like this thing isn't over. Dr. Young, we'll need your records on this man's wife to see if we can find him before he catches his next victim. We're going to put surveillance around your family, Wes. You should be safe. Looks like he took you at your word, Mrs. Young. We'll put a man on her to watch her. It's been a long night. Let's wrap this up and let these good people get some rest."

"Mandy, hold on there just a minute," Raymond said, walking toward her. "You stood up to me tonight to save my son. I appreciate that. If there is ever anything I can do for you—"

"As a matter of fact, there is. Do something about Chad. He's destroyed enough lives. Wes is my husband and the father of my child. I won't allow a spoiled brat to break up my family. If you'll excuse me, I'm tired. It's been a long day." Mandy pushed past Raymond and headed upstairs.

"I like that woman, Wes. You did good with that one. She's a woman after my own heart," Raymond proudly declared.

"She's serious, Father. Mandy doesn't make idle threats. She means it."

"I know she does."

Wes joined Mandy upstairs; they held each other and cried. Wes had never been so scared in all of his life. He'd thought the kidnapper was going to kill him. Dr. Boyd came in and wanted to look at Wes' head. She examined him, stitched him up, and left the two them alone.

They slept in each other's arms. The morning brought rain; the skies were dark and angry, and the wind was blowing a gale. The house was quiet when Wes awoke; he watched Mandy sleep. He had thought he would never see her again. He ran his fingers over the curves of her face; she moaned. He kissed her on the forehead then on the lips. She had fought his father for him; she truly loved him. He knew that now; how could he ever doubt her love again? She had risked her own life for his. How could he ever repay her for what she had done? To her it was what she had to do, to preserve her family. She was a strong woman; she had tenacity. Every day he learned something new about her. She had been through so much. He was the one who was supposed to protect her; yesterday it was the other way around.

She reached over and kissed him, she ran her hand over his face. She smiled at him knowing God had given her a second chance at happiness. She wouldn't waste it; she would cherish the gift she had been given. She held him close to her, and the baby kicked. They both laughed; he reached down and kissed her stomach. He kissed his son for the first time.

Chapter 14

The morning was bright; there wasn't a cloud in the sky. The weather had turned warmer. The birds were singing, and the house was buzzing with the staff getting ready for the big wedding. Mandy had wanted their wedding to be in the garden near the beach. Crews were finishing up the last details when Wes walked down to see what they had done. This would be the place they would make new vows to each other. Everything looked beautiful. It was a perfect day for a wedding.

He remembered just a few weeks ago he had thought he would never see his family again. The kidnapper, Jessie Wells, had been caught and charged with kidnapping. He would be serving time in a maximum-security prison.

But Chad had not changed at all. The whole incident didn't seem to bother him. He had laughed about it to his parents. He had put Wes' family and his life in jeopardy and had not even apologized to them for it. Up to this incident, Wes had been forgiving of Chad, even when he carried on an affair with Kay. But now, Wes had lost all respect for his younger brother.

Raymond walked up to his son and put his arm around his shoulders. "This is the big day."

"Yes, this is for Mother and Mandy. The vows we took Christmas Eve were enough for me. I'm so blessed, Father. I stand here and realize that had I not come down to pull the *Katie I* out for cleaning, I would have never met Mandy. Isn't it funny how life works out? I had a booming practice in L.A., I was on the board of the Cancer Society, and still I was not happy. I moved to Spring Hill and practiced there, then I run into a screaming lady on the road, and look at me now. I have a beautiful wife, a son on the way. I have my brother working with me and living next door. What more could a man ask for?"

"Speaking of beautiful women, where are the loves of our lives?"

"Mandy is upstairs in the master's suite, and Mother has gone to Rachel and Raymond's house for something."

"Just how many people did your mother invite?"

"I don't know, but it looks like a lot of chairs out there. Look, there's Grace. Let me help her," Wes said, going over to help Grace.

Raymond watched his son help the little old lady. He was proud of him. He had struck out on his own and had made a man of himself. He remembered when he was young; he smiled. He had taken the world by the tail and hadn't let go. Wes was a chip off the old block.

Wes helped Grace up the stairs to the house. Mandy was waiting for her. Grace was like a mother to Mandy, and she depended on her for guidance and approval. Mandy was sitting on the bed when Grace arrived. She was crying. She couldn't get her dress zipped up; she had gotten bigger, and the dress just wouldn't fit. Catherine had gone to get the other dress Mandy had picked out.

"Now, now, what's this all about?" Grace said, comforting her.

"I can't get my dress zipped in the back. My stomach is too big. I don't like the other dress, and Catherine says I have to wear it. I don't want to wear it," Mandy cried.

Grace smiled; she knew Mandy's hormones were raging at this point in her pregnancy, so crying seemed the best thing to do. "Now, lets look at what the problem is and see if we can fix it. Look at your face. It's all red and blotchy. You've got to stop that crying now, you hear?" Grace looked at the dress; she could fix it. All it needed was a little altering. "Do you have a sewing kit ?"

"Yes, in the closet. Catherine went to get that ugly dress." Mandy's tears started again. Grace placed her hand on Mandy's shoulder and started humming her favorite hymn. It seemed to calm Mandy; Grace smiled as she called Catherine.

Catherine marveled at the house and gardens; the decorators had done such a wonderful job. The food looked wonderful. Everything was going according to plan, except the bride's gown didn't fit anymore. Catherine chuckled at the thought of being a grandmother; her daughter-in-law was the most wonderful person. She picked up the jewel crown that went with the bridal gown.

As soon as they returned Sally started fussing around in the master's suite, making Mandy nervous. "Sally, could you just sit down or do something? Just stop fussing around," Mandy barked.

Sally looked at Mandy. "I declare, Ms. Mandy, you are the meanest thing this morning."

"Sally, you go on downstairs, and we'll handle the bride." Catherine ushered her out the door.

"Thank you, Catherine, I don't think I could have stood another minute of that squeaky voice." Mandy smiled.

Grace brought the dress back into the room. "Now, let's try this," she said, holding the dress up to Catherine and Mandy.

"It's not going to work. My grandson is too big for that dress," Catherine insisted.

"Come over here, little lady, and let's try this dress on. Come on, it's getting late. The wedding is supposed to start in a half hour." Mandy got up and held her arms in the air so that they could put her dress on her. It was a lovely off-white bridal gown; it had jewels around the neck, a clear mesh to her cleavage, and long fitted sleeves that were belled at the end with jewels lining the edges. The front of the dress had jewels forming her figure to the floor. The back had a six-foot train that had hand-stiched designs and jewels placed throughout the design. She looked beautiful in the gown. Grace had used some of the train to extend the waistline in the back. You couldn't even tell she had altered the dress. It was a perfect fit.

Catherine was amazed. "How did you do that? I mean, you had to add four inches to the waistline, and you can't even tell it." She examined the dress; there was not sign of a stitch.

"I used to do alterations work when I was younger. Haven't lost the touch. Back in my day, you couldn't just go out and buy another dress, you had to make the one you had work. Now you look beautiful, little lady. Let's get this crown in your hair, and you're all done, ready to be handed over to that handsome groom waiting outside."

Raymond was going to give her away, Ben was the best man, Rachel was her maid of honor, and Judy was a bridesmaid along with Dr. Boyd. Amy was her flower girl and little Eric, Glenn's son, was the ring bearer. Richard and Chad were Wes' groomsmen. Everyone was ready; it was time for the wedding to start.

The patio had been cleared for the bridal party, and chairs were set in rows under a tent along the walkway for the guests. Excitement filled the air. Mandy felt sick to her stomach. Dr. Boyd calmed her down by making her take deep breaths. It was time.

The music began to play, and the wedding party marched out one by one. She stood in the back of the house with Raymond. "You know Wes' mother came from a wealthy Greek family; I met her on a trip with friends after college. We fell in love, and when I had established my practice in the U.S., I sent for her. We have been happily married for forty-five years. I want you to know how proud I am of you. You have made Catherine and I so proud. You're the best woman for the job of taking care of our Wes. I am forever in your debt." He reached down and gave her a kiss on the cheek, and then it was time for them to march out.

Wes watched as Mandy walk through the door with his father. His eyes were fixed on the beautiful woman he was marrying for the second time. He had waited all of his life for a woman like her. She was so beautiful in her gown; he couldn't take his eyes off of her. When she reached him, he felt his legs go weak. She smiled up at him and whispered, "Grace fixed my dress."

He chuckled at her. *She would say something at a time like this*, he thought. Richard looked over at Rachel; she had tears in her eyes. He loved her so much, and standing there in that dress she was breathtaking. Dr. Boyd looked at Ben; she thought he was so handsome in his tuxedo. He looked over at her and caught her staring at him; he smiled at her and winked. She blushed and looked back at the minister.

Mandy and Wes had written their own vows.

"The day I saw you, I knew God had sent an angel to repair the brokenness of my life. He placed your hand in mine, and I gently took it from his. As we walk hand in hand through life, I pledge to keep you, to love you, to honor you, and to share with you all that I have. You have my heart, my soul, and my life in your hands. I promise you and God from this day until eternity I will be there for you, no matter what life may bring our way. We will endure it together. I love you today and for always, my love," Wes vowed.

"I prayed, and God sent you to me. In the darkest moment of my life, God sent you as a ray of sunshine. You are my heart, you are my soul, and you are my life. I promise that no matter what life may bring, I will stand beside you. That wherever you go, I will go; your people will be my people; your God my God; and wherever you lay your head I will lie beside you. I will love you and cherish you all the days of my life, till death do us part," Mandy vowed.

They exchanged rings. "Now you may kiss your bride," Pastor Johnny instructed.

Wes swept her up in his arms and gave her a long kiss. The crowd cheered and clapped.

"May I introduce to you Dr. and Mrs. Young?" Everyone clapped. "There will be a reception inside the house, and everyone is invited," Pastor Johnny instructed.

Ben looked over at Dr. Debra Boyd; she was staring at him. She smiled and walked over to him. "Well, hello again. How is the landscaping business?"

"Why, it's just fine, how is the baby business?" Ben replied, watching her emerald eyes sparkle in the sunshine.

"Well, as you can tell from the bride, it's going well. As long as people fall in love, I'll have a job." They laughed.

"Do you have a date for the reception?"

"As a matter of fact, I don't." She smiled.

"Would you like a date with a landscaper?"

"Why, I couldn't think of a better profession to go with." She put her arm in his, and they walked inside together Judy watched as the two of them walked off. She knew she would never have Ben's affections; she shrugged and walked to her car. She heard someone calling her name. She turned around and Blake, one of her research assistants, was calling her name.

"Judy, good. I didn't think I could catch up with you. Would you like a date for the reception? I have my BMW over there. You sure would look pretty in that BMW."

Judy laughed. "Get a life, Blake." She walked off. She noticed Chad was standing alone. "Now, that's a man." She put her arm in his. "Chad, I don't have a date for the reception. Can I go with you?" She batted her eyes at him.

"Sure, Judy."

Wes and Mandy were still standing in the garden, intertwined in each other's arms. They looked over the horizon. "This is what life is like, my love. We think we can see clearly, but there is more on the other side of the horizon, more than we can ever imagine. Just think: in a few short months we will be parents for the first time in our lives. I can't even conceive that, but I know I want to go there with you. You've made me the happiest man on earth. If God took me today, I could say that I have had a full life. You made it full. The day I met you was the first day of the rest of my life. I never dreamed you would be mine, and here we are together for always." He kissed her.

"I know what you mean. I feel like I stepped out of reality into a fairy tale. You have given me so much. You've stood with me when things were tough, and you have been patient with me through everything. I love you, Westbrook Young. I always will."

"It was a noble thing of you to invite Sarah and Amy, but when you wanted Amy in the wedding party, I was awed by your forgiveness."

"If it had not been for them I could have never loved you the way I do right now. It was closure to an old chapter in my life and the beginning of a new one. Besides, Amy thinks I'm her aunt. I had to have her here to stand up for me on this day." Mandy smiled. Wes kissed her again and again.

"You're incredible, my love. Now we need to go in to our reception. Everyone else is already inside. Since it is in our honor, I think we should attend, don't you?" They laughed.

When Mandy walked inside, she couldn't believe her eyes. They had decorated the house with the theme of Cinderella. She looked at Wes. "You did this, didn't you?"

"No, actually, Sharon did. She came to me a couple of weeks ago and told me what you said to Rachel on Christmas Eve. She just had to recreate the fairy tale for you. She loves you, you know."

"Yes, I do know. She's a wonderful person, and I love her too. Sally, on the other hand, is driving me crazy. "Okay, you've made your point. "Dr. Boyd and Ben have been making eyes at each other. Did you notice at the ceremony?"

Will you ever stop trying to match up our friends?"

"No."

They joined everyone at the reception. Raymond wanted to dance with the bride. He swooped Mandy in his arms and glided across the dance floor. If he had of been a little younger, he would give Wes a run for his money. He owed her for his son's life. He owed her so much. He knew she would be an asset to his family.

Rachel and Richard were dancing; Ben and Dr. Boyd were dancing. She looked over, and Judy and Chad were dancing. She thought, *What a good couple they make. They deserve each other. Both of them are cold and cunning.* They laughed as they danced around the floor.

The loudspeaker came on: "It's time for the bride and groom to dance." The band played Jim Croce's "Time in a Bottle."

"They're playing our song, my love. May I have this dance?" He bowed before her.

"Indeed, kind sir." She clumsily curtsied before him.

The crowd moved off the dance floor and let them dance. She felt like she could melt in his arms. They felt the baby kick, and both laughed. "I guess he has to get his say in." Wes laughed.

Ben was ready to make his speech. He instructed everyone, except for Mandy, to raise their champagne glasses. Mandy had milk. "To the two most special people in my life, this is the day dreams are made of. Your love and generosity have touched the lives of everyone here, especially me. I pray that God will grant you long life and lots of children." He laughed.

Wes shook his hand. "Ben, if it hadn't been for you being gun shy, I would have never met Mandy. I drink to your happiness, because you've sure given it to me." They hugged.

Raymond and Catherine would head back to L.A., but first

Catherine needed to do something. She went upstairs to the master suite and knocked on the door. Wes answered.

"I wanted to give Mandy something special, if you wouldn't mind. I know you gave her rings, but this set was my grandmother's. I would be honored if she would wear them. I've been keeping them for a special occasion. Mandy is the special occasion. Oh son, I love you both so much. You have made me a proud mother today." She kissed him on the forehead.

"Mandy, Mother has something she wants to give you."

Mandy walked out of the bathroom in her farewell dress. "I know Wes gave you rings, but these were my grandmother's wedding rings. I had them sized, and I would be honored if you would wear them. I've been saving them for a special occasion, and this is it," Catherine said nervously.

Mandy looked at the old world rings. Beautiful masterpieces, the yellow gold was inlaid with diamonds, interlocking to make one ring. Tears began to stream down her face. She took the rings from Catherine and handed them to Wes. Wes placed the old rings on her right hand ring finger. Mandy hugged her mother-in-law's neck. "I would be honored to wear them." She hugged her again. "Thank you. This is the best present you could have ever given me."

"You are the best present my son has ever given me. I love you, Mandy. I hope you will feel a part of this family; we already feel like you're a big part of this family. You saved my son's life. You're carrying my first grandchild. You are indeed a special woman. My grandmother is smiling down at us right now. I know she is proud to have you wear her rings."

"And I'm honored that you would give them to me." They both cried.

"Okay, that's enough tears. It's time for us to have a real honeymoon. I love you, Mother. Take good care of Father and Chad. We're off to the island." Wes hugged his mother's neck. "I love you."

· · · · ·

The sun was beginning to set over the horizon. The sky was deep orange, the wind was calm, and the weather looked good. Everyone was waiting outside for the farewell; they all had lace bags of birdseed to throw at the couple. The Hummer was sitting out front all decorated with "just married" and cans strung along behind. Mandy and Wes bid their goodbyes and climbed inside.

The driveway was lined with people who wanted to see them off. Raymond and Catherine had their arms around each other as they proudly sent their children off.

"I remember when it was you and I sailing away," Raymond said, kissing his wife.

"Yes, it brings back memories of years gone by. Raymond, our son has done well for himself. We can be very proud of him, as my father would say. I'm glad I lived to see this day." Catherine squeezed her husband.

Raymond held her close, remembering forty-five years ago when he took his bride to a strange country for a new life. She had gladly gone with him. He had never regretted a day of his life with her. He looked into her dark eyes. She was still as beautiful as the day he married her. He held her close; she smiled.

As they cruised their new houseboat into the sunset, Mandy and Wes stood on the deck watching the land disappear. This was the beginning of a new life for them together. She looked down at the rings on her finger. She held them close to her heart.

"Wes, did your mom let Kay wear these rings too?" Mandy asked, holding her hand out to look at them.

"No, I didn't even know she had them. It was as much a surprise to me as it was to you," he said, drawing her near.

"Did you see the way your parents were holding each other as we drove away?"

"Yes, that too is a first. I don't ever recall my father showing affection for my mother in public."

"They looked so in love, didn't they?"

"Yes, my love, they did."

"You look a lot like your mother."

"She says I look like my grandfather."

"He must have been a handsome man."

"You know he was, look at me." They both laughed while they watched the last bit of daylight give way to darkness.

Debra stood at the window. She walked over and sat on the couch; Ben came in and smiled at her. "Come over here and sit down. I don't bite," Debra said, patting the couch beside her.

"It feels strange being here without Wes and Mandy. Those two, you just never know what they will do," Ben said, sitting beside Debra.

"They're fine people indeed." She sipped her drink. "I wonder what it would be like to have a boat named after me. That's true love, don't you think?"

"Actually, Raymond bought the boat for Mandy's wedding present. Strange, don't you think? He gives one to Kay because she's dying, and he gives one to Mandy when she gets married."

"He definitely likes Mandy, that's for sure. I think Catherine does too. She gave Mandy her grandmother's rings, you know."

"No, I didn't know. That's an honor. The Greeks, they are very strict people. They're hard headed. Could you imagine trying to put up with one of them?"

"Looks like Mandy does. But I think she has Wes wrapped around her little finger." Debra smiled.

Ben knew it was over, Mandy would never be his. She had declared her love to Wes for eternity. He would have to move on with his life. He had tried, but just her presence near him made his heart race. He looked over at Debra; she was a lovely woman. *What was it she saw in me? I can tell she is attracted to me, and she would be a fine catch*, he thought. He had to let his heart heal from Mandy. He had to; he couldn't go on with the secret of his feelings forever.

"Looks like you have an eye for our bride."

"What? I'm sorry, I didn't hear you."

"I know you were somewhere out there with lost love. You love her, don't you?"

"Don't be ridiculous. Wes is my best friend. Mandy is his wife."

"I know, but you let her slip through your fingers. I heard Wes at the table. It's hard to get over someone like her. Don't you think?"

"I thought you were a baby doctor, not an analyst. What has happened has happened, and there's no going back and changing things. Wes and Mandy were made for each other."

"Yes, they were. You could see the two of them dancing with no music at the reception. When you're in love like they are, you don't need music. Just the rhythm of your heart is enough music. Want to have dinner?"

"Dinner sounds nice. Would you do me the honor of having dinner with me?" Ben said, holding out his arm.

"I would indeed, kind sir." She wrapped her arm in his.

•   •   •   •   •

Grace sat at the kitchen table, watching Sharon clean up the last of the reception dishes. She had tried to help her, but Sharon wouldn't hear of it. She watched as she took care with each piece of china. Sally was sitting at the table, pouting. "I can't believe Mandy said I drove her crazy."

"Well, believe it. All you do is complain, Sally. You complained about her breakfast, her clothes, the fact she likes a bath instead of a shower. You just complain about everything. It's enough to drive a person insane. I knew it was coming, and I even tried to warn you, but you won't listen to reason," Sharon said, warming up Grace's coffee. "If you want to whine, please do it somewhere else. I'm too tired to listen tonight."

Sally got up from the table and walked out, complaining.

Grace and Sharon laughed. Sharon sat down beside Grace. "You know, Ms. Mandy really loves you. She wants you to come and live with them. I heard her telling Dr. Young just the other night. She wants you to be here when the baby is born. You're kind of her second mother. She's a wonderful addition to this household. There was so much sadness until she came."

"Have you been with Wes very long?" Grace asked, sipping her coffee.

"Oh, yes ma'am, I've been with Dr. Young going on eleven years now. Ever since he graduated college and moved out on his own. I assisted his mother's chef before that for six years. I've known him about seventeen years. He's a kind, generous soul, unlike the rest of his family. Money and wealth really don't mean a lot to him. He just loves helping people. He loves Ms. Mandy. I've never seen him fall all over himself the way he does when she's around. How long have you known Ms. Mandy?"

"Oh, about a year. I don't know about moving into this big house, I'd get lost." Grace looked around the huge kitchen. "How many rooms does this house have anyway?"

"It only has eleven rooms. It's considerably smaller than what I'm used to. But I love living by the bay. On my days off I take long strolls on the beach. It's wonderful here. We've met so many new friends."

"You had your work cut out for you today, young lady. I'll bet there were two hundred people you fed today."

"Yeah, I'm used to it, though. Ms. Catherine used to throw really big dinner parties. This was just a drop in the bucket. She would follow you around to make sure everything was done just right. Not Ms. Mandy. She lets each one of us do our job. She trusts us to do what we're supposed to do. She never comes in hanging over me. I like that I always try to make her proud."

"I know you do. She loves each one of you. She's a fine little lady. She's like the daughter I never had. I did have a little girl. She died at birth. I always wanted a girl."

"Now you have one. She's a keeper. That's what I always tell Dr. Young." Sharon paused as Grace finished her coffee. "I'll show you to your room if you wish. Ms. Mandy decorated it herself. She won't let anyone stay in that room. She says she's keeping it for you."

"I am tired. These old bones hurt in the wintertime. It would be nice to lie down."

Grace followed Sharon to the room Mandy had designated for her. She opened the door and left Grace alone. Grace walked into the large bedroom; it had a four-poster bed with fine linen draped from the ceiling, and it had its own bathroom and dressing room. A large floor-length window overlooked the lighthouse and levee. It had antique furnishings that looked like her house, including a large easy chair over by the window. There was an envelope on the pillow with a dozen roses next to it. Grace opened the note.

Never in my life have I had a mother like you. You deserve the best life has to offer. This is your room always. I owe you more than I could ever repay, I love you more than words can express. Sleep well, my old friend.

Grace felt a tear roll down her cheek. "Lord, truly this little lady is my daughter. I may not have given birth to her, but she's mine. Thank you, Lord." Grace dressed for bed and slept.

· · · · ·

Richard and Rachel were dancing to soft music in their new den. They had turned the old pottery shop into a den for entertaining. Rachel had done an excellent job of redecorating the house for her and Richard. Mandy gave her half of all the proceeds from the shop. She had made her a partner. She was proud, and she kept their shop as if Mandy were there.

Richard drew her near. "Life is so wonderful now. When Mother sent you away, I thought my world had come to an end, but Mandy wouldn't allow that. She wants everyone to be happy. She stood up to my parents for us. Wes and I are truly blessed men to have wives like you and Mandy. Both our women play in clay all day. I love you so much, Rachel, and if you want the big Cinderella wedding, you can have it."

"All I want is you. When Wes was missing that day, your mother came over and hugged me. She told me that I was the woman for you all along. It seems like they have accepted us. You don't have to worry about losing your family over me. It blessed me to think that you gave up everything for me."

"I didn't give up anything, I gained a family."

"Oh, Richard, you're such a romantic guy." He drew her closer, and they swayed to the music.

· · · · ·

Sarah tucked Amy into bed. "Mommy, I love Aunt Mandy, she's the best aunt. Did you see that beautiful dress she bought me for the wedding? I was the prettiest girl there. She gave me these too." Amy unfolded her hand, and in it was a pair of diamond earrings. "She said that diamonds are a girl's best friend, so I'm going to keep them close. I don't want to lose my best friends."

Sarah kissed her daughter and turned off the light. "Your Aunt Mandy sure is a special person."

Glenn was waiting for Sarah to return to the living room where he was still in his tuxedo. Sarah still had on her gown. Glenn had the music low and the champagne chilling. He got up to greet Sarah when she entered the room. He reached out for her, and they danced. Sarah laid her head on Glenn's shoulder. "Today has been a fairy tale. I know why Mandy loves Cinderella so much. You never want to come back to earth. I was watching Mandy today. No wonder Clay wouldn't leave her. She has a heart of gold. I was surprised when she invited us to the wedding, but when she asked Amy to be in the bridal party, I almost fainted. She told me she wanted to be Amy's aunt. She was honored. Your boss is a blessed man."

"I'm a blessed man. Let's not talk about the newlyweds. Let's be newlyweds."

Sarah laughed. "We're getting married, Glenn, remember?"

"How could I forget?" He kissed her.

The moon was full. It hung high in the sky; its silhouette across the water looked like jewels. Mandy and Wes danced in the moonlight. The night air was getting chilly; he drew her closer to him. He could feel her heart beating. It was a perfect day, the wedding was beautiful, his parents had completely accepted her, how could they not? He envisioned his parents in the garden that afternoon. His new bride had even helped them find the passion in their marriage again. She was magical. He thought of her as an angel come down to fix all the brokenness in his world. She had done that. He thought about Grace and how she had led Mandy back into life after her loss. He loved Grace; he wanted her to live with them. She made Mandy so happy. Mandy missed their morning coffee talks.

"Mandy, are you hungry?"

"Starving."

"Why haven't you said something?"

"And mess up this perfect mood? No way. But I think the baby is hungry. What time is it?"

Wes looked at his watch. "It's after twelve."

"Let's go raid the refrigerator." They laughed and went into the kitchen. They opened the refrigerator and pulled out all kinds of food. They placed it on the table and had a midnight feast. They cleaned up their mess and went to their quarters.

Wes started singing. "Tonight's the night so sweetly, you give your love completely—"

"Don't quit your day job. You need to leave the singing to someone else."

He chased her around the bed and grabbed her. He fell on the bed with her; they were giggling.

"Shh," she said. "We'll wake everyone on the beach up."

He stood on the bed and yelled like Tarzan, beating his chest.

"Dr. Young, control yourself."

"I am controlling myself. You want to see what it's like when I lose control?"

Chapter 15

Wes looked at the clock on the wall; it was 10:00 a.m. He looked over at Mandy. She was still sound asleep. He didn't know whether to wake her or let her sleep. He went in and took a shower. She was still sleeping soundly. He crept out of the room and went upstairs to fix breakfast.

Mandy walked into the dining area about noon; she looked tired and a little pale. She sat next to Wes; he noticed she didn't look her normal perky self. "Are you all right?" he asked "I feel funny. I think I'm going to be sick." She got up and ran to the bathroom.

Wes thought, *It's probably just morning sickness. She's not past that stage yet.* Mandy came back in and lay back down on the couch. Wes checked her vital signs; her pulse rate was high, but that was to be expected after throwing up. Her blood pressure was fine, but her lips were white. "Just lay here on the couch and rest. I'll get you something to eat and a cool cloth for your head."

Wes went into the kitchen and returned with a tray of fruit and a cool cloth. "Thank you, Mandy whispered. "You're so good to me."

He sat beside her on the couch. "Can I get you anything else, my love? Do you need another pillow? What can I do?"

Mandy smiled. "You're so funny, Wes. Calm down, everything is fine. I just have a little morning sickness. I'm going to rest awhile, you go fishing. Enjoy the day. I just need to rest." She closed her eyes.

Wes walked out on the deck; he seemed lost.

Mandy was sick all day; by that evening she was feeling much better. She ate dinner and even danced under the moonlight again with Wes. Mandy and Wes sat on the deck drinking orange juice. The evening was wonderful; the stars filled the sky, the moon high overhead. The water was calm, and there was a warm calm breeze blowing.

"Oh, Wes, this is the life. I love it out here. The nights are so beautiful, the quaint sound of the water lapping on the side of the boat. Everything is so romantic out here. Thank you for bringing me. "Don't you think Dr. Boyd and Ben make a nice couple?" Mandy looked up at Wes.

"Now, now, Mrs. Young, don't start matchmaking again. That's what you said about Judy and Ben. I think you just want him to have someone so that you don't feel guilty about being with me," Wes said, letting her lay her head on his chest.

"How did you know? I thought I hid it so well." They laughed.

Wes laid his hand on Mandy's stomach and started rubbing it. "That feels so good, don't stop. Sometimes my stomach gets so tight it feels like it will burst. That helps," she said, reaching up holding his arm.

It started to rain; they gathered their things and ran inside. "Where did that come from?" Wes asked, shaking himself off.

"It's a squall. They're common on the Gulf. They come up without warning. It'll pass soon." The rain lasted the rest of the night the boat was tossed by the wind and waves created by the storm. Mandy was up sick all night. In the early morning hours the storm subsided, the wind died down, and the bay was calm again. Wes paced back and forth ; he was worried. He knew they should have postponed the trip. But Mandy had wanted to come. He didn't know a lot about pregnancy, but he knew his wife was having a hard time of it. He wanted to take her pain and sickness. He wanted it to be him, not her. She was such a trooper, she would smile and tell him she was doing fine. Her face would be so pale, you couldn't distinguish her lips from her face; she would be drenched in sweat, hardly able to get up and go to the bathroom to throw up. Her smile, her eyes, and her love—he wanted her agony to stop.

He wanted Mandy checked in to a hospital. She was too weak to stand and too sick to lie down. He wasn't going to let her agony go on another day. Wes called Debra; she tried to assure him this was typical for the first months of pregnancy, that it could last her full term. The storm had added to the problem seasickness, along with morning sickness; it was a miserable state to be in. But it would pass.

He wouldn't hear of it; he wanted her in a hospital. Debra called ahead to have an ambulance waiting at the dock. When the boat came to rest up against the dock, Wes jumped off and ran to the waiting ambulance. He showed them where Mandy was. They checked her; she was beginning to get dehydrated. They transported her to the hospital. Debra accompanied them, informing them she was her obstetrician.

They took her straight to the maternity ward; there they would be equipped to handle any situation that may arise. Wes waited outside the door while Debra examined her. She came out and asked him to come inside.

"She is having a bad case of morning sickness combined with seasickness. She has become somewhat dehydrated from all of the throwing up. I would like to run a test on her. She has a lot of swelling in her abdomen, and just to be on the safe side, I would like to do an ultrasound."

Wes agreed with Debra. Wes stood by Mandy's side while they performed the ultrasound. During the test Debra saw the problem; she turned the machine off and told Mandy she could get dressed. Debra and Wes went out into the hall to consult.

"It appears the placenta is detaching from the wall of the uterus. Debra told Wes as he leaned against the wall.

"It must have just started. I checked her thoroughly before the wedding. The tear is small, but my recommendation is to terminate the pregnancy."

"What?"

"That would be my suggestion. You're both still young enough and you can try again. She would be in too much danger of bleeding to death if it detached altogether. You can get a second opinion, but this type of tear can get her into trouble really fast."

•   •   •   •   •

Grace woke up with Mandy on her heart strongly. She felt like she was in danger. She looked up and said, "Lord, I don't know what's going on, but I know something is. Lord, I ask you to intervene and stop evil from prevailing in this little lady's life. Send your angels to help her in her time of need. Thank you, Lord." Grace turned over and went back to sleep.

•   •   •   •   •

Wes and Debra went back into the room where Mandy was patiently waiting. Mandy could tell by the look on their faces something was wrong.

"So, what seems to be the problem?" Mandy asked, wringing her hands in her lap.

"It appears the placenta is trying to detach from the uterus wall. We noticed a small tear. We suggest that you terminate the pregnancy and try again later," Debra said, putting her hand on Wes' shoulder.

"No! I will not terminate this pregnancy. This child is a gift. No matter what, I'm not going to terminate."

"Calm down, Mandy. If we don't terminate the pregnancy, you could bleed to death if the placenta tears loose. We can't risk that." Debra tried to reassure her it was for her own good.

"No, do you hear me? No! I have felt this child move. He's alive and well. I feel him right now, and I refuse to kill him." She looked up at Wes. "Tell them, Wes, we're not going to let them kill our baby."

"Mandy, they're right. You could bleed to death in minutes. We can have another one."

"No, no, no! I want all of you to leave right now. I want to go home. I won't let you kill my baby!" Mandy screamed.

Wes tried to calm her, but she pushed him away. "You leave with them. How could you want to kill our child? Get away from me, all of you." She looked at Wes. "If you let them do this, I will never forgive you, do you understand? I will never forgive you."

"Let's step outside and let her calm down," Debra suggested.

Wes wanted to stay with her, but she turned her back to him. She wanted him to leave too. He stood at the door looking at his wife crying. How could he let her endanger her own life like this? She was hysterical, that's what it was. She would see reason once she had some rest. He walked outside with the doctor. He felt helpless once again. How could he not help her? He cried, leaning up against the wall in the hall. He was confused, all of his medical teaching told him the doctors were right, but his heart was with Mandy. He didn't want to terminate either. He had made her think he was the enemy, he wasn't. He just couldn't bear the thought of losing her.

He sat on the floor outside her room all day. The doctor tried to get him to go and get some rest, but he couldn't leave her. If he couldn't be by her side, he would wait right here until she wanted him with her again. Debra wanted to keep her in the hospital for a couple of days for observation; then she could go home.

Mandy cried out to God. "God, please don't take my baby. He's mine, isn't he, God? Didn't you give me this gift? I made it through the death of my husband. I even made it through finding out about his affair, but God, I can't make it through losing my first child. Not like this. Please let me keep him. Let him be healthy. Doctors don't know everything, but you do, God. You have the power of life and death in your hands. I beg for the life of my child. If you must take me, then do, but let my child live."

Wes heard her desperate prayer through the crack in the door, and he wept. How could he have not known what this child meant to her? How could he let his medical training outweigh his heart? But he wouldn't fail her, not now, not ever. He opened the door and walked over to the bed. She was still crying; she tried to turn away from him, but he wouldn't let her. "You listen to me, Mandy Young. If we're going to do this thing, we're going to do it together. Do you hear me, my love? I'm with you. We'll have our child together."

She looked into his eyes; she knew he meant it. He wouldn't let them take the baby. She smiled and reached up and hugged his neck; he kissed her. "Together?" she whispered.

"Together," he said, holding her close to him. "We're in this together."

Given his prominent reputation, the hospital provided him with a bed because he refused to leave her side. She was gaining her strength back every day. Debra wanted to do another ultrasound before she left the hospital.

Mandy and Wes waited patiently as he went through the procedure of the test. She looked and scratched her head. She went over her stomach several times; she had her lay on her side so that the baby would move. She looked again; she looked up at the anxious couple.

"I know you're going to think I'm crazy, but I don't see the tear anymore. The swelling has gone down, and the baby seems to be doing fine. I want to run one more test that will conclude what I have just told you. It's an amitosis."

They both agreed to the test. "See, God will protect our baby. He's a gift, and you don't throw away a gift," she said, smiling up at him.

Wes agreed and kissed her on the forehead. He watched as Debra stuck the large needle into Mandy's stomach and pulled the fluid out. She sent the specimen to the lab. Debra informed them they would not have the test results for a few days.

Wes knew he needed to call Grace and let her know what was going on before they got home. He went into the hallway to call her while the nurses got Mandy ready to go.

"Grace, this is Wes."

"Hello, Wes, how's Mandy? Is there a problem with the baby."

"Yes, and she's been pretty sick. They wanted us to abort the baby, but Mandy wouldn't hear of it. It appears the problem has rectified itself for now. The reason I'm calling … would you consider staying at our house and helping Mandy when I get her home?"

"Sure, you know I'll do whatever you need me to do"

Wes dialed the Foundation's number. "Richard Young, please."

"Hey, Dr. Young, how's the honeymoon going?"

"Fine. Could you please get Richard for me?" The receptionist wordlessly transferred him, obviously noting the distress in his voice.

"Richard, look, we're here at Spring Hill Memorial Mandy is having a rough time with the baby. I'm taking a short leave of absence. I called Dr. Britt in L.A. to let him know. Could you keep things running there for me?"

"Sure, Wes. Is everything all right?"

"It will be. But I don't want to take any chances right now. Grace is staying over at our house to be with Mandy. If you could take care of the Foundation, and have Rachel take care of the pottery shop, it sure would be a blessing."

"Anything you need, brother."

Wes thanked him for helping and hung up. He watched Mandy getting ready to leave she was still so beautiful even being pregnant and going through all she had been through. Her color was returning, and she didn't seem as sick, but he didn't want to risk anything. He would do what was needed to keep her and the baby safe.

He wouldn't fail his family again. He would do whatever it took to make sure she had a fighting chance at giving birth to their son. If it meant staying home with her, then that's what they would do. Grace would be a big help, and he would be glad to see her friendly face. Wes hired a full-time nurse to stay with Mandy, but Grace was what she needed.

When they arrived home, Mandy was sleeping. "Where's the little lady?" Grace asked as Wes got out of the car.

"She's resting in the back right now. I know Mandy will be so glad to see you. I didn't tell her you were staying. I wanted it to be a surprise."

"No problem. Everyone sends their love," Grace said, patting Wes on the shoulder. "Things will turn out right, don't you worry yourself none. Mandy has the will of a bulldog. Once she gets a hold, she won't let go. Have faith in her, love her, and all will be well. Just mark my words."

Wes smiled. He carried Mandy inside the house and tucked her into bed; she was sleeping soundly. He walked back outside. There was something soothing about the warm breeze off the bay. It had a medicinal effect; as he sat on the edge of the deck, he wept. He let down all of his walls of manly control and allowed the tears to flow. He had needed to release all the pent-up worry. He allowed the sobs to escape; the sound of the waves on the shore drowned out the sound of his heart releasing the pain, pain that had been pent up for years, the pain of times gone by.

How could he be responsible for a life? He had tried to with Kay, and he had failed. All the lives he tried to save and couldn't. He knew the power of life was not in his hands; it was in the hands of one more powerful than him. He looked over his shoulder, and Mandy was there. She sat beside him and laid her head on his shoulder, and she let him cry.

They sat on the edge of the deck and reconnected the brokenness that had invaded their world together. He put his arm around her. "You're such a brave soul."

"No, I'm not. I'm just scared of losing the one thing in life that matters to me. Isn't it you that always says true wealth is the love of family and friends?" she said, holding his hand, looking over the familiar beautiful view. "It's peaceful here, isn't it?"

"Yes, it is. I can see why God placed us here for all of this."

"Well, I'm glad he did," Grace said, sitting beside Mandy. "How are you, little lady?"

"Much better, old woman," Mandy said, hugging Grace tight. "— When did you get here?"

"I've been here long enough. This is the life, little lady. This is the real heaven on earth." Grace said, surveying the view.

"I'm so glad you came. Did Wes tell you what happened?"

"A little, but we don't need to dwell on that. We need to enjoy this beautiful place and get you better. You have a lot of people that have missed the two of you," Grace said, patting her shoulder. "Now, this old woman is hungry. Let's try some of this food Sharon has prepared for us."

The three of them made the most of their haven. They enjoyed the sunrises in the morning, the afternoon rainstorms, and the setting sun at night. They played under the moon and stars in the luscious blue-green water. Mandy watched as the two people she loved the most in this world explored. Wes would dance with Grace under the stars; she witnessed Grace return to a time when she was young. She didn't look like the old woman she had become. She looked like a schoolgirl in the moonlight. Her eyes sparkled as she swayed in Wes' arms.

Grace's laughter could be heard all the way down the beach. She was tired, but you could tell it had been one of those things she wouldn't have missed for the world.

The amitosis came back with good news. Mother and child were fine. The two-week wait had been trying, but they had made the best of it.

Chapter 16

Spring was in the air. The morning was cool, but the bitter cold was gone. The birds were singing, and the flowers were budding; the trees were beginning to spring forth their new leaves. Mandy walked out on the patio off their bedroom. The wind coming off the bay in the winter was bitter cold, the patio was facing the water, and it had been too cold to enjoy the beauty. She looked across the yard; the pottery shop looked fine. She was proud of it.

She took a deep breath of the salt air; it smelled like home. She noticed children on the beach flying their kites. She watched them as their mothers hooted and cheered them on; she smiled. One day she would be out on the beach hooting and cheering for her son. The thought pleased her; she had been through so much and had come such along way in the two short years since Clay's death. She had learned to be independent; she had learned how to laugh and to consider others first. She had learned life was one big lesson of choices, the good and the bad.

She walked down the back stairs to the garden; the smell of amaryllis filled the air. The dogwoods were blooming, and the wisteria was everywhere. She loved spring; it was the time of year the earth came back to life from its hibernation of winter. She felt the baby move; she smiled as she rubbed her stomach. "You be still, little one, you'll be able to enjoy this beauty real soon, just be patient and let nature take its course, and you'll be walking in the gardens with your mom." She loved the sound of that … *mom.*

Duke ran up beside her. He wanted to play. She took the ball from his mouth and threw it for him. She sat on the deck that overlooked the bay; the sound of the waves washing against the shore was hypnotizing. The sun was warm on her face; she closed her eyes and soaked up the warmth. Duke brought the ball back; she rubbed his head and sent him on his way. She loved it here in the Cove on the bay that led to the Gulf of Mexico.

"Mandy, is that you out there?" Grace yelled from the patio off the bedroom.

"It's me. Come on down," Mandy called back.

"It takes this old woman a little while to come down all those steps," Grace said, out of breath.

"It's a beautiful morning. I couldn't resist coming out here and sitting a while."

"Everyone's looking for you. Sally brought your breakfast up, and you weren't in your room. I told them I bet I know where you were. Low and behold, here you are."

"You know me too well. How did you sleep last night?"

"I slept just fine in that big ole room. It's too much space for an old woman to get around in."

"Old woman, what in the world are you going on about this morning?" Mandy said, leaning her head against Grace.

"Little lady, one day you'll be an old woman like me and you'll see for yourself," Grace said, patting her shoulder.

"Isn't it beautiful here? We are so blessed to live in a place like this."

"Yeah, we sure are."

"How does Ben like having the house to himself?"

"He likes it just fine, says he don't have me to bother him all the time, cause I'm over here bothering you." Grace laughed.

"You're no bother at all. I love having you here. I feel better about having this baby with you here. I don't know anything about babies."

"It'll all come natural. Once that little boy is here, you'll know exactly what to do, mark my words. You'll do just fine. Course, I do like telling people I live at the big house on the hill."

Mandy laughed. "I still can't get used to living here. Sometimes I miss my little cottage, Duke lying by the fireplace, just he and I in utter peace and quiet. Just the sound of the wood crackling. I've almost forgot what that's like."

"You're doing just fine. Wes is a wonderful husband, and he'll be a great father. You done real good, little lady."

"Have I, Grace? Really? Because sometimes I don't want to be a wife. Don't get me wrong, I love Wes—he's any woman's dream—but all the responsibility that goes along with it. Sometimes I just want to be responsible for myself."

"You'd better get out of that real quick, 'cause once you have that baby, you won't ever be alone, for the rest of your life. You'll have that little one. Everywhere you go, he goes. Life as you know it now will no longer exist. You've had a lot of years spent by yourself, now. You'll have two lives to be responsible for. So you'd better enjoy your leisure time now. It's about to be gone forever."

"I don't know if I can do that. I love coming out here by the bay and just sitting for hours watching the people, the sights, the sounds."

"Like I said, you'll do fine. When you were on your honeymoon you stood up for that child, before he was even born. That's the way it'll be. You ever seen a mother gator when you come near her nest? Watch out, she'll get you. It'll be the same with you. You've already proven that. You have what it takes. Don't let fear dwell in your spirit. Don't let it take up space in your head. It's just a waste of time."

"I love you, old woman."

"I love you too, little lady. I'd better be getting inside to let those people know where you are before they tear the house apart looking for you," Grace said, getting up.

"I'm going to sit here a little longer. You go on in."

Grace walked inside; everyone was in tumult looking for Mandy. "I told you I knew where she was, and she was right where I thought she would be. If you ever miss her, look outside. That little lady loves to sit and look at the bay. She just wanders out there and sits for hours. She's fine," Grace said, sitting at the table. "Just let her be, she'll come in soon enough."

Rachel was sitting on her back porch enjoying the beautiful morning when she noticed Mandy sitting on the overhang deck that led to the shore. She walked up the beach to join her. She noticed Mandy seemed far away; she climbed up the steps that led to the deck. "Good morning. Looks like you're enjoying the morning."

Mandy looked up and saw Rachel coming up the steps. "Yes, it's been such a difficult winter. It's nice to enjoy the warmth of a spring morning. How are you enjoying your day off?"

"I'm relishing every moment. I'm glad the winter is over. I didn't think the weather got so cold in Florida."

"Yes, being by the bay makes it colder because of the wind off the water, makes it a moist cold, and it chills you right to the bone. In L.A. they don't have winter, do they?"

"Not much. It sure doesn't get as cold as it gets here. I told Richard I didn't know if I could stand it much longer."

"We'll have one more cold snap before Easter, then it's smooth, hot sailing." Mandy chuckled. "In a couple of months you'll wish it was cold again."

"I can't see myself wishing for cold weather ever again." Rachel laughed. "How are you doing these days? I haven't seen much of you since you returned from your honeymoon."

"All seems to be well. Wes is hard at it again. You have the shop under control. I work at night when I feel like it. The baby is fine, he moves a lot, and life is good."

"Then why the long face?"

"What long face?"

"The one you're wearing right now."

"I wasn't aware I had a long face. Everything is plump right now."

"I hear that's typical for your condition."

"I've never been fat before. It just seems strange to have a problem bending over or seeing my feet. Ah, it's beautiful here. I've lived here most of my life, and it still amazes me in the spring how beautiful everything is. Look at the gardens. They are blooming and sprouting. I love it here," Mandy said. Sadness rang in her voice.

"If you love it here, why are you so sad?"

"I don't know. I just miss the simple life. I miss my little cottage—"

"Hey wait, that's 'our' little cottage. You can't have it back." Rachel laughed.

Mandy seemed so far away; though she was talking, her heart was not in it. She just looked at the bay as if she were waiting for someone to appear to her. She tried to smile, but it seemed fake. She didn't want Rachel to detect her saddened heart. But she had, she knew everything was not well; she didn't know what it was, but she knew something was not right.

Mandy smiled at Rachel. "Have you ever had a feeling something wasn't right, but you didn't know what it was?"

"Once. I had what they call a premonition about my mother. She died the next day."

"I feel like something isn't right, but I just can't put my finger on it—"

"Ms. Mandy! Come quick, something's wrong with Ms. Grace. Come quick!" Sally yelled out the back door.

Mandy and Rachel ran to the house. Grace was lying on the floor in the kitchen.

"Call 911, now." She looked at Grace; she was pale and lifeless. "Grace, can you hear me? It's Mandy. Grace, if you can hear me let me know somehow, squeeze my hand. Call Wes, now!"

Rachel brought over a cool cloth for Grace's head; she was sweating. Mandy continued to try to get her to respond, but she wouldn't. The ambulance arrived; the emergency technician worked on her.

"It appears she's had a heart attack. We need to transport her to the hospital in Spring Hill."

"Call Ben and have him meet us at the hospital. Tell Wes where we've gone. I'll ride in the ambulance with her. Rachel, you ride in with Wes. Call Ben!" she yelled, climbing into the ambulance.

Ben arrived at the hospital. He noticed Mandy sitting at the end of the hall with her hands over her face. He sat beside her. "Mandy, where's Mom? Mandy … Mandy, look at me, where's Mom?"

"She's gone. She died about ten minutes ago. They said she had a massive heart attack. She didn't feel anything, she just went—"

"Mandy, where's my mom? I want to see her," Ben said, getting up.

Mandy pointed to the room across the hall from where she was sitting.

Ben dashed through the door. She was lying on the bed with a sheet over her body. Ben slowly pulled the sheet back; she had a smile on her face. He fell on her chest and wept. She was gone forever. He couldn't believe it, she wouldn't be lecturing him anymore, and she wouldn't hold his hand or give him a kiss. She was gone. He wept hysterically.

Wes came running up the hall with Rachel. Mandy was still sitting in the chair with her head buried in her hands. Wes sat beside her. "Mandy... Mandy, where's Grace?'

She pointed at the door; Wes could hear Ben crying. He reached over and held her in his arms and rocked her. She wept. She let all of the pain go; she didn't hold back.

A doctor came by and told Wes they could have the room next to the chair if they needed it. Wes asked to speak to the attending physician. The doctor showed him the way. Rachel sat with Mandy while Wes talked to the doctor.

He returned to where Rachel and Mandy were sitting. He told Rachel he was going in to check on Ben. He opened the door; Ben was sitting in the chair next to her bed. He had the sheet pulled down so that he could see her. Wes pulled the sheet back over her head. He kneeled beside Ben and placed his arm around his shoulder.

"She was a fine woman, your mother. The finest I've ever met. She's taught me so much. She has helped so many people." Tears began to roll down his cheeks. "Ben, I know this must be hard, but we need to make arrangements for her to be transported—"

Ben looked down at Wes; he stood up, and they hugged. He began to cry again. "I didn't know she was even sick. She never tells me anything. She just acted like everything was okay. That woman! What to do with her sometimes? Wes, I don't know if I can make decisions right now, any help you could give me, I would appreciate it. How's Mandy? I didn't mean to yell at her. I know she will miss Mom as much as me."

"She understands. She's pretty shook up right now. Everyone is. We just need to stick together like the family Grace made us. She had been having some chest discomfort for a couple of weeks now, nothing major. We started her on some medicine to help, but it was just her time to go. It's hard for us to understand, but we all have a time to go. It was just her time. She loved you, you know that, don't you? She was so proud of you. She always wanted you and Mandy to get together. She wanted Mandy as her daughter, but she got that anyway. Mandy will always be her daughter."

"You knew that she wanted us to be together?"

"Sure, she told me. She said that since Mandy was going to be with me, she'd have to adopt me so that she could have Mandy."

"Wes, you're such a special person. If I had to give Mandy up, you'd be the only one I would have let have her. Or I would have gone after her for myself." They smiled. "Can you imagine us talking like this, now?"

"Well, if I had to give her up, it would be to you. But since I don't, better luck next time." Wes patted his back. They smiled.

"It all seems so unreal. I had to see her. I watched to make sure the doctor didn't make a mistake. She has a smile on her face, did you see that?"

"Yes, I did. She knew where she was going, and she was glad to finally be able to go," Wes said, leading him into the hall. "Sit here with my wife," Wes smiled, "and I'll make the arrangements."

Ben reached for Mandy's hand; she looked up at him. "I've loved you since the day I met you. I love you even now. I was heartbroken when you and Wes got married, but Mom told me it was for the best. She knew. She knew that you would be better off with Wes than me. She knew you needed a gentle soul to be your mate. That wasn't me. I wanted to tell you that night at your house when you were so upset and suspected things were not right, but I just couldn't tell you."

"Why are you telling me now?"

"Mom told me a long time ago I needed to tell you. I didn't, you got married, got pregnant. But I want you to know that Wes is the best man for you. I want you and I to stay as we are, brother and sister, you know."

Mandy was shocked; she didn't know what to say. She reached over and hugged Ben tight. "You will always be a part of my life. I'm glad that you told me. I always wondered. I thought something was wrong with me. I remember the day I picked you up at the airport. Remember? You laughed at me. It's amazing how far we've come." She kissed him on the cheek.

He reached out and held her; they cried together.

•   •   •   •   •

The day of the funeral was a beautiful spring day. The birds were chirping; the flowers were in bloom. Children were playing on the beach, and the sound of laughter filled the air with the sound of the seagulls. Mandy walked around Grace's house, looking at the life of the woman who had forever changed her. She touched her favorite clay pot and smiled. She was so grateful that Grace had been a part of her life. She had enjoyed her last days beside the bay, the place she loved so much. Mandy knew her life was richer for knowing her. She would be eternally grateful to that Old Woman. She would always remember she was her Little Lady.

She walked up the hill to the pottery shop; she went inside and put on her apron. She opened the large picture windows to let the breeze in. She sat at the wheel, watching the lighthouse they had watched together so many times. She turned on the wheel and started to mold the clay ball. The cool wet clay spun within her hands. She realized that she too had been formed by the Master's hands, just like the clay. She looked out at the lighthouse; she formed each intricate detail and gently rubbed it with her hands.

She stood up and walked to the window. It was hot, and sweat had begun to run down her forehead. She reached up with her arm and wiped it away, clay dripping from her hands. She looked into a distant place that she could not go yet; she saw Grace … basking in the sunlight, wading in the surf.

"You told me that I was the potter's wife. That changed my life forever. You taught me to reach beyond myself and look into the depths of God's creation. There I would find life. A life full of happiness and contentment. I found so much more. I found you, and you taught me about sharing my life with others. In doing so, I became a wife, and soon I'll be a mother. I love you, old woman."

"I love you too, little lady." She could feel her hand on her shoulder, like so many times before. When she turned around, it was Wes.